CRY OF THE RAIN BIRD

Also by Patricia Shaw

Valley of Lagoons
River of the Sun
The Feather and the Stone
Where the Willows Weep

Pioneers of a Trackless Land
Brother Digger

CRY OF THE RAIN BIRD

Patricia Shaw

St. Martin's Press
New York

ISBN 0-312-13457-6

First published in Great Britain by Headline Book Publishing

First U.S. Edition: December 1995

10 9 8 7 6 5 4 3 2 1

So many gods, so many creeds,
So many paths that wind and wind,
While just the art of being kind
Is all the sad world needs.

'The World's Need', E.W. Wilcox (1850–1919)

Chapter One

Dark skies hung glowering over grey streets, watching grimy sleet harass hurrying crowds, boxing ears with stinging cold, sending Londoners racing for shelter.

Corby Morgan scrambled along the slippery pavement wrestling with his umbrella. He was angry that he'd been unable to find a horse-cab, fretting about the time, aware that his father would open the door and say: 'Late as always, Corby!'

As he lurched round a corner into fiercer winds his umbrella blew out, snapped ribs and black cloth flapping helplessly like a wretched mauled crow. Pinched faces drew some cheer from his predicament as he tried to haul it in, grinning at him as though he were a jester placed there for their entertainment, and Corby flushed with embarrassment. He hurled the useless appendage away from him, grimly satisfied to hear it crunched under carriage wheels in punishment. Cold and miserable, and very wet now, he crossed the road to Luton Street for the most important meeting of his life.

Corby Morgan, they'd said, was just a dreamer, yet another disenchanted young Englishman yearning for Utopia, for the romantic sun-drenched serenity of the South Seas – a madness, they said, common to many of these spoiled Cambridge graduates for whom the grass was always greener, be it in Italy, Spain, or in his case the South Pacific. Specifically a tropical idyll called Trinity Bay.

But they were wrong. He clenched his teeth and forged on. He and Roger McLiver had investigated and planned this move with the utmost care. They had no intention of idling away their lives and funds on a deserted beach; they had sought a place where they could make money *and* enjoy the leisured existence of gentlemen. And by God they had found it! Corby could still recall their jubilation when Roger had come to him with that clipping from *The Times*. The very thing! Exactly what they were looking for. They were so excited, they'd drunk two bottles of champagne before penning a reply. Even then they'd been cautious, destroying the first letter and composing a simple expression of interest rather than allowing their enthusiasm to leak on to the page and cause the owner to ask a higher price or attempt to hoodwink them.

Holding to that caution, they had moved to purchase the advertised sugar plantation near Trinity Bay in north Queensland, far away in Australia. Although neither of them had as yet visited the Antipodes,

1

they'd been able to make further enquiries by telegraph to referred bank officers, who had replied that Providence was indeed an established plantation with reputable management and steady export figures, and not just another one of those get-rich-quick schemes so often proffered by scheming johnnies.

Everything had been under control until yesterday. God Almighty, he and Jessie were packed, ready to go, and now this! Roger, his friend, his partner, had reneged! Had let him down.

'Damn his reasons!' Corby muttered as he punched his gloved hands together. 'And damn that bloody wife of his and her interfering family. Damn them all to hell! He'll be sorry,' he went on, fuming. 'Sugar plantations out there are making a mint of money. I'll be a rich man while he's still poking about here in London tied to his wife's apron strings.'

At least Jessie supports me, he sighed. My wife has the sense to know this is a golden opportunity. I won't let go now.

That was a disquieting thought. He had no choice but to proceed. He had said his farewells, given up the lease on their rooms, paid the agent and signed the contract. Roger's responsibility in this enterprise had been to match Corby's investment, thereby taking up a half-share. Since Corby had used up all of his own funds on the purchase price, the balance of the partnership agreement was urgently required now for their fares, transportation of their goods and chattels, and capital for preliminary commercial expenditure. Too many tales had filtered back of gentlemen purchasing various enterprises and failing within months due to lack of capital for unforeseen expenses, so Corby had made certain that this would not happen to him. They owned the plantation outright and he had been relying on Roger's investment to keep them covered financially until the next harvest.

But now the proprietor of Providence was stony broke! What a comedown for Mr and Mrs Corby Morgan, owners of a vast estate, to have to spend three months or more travelling steerage to Trinity Bay.

'Blast his hide!' Corby spluttered, rain wet on his face and a lady coming towards him caught his words. 'Sir!' she accused, shocked, jostling him aside.

'And blast you too!' he retorted. Damn her! He had more important things to think about than uppity women. He'd been worrying for weeks about Roger's tardiness in putting up his share, making excuses to his father for his friend. 'He'll come through. He's a reliable fellow, there's just some delay in the transfer of funds.'

'More like some delay in making his missus toe the line,' Colonel Chester Morgan had snorted.

'She has nothing to do with it.'

'Oho, my lad! Never underestimate the little woman. You should have had his cash in the bank before you threw yours overboard.'

'It's not overboard. I own the estate, and I don't need your Jeremiahs. I know what I'm doing.'

2

'If you knew what you were doing and you are so keen on farming you should have bought that sheep farm in Surrey.'

'A plantation is not a farm, sir.'

'Same thing. You till the soil and gamble on the weather and rely on farmhands who don't know their place these days.'

Exasperated, Corby had tried to explain to his father: 'That's the beauty of my plantation. It's in the tropics so I won't have a problem with weather, with frost and snow and all that – the weather is always the same in the tropics. And natives work the fields for their keep. White men can't work in that climate and Australia has a large population of natives, a ready-made work force.'

'If they don't shove a spear in you.'

'Sir, I don't wish to argue with you,' Corby had said at length, 'but might I point out, once again, that Providence is only one of many sugar plantations operating in the state of Queensland, and they all use native labour with excellent results.'

And now . . . Corby was on his way to seek his father's help. Who else could he turn to? He hoped Jessie had arrived on time. The Colonel liked her, they got along well, so Corby had given her the task of breaking the news to him that Roger had pulled out.

Corby smarted at the forthcoming humiliating backdown. It was easier to have Jessie pave the way for him. In the meantime he'd spent the day trying to entice other friends to join him in the enterprise, not without enthusiastic response, but none of them had the necessary cash. He would never forgive Roger for this betrayal. Never!

As he walked into the parlour his father was standing by a roaring fire, glass of brandy in hand, grinning like a Cheshire cat: 'Late as always, Corby.'

Jessie fussed about him, taking his coat. 'Darling, you're freezing. Do come over by the fire or you'll catch your death.'

'Perturbations,' a voice intoned from a deep armchair. 'Always perturbations.'

Jessie's father! Lucas Langley! 'What's he doing here?' he hissed at her. The last person he needed now was her bewhiskered eccentric old parent. Chester couldn't stand him. A bombastic retired officer with a wealth of rock-solid opinions, he had no time for Professor Langley, who, when he did have something to say, invariably disagreed with him. Corby neither liked nor disliked the old man; he was of no consequence, except for now, when as an irritant he could only hamper Corby's chances of prising much-needed funds from the Colonel. He nodded a grudging acknowledgement to his father-in-law and turned to Chester for the expected lecture of doom.

And his father didn't disappoint him. 'Trouble with you young chaps, you think you know everything.'

Corby ignored the opener and poured himself a brandy to help muster the necessary humility. He'd beg if he must but it would take a few more snorts to reduce himself to that state. At this moment he hated his

3

father. He hated his self-satisfied, cosseted life, thanks to the family fortune and an undistinguished career in the army.

The Colonel never had to worry about money. He lived high on the hog with these rooms in town, a pleasant country estate and his God-awful club. His son had received a small inheritance from an uncle and Providence had taken the last of it. Chester had always made Corby ask for money when he needed it; he'd never volunteered a penny, claiming that his son would eventually inherit the lot. Or what was left, he was wont to chortle. Corby feared his father could live to be a hundred and leave him with only bills and bailiffs.

'It has been a great blow to me,' he said sadly. 'It is hard to believe that a gentleman would renege like this, Roger has all but sabotaged my plans.'

'Ah yes,' Chester smirked. 'You always were a blamer. It's always the other fellow. Never you. Didn't I tell you to pin him down? Didn't I warn you a month ago that he was likely to run for cover, that he couldn't be relied on at the cannon's roar? But would you listen? Oh no! And now your pal has left you with a plantation that's probably not worth a whisker and no cash to run it. Have you got any money left at all or have you sent the lot into the gaping maw of the Antipodes?'

'I have some money, sir.'

'Speak up then. How much? To the penny.'

'We have some money,' Jessie said quietly. 'I have a nest egg of two hundred pounds.'

Chester's monocle gleamed. He was enjoying this. 'Ah well, let's see, that will probably get you down around the Cape, over to Tasmania and maybe to Sydney. Then what? Do you intend to walk the rest of the way?'

The Professor poked the air with the stem of his pipe and announced: 'From the Cape across the Indian Ocean to the Torres Straits and south to Trinity Bay.'

'What's that?' Chester challenged.

'Their route,' Lucas muttered. 'The sugar route.'

'Well, whatever,' Chester said, dismissing him. 'It doesn't alter the fact that you've let yourself be dumped, Corby. You can't afford this enterprise, so you'd best tell the agent to sell that place fast and count your losses.'

'No,' Corby said, trying to keep his temper. 'I can't afford to lose this opportunity. You can afford it, Father. Why don't you come in as my partner? You won't be sorry, I promise.' This was the very line he knew his father would pounce on, but there was no alternative.

'So. Now you need my money for your harebrained scheme. Why would I send my son off to be a South Seas layabout? That's how they all end up.'

'You've got it all wrong,' Corby cried. 'This isn't really the South Seas. It's a civilised British community.'

'Civilised? I call it decadent. I know what you're up to. You were never in love with work.'

4

'And you were?'

'I accepted discipline. I can see you now, lying there in a hammock, wearing a white hat and shouting at your Aborigines.'

The Professor looked up and blinked. 'There are no Aborigines working on Queensland plantations, gentlemen. None at all.'

Corby and his father exchanged glances. For once they were in agreement. The old gent was practically senile, he didn't know what he was talking about. It was common knowledge that natives worked plantations.

Jessie came to Lucas's rescue. 'It's late, Father. We'll take you home shortly. Are you warm enough there?'

Corby took a deep breath. 'I beg you, Colonel, don't refuse me. I'm so close now. At the very least I need two thousand pounds. Roger said he was good for three but I can make it with two, I know I can. I'm offering you a partnership at one-third less than Roger was paying, a half-share.'

'There's no such thing as cheap money,' Chester replied, 'only desperate. And desperates are dangerous investments. No, your mother and I have our lives to live, we can't be throwing good money after bad.'

'How can you refuse me?' Corby shouted. 'You're crucifying me! I'll lose everything!'

'Then you should have listened to me in the first place. Get yourself out of this mess and I might be able to help you with that sheep farm.'

'I don't want a bloody sheep farm!'

The Professor tugged at Jessie's sleeve. 'Tell your husband we'll invest.'

'We?' she asked, confused.

'Yes,' he smiled, licking his pink lips. 'We'll take up the half-share at his bargain price.'

'But, Father, you can't afford even that.'

'I can raise it,' he whispered.

Jessie was frantic that he'd make a fool of himself and, worse, compound poor Corby's problems. This could easily be just another example of her father's spontaneous kindnesses, emanating more from emotion than common sense – he'd been known to give away his boots to a needy fellow and arrive home, unconcerned, in his socks. And then there was the time he'd invited poachers, of all people, to share their Sunday dinner. A botanist, he could not be expected to grasp Corby's financial dealings, but it was sweet of him to offer. 'Don't worry, Father. Corby will work it out.'

His eyes were wistful, sad. 'I'm not dead yet, Jessie, but since your mother died, everyone seems to have written me off. They put me in chairs facing west to wait for my sunset. Don't you see that this is my chance too?'

Jessie felt a pang of guilt. She knew that her eighteen-year-old sister, Sylvia, resented having to care for their father on her own since Jessie had left home. Sylvia could be cold and ungracious with him, but as a married woman now, there was little Jessie could do about that –

5

except to give Sylvia a gentle reminder now and again that she ought to be a little more patient with him, comments that were not appreciated and probably made the situation worse.

He was becoming agitated. 'Tell them!' he insisted. 'This is my chance to see the Antipodes. To start a new life.'

'You want to come too?' Jessie was astonished.

'I was hoping you would ask me, but now I can buy my way in. I am needed. I don't have to be a mathematical wizard to spot this bargain. Tell him we'll take up the offer.'

Still Jessie hesitated. It was the brandy talking, she was sure. But when the argument between Corby and the Colonel descended into a fuming silence, Lucas intervened. 'Mr Jess,' he called, a title that infuriated her husband, 'would you give me a word?'

Concerned, bewildered, Corby was forced to accept his father-in-law as his partner in the face of the Colonel's amused derision: here was proof to Chester that his son would grasp at straws to dig a deeper hole for himself into bankruptcy. And Corby was angry too that Lucas, the old villain, had taken advantage of the situation. It was damned bad form to eavesdrop on a private conversation and then claim the same financial terms, and more. Had Corby managed to persuade his father to invest, he would have been a silent partner, remaining behind in England. Now he'd let half of Providence go at a low price to an old dodderer who intended joining them there. If nothing else, he was another mouth to feed, because already Corby made up his mind not to brook any interference from the Professor.

As soon as he could, he put Jessie and her father into a carriage and sent them off so that he'd be free to collect his thoughts.

A warm, cheery tavern offered refuge, so he found a dim corner and after a few drinks his despondency eased. It was possible that Jessie could talk the old boy into doing the right thing. If he could raise two thousand, surely he could find three, and pay the full price as any gentleman would do. Yes, it was possible. But still the other worry niggled. Besides being angry with Roger for backing out, Corby was very nervous of going it alone. He had been relying on the experience of his friend, who presently managed his uncle's large estate in the north. Corby had never managed so much as a duck pond. It was all very well that Roger had handed over his copious notes and books on the subject of sugar-growing – good reading for the voyage, he'd said – but that wasn't the point. Deep down, Corby had expected to enjoy his occupation as a gentleman planter while allowing Roger to make the decisions, and now the whole load had fallen on his shoulders like a dump of snow from eaves, and a twist of panic writhed within him.

By the time he staggered away from the King's Arms, he had adjusted to the fact that instead of two enthusiastic young couples, a trio would sail for Trinity Bay – he, Jessie and that old leech, Lucas Langley. He almost wished he could leave both of them behind, irritated that he'd have another parent looking over his shoulder, having at last, and at

6

least, escaped the Colonel's sardonic glare.

But Corby had a further mental adjustment to make. He had forgotten Sylvia. Not that she was a willing voyager by any means.

'I can't believe you're telling me this!' she shouted at Jessie, appalled. 'You've tricked Father into handing over his money just to get your husband out of a scrape!'

'It wasn't like that,' Jessie said. 'He wants to come with us. It's important to him.'

'I see. And what's going to happen to me? He's putting every penny he's got into this madness. Where am I supposed to live now that he's selling the house?'

Jessie tried to calm her. 'Sylvia, you mustn't take on so. Surely you don't imagine we'd go without you? Think what's ahead of us . . . a wonderful sea voyage and then our own estate out there in that beautiful climate. You'll love it.'

That hadn't occurred to Sylvia. 'You expect me to go too? To leave London and live in the wilds?' She burst into tears. 'I've always said you're the most selfish person in the world and now I know I'm right. You'd do anything to suit your own purposes. Well I won't go! I won't!'

'You haven't any choice, I'm afraid,' Jessie said quietly. 'I'm really sorry that this has upset you, but do try to look on the bright side. You might just enjoy yourself, and Corby says we'll make a lot of money. You can always come back here to visit, and you never know who you might meet in our travels.'

'I know *what* I'll meet,' Sylvia wept. 'Blackfellows and snakes! I won't let you ruin my life like this. I'll insist Father comes to his senses. He's too old for all this!'

In vain Sylvia begged and pleaded but the Professor took little notice beyond telling her to include mosquito nets in their sea chests. He was far too busy sorting his books and making lists for what was, for him, a fascinating botanical expedition.

Thoroughly dejected, Sylvia was left to do the packing, contrarily refusing to allow Jessie to help her, and when the departure day dawned she boarded the brig *Caroline* with them and went straight to her cabin to sulk. The Professor popped his head in, but misread her attitude: 'Ah! Good girl. I see you're nicely settled,' and rushed away to explore the ship.

For Jessie, however, this was the most exciting event of her life, a day she wanted to remember forever. Sails billowed above them like wild, beautiful wings that would carry them to a new and wonderful life, and the dark green sea raced beneath them. She clung to Corby's arm and looked up at his handsome face, still in a state of euphoria that this man, whom she loved so dearly, had chosen to marry her. There had been worries in this, the first year of their marriage, as to how they would survive with Corby's capital diminishing at an alarming rate but she'd had faith in him. Jessie understood his reluctance to go into trade and his refusal to go cap-in-hand job-seeking, and she was eternally grateful

7

that he'd rejected military service. She had known he'd find a way eventually. And when he and Roger, that cad, had come home full of this marvellous idea of purchasing a sugar plantation, Jessie had celebrated with them. Later that same night, with their problems solved, she was able to tell Corby her good news, that she was with child.

He was delighted. 'See! Everything is falling into place. We'll have our plantation, a great estate, and a son to carry on the family name.'

'What if it's a girl?'

'No, you must have a son. I am told that if you concentrate you can produce the required gender.'

Jessie had laughed, but realised that he was serious.

Now she drew her heavy cloak about her as the wind rose and the swell deepened.

'How are you feeling?' he asked her.

'Wonderful,' she smiled. 'Just wonderful.'

'That's a good start. I notice some of our fellow passengers are already green about the gills. By the way, I've thought of a name for our son: we shall call him Bronte. Bronte Wilcox Morgan, after my late uncle.'

'Whatever you say dear.' She kissed him. She was too happy to bother him now. She supposed that was the way with men, which was fine; it left her free to choose a girl's name, just in case.

Chapter Two

The aquamarine waters of the wide lagoon lapped lazily at the exposed reef and drifted back to its crystal depths, resting mildly, awaiting the tidal rush. Already the great ocean out there had begun to sing, preparing to surge and then thunder high over the reef in a welcome invasion of invigorating surf. The lagoon tingled in the blazing sun under weightless blue skies, diamond peaks blinking across the mile of sea to the long arch of beach. Here the sand dazzled, as pristine as the polished creamy-pink interior of a large conch shell that lay at the edge of the jungle.

Sea birds hovered over the tousled green palms that leaned loftily over the beach. They were waiting too, playing their gliding games in hot airstreams, wafting effortlessly into the blue. Soon the ocean would rouse the silent lagoon, delivering fat silvery fish over the reef, and they would be ready for the catch.

A man emerged from the shade and strode down the beach, his large bare feet squeaking sand as he plunged along. This was Ratasali, the 'big man' of the coast-dwellers of this area. He was a big man in size too, a huge, bronze-skinned Melanesian, his body rippling with muscles. In his time Ratasali had been a formidable warrior and that, combined with cunning and foresight, had assisted him in retaining power over lesser mortals for many years. That, and his famed friendship with the gods, who appreciated his advocacy.

Ratasali saw to it that all of his people treated the gods with the utmost respect and in their worshipping tendered the very best of offerings. In this manner they had fended off devastating winds, great sharks were unknown in their lagoon, plentiful rains fed their waterfalls and pools, and, perhaps more importantly, his warriors were blessed with the courage and strength to fight off constant attacks by bushmen, hill people and other islanders. In fact these men of Malaita were known throughout the Solomon Islands, indeed the Pacific, as fearsome warriors and their 'big man' to be savage in retribution.

Ratasali stood by the conch shell, which was there for a purpose, exercising his arms and legs after a heavy meal, the palm leaves on his wrists and ankles rustling as he stamped. He wore a headband of shells to hold back his woolly hair, his nose and ears were pierced to accommodate adornments made of human bones, and on this day he was sporting his favourite necklace of human teeth. Even in his

9

everyday regalia, his ceremonial headdresses and ornamentations carefully placed in the long house, Ratasali, with his broad nose, iron jaw and massive white teeth, and those deceptively soft brown eyes, was a man to be reckoned with.

Deciding it was time, he picked up the conch shell and blew into it, trumpeting a signal. A few minutes later the high carved prow of a war canoe shot out into the lagoon, slicing across the languid waters like the sudden chop of a tomahawk.

Ratasali danced with delight, clapping his hands as his new *tomaka*, his war vessel, on its first practice run sped towards the reef, its forty warriors dipping their paddles in swift precision. It was perfect! Wonderful! He shouted encouragement, thrilled with its speed as it turned towards him, the gruesome carved shark mask above the waterline baring its teeth to strike fear into the heart of the enemy.

He flung out his arm and as the canoe skimmed back across the lagoon, he beamed with satisfaction. This was the best vessel ever, beautifully constructed and carved by craftsmen. Before trusting it to the sea, he had taken the precaution of dedicating it to the gods, with the sacrifice of two women and a fat child, and there was no doubt that the gods approved. This had to be the fastest vessel in the islands.

He patted his stomach. The ceremonies to the gods completed with meticulous care, the sacrifices had made an excellent meal for his people.

Signalling to the men to keep practising, Ratasali replaced the conch shell and disappeared from the beach, making his way through the village to the long house to give thanks to the gods.

The thatched building, lined with skulls, was empty at this afternoon sleep-time so Ratasali squatted cross-legged on his mat to think things over. Now that the new *tomaka* was launched he had several important matters to explore.

White-men ships were due any day, recruiting men to work on the sugar plantations of Fiji and of Queensland, in the north of the big country, Australia. Ratasali knew all about the canefields. As a young man he had been kidnapped from a nearby bay and taken to work in Fiji. Three of his kin had died of dysentery in the hold of that ship before they even reached land, and of the forty-four men taken from Malaita that day, supposedly indentured for three years to white planters, only seventeen had made it home again. The others, unaccustomed to hard labour and poor rations, had died, exhausted, in the fields, or wasted away of disease, left neglected in their huts.

Ratasali had survived, but more than that, he'd watched and learned. He had learned the white man's language, and had discovered that the British had laws covering the recruitment and employment of Kanakas, an island word for 'men'. At first he'd thought this was just a tale. He'd laughed about it, in fact. 'Imagine,' he'd said to his friends, 'having laws in our country for stealing men! Or women, for that matter. Would we have to beg permission of our enemies to grab them for sacrifice? Or even for meat when pigs are in short supply? These people are mad!'

It had been a surprise and a relief to find that the blackbirding ships were only seeking men to labour in the canefields. And it was indeed true that if they survived the three years they were free to return home, for the planters were bound by law to send them back.

Then he'd found out about the 'passage men': islanders who were paid two pounds or more for each recruit they delivered to the ships. Money they could use to buy supplies and oddments from the same ships! Some men volunteered to go, for the excitement of it, but most, like himself, were lured aboard and kidnapped.

Blackbirding had become a savage trade on both sides, with white men shooting opponents on the beaches and murdering belligerent natives aboard ship, while the islanders fought back, attacking any white men they could get their hands on . . . even the missionaries who tried to defend the islanders from marauding whites.

At the end of his indenture Ratasali was paid off in tobacco and tea, but the captain of the ship that brought him back to Malaita had refused to wait for canoes to come out to collect him, fearing retaliation, since several ships had been burned to the waterline by natives. Instead he had thrown Ratasali overboard outside the reef, forcing him to swim the rest of the way.

So he had arrived home shamed, knowing that while others had returned with gifts for their families, he had come back with nothing but rage in his heart.

His first move had been to take a knife and kill the passage man who had sold him, one of his own kin; not on his own behalf but for the three who had died when they were first kidnapped. Or so he told the villagers, who accepted that this was atonement to the gods. Then he went into the hills, captured two enemy warriors, and presented them to the families of the dead men. Grateful relations, still mourning their men who would never return, were able to sacrifice the hillmen to the gods as offerings for the loss of their sons.

From that day Ratasali became a passage man for the plantations, the wiliest in the Solomons, demanding payment for his volunteers and inflicting swift punishment on white men who reneged on agreements. Nor would he allow any of his people – because soon Ratasali rose to become head man – to work in Fiji. He knew that conditions were better in Queensland because old hands who came home often volunteered to return, thus adding to Ratasali's riches. There were still losses, many men still did not survive, but Ratasali, like any general, saw them as acceptable casualties in the business of trade.

He was waiting on the labour schooner *Medusa* out of Trinity Bay, Queensland, which was due any day, but there were problems. He had promised Captain King fifty men and six women at the agreed price of two pounds each, but as yet he hadn't assembled the required number and that would make the captain angry. He had to meet a quota for eager planters, or lose money on the cost of the voyage. Ratasali understood this and he was doing his best. As well as the group he'd rounded up, he had nine old hands who wanted to go back to Queensland, finding life on the island too dull after their three-year stints in the white man's world.

Ratasali was contemptuous of their attitude. He couldn't understand why they'd be willing to break their backs labouring six days a week in those dirty canefields for any earthly pleasures. Not even the availability of Japanese women in the Chinese brothels that proliferated in Cairns. They had to pay for those little brown women when there were clean islander women available free. It was a mystery to him. He had hated every day that he'd been forced to slave for the whites for a measly three pounds a year. Then again, he mused, it was obvious that he was of a higher birth rank than any of them, since it was not in his nature to bow to any man. Ratasali would never volunteer to go anywhere near those ships, not even in a canoe to exchange gifts. It was well known that blackbirders would often run down canoes to kidnap the curious occupants.

That had made him cautious. Several times white men had tried to grab Ratasali himself at gunpoint, but he was always well protected by warriors hidden in the bush. Many men had lost their lives defending their chief but – he smiled – the would-be kidnappers had never made it back to their ships.

Captain King was a legitimate recruiter, as far as they went, since he carried a government agent, Jock Bell, aboard *Medusa*. But it was well known in the Solomons that if King couldn't meet his quota, plus extra men to make up for wastage on the voyage, then he'd grab young islanders anywhere he could find them, with the help of the big red-headed agent. So to make his money and avoid trouble, Ratasali had to have the numbers.

His friend Higimani joined him. 'The big ship *Medusa* is due,' he commented, settling himself down.

Ratasali nodded morosely.

'Let me go,' Higimani said. 'I want to go back.'

His chief was amazed. 'Why? You've been home two years now. Why would you want to go back?'

'Ah – when I see those great ships with their wondrous sails out there beyond the reef, my heart sings with excitement. I yearn to ride them once more.'

'Locked in the filth of the holds,' Ratasali growled.

'No, no. Not good boys like me. They let me roam the decks.'

'You're not a boy any longer and you'd have to work.'

'They call us all boys. I don't mind the work and I like their tucker. I am bored here.'

'You're mad. You have two wives. What will become of them?'

'I'll take them with me.'

That interested Ratasali. It was hard to persuade families to hand over their women. He sat for a long time considering this request. 'Very well,' he said at length. 'Besides the old hands, only seventeen of our

12

young men have volunteered to go. I need more.'

'What about the six hillmen we captured?'

'Yes, they go or they die,' Ratasali replied casually, 'but it's still not enough. You gather up fifty men and six women and I let you go.'

Higimani was delighted. 'I'll find them,' he promised. 'Leave it to me.'

That pleased the chief. One job less for him. The festival of the great white sharks was only a week away and he had much to do. This would be the greatest celebration of all. Wood-carvers were busy making him a new throne, inlaid with pearl shell, which would be placed high on a bluff looking out to sea, and women were gathering food for the feasting. As well as their own firewater, Ratasali had a case of white men's rum, to treat his people, and as the full moon rose with its blessings at the height of the celebrations, the offerings from the stone altar would be the most exciting in years.

Every night for weeks, chosen men had been furtively feeding sharks below the bluff, and during that time more and more of these clever animals had come in to thresh and fight among themselves for the food. When the big night came they'd be there in such numbers that his tribesmen, already whipped up by the grog and their chief's oratory, would be in a frenzy equal to the expected feeding frenzy of the sharks when sacrifices were thrown over the bluff. For on that night Ratasali intended to join the gods. In future, intercession would be made, not through him but *to* him for favours and blessings, and he would become the richest chief in the islands. His son Talua, now eighteen, would stand beside him at the altar to be anointed in blood as a god too, therefore ensuring his succession.

Ratasali grinned. Here was the real truth, the heart of the matter, the reason for his almost fanatical interest in this year's ceremonies, ordering huge bonfires and more singers and dancers than had ever been seen before. As chiefs grew older, ambitious young men cut them down. Ratasali had no intention of ending up as shark fodder. He had many sons but Talua was the best of them – beautiful, strong-limbed, of his father's build, and with unblemished god-like features. Beautiful in temperament too, staunchly loyal to his father. When the time came Ratasali would step down and hand over leadership to his son, with a fine band of warriors as back-up. Then and only then, under Talua's protection, he could live to enjoy his riches and look forward to knowing his grandchildren.

It was a magnificent plan that he had discussed with the gods, who were pleased to receive him, for they too were spirits of the earth and the seas who had gained immortality. Once he was a god, Ratasali planned to build many shrines to himself so that he would be known forever as the greatest god of them all.

Aboard *Medusa*, Captain King gave the order to drop anchor off Manu Bay, on the east coast of Malaita, and his schooner settled gently in the swell. It was just on dusk and as he watched, a great bonfire on a bluff sprang into life, flaming colour against the darkening sky.

He laughed and called to Jock Bell: 'Look at that! That must have been the light we saw in the distance last night. Old Ratasali isn't taking any chances that we'll miss him. He's lighting fires to welcome us.'

'I don't trust him,' Bell said. 'He's too oily, too anxious to please. It doesn't fit with the reputation he's got around these islands as being a dedicated head-hunter.'

'That's their business,' King said. 'All of these islanders are the same, they fight among themselves, eat one another, keep heads as trophies. We're not missionaries, we're just here to pick up cargo.'

'Cannibal cargo,' Bell retorted.

'So what? We deliver. Chief Ratasali is anxious to please, for good reason. We don't give him any trouble. We go in, collect our Kanakas, pay up and get out. And he always lines up good workers for us, so quit worrying. This one's the least of our problems.'

The following morning, though, King took the usual precautions. He studied the shore carefully through his telescope, grinning to see Ratasali done up for the occasion like a Christmas tree, in feathers and paint. He was relieved to see Ratasali was still the boss; sometimes a change of chiefs spelled danger.

Then he ordered not one but two longboats to be lowered. The first would ferry him and the agent to shore, the second had a different role. Four sailors followed them in that longboat but stayed offshore, guns trained on the beach; there was always the possibility of a sudden raid by an enemy tribe. That, the captain recalled, was the wild card in these operations. It paid to remain alert.

As his oarsmen beached the boat King sprang into the shallows and strode forward to an open-armed greeting from the chief, who almost squeezed the air from his chest.

'Welcome, my good friend,' Ratasali shouted. 'You come longa good time. All fixemup plenty here.'

'Good fellow, Chief,' King replied, deliberately jingling a bag of sovereigns as a sign of good faith. He stood back and looked at Ratasali: they were both the same height, both over six foot, but the islander was massively built. 'By God, Ratasali,' the captain laughed, 'you're a big man now. People say you're the top chief these days, plenty tucker, plenty women, eh?'

Ratasali beamed his pleasure and shouted the translation to the respectful crowd of natives along the beach, who whooped in delight, jostling and stamping with excitement. They thrust forward a shy young man whom the chief introduced as his son, Talua.

'This feller next big chief when I sit down,' Ratasali informed King, who was quick then to show proper respect to the young man. 'He speak good Englis too,' Ratasali added, but Talua dug a toe in the sand, seeming disinclined to demonstrate. Not that King cared; he was

14

anxious to load up and get moving.

As ritual demanded, he sat in the sand, making conversation with the chief, and Jock Bell was permitted to join them. This was Bell's chance to interrogate Ratasali about island problems: which chiefs had become dangerous to approach, the whereabouts of missing seafarers or missing ships, and so forth. This fellow's information was usually reliable.

While the other two talked, King glanced down the beach to where a large group of islanders were waiting impatiently. These were his Kanakas, and by the looks of them he had a fit mob this time. The planters would pay well.

Now came the usual invitation from the islanders to remain ashore for a feast, but King had worked out an acceptable routine to duck this pleasure; when meat was served it could easily be human flesh and it was ill mannered to ask. He apologised profusely to Ratasali, claiming he had to catch the tide, but beckoned to his sailors to bring out a small sea chest of tobacco, tea and beads to soften the blow.

And so to business. Assured by Ratasali that the number of natives was correct, he counted out the exact money, returned it to the canvas bag and handed it to Ratasali, who then instructed his friend Higimani to begin loading the Kanakas into the captain's longboat.

'This feller comen back!' Higimani called to King.

'Good for you!' The captain turned to Ratasali. 'You got plenty old hands coming back with me? That's good news. Trained men, they make it easier for everyone.'

'I send 'em,' Ratasali announced. 'More better others follow, do good work. Nex' time you pay three pounds for old hands, eh?'

'Fair enough,' King said.

Ratasali grinned with delight and punched his visitor in the arm. 'You bloody good fair man, Cap'n. And nex' time you bring this feller one good live sheep, eh?'

'A sheep?' King asked, astonished.

'Sheep,' Ratasali insisted. 'This feller not chief no more. This feller god. More proper respect, see? My son a god too.'

'Oh, right! A god! That is big news. You better teach me god ways, sir.'

The longboat had put to sea, heading for *Medusa* with natives crammed aboard, but there seemed to be some difficulty between the agent and Higimani, so King kept talking. 'I never met a god before. By cripes, this is important news to take our great queen.'

Ratasali nodded absently. He too was aware that something was wrong. He lifted his bulk from the sand, leaning on his spear, and looked at King's second longboat where the sailors, also disturbed, were levelling their guns to cover the captain. He picked up a conch shell and strode away with King in pursuit.

'This is a rort!' Bell shouted at King, who could have clouted him. The red-necked bastard might be a big noise back in Cairns but he was a walking disaster among the niggers; bloody hopeless with them.

15

'Calm down,' King said. 'What's wrong?'

'We sent off the first load,' Bell told him, 'then I get to look at the mob behind them. They've got ring-ins here. Look at this!' He jerked out a boy: 'No pubic hair. We can't take him, he's too young.'

'All right, leave him,' King laughed, looking to Ratasali for support. 'Kids push in, don't they, Chief?'

But the smile had gone from Ratasali's face and he stood staring sourly at his batch of would-be travellers.

'What about these?' Bell shouted, dragging out others hidden in the mob. 'They're useless. No one would buy them. Look at these two women, they're covered in sores.' He hurled them forward. 'And back here, rickety old blokes not worth a cracker. Is this what you've paid for?' One by one he hauled cringing natives from among the fit men.

Surprised, King turned to Ratasali. 'You promised good fellers.'

Enraged, Ratasali sprang forward with his spear. But it was not the captain he was attacking. He had realised what had happened, that in his eagerness to go with the big ship, Higimani had double-crossed him, had made up the numbers by hiding decrepit and diseased natives in among the fit men. Ratasali lunged at this man who had been his friend and who now was spoiling everything.

His spear lodged in Higimani's throat. At the same time the sailors panicked and shots were fired. That was enough to cause chaos, as those of the excitable natives who weren't hit joined the fray. Suddenly the quiet little beach was in uproar, with the sailors in the boat firing steadily, believing they could restore order.

Bell ran for the sea. Above the screams, Captain King was shouting at his men to stop firing, and Ratasali, fearing that this first day of his godness would never be forgiven if he didn't retaliate, raced away to blow long and hard on his conch shell. Immediately, the magnificent war canoe shot into the bay and made straight for the sailors who were firing at their people.

Enmeshed in the fighting on the beach, which had now been further aggravated by reaction from Higimani's kin, King went down with a spear in his shoulder, screaming in pain as someone tore it loose and dragged him to the sea. With all eyes turned to the great war canoe, Talua, weeping, pulled the captain, his father's friend, into the lagoon, striking out into the deep waters towards the reef. Blood washed around them as King tried to swim, but Talua held him firmly, dipping and pushing through the warm water, forging on through the choppy waves of the open sea on the outgoing tide until strong hands grasped them, pulling them aboard the *Medusa*.

Back in Manu Bay, the sailors with their rifles saw that great terrifying canoe coming towards them. They were marksmen, all four, but it would have taken a cannon to stop the forty warriors. In despair one man turned his last shot on the beach. He sought out the native chief who he believed had killed his captain, not likely to miss the great brown polished frame that had called death upon him too, and in the

16

swaying boat he took careful aim and shot dead Ratasali, the god.

The great war canoe with its ferocious teeth came for him as fast as a yawning rogue wave.

Determined not to be left behind, some of the native volunteers also swam for the *Medusa* and clambered aboard just as the crew were swinging into action. The first mate had seen the eruption of violence through his telescope, horrified that a peaceful transaction could have gone so terribly wrong, and as soon as King and the agent were safe he was ready to sail. The war canoe had stunned and fascinated him and he'd had to watch helplessly as his four armed crewmen were mown down. Now it was imperative to have *Medusa* well away before the native war party took it into their heads to collect firesticks from the beach and come after them.

Amid the confusion of hysterical natives and the busy crew on the deck, Bell rushed the captain down to his cabin, swabbing and padding the deep wound to try to stop the bleeding. 'We'll have to stitch it,' he said.

King shook his head. He couldn't spare the time. 'No, just bind it tight for now. I have to see what's going on out there.'

'No you don't,' Bell replied. 'There's nothing to be done. We're under weigh.'

Curious natives, who should have been in the hold, were peering through the open hatch at them.

'Get Talua for me,' King shouted and within minutes the young man was pushed down the timber steps. Groaning with pain, the captain reached out to him. 'Thank you, lad, you saved my life. I won't forget you. We'll drop you off at the next bay so you can go home to your father.'

'You're not thinking straight,' Jock Bell argued. 'You paid for fifty men and we'll be lucky if we've got bloody thirty with us. We're entitled to keep him.'

Talua's large brown eyes rested miserably on the captain. 'My father dead. Men say gun killem.'

'Oh Jesus!' King said. 'What a bloody débâcle! I'm sorry, son.'

'It was his own fault,' Bell snapped angrily. 'He tried to trick us.'

'No he didn't. It was Higimani who tried to pull a fast one. Ratasali was as surprised as I was. The least we can do is let his son go.'

But Talua shook his head. 'No go back now. The gods angry. Plenty fighting there now to lookout new chief.'

'Is it dangerous for you back there now?' King asked.

Talua nodded, and Bell intervened. 'Good. He stays.' He hustled the lad above decks and as the schooner swept away from the island he began to call the natives to order, taking their names one by one and sending them below. When he came to Talua, he glared. 'We lost four white men here, four good crewmen. We don't want to be reminded of Ratasali or his family. Your name is Joseph now. Got it?'

'Jo-seph,' Talua shrugged. He was too devastated by the loss of his father and the shock of the day to be able to comprehend fully what had happened. He padded humbly away and dropped into the hold to curl up in a damp corner, nursing his grief, feeling the frantic rush of the big ship beneath him.

Chapter Three

The shanty port of Cairns on Trinity Bay was never quiet. The best that could be said of it was that it allowed the occasional lull. That would be around three in the afternoon when Europeans succumbed to the blazing heat and Chinamen padded swiftly, silently, about their errands temporarily safe from harassment. But dawn was bedlam. At the first trace of light, birds hidden deep in the luxurious fronds of tall palm trees began tuning up, then honeybirds piped, waking the incessant twitterers, and songbirds joined in with their fluting tones until, like a mad brass section, the parrots took over – all manner of parrots from rosellas and corellas to thousands of flashy lorikeets and parakeets – lifting the noise level to a deafening screech.

And this was only background noise. Mike Devlin, lying on his bunk in the wildly misnamed Palace Hotel, stirred restlessly. The birds were a part of life in the north, he hardly heard them any more, but he did hear the shouts and curses as all-night roisterers tumbled out of the bars and brothels.

'Oh Christ!' he muttered, turning over to try to retrieve some sleep as fights broke out, women screamed and swore and an irate wife could be heard collaring her man. Horses neighed and whinnied, raising dust as they pranced nervously in the street, dust that permeated the already hot air, adding to the stink from fresh horse manure and the ever-present stench from Trinity Bay's huge mangrove swamps.

'Tide's out,' he commented grimly to himself. The smell was always worse when the muddy wastes were exposed.

He heard several gunshots but even that didn't move him. Trigger-happy drunks weren't unusual in this neck of the woods – gold-miners, seafarers, cattlemen and planters were a rough mix. He wondered if this crude frontier town could ever sort itself out. Sooner or later it would have to, he mused, hopefully. Providence plantation, of which Mike was manager, depended on this port.

The racket outside was escalating so he stumped sleepily across the veranda to look down at the street, still not all that interested because it wasn't Sunday. Cartloads of Kanakas came into town on Saturday nights, since Sunday was their only day off. Boozed, they were real trouble. Mike usually managed to persuade his labourers to stay home but if they insisted on visiting the 'bright lights' he wasn't permitted under the law to stop them. All he could do was send a dray in on

19

Sunday nights to collect the 'bodies' because most of the poor fools drank themselves unconscious.

'What's going on?' he shouted to men below him.

'Riot!' someone yelled. 'Riot in the holding house!'

'Holy hell!' He dragged on his clothes and raced down the rickety side steps, making for the wharf. The holding shed was first stop for incoming Kanakas, where they were identified and indentured by immigration officers. It was always a confusing, at times funny procedure, with the bewildered new boys wearing European clothes for the first time: their issue of shirts, trousers, boots and hats. Most of them had never before worn more than a lap-lap and so their struggles to dress could be hilarious for the onlookers and great fun for the cheerful islanders. Even the unfortunates who had been kidnapped managed to find some humour in these seemingly chaotic proceedings.

They stared about them in wonder, too, at their first sight of a white man's village: everything astonished them, especially the horses. They stood in line with an interpreter as the officials took careful note of the date and their destinations, because, by law, the planters had to have them available for deportation to their home islands in exactly three years' time. The time span often created a problem, since many of the volunteers had not been able to differentiate between moons and years. To be away for three moons was regarded as quite an adventure, but when they discovered they'd been hooked for three years they were understandably upset. Usually, though, the reactions were fear and despair, never riots, because other islanders were present to console them.

As he neared the shed, formerly a warehouse, it appeared that the sudden upheaval had been quelled, more or less. Battered white men, seamen and officials, were wandering, dazed, about the wharf, heads and shirts well bloodied from the fray; several islanders were cringing under police truncheons, blood pouring from head wounds, and three troopers faced the door of the shed with rifles. Inside, the natives, still protesting, hammered on the corrugated iron walls.

'What the hell happened?' Mike asked an agent, Jock Bell.

'How do I know?' Bell retorted angrily, his whisky-red face now blotched with exertion. 'We were just sorting them out and they ran amok.'

'Any booze in there?'

'Not as far as I know.'

'It's your job to know,' Mike said angrily. 'I hired thirty of these fellows yesterday and I expect to get them in one piece, not bashed about. Where's Captain King?'

'He's still aboard. He's got a fever.'

Mike strode over to one of the immigration men, and yelled at him over the din. 'What's going on, Charlie?'

Charlie, resting heavily on a crate, nursed the back of his neck. 'Some bugger gave me a chop, nearly broke my bloody neck.'

'Why?'

'Christ knows! One minute they're getting into line and the next minute they jumped us.'

'Who was getting them into line? Bell?'

'Yes, he and a couple of his mates.'

'The bully boys with their sticks?'

'Oh well, you know how the niggers muck about. Jock was just giving them some hurry-up. No more than usual.'

'Except that someone didn't like it,' Mike snapped. He looked about him. 'Where's Solly Sam?'

Solly Sam was the interpreter, a half-caste from the Solomons, son of a missionary it was said, but that was probably a joke. Mike needed to find out if there was a hothead among his newly acquired labourers. Considering that Kanakas were notoriously fierce on their home turf, they adjusted surprisingly well to the discipline of the canefields, one of the reasons planters from Fiji and Queensland competed for their labour. Neither Fijians nor Australian Aborigines would work the fields, the latter loud in their contempt for Kanakas, calling them 'whitefeller dogs'. To keep the peace at Providence, Mike chose his recruits carefully. He couldn't afford troublemakers.

Solly Sam was on his haunches beside the half-dozen sorry natives who had been dragged out of the mêlée. 'Bloody good fight,' he grinned, winking at Mike.

'Bloody stupid,' Mike retorted. 'Who started it?'

'Dunno, boss. It was all too quick. I went out that window mighty fast.'

'What about these fellows?' Mike indicated the islanders now under arrest.

'Ah, they don't know nothin'.'

Solly Sam watched as Mr Devlin marched over to the troopers and after a loud argument was permitted to go into the shed.

'Don't blame us if you get your head knocked off,' a trooper shouted after him, since he had insisted on entering unarmed.

Solly tapped two of the natives, and spoke to them in their language. 'That man is Mr Devlin. He's a strong man, good boss. You boys are lucky, you go with him.'

They raised their eyes to stare miserably at him. No one had bothered to dress their wounds and in their present state they didn't feel lucky, but Solly laughed. 'No bones broken. White men here can't do you damage, you're worth money to them. It's when you get out on the plantations you have to watch out. Some bosses bad men. No good. So you keep quiet, work hard, or they shoot you and tell the chiefs you die of sickness.'

The noise in the shed died down and soon Devlin emerged with several of his old hands. Solly recognised some friends among them, including Kwaika and Manasali, who was known in the fields as Sal.

Mike instructed Kwaika to call out men from their island, Malaita, but as he began and Kanakas crept meekly from the gloom, Jock Bell intervened: 'What are you doing, Devlin? Picking the eyeteeth out of the mob as usual.'

'No, I'm just separating them. That row could have been inter-island trouble, just local feuds. Tell King I'll take them down by the bell tower.'

Solly Sam listened carefully as the names were called and Malaita men emerged. He knew full well what the trouble was about; the injured islanders had told him, their voices steeped in dread, but he had no intention of disclosing the information, not even to Mike Devlin. Solly knew better than to interfere in tribal matters. Nevertheless curiosity propelled him forward and he noted Kwaika's hesitation as he called the name 'Joseph'.

There was a delay. None of the white men noticed. Dark eyes flicked from one islander to another until Joseph came out, and then the eyes dropped as if nothing unusual had happened. Solly caught his breath in excitement. He had never seen a god before. This wasn't Joseph; this, he'd been told, was Talua, son of the great chief and recently appointed god, Ratasali, who had gone to the sky after anointing his son as his successor.

Already the islanders believed that the fight on the beach at Manu Bay was pre-ordained, that Ratasali had been informed by the other gods of his imminent death and, after spectacular ceremonies, had gone forth to join them. It all fitted, Solly Sam had to agree: the timing of the ceremonies, the final sacrifice by Ratasali of his best friend, Higimani, and his flight into death. Now standing before him, unmistakably the son of Ratasali, whom Solly had known well, was a fine specimen of young manhood, magnificent even in a shirt that wouldn't do up across his wide chest and in half-mast trousers.

Talua moved meekly away with the others – unlike his father, who had always been an arrogant, belligerent man. Solly couldn't decide whether Talua was simply playing possum or was genuinely of gentler disposition. 'But the father will emerge,' he told himself. 'Ratasali will make a very clever god. He will be watching. And that Jock Bell is a marked man.'

He nodded sagely, intrigued, enjoying the secret. Bell had struck Joseph in the line-up! The Malaita men, mostly tribal, had been outraged that this white man should strike a god, and the eruption had been spontaneous and vicious. Moving to protect Talua they'd attacked all the white men within reach. No one man could be held responsible for the attack, nor would they disclose the reason. It was a matter of great pride among these men that Talua was with them, Talua, whom they'd already recognised as their leader, their very own god to watch over them and bring them good fortune in this strange land.

And what a strange place this was. The new boys tried to take stock of their surroundings as they were herded away from the wharf, but the clothes hindered their progress. They sweated freely in the rough shirts, they tugged at their crotches, trying to ease the constriction of these things called trousers, and they pulled off the boots because they were already raising blisters, ignoring the warnings of the old hands that they must persevere.

'Boots will save your lives in the canefields,' they were told, 'protection from snakes.' But none of it made sense to them. And they were confused by the sudden change in attitude of these white men, the boss and the two others, who were not carrying guns or sticks and who strolled along with them, passing round canvas waterbags.

While they rested in the shade of tall trees, the naming business began again, this time without any fuss, and bags of food were handed about. This food was better than the dirty rice they'd been given on the ship – bread with hunks of meat, and plenty of bananas.

By the time they climbed on to drays for the journey to their new home, Providence plantation, the islanders were less apprehensive, more contented, some even laughing and jostling boisterously as the great adventure unfolded.

The drivers of the drays were white men, millhands commandeered for this job and by no means unhappy with the chore which had given them an overnight visit to town.

'I have to stay in town to meet the new owners,' Mike told them. 'The *Caroline* is due any day. Keep the old hands, Kwaika and Sal, up front with you to give them authority. You shouldn't have any problems but be sure to give the horses a couple of hours' rest at Halfway Creek.'

He waved them off, relieved that the Kanakas had settled down. Mike had hired thirty men this time. No women. Single women caused too many problems. He and Jake had agreed on that right from the beginning. They had built small married quarters for the half-dozen fortunate Kanakas who had brought their wives, and six couples had remained the quota. The rest of the men were housed in long barracks well away from the women, and a half-mile down the track from the main house. The wives were employed as cooks for all the men.

As he made for the bank to draw the cash to pay Captain King, Mike was thinking of his friend Jake Wallace. He missed him and was not looking forward to breaking in new owners. If they decided to keep him on. For all he knew, this Englishman, Corby Morgan, might not require his services. Mike, at forty, was still a fit man, and he enjoyed his work at Providence. In fact he loved the plantation where he had worked for the last six years.

Over time, Mike had had dozens of jobs; he'd shipped out from Hobart on whalers for some years, which accounted for his abhorrence of foul smells. Clean air was almost an obsession with him. Except during the burn-off, the plantation was wonderfully fresh and green, and that beautiful river flowing past the fields of cane was as pure as crystal.

It was just a stroke of luck that had introduced him to Jake Wallace.

23

When he quit the whalers Mike had worked as a sheep-shearer, then, moving north, as a cowhand on a cattle station, then as a drover. Always restless, he'd drifted into Queensland towns and finally ended up as a barman in Brisbane, and that was where he'd met Jake and his mate Tom Swallow.

'Mr Swallow manufactures biscuits in the south,' Jake had told him, and Mike, as barmen do, had acknowledged the information politely but without any real interest.

Later, while Jake was putting away his usual pints, he'd enlarged on the subject of Tom Swallow. 'He's a smart fellow is that Tom. He's bought a swag of land in the north near Trinity Bay, to grow sugar cane. What do you think of that?'

'Very good,' the barman replied absently.

'But don't you get the point, Mike? Sugar. Biscuits. He'll have the business sewn up from go to whoa. He owns a biscuit factory.'

'Oh yes, I get it.' Mike hadn't thought any more about it until, months later, Jake walked into the bar with the news that since Tom Swallow was on to a good thing, he too was going into the sugar business. Acting on the advice of Swallow, Jake had purchased a large estate in the same area. 'It's virgin country, magnificent, tropical, ideal for sugar. Of course I'll have to get it cleared, bit by bit, but that damn cane grows fast, I'll have a harvest in no time.'

'Then what?'

'Then I sell what I can here and export the rest.'

'Sounds complicated.'

'No, it's not. Tom will keep me on the right track. You wait and see, I'll have one of the best plantations in the north before I'm through. I'll end up a bloody millionaire.'

'How much land did you buy?'

'Six hundred acres.'

'God Almighty! I hope you know what you're doing.'

'Sure I do. That town of Cairns on Trinity Bay is growing, thanks to all the gold-fields up there, and by the time the gold runs out the sugar will keep it going.'

'I haven't been that far north. I thought that was cattle country.'

'No. That's over the range. It's too wet on the coast. Why don't you come with me?'

'What?'

'You heard me. Chuck this dead-end job. Come with me.'

'What'll it cost me?'

'Won't cost you nothin'. I'll put you on the payroll.'

'How far is Trinity Bay from Brisbane?' Mike asked, interested now.

'Christ, I dunno. Couple of thousand miles, I suppose, as the crow flies. The ship sails tomorrow. I have to get my horses on board early. You can start by giving me a hand there.'

Mike took off his apron, shook hands with the publican and left with Jake.

While they were waiting for a contingent of Kanakas to arrive in Cairns, the two men rode the boundaries of Jake's estate, which he had named Providence, and then studied the terrain with care, drawing up maps to work out which blocks should be cleared first. Then they rode further afield to become better acquainted with the river that fed the property.

They explored the upper reaches of the Barron River, both of them overwhelmed by the wildly beautiful rainforests. They journeyed through ancient gorges festooned with ferns and orchids and climbed into jungle teeming with flashy birds, delicate butterflies, and, at night, cascades of glittering phosphorous plants. By the time they reached the mighty cataract known as the Barron Falls, Jake was beside himself with delight: 'Bloody beautiful, isn't it? Bloody beautiful!'

And Mike had to agree. Even though he was weary and stiff from a climb that the older man had taken in his stride. He had expected the Trinity Bay area to be much the same as Brisbane. Nothing had prepared him for this massive and spectacular event of nature.

Looking up now at the steamy green mountains surrounding the bay, that experience was still with him. It was as if nature were showing off in those impressive surrounds, brazenly flaunting its beauty to a point of decadence. A decadence that he still felt, far below at Providence, seeping over the rich lowlands and sighing through the sweep of canefields as seductively as the pipes of Pan.

He gave a snort of laughter as he remembered that foolish expedition. Two new chums riding innocently into Irukandji country, home of one of the fiercest Aborigine tribes in the north, but with beginners' luck, they'd fared well, attracting little attention from the blacks. And despite the ongoing war between blacks, and the miners and cattlemen pushing inland, Providence had been mercifully free of trouble. A few Aborigine clans still camped on the plantation side of the river but mostly they kept to themselves, while their more belligerent brothers stayed on the west side.

Jake was happy to leave them be, and acceded to the request of the Providence blacks that they be accorded their right of passage. The blacks clung to their old ways; they followed the same old trails, and when those trails crisscrossed the plantation, that was the way they had to go. Once the homestead was finished, though, a trail often took a detour, right past the kitchen where they'd get handouts of tucker. No, the blacks weren't a problem at Providence; it was the Kanakas who had to be kept calm. Every so often one or more of them would run amok or they'd break out into fights among themselves, so Jake and Mike had to keep a firm hand on them.

Finally the Kanakas had arrived and work had started at Providence. God, how they'd worked, he and Jake, side by side with fifty Kanakas, clearing the land and planting field after field of cane. Mike had never worked so hard in all his life, and had never enjoyed himself so much. It was exciting to watch those sticks grow into towering plants, jubilant

25

waving fields of cane. To bring in the great harvest and then celebrate the year's work.

Now he walked by the barred windows of the Bank of New South Wales and pushed through the heavy door, feeling resentful of change.

Between them, he and Jake had carved Providence out of a wilderness; they'd built barracks, stables, a fine homestead; and in only three years Jake's investment had shown a profit. And now that sugar was booming, strangers were taking over!

'Yes, Mr Devlin?' The teller addressed him, and Mike made quick calculations. Two hundred and ten pounds for Captain King.

One pound a head to Immigration for landing thirty Kanakas, and ten pounds per head to the same officers for return passage money, to be kept in trust for these same men in order to ensure they were returned home in three years. Five hundred and forty pounds.

'Draw out a round six hundred cash for me,' he told the teller, signing the withdrawal form. He was owed three hundred pounds but the Providence account was running low. They couldn't expect any more payments until after the harvest. The new owner, the rich Englishman, would have to top up the balance fairly smartly.

He pocketed the cash and walked out into the glare of the day, making for the saloon bar of the Victoria Hotel where all such transactions were settled.

It was still hard to believe that Jake no longer existed. Big, exuberant Jake, always the life of the party. And there'd been some swell times at Providence! After one such party, with a fiddler playing and friends milling about the front veranda in the moonlight, Jake had gone tumbling down the front steps. A shout from Jake. Laughter from the guests. Then silence.

Not a drunken fall. A heart attack. They'd carried him inside, past shocked men and weeping women, and a few minutes later Dr Leary had pronounced him dead.

Typically, Jake, who'd always thought himself to be indestructible, hadn't written a will, so Providence went to his son Tom, a Brisbane horse-breeder. Within days of the funeral Tom placed the plantation, lock, stock and barrel, on the market.

Not one to let the grass grow under his feet, Mike had made a deal with Tom, that he would stay on as interim manager until the place was sold, on condition that he could build a manager's residence on the property. As he pointed out, he could hardly expect to live in the homestead with the new owners, so his own quarters were essential.

'They won't know any different,' he explained to Tom. 'I want them to take the manager's residence for granted.'

'But what if they don't keep you on?'

'Then it's my bad luck. But if they do, I'll have a house of my own. But listen to me, young Tom! If I walk off here, this place will go to the dogs, because I'll see to it that you don't get another manager, and you'll end up with nothing to sell.'

26

'That's not fair.'

'It's bloody fair. Take it or leave it.'

While Tom searched for a buyer — without success, since the north was considered too hot and too dangerous for white men while there were better propositions going further south — Mike built himself a small bungalow up the hill from the main house, with a view of the valley, and got on with managing the plantation. Finally, in desperation, Tom advertised Providence in London and the plantation was sold. At a stupid price, Mike told him, but Tom didn't care. He wanted the money and wouldn't hold out for a better offer.

Now Mike waited. The *Caroline*, bringing the new owners, Mr and Mrs Corby Morgan, was due any day.

He walked into the hotel and bought himself a pint, hoping that the bloody ship would pile up on a reef coming down from the Torres Straits, as so many others had done.

Chapter Four

Captain McTavish of the good ship *Caroline* was taking no chances. The voyage from London had been a copybook expedition right from the start because he was a meticulous skipper. The ship was well appointed and well provisioned, and he'd hand-picked his crew. They'd sailed the Indian Ocean into the northern tropics ahead of the monsoon season, which bore with it devastating cyclones, and had reached Batavia without mishap, although quite a few of the passengers had become rather testy by this time, mainly due to boredom.

At Batavia he'd armed the crew and doubled the watch as protection against murderous Asian pirates who preyed on ships in the Arafura Sea and the Torres Straits. They'd had only one encounter with these gentlemen when a large schooner, flying a Dutch flag, had hailed them with a distress signal. The captain, observing them through his spy glass, had noticed that they were no more Dutch than he was an Eskimo, so he had sent his great clipper, using auxiliary steam, straight at the schooner, almost swamping it. Not that he would have cared had he sunk it; he had spotted the snub-nosed cannons peeping out from under canvas, fore and aft.

Do-gooders among the passengers had cried 'Shame!' and threatened to report him to the maritime authorities, but ignoring them he had turned his attention to the pilot, whom he had engaged in Batavia. This was his master-stroke. The pilot, a German, had guided the ship through the straits and around the tip of Australia and then into the deceptively safe passage between the mainland and the Great Barrier Reef as they headed south. The treacherous reefs had claimed many a ship and McTavish was determined his *Caroline* would not be one of them.

Although they had a few anxious moments the pilot did his job well and *Caroline* dropped anchor at the entrance to Trinity Inlet on a glorious sunny-blue day, as the crew gave a rousing three cheers for their captain.

Soon the lighter *Bee* came trundling out on the first of its many trips to convey passengers and freight to shore, and McTavish stood on the deck bidding farewell to his voyagers.

Corby Morgan, a contrary fellow, shook his hand. 'Well done, Captain.'

McTavish smiled. Morgan and his wife had taken a stateroom on the poop deck for the voyage, but even that, four classes above steerage, hadn't prevented him from fault-finding and complaining. When they'd encountered the pirate ship, though, Morgan had taken the captain's side in the ensuing arguments. McTavish bade farewell to Mrs Morgan, a fine woman, and to the dear old Professor, and he smiled with genuine pleasure to see the last of Miss Sylvia Langley, who had flirted outrageously with one of his officers and then suddenly switched her attentions to his first officer, Lieutenant John Mansfield, causing friction between the two men and scandalising other passengers – Mansfield was a married man. She was a very pretty girl, with her dark curls and almost cobalt-blue eyes, beset with long dark lashes, but she was rather scatterbrained and impetuous. And unfortunately she'd shared her stateroom with Mrs Lita de Flores, a languid, sophisticated young widow who was returning to her family plantation at Trinity Bay. Not the ideal company for an impressionable miss like Sylvia.

But they were out of his hands now. Lita, being Australian-born, was going home. The Morgan party were seeking a new life here in the tropics. And God help them, he mused. They were in the hands of the furies here, man and nature at their best and worst.

Mike saw her standing alone at the edge of the wharf and he experienced a physical jolt at that first glance, as if some magnetism had passed between them. She didn't notice. She was wearing a long duster coat over a wide-skirted dress, and an imposing hat on thick coils of hair, and she was staring out to sea as if loath to leave it. But it was the stillness of her that held his attention; she had a serenity not often encountered in this turbulent town.

With an effort he turned away from his study of the calm and lovely profile to join the crowds further down the wharf. Passengers were being landed from the *Caroline* and he had to find Mr Morgan in the confusion of newcomers and welcomers, wharf labourers, sightseers and scurrying Chinese bearers.

Lita de Flores sneaked an arm through his as he joined the throng: 'Mike, darling! How wonderful to see you! God, I'm glad to be home! Europe was deathly. Absolutely bloody freezing! You heard my husband died?'

'Yes, I'm sorry, Lita, my condolences.'

'Oh well, it was his fault. He insisted on going back to Paris to see his family. He had a weak chest. Daddy warned him not to go, but you knew de Flores. Bloody spoilt, had to have his own way.'

He grinned at her. Lita, sleek, self-assured, was the most ladylike rascal he'd ever met. 'Look who's talking!' he commented.

'Oh, get out with you! I'm not spoilt! Darling, I sat with him in that dreary Swiss sanitorium for four months, right to the end. No one could have done more! And all the time I was petrified I'd catch that sickness too. But I must fly, Daddy is waiting. Now, I insist you and Jake come over to Helenslea as soon as I get settled.'

29

'Jake's dead.'

Lita stepped back to stare at him. 'Jake? He can't be! Oh damn! How bloody awful! But some people on the ship told me they'd bought Providence from him . . .'

'From his son.'

'Good God! What are you doing then?'

'I hope to stay on.'

'They'd be mad to let you go. That's Corby Morgan over there, the fellow in the grey jacket and topper. He's rather a stuffy character, Mike. I'll get Daddy to put in a good word for you.'

She kissed him on the cheek and hurried away, her white skirts billowing in the breeze. She looked cool and crisp in that elegant dress with a matching parasol. Mike smiled, for the Lita he knew usually wore jodhpurs and silk shirts and rode hell-for-leather about the plantations like the wild bush girl she really was, despite her terms at expensive boarding schools and her two-year sojourn in Europe.

But now it was time to meet the new boss. He walked quietly over to the gentleman who was watching anxiously as luggage was being slung ashore. 'Mr Morgan?'

'Yes?'

'Welcome to Cairns, sir. I'm Mike Devlin, manager of Providence plantation.'

'Oh, you are? Good. Excellent. I was hoping we should be met. I must say you've put on a fine day for us. Bit warm, but one imagines that's to be expected.'

'Yes, our winters are kind,' Mike replied.

Morgan blinked, surprised at the comment, and then laughed. 'Winter. Of course. You're topsy-turvy down here, aren't you?'

'Very topsy-turvy,' Mike said, relieved to find that Morgan seemed an amiable fellow, and only in his thirties. He had expected a much older, sterner gent. He turned to the young lady standing with Morgan. 'And this is Mrs Morgan?' he asked, smiling down at her.

'No. This is Miss Langley, my sister-in-law. My wife seems to have disappeared somewhere. Go and find her, Sylvia. And where's your father?'

The girl ignored him, stretching out a dainty hand to Mike: 'How do you do, Mr Devlin? I'm most pleased to meet you. I have my little dog in a cage here for fear he might fall in the sea, but it's rather warm for him. Do you think you could put him in the shade for me until we're ready to depart?'

A dog? Mike peered at the sad-faced spaniel with alarm. Hadn't anyone told them what happened to dogs here? There wasn't one left in the town, except for a few bush-wise dingoes that only the blacks had managed to tame. But this was no time for explanations of that sort, he had to keep these people happy. He picked up the cage, looking helplessly about. What shade? On a wharf?

Fortunately Morgan countermanded her instructions. 'We are all in

30

need of shade, Sylvia. If you could find us a porter, Mr Devlin, we could set off.'

Glad to oblige, Mike commandeered a long wheelbarrow and piled on it the cabin luggage which Morgan identified. As he added the last piece, the missing father, introduced as Professor Langley, made his appearance; a small man with a fluffy beard and sideburns, and sharp twinkling eyes.

'So you're the manager of our plantation,' he said enthusiastically, and Mike noticed Morgan stiffen. *Our* plantation? he thought, I was under the impression that Mr Morgan was the sole owner. But I guess I'll figure this out in time.

'Yes,' he replied. 'I'm looking forward to showing you around.'

'I can't wait,' the old chap replied. 'It's all very exciting.'

'Then can we please go?' Morgan said. 'I see my wife has wandered on ahead of us.'

As he trundled the wheelbarrow along the uneven planks of the wharf, Mike saw the sweet-faced, gentle woman coming towards them. But disappointment set in when she was introduced as Morgan's wife.

'Haven't you had enough of the sea?' Corby asked her petulantly. 'You've been staring out there as if you might miss it now.'

'Oh no, dear,' she said. 'I've been admiring this bay. It's truly beautiful, the colours are so strong with those mountains in the background.' She turned to Mike. 'The light is different here,' she observed, falling into step beside him. 'It's so sharp, Mr Devlin.'

She seemed unconcerned that her husband was striding on ahead of them, with her sister and father in tow. 'How long have you been at Providence, Mr Devlin?'

'From the first day, ma'am,' he replied. 'Six years.'

'Thank God for that,' she commented. 'Mr Morgan has been making a study of the sugar industry on the voyage and I'm sure he'll make a success of his endeavours, but he'll be most grateful for your guidance, so I do hope you'll stay on with us, at least for a while.'

His first flush of infatuation for this lady was fading. What did she mean? For a while? What were they up to, this lot? Did they intend to pick his brains and then chuck him out? Like hell they would. Still . . . slowly, slowly, catchee monkey, he mused. A manager could be sacked at any time, so his best bet would be to shut up and feed this paragon of book-learning with information bit by bit. Make himself indispensable.

'Where do we go from here?' Morgan asked.

'I've made arrangements for you to stay at the Victoria Hotel here in the town for a few days,' Mike told him. 'To give you a chance to get your bearings. It's a new hotel, only been built six months, and they serve decent food so you should be quite comfortable.'

'Why do we have to go to that expense?' Morgan demanded. 'The plantation is our home now. We should prefer to go straight home.'

'I can see your point,' Mike said, placating the man, 'but there are

31

quite a few people in town who wish to make your acquaintance. You know the drill . . . a couple of bank managers, councillors, other planters. I thought a gentlemen's dinner might be in order.'

'And who pays for this gentlemen's dinner, Mr Devlin?'

'It'd go on the Providence account. Jake used to entertain leading citizens four times a year. And they reciprocate, of course.'

'By Jake, I understand you mean the former owner, Mr Devlin. But I am not Jake. We have come a long way, we've crossed the world. I am not in the mood to entertain and I am simply not ready. Forgive me if I appear ungracious. I appreciate your thoughtfulness, believe me, and in other circumstances it would be a quite splendid idea, but not now.' He drew Mike aside. 'Don't get me wrong. I thoroughly enjoy a good smoke night but I have to get the family settled. We'll leave right away.'

'It's no trouble to cancel the dinner,' Mike said, knowing that he was bringing down the wrath of the proprietor of the Victoria Hotel, Clancy Ahearne, who was expecting them, 'but I think you should stay here overnight.'

'Why?'

'It's not a good idea to travel when the sun's high. It's nearly eleven o'clock now. It's better to leave first thing in the morning.'

Corby patted him on the shoulder. 'Come now, Mr Devlin. Do you see me as a milksop who needs nursing? It's a glorious day. Now what transport can you provide?'

His manager shrugged. 'A bullock train will bring on your heavier trunks and other effects which I presume you have with you.'

'Indeed we do.'

'Then if you would care to ride, I have a horse for you. The ladies and Professor Langley can ride in the wagon with the cabin luggage, and I also have some packhorses organised.'

'Well . . . there we are. No problem at all. We shall be home in no time.'

'In six hours,' Mike corrected, 'all being well.'

The shock on Morgan's face was some recompense to Mike for his dawning realisation that this was a man not given to accepting advice.

'Six hours, you say?' Morgan remarked lightly, with an attempt at bravado. 'I was under the impression that Providence was much closer.'

'The wagon will slow us up,' Mike told him. 'It's much faster on horseback.' But then to rattle the man and consolidate his own position, he added: 'That's now, I mean, in the dry season. In the wet it can take a lot longer, that is if we aren't completely cut off.'

'Then we shall just have to suffer it, won't we?' Corby replied firmly.

'Not much choice,' Mike said with a grin. Despite the fancy clothes and his obstinate attitude, the Englishman wasn't short of spunk. Having made his decision, he was prepared to tough it out rather than back down, and Mike awarded him points for that. Of course they had a long way to go — the journey to Providence, though hazardous, was just the beginning. Providence itself could be a volatile mistress, gleeful or grim, totally unpredictable. Mike always felt that if he could get through a day without some drama or problem he'd done well. It would be interesting to see how Morgan coped with the physical exertion and the pressures of a workforce of ninety Kanakas.

Sylvia thought the plantation manager, though old — forty at least — very handsome, with his black hair pegged at the back, dark eyes and tanned skin, and a warm smile under that thick moustache. He wasn't wearing a jacket, as gentlemen should, so his wide chest and muscular arms were all too evident under an old-fashioned full-sleeved shirt which was left daringly open at the neck.

'Oo-la-la!' she said to herself — Lita had taught her that — as she watched him unpack the barrow. 'He looks like a dashing pirate!' She'd been fascinated to see Lita kiss him on the cheek for all the world to see, and his smiling, easy response, as if he were her brother, which he certainly was not. She'd have to find out all about him from Lita one of these days.

It was cruel of Corby to insist they leave straight away. Mr Devlin had tried to make life more pleasant for them by suggesting they stay at an hotel for a few days, but Corby wouldn't have it — too mean to pay, of course. At least she and Jessie had been permitted to take morning tea in the lounge of the hotel while the men made the travel arrangements.

'This seems quite a proper place,' she said to Jessie. 'You ought to insist that we take rooms and stay over, especially in your condition.'

'It won't make any difference, condition or not,' Jessie replied. 'I'll have to make the journey sooner or later and I'm feeling quite well.'

Sylvia lapsed into silence. Jessie was such a cabbage. Whatever Corby said was right, she always did exactly as she was told without a murmur. Still, she thought, primping her hair and looking over at three young men who were in earnest conversation by the door, Jessie was so plain, with her mousy hair and nondescript colouring, she'd been lucky to catch Corby. For all his bossy ways he was quite good-looking and he was always dressed elegantly, which was more than could be said for his wife. Fashion did not interest Jessie, who wore drab, correct outfits designed to last, in stark contrast to her sister, who delighted in attractive clothes.

Corby never seemed to notice how dull his wife looked beside him, and that had been a mystery to Sylvia until her new friend and cabin-mate, Lita, had whispered: 'It's quite normal, dear. Lots of men prefer dull little wives who don't make a sound out of place, because they don't attract attention from other males. It rules out competition, you know. Had your sister been a sparkling wit, she'd never have landed Mr Morgan, who prefers to be the centre of attention himself.'

From the minute she'd met Lita, Sylvia's life had changed. Here was a person who listened to her, who understood that it was callous to wrench a young lady from her accustomed social setting, and, best of all, who was such fun. She never seemed to take anything seriously,

33

especially her role as Sylvia's chaperone when the family had retired. Flirting outrageously herself, she wasn't in the least critical of Sylvia's shipboard romances. Rather, she enjoyed hearing all about them.

Corby disapproved of Mrs de Flores, of course, but Sylvia didn't care. Lita was quite divine, and her friend. Sitting there by the window, watching all manner of strange, rough people idling about the peculiar village, Sylvia hoped that Lita wouldn't forget her now that the voyage was over. She had promised to keep in touch, insisting there were plenty of jolly people living in the district who would be pleased to welcome the newcomers.

'We ought to go for a walk,' she said to Jessie, becoming bored with the delay.

'No, we'd better not,' Jessie said. 'Corby asked us to wait here. He wouldn't want to have to come looking for us. Would you like some more tea?'

'Thank you, no. I'm going to have a look out the front door. Surely that won't bother your husband!'

'Don't be like that, Sylvia. Corby has been very patient with you . . .'

'About what?'

'You know perfectly well. Your behaviour on the ship left a lot to be desired, so I suggest you don't add to his exasperation.'

'He's not my keeper!' she snapped.

At the door she met her father, who took off his cap and mopped perspiration from his face. 'Oh my dear, that sun is hot. I've been exploring. They're making quite a town here . . . a new court house and post office, and a police station . . .'

'I should hope so,' Sylvia retorted.

'Yes, quite.' He blinked. 'Come and have a cup of tea, dear.' With a sigh of frustration Sylvia went back inside with him.

Reminded of Devlin's suggestion that they should defer travel until the early morning, Corby was disconcerted to find that the women would have to travel in a lumbering German wagon without cover. He wasn't worried about Sylvia, but Jessie was nearly seven months pregnant and could be affected by the heat.

'Surely we can do better than this,' he said. 'I thought a gig or a jinker with a canopy might be more appropriate for the ladies.'

'Afraid not. Once we get away from the town the road deteriorates. In the dry weather it's like driving over a ploughed field. A lighter vehicle would rattle their teeth out, the wagon is much safer.'

He introduced the driver, a grey-haired blackfellow. 'This is Toby. He's got hands of steel, he'll take it carefully, won't you, Toby?'

'Go real steady, boss,' Toby grinned. 'These two feller horses good boys.'

Corby watched as the wagon was loaded, and bags of spare provisions were strapped on to the packhorses. Two Chinamen came running with a hamper and three umbrellas.

'Our passengers will need some shade,' Devlin explained, 'and there's some food in the basket, we can have a meal on the way.'

'That's very thoughtful of you,' Corby replied. He was feeling quite adventurous; two fine horses were saddled ready for them and he had noticed that there was a shot-gun under the driver's seat in the wagon. But when Devlin armed himself with a handgun and stuck a rifle in a leather pouch by his saddle, his excitement changed to unease. 'Are these guns necessary?'

'Best to be on the safe side,' Devlin said.

'From what?'

'Snakes,' the manager replied, but Corby wasn't to be put off so easily.

'You need an armoury to defend yourself from snakes?'

The manager hesitated. 'I didn't want to worry you. Sometimes the tribal blacks out in the bush can be a bit difficult, and there are always bushrangers to watch out for. But we're not much of a target, they're usually out for gold.'

'And provisions?' Corby indicated the packhorses.

'It's possible.'

'Then I should prefer to be armed also.' Corby wanted to impress on this fellow that he was in charge of this expedition, not just a passenger.

'By all means. What do you want? A rifle or a revolver?'

Corby wondered if the word 'sir' inhabited the fellow's vocabulary. 'The latter, please, and a decent one.' He took out his purse. 'How much do you require?'

'We'll put it on our account,' Devlin said. 'You wait here while I dive over and get one for you.'

His reply both cheered and displeased Corby. To have an account meant that credit was established and he wouldn't have to use his meagre funds, but on the other hand 'our' account bothered him. He'd have to keep an eye on Devlin, see to it that he wasn't booking goods up at town stores without a chit signed by the real boss, Corby Morgan. God knows what this slack system might cost him. In Devlin's absence he turned to the young stablehand who was lounging by a fence, minding the horses. 'Do all these horses belong to the Providence plantation?'

'Yes. Mike keeps spare mounts in town, usually half a dozen or so.'

'They're fine horses.'

'Oh, yes. Jake was a good judge of horseflesh. That one over there . . .' he pointed to one of the packhorses, a tall chestnut with a white mane, 'that's Prissy, sister to your mount, Prince.' He laughed. 'And do you reckon she isn't put out, being turned into a workhorse, even though we've only given her a light load! They know, the buggers. Mike had her brought in because he thought your missus would like to ride. But when he woke up she was in the family way, he had to rethink, didn't he?'

Corby turned away in disgust, offended by this lout's casual reference to his wife's condition. God, how he wished Roger and his wife were with him to give him the reassurance he would need to cope with these awful people.

Nevertheless, he couldn't resist a slight swagger as he walked up the main street to collect the women and the old man, with a gun slung on his hip, his well-cut jacket flapping open to accommodate the bulge. None of the other men in the street seemed to notice – quite a few were wearing guns themselves – but as soon as Sylvia saw him she burst out laughing. 'My God, Corby! You look like a highwayman! Stand and deliver!'

He ignored her and took Jessie's arm. 'Don't be concerned. I'm advised that one could encounter snakes in the countryside. Now come along, it's time to go.'

'Shouldn't you have changed into riding clothes, dear?' she asked, but he shook his head.

'We are not going to the hunt, Jessie. I don't own the rough-and-ready stuff they're wearing here, so this will have to do.'

The journey was appalling. The men on horseback could do little but trot along within sight of the wagon and the packhorses hitched to its rear, and Corby yearned to get the hell going, thinking they might not make Providence by nightfall. They followed a narrow track through withered, dry countryside that had a stultifying sameness of scrub and gaunt trees without a farm to be seen. If it hadn't been for the armies of flies that travelled with them, Corby thought he might fall from his horse in sheer boredom.

He had cross words with the Professor, who had chosen to sit up by Toby and was therefore able to ask him to halt whenever he spotted some peculiar plant to commence his collection. Corby instructed Toby that he was not to stop the horses at the old man's whims, but the Aborigine was confused and continued to do so until Mike spoke to him, with apologies to Corby's father-in-law.

Sylvia, who'd ridden out the whole voyage without a sign of seasickness, demanded they stop on several occasions because she felt nauseous thanks to the bump and sway of the wagon. On the third stop, Devlin produced their meal of sandwiches, and tea boiled in a tin dipper, called a billy, over a campfire, while Corby fumed. He also produced some fruit cake and two bottles of white wine which they were able to enjoy in blessed shade. It was hot, it was bloody hot! Corby was sure sweat was ruining his clothes, and the gun rubbed at his hip like a scorching iron. And then Sylvia was sick, vomiting down the side of the wagon, having drunk too much wine.

A nightmare, Corby fumed. A bloody nightmare! Despite the fact that his wife had not complained – even though her face was burning from the sun since she'd become too tired to hold up the umbrella – he vowed that he'd never take the two women into town unless they were able to ride. Absolutely bloody never! They were making a fool of him in front of Devlin, who seemed to be taking all these miserable mishaps

36

for granted. And to make matters worse, Langley was carrying on an animated conversation with the grinning black driver as if they were old school chums suddenly reunited.

From the road they had only sighted a few houses in the distance, dull-looking bungalows with no attempt at style, probably belonging to tenant farmers. And that reminded him: 'How many tenants do we have on the estate?' he asked Devlin as they rode along together.

'None,' Devlin replied. 'It's more practical to run the place ourselves.'

'But surely the whole property isn't under cultivation?'

'No, a lot has to be cleared yet and some of the land is too wet or too hilly to bother with, but we are extending the canefields each year.'

'One would think the rents would be useful,' Corby said. 'And to have tenants working their own fields would save us a deal of expense.'

'Think of it as a factory,' Mike told him. 'It's better to own a factory producing merchandise than to rely on the dubious standards of piecework. It's essential that we produce a high standard of cane. The sugar refinery in Brisbane is always experimenting with new varieties, looking for hardier canes for a better crop, and they often send cane inspectors up to advise us.'

'How long does it take a crop to mature here?'

'About twelve months, thanks to the climate and the rainfall. After the first cut we ratoon, allowing the cane to grow again for three years before the sugar content lowers so that we get four crops out of each stick of cane planted.'

As they came to the crest of a hill Corby stared. 'Good God! These are canefields?'

'They surely are.'

Ahead of them, spread out like a shifting sea, were acres of cane against the backdrop of distant mountains. Corby was stunned and impressed by this display and knew, with a sense of pride, that he'd made the right decision. He sent his horse cantering down the hill to ride alongside the crops, surprised at their height. Even on horseback the wall of leafy canes towered over him. 'Is this Providence?' he called to Devlin.

'No, this is our neighbour, Helenslea. It belongs to Edgar Betts. He's a tough old coot. You met his daughter, Mrs de Flores, on the ship, I believe.'

'Yes,' Corby said curtly. 'Is Helenslea the same size as Providence?'

'No, bigger. It's two thousand acres, which is in our favour since it gives us enough cane to share a mill.'

Now Corby didn't mind the blazing sun or the stifling dusty tang of the cane or even the clouds of insects that buzzed about him. He raced down the road, eager to see, to touch, to enjoy his own fabulous estate.

Devlin joined him as they splashed across a shallow creek and up a small rise. 'This is Providence,' he said. 'This track goes right on up to the house.'

37

On one side was the creek, bordered by tall stringy gums and scrubby undergrowth, and on the other, row after row of bushy canes that seemed to Corby like a guard of honour. He was pleased they'd left the wagon far behind, for he wanted to enjoy this experience to the full without the distraction of the others.

When at last the canefields gave way they were confronted by a large unkempt clearing, and in the centre another of those bungalows, a large timber cottage perched on stilts with a wide veranda across the front.

'Home sweet home,' Devlin remarked as he dismounted, oblivious to Corby's dismay. This was not a gentleman's residence, the substantial house he had expected. It was just a workhouse dumped in the clearing. And no attempt had been made to soften the aspect with gardens or lawns, except for a few shrubs that peered limply from under the front steps.

Pushing aside his disappointment Corby stood by in front of the house. 'Now let me get my bearings. We have come south and turned inland, that means the sea is over there to my right.'

'No,' Devlin said. 'The Providence track from the road, between the canefield and the creek, comes west towards the river and then veers right to arrive here at the front of the house. Although it's half a mile away through that scrub, we are facing the river.'

'We don't face the road? That's strange.'

'We're a good way from the road,' the manager explained. 'And Jake planned eventually to clear all of the scrub in front of us, right down to the river, and turn it into home paddocks for horses.'

'That sounds more civilised than this,' Corby replied. 'We seem to be totally surrounded by wilderness.'

'And canefields,' Devlin added. 'But it would have been pleasant having a clearway to the river and the possibility of a breeze.'

'It's a big river?'

'Oh yes. It rises far to the north-west, a tributary of another one, I'm told, and cuts through other plantations to give us a natural border. It flows on to the sea about forty miles south. We have several creeks flowing through the estate so we're not short of water, but there's a rainwater tank for drinking water at the rear of the house.'

'I see,' Corby said. 'Now let me get this right. I am facing the river, therefore the coast is at my back.'

'Yes, it's about twenty miles across country to Elbow Bay. A very pretty little bay.'

'Are there any roads to it?'

'No, not yet.'

'Then we must see to it one day. And get this forest in front of the house cleared away too. Good God! Who are they?' He was startled to see a motley group of blacks standing shyly by the corner of the house, dressed in odd scraps of clothing.

'They're local blacks. They camp over by the creek.' Mike took Corby over to meet them. 'This is the new boss, Mr Morgan.'

38

They grinned enthusiastically at him and Corby managed to acknowledge them politely, although finding, on closer inspection, that they were a wild-looking lot.

Devlin drew forward a tall slim girl with tangled black hair and large nervous eyes. 'This is Elly, your housegirl.'

Then a Chinaman and a tiny Chinese woman pushed through the crowd, so he had to meet them too. 'And this is Tommy Ling, your cook, and Mae, his wife. She tends the laundry and the vegetable garden.'

'How do you do?' Corby said, standing back as they both bowed to him, their hands shoved in large sleeves.

Weird, he thought, quite weird, all of them, and he turned back to inspect his new home as black stableboys rushed out to take charge of their horses.

The house itself was deathly plain, devoid of character, and yet Devlin seemed quite proud to show him through. A passage ran down the centre, with a parlour and dining room on one side and three bedrooms on the other. That was it! Tacked on to the back veranda were a large farm kitchen and a bathroom.

The manager pointed to nearby buildings. 'That's the guest rooms, with the laundry next door.' Further across the hard dry yard were a dairy, coolroom and several sheds, while the continuation of the track to the house led on to stables almost hidden by a clump of trees.

Corby surveyed all this without comment. 'Where do the labourers live?'

'The Kanakas have barracks about a half-mile on from here.'

'*Kanaka* I presume means labourer?'

'No, it's an island word for man, Hawaiian I'm told.'

'Why island words?'

Devlin glanced at him, surprised. 'We import our workers from the Solomon Islands.'

'What the hell for?' Corby was taken aback. 'Surely you've got enough Australian natives?'

The manager laughed. 'Any amount, but they won't work the fields. They reckon it's a dog's life and they're right, of course, it's damn hard work. The Aborigines can find their own food, they can't see the point in cropping. The lads you met outside, they're Aborigine, they all love working with horses, but they won't go near the cane.'

This was an aspect that hadn't occurred to Corby, or to Roger for that matter, for all his research into sugar production. The very idea made Corby nervous. What must it cost to import labour? To cover his irritation he strode out to the front veranda just as the wagon came into sight. 'First thing I want done,' he said to his manager, 'is fencing. I require the whole area around the house to be fenced and those people kept out. This place is desolate, a garden will have to be planted here without delay.'

'By all means,' Mike said amiably. Morgan was right, a garden would be very nice. He and Jake had never given it much thought. The men were always needed for other work.

When the rest of the family arrived, Mike was interested in their different reactions. Mrs Morgan was quiet, she was very tired and only wished to rest but she did remark that the house was 'nice and clean'.

'That's Elly's work,' he told her. 'She's only young but a good housemaid.'

Her sister, Miss Langley, turned her nose up. She seemed to enjoy baiting her brother-in-law. 'So this is the family mansion, Corby? Hardly the place for a squire. I can't imagine what you were thinking of, bringing my sister to a place like this.'

'You take the room on the end,' he said angrily, 'and your father can have the middle room.'

'Oh no,' Langley piped up. 'I've been looking about. I should prefer to take that guest room outside, if that is permissible, Mr Devlin?'

Mike shrugged and looked to Morgan, who only replied: 'Sleep where you like. I couldn't care less. Mr Devlin, tell the cook we should like tea right away.'

Miss Langley giggled. 'A Chinaman for a cook! How incredible! Does he know how to make tea?'

'That's one thing he can do.' Mike smiled, preferring not to add that Tommy Ling, who had been with them for years, was a very erratic cook. When he put his mind to it he could serve excellent baked dinners or tasty Chinese fare, but on off days, usually when he had a new supply of opium, his failures could be spectacular.

'And where do you live, Mr Devlin?' the girl asked, her blue eyes gazing up at him.

'Up the hill,' he replied, careful not to respond to an obvious flirtation.

'Then you must show me in the morning,' she said.

'He'll have better things to do in the morning,' Corby told her. 'Go and see to your sister.'

Chapter Five

Mike had managed to get his charges out to Providence without any major upsets, and now he was anxious to escape from them, in order to see how the new batch of Kanakas had settled in. Normally he collected them at the port and brought them out to Providence himself, giving them a day to settle in before sorting them into gangs to begin work, but this time he'd had to leave them in the hands of Ted Perry, and that worried him. Ted was an experienced foreman but a hard taskmaster. It was essential to employ a foreman who could control all the gangs and keep them working, but Ted was too handy with the whip, and since Jake died there had been far too many complaints about Ted's cruelty. Several of the Kanakas had been beaten up so badly they'd been unable to work, and their spokesmen reported this treatment to Mike.

Jake would have fired Perry on the spot, probably after giving him a taste of the whip himself, but all Mike could do was demand that the foreman ease up. This had almost resulted in a fight between the two men since Perry resented any criticism. Mike couldn't fire him, as he was on a contract, one that could only be revoked by the new owner. In fact, Mike mused crankily as he answered Morgan's stream of questions, Perry was in a better position than he himself was, since he didn't have a contract. To get rid of Perry, Corby Morgan would have to pay him off.

Having finished tea, one of Tommy's better efforts, served with scones and cake, Corby was pleased to discover that Mike had the spirits cupboard well stocked. He opened a bottle of brandy and settled back in Jake's big leather chair for further discussions with his manager. So Mike, determined to give the impression that the plantation always ran smoothly under his management, was cornered.

'I'd better go,' he said at length. 'I like to do the rounds at this hour, see that everything's shut down nice and quiet.'

'You've got a foreman to do that, haven't you? Have another drink.'

'Yes, but I've got to see he does his job too.' Some other time he would talk to Morgan about the disruptive activities of their bad-tempered foreman.

'I don't know why I need a manager *and* a foreman,' Corby said petulantly.

'Most plantations have several foremen,' Mike explained. 'We can manage with one, but it's tough going, this is a big operation.'

'Nevertheless,' Corby replied, 'you seem to have managed admirably for the last few months without the assistance of the former owner, so why do we need three men now? I am not exactly useless.'

Jesus! Mike thought. Jake worked like a Trojan, and I'm only just managing to keep the place at par. If anything, we need more Kanakas. 'I'm sure you're not,' he replied. 'But there's a lot to do at various levels. I'll show you round the plantation in the morning.'

'It doesn't alter the fact that as owner I should be manager with a foreman working under me. That seems to make sense.'

If you've got eyes in the back of your head, and you're prepared to sit your horse all day or muck in when needed, and forget sleep and your fancy garden, sure it does, Mike thought. And then when the wet comes you'll be so bloody tired you'll wish you were dead. But he only replied: 'That's up to you, Mr Morgan. I'm here to keep the show moving for you, and get that cane to the mill. I usually start at four thirty in the morning. What time should I call for you?'

'Have a horse ready for me at nine sharp, Devlin. I'll begin my inspections bright and early.'

'Bright and early!' Mike muttered to himself as he made for the stables. 'Brother, are you in for a shock if you want to be manager.'

He followed a bridle track through open scrub to what they called the compound. Though not fenced, it was an area set aside for several barrack-like buildings and an open thatched long-house which the islanders had built for themselves as a community centre for meals and gatherings. Normally at this hour it was alive with chatter and laughter, but an ominous silence greeted him as Kanaka gangs filed up to the shed to replace their hoes, spades and picks and join the others in the long-house.

Even the women who were preparing their supper over open fires wore blank, sullen expressions instead of their usual cheeky bantering air. These were Kanaka wives, plump, nut-brown women who wore colourful sarongs with a confident flair and were never averse to whacking male miscreants with their large wooden spoons.

Mike could always get a laugh out of them, so he hitched his horse to a tree and approached them first. 'What did you girls do? Give all these blokes tummy aches?'

They shook their heads and kept on stirring pots of rice and stew, chopping fish and fruit at the far bench with a gusto that threatened to remove fingers. None of them would look at him.

'Cat got your tongues?' he joked.

Pompey's wife Tamba rolled her eyes at him. 'No, massa.'

'Where's Pompey?'

He followed her glance towards her brawny husband who was trying to appear inconspicuous. 'Out here, quick smart,' he called, and reluctantly, all eyes on him, Pompey rose to his feet and padded over to him.

'You're head man, Pompey. Tell me the trouble.'

42

Pompey sighed. 'Trouble all finish now. All fixem.'

That worried Mike even more. 'Fixem' could mean anything. 'Fixem finish' often meant dead. 'Nothing's fixed,' he said, and then he realised there was an air of fear around him. 'Why are all these people frightened?'

Pompey shrugged, unwilling or afraid to speak. Mike marched over and kicked one of the large pots of rice, making the contents splutter into the fire. 'No supper for anyone,' he shouted to Pompey so that all the others could hear, 'unless you tell me the trouble.'

Pompey looked as if he were about to bolt. Mike grabbed him by the arm to hold him while he kicked over another pot. A great sigh went up from the crowd; the islanders loved their food and this waste was a terrible punishment.

'Is it the new boys?' he asked, remembering the riot at the port.

'No!' Pompey cried, petrified. 'All good fellers them.'

'Where have they been working?'

'All clear out scrub in new block, longa downways. Doing good until one fellow he . . .' Pompey hesitated. 'He hurt.'

'Which feller?'

But Tamba was becoming impatient. 'His name Joseph. He in hospital.'

'Right,' Mike said to Pompey. 'Let's go and see him.'

'Supper give out now?' Tamba asked him, and as Mike nodded there was a scamper for the tin plates before he could change his mind.

The hospital was another long building, but with hessian walls that were only rolled down in the wet. Two of the wives were paid to act as nurses, caring for the sick. In an emergency the doctor called, if he happened to be in the district. The patients, unused to the climate and hard work and the strange food, suffered from exhaustion, dysentery or pneumonia, when not brought down by accidents or snakebite, but they could only be nursed here. No white hospitals would take coloureds, be they black, brown or yellow, and they had to survive somehow. A small cemetery on the hill was a sad testimonial to the lack of medical facilities. Jake had suggested to the town council that they build a hospital for coloureds in Cairns but the proposal had died on the floor. There were no doctors available for such an establishment even if the council were willing to spend money on such an unpopular plan.

At least, Mike told himself as they toiled up the hill, all of the Kanakas at Providence were volunteers. Before he took any on Mike always questioned them, through an interpreter if necessary, to make certain they hadn't been kidnapped by blackbirders. Not that that was much consolation when he had to watch poor fellows waste away in hopeless bewilderment.

He stooped to enter the shed and stopped at each bunk for a quiet word with the patients and the nurses, pleased that the women were keeping their makeshift hospital clean. Towards the back he found the

43

new man, Joseph. He remembered him now as the tall, proud young fellow who had stood quietly with the others, and had smiled happily at being taken on. Mike was certain this was no trouble-maker, and yet . . . look at him now! He was lying flat on his face, his back a bloodied mess from a whipping.

'Oh, Christ!' he said, as he gently replaced a sheet of cheesecloth used as protection from flies. 'Did Perry do this?'

Pompey nodded.

'That bastard! Why?'

'Perry bash up new bloke. This feller he say: "Leave him 'lone. Doin' his best."'

'He speaks English?'

'Yes.' Pompey hurried on. 'Then Perry go mad yellin' at this feller. Tied him to a tree for the beltin'. Perry say he show good example.'

'I'll show him good example,' Mike growled. He squatted on his haunches by the bunk and touched Joseph on the shoulder. 'I'm sorry about this. We'll look after you. I'll see it doesn't happen again.'

The lad stared at him from his prone position and Mike was struck by the calm resignation in his eyes. 'No matter,' Joseph said. And then he appealed to Mike. 'You big boss, you don't send me back.'

'Of course not. You get better and I'll find you a good job. Speaking English you get more pay.'

Joseph smiled, and closed his eyes to rest.

Perry wasn't in his hut, and Mike searched everywhere for him until one of the Kanakas told him that the foreman had gone to visit the new boss.

'Damn!' He rode to the edge of the clearing and saw Perry, large as life, standing by the front veranda talking to Corby Morgan. No doubt he'd get in first with his story of how a Kanaka came to be whipped like that. He was a fast talker and quite a genial gent away from the canefields. Having taken his leave of Morgan for this evening, Mike could hardly intrude now, so he detoured to the rear of the house where he spotted Perry's horse hitched by the horse trough.

When the foreman finally came tramping across the yard he found Mike sitting waiting for him. 'Ah, Devlin,' he said. 'I was just coming to look for you. What about a drink?'

'Not right now. You've been talking to Mr Morgan?'

Ted laughed. 'If you can call it that. He's a few sheets to the wind, I'd reckon.'

'He's entitled,' Mike replied curtly. 'He's come a long way. I suppose you told him you put one of the new Kanakas in hospital today?'

'Ah, Jesus, they're a pack of slackers. That bloke got what he deserved. Anyway, it's nothing to do with you. I run the gangs, and you'd be the first one to yell if the work wasn't done.'

'I've told you before, Perry, to stop the rough stuff. That kid is in a hell of a mess . . .'

'So what?' Perry flared. 'One bloody nigger gets a hiding, the rest of them take notice and get their backs into the work. They're not here on a bloody picnic.'

'The one you whipped won't be able to work for a week!'

'Oho! That's more like it!' Perry sneered. 'You're only worried about where your bread's buttered. I'll get him a salt bath tomorrow, that'll cure him.'

'You're a bloody mongrel,' Mike said, but Perry wasn't fazed.

'Come off it, Devlin. Cool down. If any of these Kanakas don't want to work here, let them swap jobs with some of the Helenslea gangs. Old Edgar Betts'll show 'em what plantation work's all about.'

Before Mike could reply, Corby Morgan came striding over to them. 'Gentlemen. My ladies are about to sit down to dine. They do not need this shouting match outside their window. Kindly take your arguments elsewhere.'

As they rode away, Mike felt chastened like a naughty schoolboy, but Perry was hugely amused. 'Did you get on him? "Kindly take your arguments elsewhere!"' He laughed. 'What a ponce! He's not going to last long.'

'He's still the boss,' Mike warned, 'and I wouldn't underestimate him. There's flint in that skinny frame.'

'What are the women like? I didn't even get a look at them.'

'Very proper. You'd do well to keep away.'

'What about that drink?'

'No. I'm buggered, I want to get home.' And he did. He'd been surprised to find that living alone in the smaller bungalow was very pleasant.

At first he'd found it lonesome, wandering about not knowing what to do with himself of an evening. He'd spent years in the company of the restless, tireless Jake, who had to find things to do, be it cards, or night hunts for game, or prowling down to sit with the Kanakas, swilling their home-made brews. Or just knocking over bottles of rum, the pair of them out there on the veranda of the main house, talking over the day's events. And those were the quiet times. Because Jake loved women.

For a while, Lita Betts had been his mistress, staying over for days at a time, completely at home at Providence. Edgar, her father, hadn't cared; his daughter did as she liked, and it would have pleased him to see her marry the widower who owned Providence and so amalgamate the two properties. Lita had caused the only bust-up between Mike and Jake by climbing into Mike's bed when she'd thought Jake was too drunk to notice.

But he'd noticed! He'd come roaring after her with the horsewhip, and it was Mike who'd taken the first lash – he still had the scar across his back – while he was trying to persuade Lita to leave.

'But, darling,' she'd said to him – they were such mad days – sitting on the edge of his bed, ignoring Jake's shouts of rage, 'you're so much more interesting. Jake only wants a woman when the moon's up. Haven't you noticed?'

They'd ended up laughing about it, Lita and Jake, while Mike called for Elly to minister to the cut with the age-old stinging salt cure. And Jake had apologised to his angry friend.

But Lita had been right. Come full moon, with Lita away on one of her jaunts to Brisbane, Jake would invite other planters, without their wives, to what he called his 'weekend conferences', which also included the cream of Cairns' chippies. And, by God, they were a wild lot, hilariously matching Jake at every turn and charging him heaps for their company. The guests drank anything and everything; they dined on the best Jake could supply, and they smoked Cuban cigars, unless their preference ran to opium, which was always available.

At one stage Mike had fallen madly in love with a pretty little Chinese girl, who, at Jake's insistence, had told Mike point-blank that he couldn't afford her. That had hurt. It was shortly after that that Lita had delivered the same message to Jake from Brisbane. She had met and married a wealthy young Portuguese gentleman who was sailing the world in his father's clipper ship, out of Lisbon. The parent, who owned rich gold mines in South Africa and who was now investigating prospects of gold in Java, apparently held court in Bermuda in the summer and Lausanne in the winter, which intrigued the adventurous Lita. The world cruise on the beautiful clipper, though, was designed to benefit his son's failing health.

As a farewell gift, Lita sent Jake a gold-plated horseshoe, which he immediately, in disgust, handed over to Mike. It was now nailed over Mike's front door, for good luck, and in remembrance of those rollicking times.

He tapped the horseshoe as he walked into the house, dumping his pack and guns and settling on to a chair to remove his boots. The high-set house was cool and quiet – or as quiet as it ever would be, given the croaks, squeals and whispers perpetually emanating from the busy forest surrounds and the soft shuffle of water slipping downhill in the nearby rocky creek. Maintaining the tranquillity that now gave him so much pleasure, he moved quietly to light the lamp and gaze at the wide, comfortable room that was his parlour, his dining room and his office. In contrast with the heavy cedar furniture of the main house, Mike had purchased a job lot of cane furniture for his bungalow – or, rather, a Chinese friend had practically bullied him into it, claiming it was more appropriate for this climate. Having little idea of how to decorate a house Mike had had to admit eventually that the lighter furniture did look pretty good, especially since bamboo blinds had been included.

Hungry now, he inspected the food safes which Tamba kept well stocked for him since he preferred to prepare his own meals. He decided on salt pork and Tamba's collation of rice, tomatoes, onions and green peppers, with slices of damper. As he poured a long glass of rain water from the jug, he winked at the coiled carpet snake that was watching him from under a day bed: 'You been looking after the place for me,

Snake?' he asked. 'If I find any mice or cockies around, you're fired. Don't forget that.'

Losing interest, Snake allowed his head to rest contentedly on the floor as his master set the lamp on the table with a couple of newspapers to finish his evening in peace.

Since neither of the women had any idea how to address the Oriental who lurked in their kitchen, and Corby made it plain that domestic matters never had been, nor would, in future, be his responsibility, it was left to the Professor to approach Tommy Ling and advise him that the family would have a simple supper of scrambled eggs, toast and tea.

Tommy was aghast! 'No, no, no,' he shrilled, swooping over to the oven to display a succulent leg of lamb sizzling softly in a barricade of potatoes and pumpkin. 'Boss say English dinner for important English peoples,' he declared. 'You look see, look see!' He popped lids of saucepans on the wide range: 'Peas! Beanies! All good Chinee garden vegetables! And plum pudden!'

'Oh, I am sorry,' Lucas Langley replied. 'How very kind of you to go to this trouble. We must certainly eat what you have prepared, it looks delicious.'

The cook bowed in relief. 'You new boss here?'

'No, Mr Ling, I do not wish to be a boss. I am Mr Langley.' He proceeded to explain the members of the family to Tommy, who listened carefully, repeating the names. 'Now,' he continued, 'do you need any help here?'

The young Aborigine girl came in. 'Tommy doan like people in his kitchen,' she grinned. 'Missus better tell him what to cook in the mornings then keep out. I watch him for her. You go now. I'll ring this here bell when dinner ready.'

Disappointed, the Professor retreated. He was interested in everything and everyone in the place and he would have enjoyed a chat with the Chinaman to find out who he was and how he came to be in the country, but he supposed there'd be time enough. He was delighted with his plain little hideaway outside, which would spare him the overpowering presence of his son-in-law and allow him the freedom he'd been hoping to find. To Lucas, Providence was all that he had expected, and more . . . a wonderland of strange flora and fauna with the added mystery of this exotic collection of human inhabitants. He couldn't wait to begin his explorations.

But his daughters were less enthusiastic.

Jessie had slept fitfully in the strange bed for a few hours, troubled by confused, almost nightmarish images, and she awoke nervous and shaken. The room was cool, with a light breeze wafting in from open french doors that led on to the veranda. There were no curtains, she noticed, and no provision for them either. She shivered at this lack of privacy but that was only part of her dismay. Jessie was frightened. She so wanted to please Corby but it was beginning to dawn on her that she

47

had no idea how to run a house so far from civilisation, so far from the comforting proximity of the butcher, the baker and, yes, the candlestick-maker.

And who would help her with the birth of her first child, that terrifyingly lonely event she had yet to face? Not Sylvia; she hadn't any experience either, and anyway, she'd run a mile. Would she have to go into that dreadful raucous town to have some stranger deliver her child? A forest of worries pressed in on her as she struggled to her feet and poured water from a large jug into a china dish, sloshing her face, her neck, under her arms, with the tepid liquid as if to wash away these fears.

Sylvia didn't help. She had changed into a low-cut and very pretty Swiss cotton dress that she'd had made for her on the ship — one of many dresses designed by Mrs de Flores. Now she came swanning in to show Jessie. 'Isn't this just divine? I couldn't make up my mind whether to wear this or the white organza, but I'll save that up for a better occasion. The floral pattern on this is really lovely, though. Blue does suit me.'

She twirled in front of the mirror set in the large wardrobe. 'God! The furniture in this place is just appalling, isn't it?'

'Father says it is made of excellent red cedar and quite expensive,' Jessie replied as she pulled on a long skirt and covered her expanding waistline with a cream linen smock.

'Good, then you ought to sell it right away. It's easy to see it was chosen by men. Poor Mr Devlin was so proud of it. I didn't have the heart to tell him it belongs in a manor house, not in a flimsy cottage like this. You look dreadful. Are you all right?'

'Yes, thank you. Just a little hot.'

'My dear, this is winter! Lita said it gets ten times hotter when their summer comes. What does Corby really think of this house?'

'He didn't say. I expect it just has to do.'

'It's revolting and you know it. If Corby won't build us a suitable home I intend to speak to Father. Don't forget he owns half of this estate.'

'You're wasting your time,' Jessie flared, pleased to have some comeback. 'Father can't see anything wrong with it.' She made a deliberate effort not to look up at the bare rafters that hung over them. 'And you might remember that there is no money for anything new, let alone another house. Please, Sylvia, try to make the best of it.'

'But how can we entertain in a place like this?'

'I have no idea,' Jessie said, as she put on her shoes and stood up to begin this new life. 'Nor who we might entertain.'

Dinner was, however, a cheery occasion, with Corby in the best of moods. The black girl had set the table with the bare essentials, including, Jessie noted, a snowy-white tablecloth, so her first question went to Elly: 'Do you do the washing and ironing?'

'No, missus. Tommy's missus done that. Chinee lady our washer-woman.'

'Will you look at the silver?' Sylvia giggled. 'I swear it's tin.'

'It will suffice until ours arrives,' Corby snapped. 'Tell the girl to serve, Jessie.'

The table was set for five. Sylvia took her place. 'Shouldn't we wait for Mr Devlin?'

'I have not invited him,' Corby replied. 'I gather he lived here with the former owner. He now has to learn his place.'

'That's a pity,' Lucas remarked. 'A conversation with him would have been most enlightening.'

'You can talk to him any time.'

When Elly confronted Corby with the lamb roast on a platter, Jessie apologised. 'Oh dear. I'm sorry, Corby. You did order scrambled eggs.' She looked to her father. 'I thought that was what we were to have.'

'Never mind,' Corby told them, picking up the carving knife and fork. 'I do believe this is more fitting. And it smells so good I'm suddenly extremely hungry. Jessie,' he added, 'tell the girl to serve us some red wine.'

Elly stared at them mystified, so Lucas jumped up. 'What if I appoint myself wine-master to the household? Just as well we brought our own, there isn't a wine cellar, but I'll attend to that.'

'Good idea.' Corby smiled, then excused himself for a few minutes to investigate an argument that was taking place outside. On his return he made no comment about it, but he did tap Jessie on the shoulder to whisper: 'Do you think you could see that our waitress wears shoes?'

After the stale and salty shipboard fare, the roast dinner with fresh vegetables was a joy, and they all ate well, even Jessie. 'We have to thank Corby for this,' she told the others. 'He did the right thing bringing us straight on home. I must admit the journey was trying but the worst is over, we're home at last.'

They were dining by candlelight and no one noticed that Sylvia's little dog, scampering about the floor, was having a fine time chasing skinks and inch-long cockroaches, while high above them little geckos peered down with their innocent round eyes. It wasn't until much later, when Jessie and Corby were already slumbering, that Sylvia's screams rent the night.

'There are things in my room!' she shrieked. 'Wild things, snakes, moving about everywhere, waiting to attack me!'

But when Corby came rushing in, the mantle turned up to bright lamplight, the nocturnal invaders had disappeared. Even the gentle bat, or flying fox as it was known here, had taken fright and fled through the open eaves.

'It's just the wine,' he snapped in disgust. 'You're seeing things. There's nothing here at all. Now go back to bed.' But his eyes had been drawn more often to the girl herself as he prowled the room. Too alarmed to remember to cover herself further, she stood stock still in her lawn nightdress while he searched, the enticing curves of her naked body silhouetted through the almost sheer material. Coming closer to her, eyes downcast, pretending to search, he was tantalised by the high, taut breasts, the tiny waist and that eye-catching patch of black above the long slim legs.

'Do I have to stay in here?' she pleaded.

Kinder now, he took her arm and led her to the bed. 'Yes,' he said, feeling the warmth of her. 'It might have only been a mouse. I'll have a better look tomorrow.'

He hurried from the room, that warmth still with him, so soft and sensuous, and he was unwilling to push it away.

That same night the Malaita men did not so much meet as meld into the tropical cavern of forest that had little in common, except for a sullen heat, with the rubbery softness of their island flora. This tangled scrub with its skinny gum trees, white in the moonlight, refused to give way to jungles of interloping palms and creepers, remaining a mix of breeds knee-deep in sharp grass and ferns. Ancient tree-ferns stood apart, dark survivors of the ages, hardy and watchful like their contemporaries, the black tribes.

Kanakas were jungle people, rounder and sleeker than the Aborigines but wary of these natives who treated them with contempt as well as a certain amount of fear. For the strangers had brought with them a god-awe dedicated to blood sacrifice, which confused the locals, who revered the earth and its wonders.

Gradually, though, the white men were clearing out the forests, forcing local tribes to retreat, and through their labours fining down that gleaming islanders' flesh into clothed, lean and hungry imitations of their peasant class.

As the Kanakas gathered silently in the forest, local natives withdrew. They were not interested in Kanaka affairs unless they presented a threat, and these days they seemed to have learned their lesson. In the early stages, these Kanakas had stolen fat Aborigine children for sacrifice and feasts, their cannibal feasts, and they'd met with sudden and fierce reprisals first from the Irukandji people, and then from the whites who were quickly informed of this imported terror.

There was no spokesman as such, as groups discussed the shocking attack on Talua in whispered angry tones. They recalled that the white man Jock Bell had also struck their young god, and many were the voices demanding retaliation, but Talua himself had refused to permit any such action. They reminded each other that he had said: 'We are in a new world. We must learn their ways and obey their laws so that when the time comes we can come and go freely, like Kwaika and Manasali, bringing blessings and knowledge back to our own people.'

And so Jock Bell had been spared.

But now this white boss, Perry, had not only flogged Talua without mercy, he had broken his own laws. Hadn't Manasali, known as Sal, heard Mr Devlin roaring at him over this? And Mr Devlin was right. The old hands knew the law as well as he did. Bosses were not supposed to flog Kanakas, even though plenty of floggings went on at other plantations; it was the talk of the town brothels. Brutality by white bosses often caused riots but they were quickly put down by men with guns, so the unfortunates just had to suffer. The beating of Talua, though, was a special case.

There was no talk here of rioting or mass payback. Only one man was responsible for this blasphemy and he should be punished. Talua was in no condition to make a decision, voices said, one to another, and anyway he should be kept out of this, for his own safety. The time to act was now while Talua was still in the hospital, safe from blame.

As they sat cross-legged in the gloom, some smoking clay pipes, most chewing betel nut, the decision spread like a sea mist, infiltrating, silently seeping into the minds of the Malaita men. No names were mentioned, for among the forty-odd dark figures in their ghostly-white shirts the secret was already safe, and they filtered quietly back to their quarters to sit by their campfires and sing their island songs with the rest of the workers.

Sunlight streamed in on him through the bare glass, pinpointing tiny particles in the air, like a sheet of golden gauze. Throwing back the covers, Corby luxuriated in its warmth as the sun nudged at him to be up and about.

What a civilised way to awaken, he mused, stretching out in the large bed which had no trouble accommodating even his long legs. The mattress was firm too, well made. He decided that when he did consider refurnishing, the bed would stay. He had slept well and so had Jessie, for a change. She was still asleep, breathing quietly.

Reaching for his watch, he discovered it was only six o'clock, and he was wide awake, ready to rise. This made for a change too. Back home it was a struggle to be up by nine. Still in his nightshirt, he slipped from the bed, opened the french doors and stepped out on to the veranda. It was very quiet, except for the occasional call of strange birds settling in the wall of trees beyond the rough clearing, and the stillness of his surrounds gave him a flutter of nervousness until he realised that the house was quite a distance from the canefields and the activity one would expect from a large labour force. What had Devlin said? More than a hundred on the staff! Amazing! He, Corby Morgan, had all those people working for him, and from this vantage point he was lord of all he surveyed. What a day!

He dressed quietly and took himself off for a stroll about the grounds. 'If they can be called that,' he muttered, pacing the dusty earth between the collection of shingle-roofed sheds at the rear of the house.

Past the stables he came to a huge home paddock where at least thirty horses were grazing. 'Good God!' he said. 'They must belong to me too. Impressive, very impressive!' He followed the simple three-rail fence until he came to a vegetable garden neatly laid out in long rows, and at last discovered a sign of life. Far at the back the Chinese woman, in a wide coolie hat, was trotting along with a watering can. 'Rather you than me,' he said to himself. 'That must take hours.' Amused, he turned to watch as six dairy cows came ambling up a track towards him, huge, evil-looking beasts, their udders swaying thickly.

He ducked under the fence to watch them pass and nodded to the two black girls in sagging grey shifts who were following their charges, armed with long sticks. They took quick, shy glances at him and hurried after the cattle, giggling noisily.

He retraced his steps, staring about him at the spacious blue sky, at the muscular greenery that hemmed in the homestead patch, and at the same mountains above him that had loomed over Trinity Bay like massive fortress walls. But the mountains were of no interest to Corby, they seemed a surreal backdrop to this larger-than-life sugar farm.

The Chinese cook yelled at him from the back veranda. 'You want your brekkie, boss?'

Startled, Corby looked up. 'Are you addressing me?'

Tommy nodded vigorously. 'Want brekkie?' he persisted.

Corby hesitated. There was no sign of the women. He was accustomed to breakfasting with his wife, and with his mail and newspapers. Now, of course, there'd be no mail and no papers for conversation pieces, so what the hell? He burst out laughing from sheer exuberance as he bounded up the steps. He couldn't remember when he'd last laughed like that, but it felt good. It felt great! And, by Jove, even on top of that meal last night, he was hungry. 'Yes,' he said to the Chinaman. Breakfast? Had anyone given cook his instructions? 'Oh well,' he told himself. 'I can take pot luck today.'

Pot luck was placed before him on the bare diningroom table without the benefit of cloth or napkin. To this gentleman, accustomed to his boiled eggs or kipper, it was nothing short of hilarious, but Corby suddenly found the appetite that had deserted him since his boarding school days. He studied the piece of steak, the chop, the bacon, the slices of lamb's fry and the two fried eggs that sat aboard the meat, and surveyed the jug of steaming gravy and the hot buttered toast, and the large china pot of tea. Then he went at it all with gusto, pleased that, being alone, he would not have to affect a little more dignity.

Tommy shuffled back in. 'You al' ri' there?'

'It's the best bloody breakfast I've ever had,' Corby announced.

The Chinaman's swarthy face broke into a toothy grin. 'You good boss. You an' me we get on plenty good.'

'Thank you,' Corby replied with whimsical cordiality as he devoured the delicious grilled chop.

'What you want for dinner?' Tommy asked.

'Good heavens. I can't think that far ahead. See my wife.'

'No, no! You say. Ladies too fussy! No good.'

Corby poured his tea and turned to the cook. 'Now see here. Mrs

52

Morgan is in charge of the menus. She will instruct you later today.'

The cook's smile disappeared. He frowned, pursed his lips and seemed to dig his flip-flop sandals into the timber floor. With a rare flash of tact, Corby solved the problem: 'I will be busy, so I will tell Mrs Morgan and she can tell you. Is that understood?'

'Ha, yes!' The grin returned. 'You want more chop? More tea?'

'No thank you, I've done very well.' Corby sat back in his chair. He had indeed, he was sure. Handling staff would be a priority here and this first foray had been a success. He would manage, having already made a good start.

Mike found him at the stables, dressed immaculately in a splendidly tailored riding outfit complete with high polished boots. He approved. Now that tough old Jake was gone, the new owner needed to display authority, and today Morgan surely looked the part.

'I've brought you a present,' he said, handing Corby a straw hat with the wide brim turned up all round. 'It's top quality.'

Corby took it gingerly. 'Thank you.' He ran a hand through his blond hair as if trying to decide whether he should wear the thing or take it for a keepsake.

'I'd wear it if I were you,' Mike advised. 'Protect you from sunburn. All the planters wear them, sort of a badge of office.' He punched at his battered old felt and replaced it on his head. 'I'm hard on hats, belting about the way I do, so I stick to this old thing when I can find it.'

'I suppose I'd better take your word for it,' Corby replied, settling it on his head. 'You're sure I don't look a bit odd?'

'No. As long as it fits.'

'It's quite snug actually,' Corby admitted, climbing on to his horse. 'Now, where do we go first?'

As they rode away from the homestead Mike remarked that Sunday was a good day to begin inspection, with the plantation quiet and everyone at their ease.

'Sunday?' Corby said. 'Jove. So it is! I'm afraid I've lost all count of the days. Do they have a service here?'

'No, but you can invite a preacher to visit when you're ready. They make the rounds occasionally.'

Soon the wide track took them past huge fields of cane divided by flattened pathways. 'These are the south fields,' Mike told him. 'The cane's looking good, isn't it?'

Corby could only nod. He presumed it was but he was more interested to learn that this immense crop was only part of his holdings, and the excitement began building in him again.

Several blackfellows in cheap shirts, their trousers tied up with ropes, came ambling towards them, and Mike reined in his horse. 'Where are you off to?' he asked, not unkindly.

'Jus' a walk, boss,' one man replied, but they were all staring curiously at Corby.

'This is your new master, Mr Morgan,' Mike told them, and they raised their hats, bobbing woolly heads in salute.

'They're Kanakas,' Mike explained, moving on, and Corby followed.

They entered the compound and dismounted, surrounded now by crowds of Kanakas, a good-humoured lot, Corby was relieved to note. He was pleased to hear several of them call out to him: 'G'day, master.' Big-bosomed women squatting in the dust grinned at them as Devlin moved easily among them, pointing out the various aspects of this community, which was quite a large village in itself.

'To differentiate,' Mike explained, 'the Kanakas call me boss and they call you master. Same goes for Perry. He's just known as boss too. That's his hut further up the side track. The women prepare his meals. I live right up the hill, you can just see my veranda from here. I prefer to get my own meals unless I'm too busy. By the way, if you ever want me, just send one of the house blacks for me. There's always someone around.'

'I hardly saw a soul this morning,' Corby said. 'Only a couple of native girls and a Chinese woman.'

'They're around. Their camp is on the boundary of the property, the other side of the homestead, and they don't come anywhere near the plantation. We don't let them mix, the Abos and the Kanakas, they get into too many fights. And in case I forget, the Abos call all white men boss, so don't take offence.'

On they went again, past more and more fields of cane, while Devlin explained the merits of this particular crop: good cane imported from New Guinea which had replaced the Cuban variety, and was sturdier and better able to withstand early wet weather. Corby tried to pay attention but he was now experiencing a sense of power, and he sat tall on his horse, silently exulting at the magnificence of his estate and his role of master. What a fool Roger was! He couldn't wait to write to his father to describe the green opulence of this land.

They crossed a small stream and Devlin led him for miles down a track through ragged bushland. 'The north fields are further on,' he said, 'and we've got men clearing land to the west, but I'll take you in that direction later.'

Eventually they came to a high bank looking down at a wide, fast-flowing river. 'This is the boundary of Providence. We used to send the cane down river but now we haul it over to Helenslea, since the mill was built. Edgar Betts and Jake built it as a co-operative, we share it. We get a better result that way. The faster the cane gets to the mill, the better, not a minute to waste.'

'How do you get it there?'

'The Kanakas strip and cut it, load it into drays and they're off. Take it over to Helenslea and no mucking about. Busy time coming up to keep them all on the move, I can tell you.'

Suddenly, out of the clear blue sky a crack of thunder split the air, and Corby jumped. There had been no lightning. The thunder persisted in one long, ear-splitting drum roll right along the mountains, petering out in the distance.

'Hold your horses, Lord,' Mike shouted. 'Give us time.'

'What for?' Corby asked.

'To get the cane in before the wet.'

'If there's a storm coming, why don't you get started now?'

'I've been watching. It's not quite ready. We need a few more days yet and plenty of sun.'

That made Corby nervous. He felt this fellow was gambling with his crops. His money. 'You won't get much sun if there's a storm.'

'We're safe for a while yet. There won't be a storm. He's just letting us know He's about to ring the changes.'

'Oh,' Corby replied, unconvinced. He turned his attention to the river and the richer, jungle-like surrounds with palms hanging over the wide sandy banks. 'It's very picturesque here,' he commented. 'Shall we ride down?'

'Yes, we can,' Devlin said, leading the way. 'The horses could do with a drink. So could I, for that matter. It's noon. I ought to be getting you back for lunch.'

Corby was surprised that the time had passed so quickly; as far as he could make out, they'd only covered a small section of the property. He didn't need lunch, but he was tiring. He noticed that Devlin now had his rifle across his lap. 'What's that for?'

'Crocodiles,' he replied. 'The bloody river's alive with them.'

'Jesus!' Corby exclaimed, hauling in his horse. 'I'm not that keen to see the river.'

'Don't worry, I'm watching. We've shot quite a few here and they learn, but always be careful. They're fast out of the water, they can come up the banks like trains. The Kanakas fish here when they can get their hands on a stick of dynamite. They stun the fish and scare the hell out of the crocs at the same time.'

Ashen-faced, Corby allowed his horse to drink for a few minutes, but obviously the animal was also aware of the problem, because after a few thirsty swills it turned about and jumped quickly back up the banks.

'We're not supposed to know about the dynamiting, of course. It's a fishing trick the Kanakas learned from white men, but some don't get it right. They either filch the dynamite or pick some up in town, and away they go. We only hear about it when someone blows his hand off.'

'Dear God!' Corby said.

Devlin shrugged. 'I try to tell them but there's always some smart bugger. We can only patch them up and send them home in disgrace.'

Corby was hot now. The midday sun was scorching, and although he wouldn't admit it he was glad of the shade from the light straw hat.

They began the ride home, but not far along the track, Devlin stopped. 'What's that?'

'What's what?'

'I thought I saw something in the bush.' He wheeled his horse and plunged into the undergrowth between the trees.

'Oh Christ!' Corby heard him shout. 'Oh Christ!'

'What is it?'

'Stay there,' Devlin warned, dismounting, but Corby had to know. He followed Devlin and found himself staring at a man, lying half-hidden in the brush.

'What's the matter with him? Is he drunk?'

'No, he's not drunk. He's dead. It's Perry.'

'Oh no! Good God, no!' Corby didn't want to look. He turned away. 'What happened to him?'

When Devlin didn't reply, he insisted. 'What's happened to him, man? Is it snakebite? And what would he be doing right down here without his horse?' Another thought came to him and he whispered, 'Could he have committed suicide?'

'Not unless he figured out how to cut off his own head.'

'Oh my God!' Disbelieving, unthinking, Corby leapt down to see for himself the bloody torso without a head. He fell away, clinging to trees to vomit as a fierce headache overtook him, and his body shook in fear. As his stomach rebelled again and tears dripped salt down his face he fished out a handkerchief, trying to pull himself together. Then he turned to rage at Devlin: 'How could a thing like this happen? You're the manager, what . . .'

But Devlin, his rifle in his hand, was beating at the surrounding bush, and when Corby realised why, he clung to the saddle of his horse, his face resting against the soft leather away from that awful smell. Devlin was searching for the head.

The women were busy, immersed in familiar chores, other concerns put aside for the time being.

Jessie awoke to find the maid, Elly, standing by her with a breakfast tray and instructions from the cook: 'Tommy say you drink plenty milk.'

'Oh, yes, thank you. Just put the tray on that little table over there.' Jessie climbed out of bed, almost blinded by the glare of the sun which seemed to be focused on her windows. She pulled a wrapper on over her long flannel nightdress and was just in time to stop Elly, who was headed for the door. 'Don't go. Sit down, dear, and we'll have a talk.'

Elly sat awkwardly on the edge of a chair, clutching at her shapeless grey shift.

To put her at her ease, Jessie commented on the breakfast of boiled eggs and toast and a large glass of milk. 'How nice. Just what I wanted.' Since that didn't bring any response she broke open the eggs, genuinely pleased now. 'Oh, heavens. Fresh eggs at last! And fresh milk too, I'd almost forgotten they existed.'

The girl, whom Jessie guessed to be about seventeen, nodded dully and Jessie smiled. 'I'm sorry. How silly of me. You wouldn't have experienced shipboard food.'

She wanted to know all about this girl, and decided to start from the beginning. 'I haven't met any of your people before,' she began. 'You're Aborigine, Elly?'

The maid seemed even more confused. 'No, missus, Yindini.'

Jessie didn't know what to make of that word, so she went on with her breakfast while Elly waited obediently. She was a tall girl, her skin like anthracite, and she looked very healthy. Those dark eyes were clear and quite lovely, and her large white teeth were dazzling against her skin. Her taut neck and bare arms were well formed. Strong, Jessie thought, but oh dear! The calico shift was far too tight across her bosom . . . and that gave Jessie an idea. She needed to gain Elly's confidence and all women had a common denominator.

'Who makes your dresses?' she asked.

Elly shrugged. She obviously didn't know. But she did volunteer some information. 'Got two dresses,' she announced. 'One on, one in wash.' The words were recited as though from instructions.

'Oh good,' Jessie said. 'But would you like me to make you some more dresses? Pretty dresses?'

The eyes lit up. 'For me?'

'Yes, if you wish. And for the other housemaids too.'

Elly pouted. 'Them other girls only bush girls. I am the house-girl.'

'Oh well.' Jessie hurried to correct her mistake. 'I'll just make them for you.' So the house staff consisted of only a cook and a maid. Someone had told her that these houses were overrun with native staff. Obviously not.

Just then Sylvia, already dressed, came in. 'Oh, there's the maid,' she said. 'I was looking for her.'

'Have you had your breakfast?' Jessie asked.

'Yes, she brought it in. Quite weird, boiled eggs and bacon, but I enjoyed it. After the dreadful night I put in I needed some decent food to face the day. And now I don't know how I shall cope.'

'Why? What's wrong?'

'It's our clothes,' Sylvia wailed. 'I didn't notice on the ship, we must all have been the same, but they have the most *horrible* odour.' She flung open the wardrobe where Jessie had hung some of Corby's jackets. 'And it's not just our things, smell these coats!'

Jessie obliged. 'Oh dear, they do have a musty smell.'

'Not musty, mouldy!' Sylvia opened the lid of a trunk. 'It's in everything! Even our linen.'

'Yeah, stink!' Elly chimed in, wrinkling her nose.

'We don't need her opinion,' Sylvia snapped. 'Every single thing we own will have to be washed or cleaned or aired somehow. We can't possibly go into company with clothes that reek. What are we going to do?'

'We'll just have to get to work,' Jessie said. 'Elly will help us.'

'No fear,' Elly said. 'Chinee lady washerwoman.'

'Then get her,' Sylvia commanded, and Elly was out of the door like a shot, glad to escape.

57

Between bows and head-shaking Mae examined their clothes, holding several items at arm's length as she came to the bottom of their sea trunks. 'Pooh!' she said, squatting down in her black cotton pyjama suit. 'All nice things spoil.' But she had a gentle, almost defensive admiration for the fine materials she encountered. Jessie studied her plastered-down black hair and her thin, lined face, and guessed that the woman had seen better days.

'Can they be cleaned?' she asked, staring in horror at the green mould that had settled on some of the garments during their long sojourn in the airless heat of the cabins.

'Number one, sortings,' Mae announced, and under her guidance, the two women set to work.

Eventually the exasperated cook burst into the room, ignoring the mounds of clothes scattered about the room. 'You come!' he said to Jessie and Sylvia. 'Sun high!'

'Little dinner time,' Elly explained, her arms full of washable clothes to be taken down to the laundry. 'Night time big dinner.'

Encouraged by Mae's obvious expertise, Sylvia was in a better mood. 'I think lunch is ready,' she laughed. 'We'd better turn up or he might attack us.'

Mae seemed to find this remark about her husband outrageous. She cackled with mirth and patted Sylvia's hand.

'Shouldn't we wait for the men?' Jessie asked, but Elly shook her head.

'Boss gone off with Mike. Your daddy gone walkabout with Toby.'

As the sisters settled down to a lunch of cold meat, bread and pickles and banana custard, Sylvia whispered to Jessie: 'Did you hear her call Mr Devlin "Mike"? Do you suppose she's his girlfriend? Lita says a lot of white men out here have black women.'

Jessie was shocked. 'How can you talk like that? I don't suppose any such thing. And I don't want to hear another word about that Mrs de Flores.'

'I wouldn't take that attitude,' Sylvia said sagely. 'There's nothing on past here but forests. Mrs de Flores is our nearest neighbour. I, for one, will be glad of her company.'

Jessie took another slice of ham. 'Yes, I suppose you're right. I'm sorry. I shouldn't be so quick to judge. It's just that she's so . . . different.'

In the meantime their father was in his element traipsing about with Toby, wanting to know everything about his surrounds. Earlier they had met Mr Devlin.

'Good morning, Professor,' the manager said. 'You're out early.'

'So much to see,' Lucas replied. 'Toby has offered to take me down to the Aborigine camp. Is that all right with you?'

'By all means,' Devlin replied. 'Our blacks here are Yindini people. They'll make you welcome.'

So, stout staff in hand, the Professor continued on his explorations.

He progressed very slowly, examining different plants, taking notes, and finding a special delight in the tumbling fronds of bush orchids. He was not surprised to encounter them, but already the variety was exciting him. 'I shall make a study of orchids,' he told Toby. 'I can have a grand collection and I won't even need a hothouse.'

It didn't bother either of them that half of the time Toby had no idea what he was talking about, because they both shared a love of nature. Toby was interested in the Professor and happy to divulge his expert bush knowledge.

'You call them fellers "orchid"?' he asked.

'Yes. Very rare in my country.'

'Plenty more up high alonga river,' Toby said, pointing to the high mountains.

'Then we must go and find them.'

Toby shook his head. 'Them Irukandji mob up there. Bung a spear in you plenty bloody quick.'

'How very interesting,' the Professor smiled, watching a gorgeous parrot stump along a tree branch. A little dazed at his answer, Toby hoped he meant the bird.

Corby was feeling a little better. As he sat by the track to smoke the cigarette Devlin had rolled for him, his heart stopped pounding and some colour returned to his face.

Devlin had covered the body with brush. 'Would you mind staying here while I go for help, Mr Morgan? I've searched the area, and there's no one about as far as I can make out, but I'll leave you the rifle.'

'No, wait,' Corby said. 'Just hold on a minute. What happens now?'

'I'll get a couple of Kanakas to collect the body. All we can do is wrap it in canvas and wait for the police to come.'

'How will the police know?'

'I'll send a rider to town.'

Corby finished the cigarette and sat staring at the ground. 'Why do we need the police?'

'They have to be informed.'

'Why? I don't need a scandal like this. Good God, man, I've just taken over this place. I don't want police on my doorstep. That would mean an inquest. I'd have to go to court. I've never set foot in a court in my life! Can't we handle it here?'

Mike was beginning to think the shock had addled this man's brains. 'No way!'

'Mr Devlin,' Corby said, getting up to pace across the track. 'Why was this man murdered? You must have some idea. The police will ask you that.'

'I don't know why,' Mike said cautiously. 'Not yet anyway. But I'm guessing it was done by one of the Kanakas.'

'Why would they kill a foreman?'

'Beats me. If they're badly treated or they get a bee in their bonnet, they're likely to play up a bit, if they're game enough. But they've never murdered a boss before. Not around here anyway.'

Corby groaned. 'And it had to be my plantation.' He was becoming angry now, resentful of this awful event. 'You were arguing with him last night. What was that about?'

'Perry flogged one of the Kanakas. He could be brutal at times.'

'Well, there you are. There's your man. Bury the body and then take that fellow into town and hand him over. Make an end to it.'

'It wasn't Joseph, he's still in hospital. But it's peculiar. That's not just a murder, it's an execution. And it's not a normal reaction from Kanakas. Jesus, if they killed a white man for every flogging handed out there'd be none of us left.'

'Oh dear God! Are we in danger now?'

'I don't know. That's why we have to call the police.' He led the two horses from the shade. 'Perhaps you'd better come with me.'

But still Corby delayed. 'Aren't you worried the police might interrogate you? After all, you did have a row with him, and I did mention that I would only need one overseer now.'

Mike stood very still. 'Mr Morgan. Don't pull that on me, or you'll end up with no overseers. I'll ride out of here right now and you can sort things out yourself.'

'There's no need to become aggressive. I was simply pointing out that the police could be a nuisance for you too.'

'I'll take my chances.'

'So you might. But what about my wife and her sister? If they hear about this they'll be frightened out of their wits. They're not accustomed to such horrors.'

'I know. I'm sorry about that but it can't be helped. We simply can't cover up a murder. It's a bloody awful start for you but it's better in the long run to let the police deal with it.'

Corby remembered that Devlin had said they'd be very busy soon, burning the cane and then cutting, and it irritated him that interference by the police would upset, even slow down, the workforce. 'For all you know wild blackfellows might have done this.'

'No, they use spears. It's definitely the work of one or more Kanakas.'

'How can you be sure?'

'Because back on their home islands, they're head-hunters. Whoever did this has got his trophy hidden somewhere. And I'll damn well find it.'

Corby thought he was going to be sick again. And he certainly wasn't staying in this dreadful spot alone. He mounted his horse and followed Devlin, who was already cantering down the track.

The women weren't told. Corby wanted to keep it from them for as long as possible. In his wife's condition it could have a dreadful effect on her, and on the child she was carrying.

Devlin agreed to speak to the house staff to make certain they made no

60

mention of the dreadful business, which they were bound to hear about, and then he went down to begin interrogating the workers.

Corby stayed at the house, sitting in the office trying to concentrate on the plantation books which Devlin had set out for him, but he kept a loaded gun nearby. What if Perry were only the first? What if some murdering hound was out to kill all the whites? He spent sleepless nights and wasted days hanging about the house, and in the end was much relieved when a policeman arrived with two troopers, explaining to the women that it was just a routine visit.

Chapter Six

' 'Tis the first time I've not been put up at the homestead,' Sergeant Dennis McBride growled as he mounted the steps to Mike's bungalow.

'What's wrong with my place?' his host laughed.

'Nothin' at all, it's a fine spot you've got here. Like an eagle's nest. But it's still not the rules.'

'Don't take it to heart,' Mike said. 'It was my idea. Since he doesn't want the women to know what happened, you'd have had a job making conversation with Morgan and his family all evening. We can talk better up here.'

'The man's mad. The women will find out sooner or later. And they look a healthy pair of girls. I always say if women have got the guts to come to places like Trinity Bay, even to take on that bloody sea voyage in the first place, they're no namby-pambies.'

'Don't worry about it. Morgan's doing his best. It was a mighty shock for him.' Mike produced a bottle of whisky and a jug of water and the two men sat down at the kitchen table. 'So let's start from the beginning again.' He related the finding of the body, the flogging of Joseph and his certainty that the murder was the work of one of the Kanakas. 'I put a couple of black trackers on the job right away,' he continued. 'And they say that Perry walked down there in the company of another man who was wearing boots, so that cuts out the Abos. And he was killed there with a machete.'

'All right. But Perry's bed had been slept in. Why would he suddenly get up in the middle of the night and go traipsing into the bush with a Kanaka? He was a big feller, it'd take a team of them to make him go voluntarily, and there's no sign of a struggle.'

'Unless his attacker had a gun,' Mike said.

McBride frowned. Although it was forbidden, both men knew that Kanakas did have ways and means of obtaining and hiding guns, just as they managed to get their hands on dynamite. It was more of a status symbol than aggression, since a pistol could be used to shoot game. Possession of firearms was punishable by long jail terms, which terrified both Kanakas and Aborigines, so there were few natives who would take that risk.

'The trackers seem to think the machete was already in place,' Mike said. 'And that after the murder the killer went on to the river to get rid of the weapon and to wash himself down. They say he entered the water, then made for the track and followed that back. They couldn't pick up his trail on the flat open path.'

McBride took a gulp of whisky, enjoying this respite. It had been a long, hard ride out to Providence, and at fifty, he was feeling his years and the extra weight that had accumulated over the last decade. 'Why didn't he finish the job and chuck the body into the river? It was risky enough going down there at night in the first place, but the crocs would have disposed of the body for him.'

'And him too, hauling a body down the banks,' Mike said. 'I'm inclined to think it was meant to be found. Execution style.'

'Maybe so. You're certain this Joseph bloke couldn't have done it?'

'Yes.'

'But it was one of the new boys?'

'I thought so at first. But none of them had guns, and they don't know that area. They've been working out in the other direction. They also don't have machetes. They're marched out with all the implements in the mornings and everything has to be accounted for and locked in the shed before they go off. Perry was strong on that. He'd keep them there half the night if they so much as lost a spade.'

'Someone could have supplied the weapons to the new chum.'

'Yeah? So now we've got two to worry about.'

'Or more,' McBride said morosely. 'Maybe one of the old hands had it in for Perry and bashing up that Joseph kid triggered him off. Or gave him the opportunity to push the suspicion elsewhere. I hear Perry wasn't too popular, he was a bloody tyrant when he worked on that Mackay plantation. I thought he'd cooled down out here.'

'Until Jake died. He's been up to his old tricks again lately, and that's what got him. Oh Christ! I just remembered! We took on quite a few Kanakas from Mackay! Where do we look for Perry's killer? I've questioned every bloody one of them, over and over. Yesterday and today. They say they don't know nothin'.'

'And you reckon this killer chucked Perry's head into the river?'

Mike looked surprised. 'No! No, I don't! I reckon it's a trophy and that's bloody bad medicine. We have to find it, we can't have cults starting up or we'll be in real trouble.'

'Oh Jesus, yes!'

'I got the black trackers on the job and two old blokes from the Abo camp. They've searched every inch of the Kanaka compound and all around. So far no go. Bloody bastard, whoever it is, we have to find him and his trophy.'

'Well, I'll start questioning them all over again tomorrow, try to put the fear of God into them, threaten them with jail if they don't cooperate. But I don't like my chances with a mob like this. By the way, does the old man, Morgan's father-in-law, know about Perry's demise.'

'Yes. He's an odd one. "What a tragedy, Mr Devlin," he said. "But I'm sure you'll see to it." And then he wandered off.'

'Taking it better than Morgan.'

'Oh, fair go. Morgan's rattled and he's got every reason to be. I don't think he has any idea what he's up against here. He still sees the place as a neat English estate with born-and-bred farmhands. He's no idea how the Kanakas can muck everything up if they're not watched.'

'Or nature,' McBride added.

Joseph was frightened. First the boss and then the three policemen had harassed him for days with questions and more questions, threatening that he could be put in a lockup in the town if he didn't point out the murderer. But he could tell them nothing. He dare not tell them anything. He didn't want to be a god; his father had thrust this upon him even though he'd known that human sacrifice revolted him, that the agonised screams of the victims caused Talua to endure frightful nightmares and an overwhelming sense of guilt. As a child he had wept and begged to be excused from these ceremonies but his father had been adamant he attend, and even his mother had had no sympathy for him. 'Run along,' she'd say impatiently. 'Ratasali is right. It will make a man of you.'

To compensate, to make his father proud of him, Talua had practised the manly skills attendant to hunting and game-playing to a point of desperation, until he could outrun any of the other lads, could dive deeper and stay under water far longer than them, and his prowess with the spear became legend. All this effort turned a rather plump boy into a tall, immensely strong youth who became his father's pride and joy. Talua groaned, remembering that all he had achieved was his father's insistence that he remain by his side as his favourite son, especially at those horrifying ceremonies. He'd known that the rituals would continue, even after Ratasali's death, and there was every chance he'd be a victim himself, so that swim to the ship, dragging the white man, had been a dash for freedom.

Many of the old men had told him that to enter the white man's world was a magnificent adventure, and they had spoken the truth. The great ship, regardless of the foul dark hold, was a wonder in itself, and to see an entirely new world as they were brought ashore at Trinity Bay was exciting. He had felt another pang of grief for his father, mixed with gratitude that Ratasali had taken the time to see that his son, his successor, learned English. And then he had stepped curiously on to another wonder of construction called a wharf, looking forward to a land where he was determined to live his life as he chose.

The trouble had started almost immediately, in the first big hut. The man with the whip hadn't bothered him. He was mustering island people in much the same way as they herded up their own prisoners in the usual initial confusion. But when the whip had struck him, Malaita men had sprung to his defence, protecting their god.

Talua was appalled by the fight and he had shouted at the people in their language not to do this, but he was hustled to a far corner out of danger. From there he begged them to leave him be; he insisted that since they'd left their island shores far behind, he was no longer a god – indeed he wished to be known now as Joseph, a Kanaka, a working man, one of them.

And now it had started all over again. Mr Perry had been sacrificed, punished for the flogging, and his head taken in retribution. No one needed to explain this to Joseph. He knew, as did all the other Malaita people, and he despaired. He had been in a rage with Perry for flogging him, but despite the pain had refused to cry out, and as the vicious cords had ripped his back he'd plotted revenge of some sort, one day. But as a man, face to face. Not this way. He resented the intrusion of the Malaita people in his new life and wished he could get away from them. There were other plantations; maybe he could work somewhere else.

But in the meantime the white men were suspicious of him, tying the killing in with his flogging. It was some small mercy that Perry had lashed him so badly he'd been too weak to move and so couldn't be blamed. All the same, just when he'd wanted to be accepted by the white men, the Malaita people had brought trouble down on him. He did not know who had done the killing. And even if he did . . . could he hand over one of his own people to the white police?

That gave him an idea. This business had to be stopped, otherwise he'd spend his time here worrying that any white man who didn't treat him well could suffer the same fate. And in the end the white men would turn on him. So from now on, if that was what the Malaita wanted, he would be their god. And he would issue his first laws and instructions as soon as possible.

He walked stiffly down the leafy path to the compound, carrying the new shirt provided by the hospital women. He held his head high and his shoulders pulled back to curtail muscle movement and ease the scorching pain of the torn skin. And in doing so he gave the opposite impression to the apprehension he really felt.

It was just on sunrise and the workmen were massed in the long-house to collect their tea and buns before heading out into the fields. The serving women waved to him and the men grinned encouragement, nodding appreciation at his apparently stoic progress.

Mike Devlin was observing them all carefully and he too interpreted Joseph's erect bearing as haughtiness, believing that the young bloke was deliberately putting on a brave front. Several Kanakas broke from the queues to greet Joseph, insisting he sit at one of the long benches where his mug of tea was brought to him. Acts of kindness or collaboration? Mike wondered.

They'd buried Perry, and after three days of threatening the Kanakas with dire punishments if they didn't bring forward the murderer, Sergeant McBride and his troopers had given up and left, the mystery unsolved. McBride had interrogated all of the Kanakas, one by one, without success, so finally he'd addressed the dusky assembly: 'You blokes listen to me. You've got a murderer among you. So until we find him, all Providence Kanakas are banned from town.'

There was a mutter of dismay from the crowd but McBride persisted: 'If we see any of you buggers in town you'll be shot on sight. Savvy? We don't want no murderers in our town and since we don't know which one it is, you can all bloody stay out.'

Mike had added his punishment. 'No more free baccy on Sundays either. That all finish too.'

Disconsolately, the workmen wandered off and McBride turned to Mike. 'You ought to cancel their Sundays. Twist the knife. Make them work the full week, that could get a reaction.'

'Yeah. And bring the government agents down on my back.'

'I wouldn't worry too much about them these days. The regulations are becoming old hat. There's a big push on to deport all the Kanakas and Chinese from Queensland.'

'That's crazy. Who by?'

'Not so crazy. Labour politicians are getting plenty of mileage, claiming the Kanakas and the Chinks are taking white men's jobs. They want the lot out.'

'But the Premier himself is forever issuing new regulations to make certain the Kanakas are well treated. Why would he do that if they're even contemplating getting rid of them?'

McBride grinned. 'It's called "two-bob-each-way".'

This was all news to Mike. 'It still doesn't make sense. White men won't work the canefields and the government is making a packet on the import fees with so many Kanakas coming and going all the time.'

'Ah, but the politicians from the south, who don't own plantations, are more interested in votes than the economy of Queensland. You mark my words, Mike, stirrers are infiltrating the sugar towns right up the coast. They're holding meetings, calling on all our white layabout workers to unite under a Labour flag.'

'To do what?'

'I told you. To deport the Kanakas and the Chinese under a White Australia policy.'

Mike laughed. 'That'll be the day. Can you imagine white men working for three pounds a year?'

'More like it,' McBride snorted, 'can you imagine the plantocracy paying white men three pounds a week to cut cane?'

'Stalemate,' Mike had said. And at that point the conversation had drifted into more pressing matters. They had decided not to mention publicly the subject of the severed head, to play down any hint of a cult killing and so avoid panic. And Mike had persuaded the sergeant to allow him and Corby Morgan to make written statements rather than have to go to town and meet with the magistrate, who was also the coroner. Morgan had been greatly relieved. The new owner still held the peculiar opinion that this murder was a slur on his reputation, and he seemed more concerned about that than Perry's death.

But now, Mike worried, they'd wasted three days, so there was no more time to be lost. He strode among the Kanakas, appointing gang

66

leaders to take the men off on various jobs, and called Pompey over to him: 'With Mr Perry gone, I'll need an overseer. You take charge for today.'

'And more days?' Pompey asked enthusiastically.

'I'll see how you go.'

'I get a horse?'

'Yes, and hurry up.'

'More pay too?'

'No one gets a dead man's pay,' Mike retorted.

The shed was unlocked, tools and implements handed out and the men began tramping away, leaving a few stragglers, including Joseph.

'You blokes,' Mike ordered, 'fill in the first latrine trench and dig a new one.' To combat dysentery he was very strict with the sanitary arrangements, basing rotation of the trenches on the life of the fly. There was always work about the compound.

But he had other plans for Joseph. 'You come with me,' he called. 'I'm going to teach you how to build a fence. Grab one of your mates there.'

Later that day Mike took Morgan on a further inspection of the property. 'The blacks still haven't been able to find Perry's head, poor bugger,' he said. 'Maybe it *was* thrown in the river.'

Corby shuddered. As far as he was concerned that subject was closed. 'Do you think there'll be any more attacks?' he asked.

'No,' Mike said, hoping he was right. 'But you wanted the homestead fenced, so I'm getting some men on to it. We can do with a fencing gang anyway, so I've got a couple of Kanakas started splitting logs. If you show me exactly where you want the fence I'll mark it out myself.'

'Excellent,' Corby replied, somewhat cheered by this news. 'Now that everything seems to be returning to normal, could you come over this evening? I want you to explain the bookwork to me in the presence of my wife. Thanks to her father's insistence, she is an educated woman and has studied mathematics. If we could train her to attend to the office work it would leave me free for my own duties.'

'Be glad to,' Mike said.

Since he'd had very little contact with the women, Mike was interested to find out more about Mrs Morgan and assess the role she'd be playing at Providence. But the evening proved difficult.

Mrs Morgan sat quietly as Mike brought the ledgers and journals from the desk in the parlour and placed them on the dining room table. Corby immediately took charge and began rifling through the pages, asking rapid questions about everything related to costs, and challenging bills for food and equipment.

'I was under the impression that places like this were self-supporting,' he said.

'Hardly,' Mike replied. 'If we were to grow enough to feed everyone here we'd have to take them off the cane and turn it into a farm. Mainly the Kanakas need rice, tea and flour, and we buy our meat on the hoof.'

'These general store bills are far too high,' Corby complained. 'Why do we need all these things?'

'General maintenance and working implements,' Mike said.

Corby kept peering impatiently at the ledgers. 'Why do some men get paid more than others?'

'After two years we give them a rise in pay, for experience. And the ones who come back for a second term start at that rate.'

'Well, that's going to stop right now,' Corby snapped. 'They all work the same hours for the same pay in future.'

Mike shrugged. 'Whatever you say.' Most plantations did keep wages at the same rate but Jake believed in incentives.

'And your wages here,' Corby continued. 'What is this amount?'

'Two hundred and sixty pounds,' Mike said. 'That's owed to me in back pay.'

'I don't understand. What back pay?'

'We've been running short on ready cash,' Mike explained, 'waiting for you, so I forwent my pay for the time being.'

'And you expect me to pay this?'

'I hope so,' Mike grinned.

'Well, you'll simply have to wait,' Corby said. 'Since you didn't draw your pay, you obviously didn't need it. Where has all the money gone?'

Mike noticed Mrs Morgan's intelligent eyes. She was following all this carefully but her expression gave away nothing but interest. He tried to hide his own irritation. 'When Providence was sold the previous owner was entitled to the profits from the last harvest, but he did leave me some working cash to keep the place going. There are only a few pounds left now, and there won't be any more cash coming in until we sell the sugar.'

'And when will that be?'

'The agents start buying from the mill about December.'

'That long?' Corby was aghast. 'I can't wait until then. I have to tell you, Mr Devlin, I am not a rich man. I don't have the funds to last out until December.'

Mike didn't show his surprise. He had taken it for granted that these were wealthy people. 'That doesn't really matter,' he said. 'Our credit is good here. The stores will supply us. You can pay them after the harvest.' And you'd better pray that nothing goes wrong, he added to himself. Like heavy rain, or blight or bugs that can wreck crops. With that he made the decision. 'We'll start burning off tomorrow,' he told Morgan. 'Better to be safe than sorry.'

Mrs Morgan spoke for the first time. 'What are you burning, Mr Devlin?'

'The cane,' he told her. 'We burn each field separately to get rid of the undergrowth and dead leaf trash.'

'But wouldn't that ruin the cane?'

68

'No, ma'am.'

'Can we come and watch?' Her question was addressed to Corby.

'I'm not sure about that,' he replied. 'It could be dangerous.'

'Not really,' Mike said. 'As long as you keep well back. It's quite a sight.'

Just then the little dog came scampering in, with Sylvia giving chase.

'For God's sake, Sylvia,' Corby snapped. 'I told you we were having a meeting!'

'I know,' she said, 'but he got away.' She scooped up the spaniel and nuzzled it close to her face. 'Poor little thing, he's got lumps all over him.'

'Let me see.' Mike took the dog, and ran his hands over it.

'They're ticks, miss. You'll have to get them off quickly or they'll kill him.' He went to the door and called to Elly, who came running. 'It's got ticks. You get them off, eh?'

As she took the dog away, Sylvia clutched Mike's arm. 'What do you mean, they'll kill him? What are they?'

'They're mites that burrow into the skin, head first. Bad news for dogs but they can get on humans too.'

'What?' Corby exploded. 'I told you you shouldn't have brought that dog, Sylvia. I won't have it bringing ticks into my house.'

'The dog doesn't bring them in,' Mike said. 'Anyone can get them brushing past trees or in the bush. Usually on the neck or the back. Miserable things they are, you can't just pull them off, the heads stay in. You have to douse them with kerosene first.'

Corby and his wife looked shocked and Sylvia was horrified. 'How utterly disgusting, I shall be frightened to go out of the door.'

'At least we know what to look for, and what to do,' Jessie said quietly. 'Would you care to stay for supper, Mr Devlin?'

He saw Morgan cast a stern glance at his wife, but he ignored the warning. 'Thank you, Mrs Morgan, I would.'

'Good,' Sylvia said. 'While we're waiting, you really must have a look at my room, Mr Devlin. I'm sure it is still full of dreadful crawling things.'

She tugged him away and down the passage, taking no notice of his smiling objections. 'It's a waste of time,' he said as she threw open the door. 'You can't keep them out, but they won't hurt you. They're only little geckos . . .' He stepped inside and searched about until he found one and picked it up. 'See, they're pretty little things. And they're so shy. If they're scampering, they're scampering away from you.'

Sylvia wasn't impressed. 'They're awful. And there must be spiders too.'

'Elly keeps an eye out for spiders, there aren't any webs about. Just keep that mosquito net tucked down all around your bed and nothing will bother you.'

By the time they returned, the Professor had arrived. He too was looking forward to seeing the burning of the canefields. With the bothersome plantation books removed, Corby's spirits rose, and they had a pleasant supper, the women taking the opportunity to ply the manager with questions.

Corby himself showed Devlin out, strolling down the front steps to survey the clearing. 'I'd like the fence to extend beyond that large tree down there,' he said.

'The fig? That's more than two hundred yards.'

'I'm aware of that. And for balance take it fifty yards either side of the house, ending it level with the rear of the house to shut off the service area.'

'You'll have a big garden.'

'Or small grounds,' Corby replied, 'with a gate up here for carriage access. And a picket fence will suffice.'

'A picket fence? You really only need a split timber two-rail fence.'

'It is not a horse paddock,' Corby said.

'In that case I'll have to order the palings from the sawmill,' Mike replied, wondering what happened to all those calls for economising.

'Yes, do that. I want the fence up as soon as possible.' Corby looked up at the clear starry sky. 'You were right about that threat of a storm. It's a beautiful night. I shall see you in the morning then.'

As he walked back into the house he caught sight of Sylvia. 'Just a minute, young lady. A word if you please.'

'Yes, what is it?'

'I'll thank you not to be flirting with the help. You made an absolute spectacle of yourself with Devlin this evening, practically mauling the man.'

'I did not,' she flared. 'And anyway, what I do is my business.'

'Not when it comes to my staff. I won't have you flaunting yourself in front of men like that.'

'Stuff and nonsense,' Sylvia said. She picked up her dog and flounced away down the passage with a small smile on her face. 'I do believe, Tuppy,' she whispered to the spaniel, 'that our Corby is jealous. How very interesting.'

They were all out on this special day.

The women were hatless but wore long cloaks over their summer dresses, and they stared at the Professor, who had now decided it was time to wear the tropical clothes he had purchased in Cape Town from an army store: khaki shirts and shorts, teamed with long socks and solid boots.

'Father, you look ridiculous in those baggy short trousers,' Sylvia laughed, but the old man was unconcerned.

'What's good enough for the army is good enough for me. I find these trousers quite comfortable. They're very airy.'

'I'll bet they are,' Corby sniffed. 'Apparently the first burn-off is quite an occasion on a plantation so I thought we should introduce our own customs to set the tone. I myself have prepared a claret cup.'

70

'At this hour?' Jessie said impulsively, not meaning to criticise her husband.

'Why not?' Sylvia said. 'God knows it's dreary enough living here. Corby is only trying to cheer us up.'

'I second the motion,' her father smiled. 'I'm partial to claret whatever the hour. Let's drink a toast to Providence.'

'Hear, hear!' Corby said.

Sylvia thought he had never looked better. This soft pink light on his fine fair hair, silky eyebrows and moustache gave a most pleasing effect, and his previously rather parchment-like skin had a warm tan now from the sun. Back in London, she mused, as she sipped her claret, he wore a permanently forbidding frown, but look at him now! He was far more amenable.

But Jessie saw something else. She saw a husband who was relaxed enough outwardly to be wearing open-necked shirts and breeches and that odd straw hat; a picture of ease, even with that gun strapped to his hip. But he still kept a loaded rifle in the parlour and roamed the house during the night.

Why were those policemen here? Corby had said they did the rounds of the plantations as part of there duties, but if so, why had they avoided the house? Surely they could have extended hospitality to the sergeant. When she'd suggested they invite him for a meal, at least, Corby had practically told her to mind her own business. 'He's not of our class!' he'd snapped, but somehow, out here, that hadn't seemed to ring true.

Finally, in answer to her questions, Corby had become angry. 'Leave me alone, woman, for Christ's sake! Haven't I got enough worries!'

'But, darling, that's why I'm asking. Why are you so worried? Is there anything I can do to help?'

'Yes, you can bloody stop quizzing me! I've had enough of interrogations. I have huge responsibilities here, can't you see that?'

Why had he had enough of interrogations? What interrogations? What were the police really after?

Having listened to his business discussion with Mr Devlin, Jessie understood why Corby was so on edge. This harvest could make or break them. His present jollity seemed to her more like bravado, and she couldn't blame him for that, but she had noticed that his humour improved with alcohol. And even though it was rather mean to think such a thing, she guessed that he'd already had a few while preparing the claret. She was afraid he was relying too much on alcohol, and that was a worry, because, harking back to their London days, when Corby overindulged he could become very nasty. She prayed that now he had all these responsibilities he would remain the pleasant social drinker that he'd been, so far, at Providence.

Corby was eager to get down to the fields. He rode off ahead, leaving Toby to escort the family on foot. Elly joined them on the walk to the first of the canefields, and soon a mob of Aborigines, at least thirty men, women and children, were bringing up the rear.

'Don't worry about them,' the Professor said. 'I've met them all and they're very interesting people. They want to see the fun too. Turn about and give them a wave.'

The women did so, and were rewarded by grins from the adults and the sudden company of the children, who raced forward to march along with the white folks.

Jessie smiled down at their happy little faces, reminded that she'd soon have a child of her own to care for in this strange place. And watching Sylvia stride on ahead, she was glad, now, that her sister was here, a comfort for the months to come. Mr Devlin had told her quietly that he had alerted the local midwife, a Mrs McMullen, wife of the manager of Helenslea, and that she would ride over whenever she was needed. That was a relief. But at least in the meantime she had her sister to turn to. Lately she'd been feeling very tired, and her ankles were swelling in this unaccustomed warm weather, so she was resting as much as possible, allowing Sylvia to take over the running of the house. As Corby had said, it gave Sylvia something to do, but Jessie was grateful and she determined that, after the baby was born and the household settled down again, she would make an effort to provide some social life for her sister.

Whoosh! It was as if a great dragon had suddenly breathed fire on the wide green field, and in drawing breath for another onslaught had sucked in the surrounding air, leaving the onlookers gasping in a cold and fearful vacuum.

And then it came again.

Whoosh! The sea of tall leafy cane wavered for a second, leaves fluttering helplessly, before it exploded in a deafening roar. Fire charged through the foliage in a savage fury. Flames flared and leapt, hurling debris skyward in their destructive progress.

Men were shouting; small dark figures running along the perimeters, silhouetted against the blazing light. Overhead, ignoring the smoke, knowing owls soared gleefully, while higher still, red hawks hovered and a lone eagle sped swiftly down from the mountains to investigate. To these birds, fire was a bonanza, and well the terrified denizens of the bush knew it.

Little wallabies bumped and zigzagged from their treacherous shelters, heading for the scrub, and reptiles sought frantically to escape. Lizards took off blindly, tiny legs scampering, some into the flames, others making it to the clearing only to be swooped on by triumphant birds. Snakes lashed their way out of the inferno to face the double danger of men and birds. But ignoring these life forms, the fire, with a life of its own now, tore madly through the tinder-dry undergrowth, enveloping the cane-stalks, scorching the leaves, on and on in a mad crackling caper until it came to an abrupt end. Men with handkerchiefs tied about their faces were waiting with splashing buckets, with water-soaked bags, with heavy stamping boots to force an end to the rampage. The fire had done their bidding.

At first the women had reeled back in shock as the canefield exploded, and Jessie had turned to her father. 'Are you sure they know what they're doing? How can a harvest survive this?'

Even the Professor was taken aback. It had seemed reasonable in a book, but the reality was unnerving. But now, with clouds of smoke billowing against the blue and Devlin riding casually over to talk to Corby, he relaxed. All appeared to be proceeding as scheduled. 'My word,' he said to Jessie, 'it does seem a robust way of dealing with the problem, but obviously it works. No one seems to be concerned.'

The burn-offs continued, even at night, with flames lighting the dark sky and showers of sparks like fireworks shooting up in the distance. Gangs of cane-cutters went to work, slashing and sweating their way along the dirty blackened rows, backs straining, limbs aching, but no sooner had they worked through one field, piling the cane into the drays, than another was burned and ready for them. This was the hardest work of all on the plantation, but there was no let-up. The Kanakas laboured from dawn to dusk in the smouldering heat, while their master and their boss rode from field to field to keep them going and get those packed drays on their way to the mill.

Every available man was put to the task, even the trainee fence-builders, and Joseph found himself in old Sal's gang. Having seen the fire, he was astonished that the cane was only slightly blackened, but there was no time to think about that; the work had to be done, and fast. There was a competitive edge about this frantic slashing.

'You big strong boy,' Sal had said. 'You come with me. I show you how to work good.' He gave Joseph one of his own wide, sharp knives and instructed him on the best way to go at the cane, bending to get the full stalk, and striking with clean cuts.

As for the other new men, no one wanted them, they were too slow, so Pompey had them divided into gangs under his control. His horse tethered, he swung among them, a tyrant now, herding them at the cane, belting stumbling, inept workers with his stick.

Despite the sweat and toil and the filthy blinding ash that clung to their skin and their wretched clothes, the more experienced men were crowing as they filled the drays, jeering at weaker gangs. This had become a test of strength and endurance; a way for the men to prove themselves and so relieve the monotony of their servile existence.

Waterbags were passed along and Sal took a minute to explain to Joseph that the cane had to be taken to a special place to be crushed within fourteen hours or it would begin to spoil and the white men would become angry. 'As if we're not in enough trouble,' he added darkly. 'No more Sundays in town. No more little Jappie girls.' He prodded Joseph cheekily. 'You like girls, huh?'

Joseph nodded. That was another problem. As the chief's son, there were always women ready to share his bed and play sex games with him

73

on the island, but here! No women. The few Kanakas who did have wives guarded them jealously and, as he had already heard, would only permit favours with them to their own friends, even then demanding high prices. He wouldn't mind a Jappie woman, he'd never even seen one, and he daydreamed that maybe he could find a wife among them.

As he worked, he listened to the comments around him. It soon dawned on him that to be allowed to re-enlist after their terms were up, Kanakas had to prove their worth to the white men so that they would be known by name. Few asked to stay. They were glad to be free after all that time; it was only when they got back to the islands that some became bored or disillusioned and yearned for the big ships to come for them. He was determined to be noticed, to be permitted to stay; apart from the fact that Malaita could be dangerous for him now, the more he saw of the white men's world, the more it intrigued him, and a spark of ambition fired his soul. He took hold of the cane, bent and slashed, bent and slashed, deciding he would be the best. He would have a gang of his own and show the master that he could, and would, be one of the elite of the Kanakas.

Sal was delighted. 'Look at him!' he shouted as Joseph forged on. 'I told you he would fix you. Now we keep up with him!'

Joseph slashed the heads from snakes, he kicked rats aside, he ignored the swarming stinging insects and the streaks of pain still present in his back. As the days wore on he saw men crumple with exhaustion, with muscle cramp, with sunstroke; he heard the screams of 'Snakebite!' and agonised shouts when knives slipped and cut into legs or arms, but he kept going and when Mr Devlin came by he hid the strain and grinned: 'Good job this, hey?'

Surprised, Devlin nodded. 'You feeling better now?'

Joseph stood up, stretching his muscles. 'Yes, boss. Pretty good.'

As the boss rode away Joseph went wearily back to work. He reasoned that if other Kanakas could keep this up, then so must he. After all, he was Ratasali's son. And that gave him something else to think about.

At night everyone was too tired to care, so Joseph chose the day off that white men named sun day to make his mark. He called the Malaita people together near a lonely field of stubble. There was a lethargy about them as they lay on the grass in the settling orange-ribbed dusk. But they sat up to take note as he stepped quietly out to address them, his strong body oiled and gleaming and a pink sarong tucked about his hips. This was not Joseph, this was Talua, and his approach had been well thought out.

'Who among you,' he hissed, his voice more threatening for its sibilant whisper, 'dares to usurp the domain of the gods?'

They shrank into fearful silence as he continued: 'Who among you says that I am less of a man that I cannot defend myself?' His voice rose. 'Who among you takes it upon himself to interpret my wishes? What son of a flea-ridden hag dares to foul my name with his deeds? Did I order that killing? No. I did not. Did the great Ratasali use unclean,

74

unanointed scoundrels at his altar? Never! Did he expect those same scoundrels to choose and inflict their own revenges on his behalf? Never! It would have been an insult to him as a great chief and a god.'

He stopped to glare at them. 'So who has done this to me?'

His voice thundered with an emotion that had at first been pure theatre. He had to exercise some control over these people, otherwise the ordered life that he envisaged would turn into a nightmare. Since they were convinced he was a god, it was no use telling them otherwise. And for that matter, was he? The idea was too terrifying to contemplate. But if he didn't take control, what other paybacks would follow for slights and indignities upon his person? For which he would be blamed by the bosses, and his burgeoning plans ruined.

'I say to you,' he went on berating them, 'no one speaks for me. No one acts for me. I am Talua, and woe betide any man who dares to think he can do so.'

This was all he had intended to say, but he seemed unable to stop now, and as his words rolled on he heard not himself but Ratasali. The more formidable voice of his father rang out.

In the distance the sad tones of a koel bird called 'coo-ee' – high-pitched mournful notes – and Talua shuddered, as from within him, the god-voice vented its rage on the cowering islanders: 'Anyone who acts in my name will suffer the same fate as the pig who has already defiled my name.'

What was this? What fate? The words were tumbling out with a force Talua could not restrain.

'He is banished from us to the bowels of devils, his innards eaten by worms. A leper, despised by the gods. He is death, walking to his own dark altar to retrieve that which is hidden. I turn my face from him.'

There was a rush as if a wind had swept over them, brushing them to their knees, foreheads pressed to the ground. Joseph was stunned at this reaction. He wanted to run among them and drag them to their feet, to their senses. His play-acting had gone too far and they had met him with their yearning for familiar customs. Shaken and depressed, he now felt beholden to them. But what could he do for them? He too was just a lowly worker with much to learn.

That night he had to force himself to stand in line for his supper of fish cakes and rice, but no one paid any attention to him. It was as if nothing unusual had happened. Around him men were complaining about the loss of the baccy ration and being refused permission to go to the big village.

Like everyone else, with the prospect of another gruelling week ahead, Joseph slept soundly, until a persistent whispering voice woke him.

'Talua,' the man whispered urgently. 'I am Katabeti, you must hear me.'

Katabeti, Joseph knew, was a Malaita man who had been at the plantation for some years. Why was he bothering Joseph now? 'What is

it?' he hissed, disgruntled at being awakened from a good sleep.
The man was weeping. 'I beg your forgiveness. I have insulted you.'
'Go away,' Joseph replied groggily. 'Let me sleep.'
'I will go,' Katabeti sobbed. 'But I wanted you to have the offering.
The sacrifice was for you.'

He dumped a bulky sugar bag on Joseph's bare chest, and even before
his hands felt the hard round shape, Joseph knew what was in the bag.
He thrust it away, his heart pounding with terror, afraid that the others
would wake and find him with this thing. 'Take it!' he gasped, panic
rising like bile. 'Take it away from me!'

Katabeti grasped the bag again. 'What should I do with it?'

'I don't know! I don't care! Throw it in the river!'

Shocked, Katabeti fell back on his haunches, crouched beside Joseph.
'I can't do that! There are crocodiles in that river. The old gods would
require vengeance.'

Frustrated, Joseph tried to turn his back on the man. Crocodiles were
much revered by Malaita people, and special rituals were necessary if
one were to be trapped and killed for food. In the meantime their waters
had to be kept unpolluted. It was true that this would be a blasphemous
act but he didn't care, he was tired of the old men and their old ways.

But Katabeti would not go away. 'What should I do?' he persisted.

'Take it to the white boss then,' Joseph whispered angrily. 'Tell him
what you have done. Release the rest of us from the punishments and
suspicions you have inflicted on us.'

It was with relief that Joseph realised Katabeti had gone, had slunk
away in the darkness. He knew the man wouldn't go to Mr Devlin and
face the dreaded white man's death by hanging. He felt about him in the
darkness. The bag was gone too. Joseph gave a sigh of relief and sought
sleep again.

To Eladji, whom Jake had called Elly when he bought her from her
mother to work in his house, this family was a strange mob.

Come to think of it, she mused, all the whites were strange. A lot of
them were plain evil, though Jake and Mike were good fellers. They'd
handed her over to Mae, the Chinese lady who had taught her about
house living. She had been like a new mother, and tiny as she was, Mae,
with her magpie screeches and flailing fists, had many a time fought off
Elly's real mother, Broula, who had come down to claim her back.

Ignoring her arrangement with Jake, Broula had tried several times to
sell Elly to tribal men because she was humiliated that her daughter was
unmarried and childless. Her efforts to retrieve Elly, who preferred to
stay at the house, had caused so many ructions that Jake was forced to
step in. He gave Broula a slap on her bare bum and sent her back to the
camp, but he followed up with a fresh supply of rations including lollies
and baccy.

That only gave Broula the impression that Elly must be Jake or
Mike's girl and therefore was worth more, but on examining her

76

daughter she discovered that this was not true. She then redoubled her efforts, offering her virgin girl to more important tribal elders until Jake solved the argument by decreeing that Elly should sleep under the house. He banned Broula from entering the homestead precincts, and he also banned Elly from visiting the blacks' camp except for a short time on Sundays. Broula was sour about this but Elly was happy; she still had time off to wander about when her chores were finished in the afternoons, and she was spared her mother's nagging.

Jake and Mike had plenty of visitors, plenty of parties, and after she had finished serving, Elly loved to lie on her bunk under the house and listen to the music and big-fun singings. Until the night the white feller, Keith, had come down after her. He'd punched her when she'd told him to go away, that Jake would be angry. 'Shut up, you stupid bitch! Jake won't mind sharing the wealth. I bet he and Mike have a good time with you.'

When she'd tried to fight him off he'd bashed her again and made violent sex on her like a mad bull. As he staggered up in the darkness, leaving her limp and battered, he warned her not to tell Jake or he'd come after her again. But the morning light told the tale. Shamed, Elly couldn't hide the bruises, and Jake soon got out of her what had happened. He'd been so angry he'd taken his horsewhip to that feller Keith, and chased him away. Elly never saw him again.

When the baby was born, Broula was overjoyed to have a grandson, so the child was given to her. She doted on the boy, Kamadji, and turned the tables on them by insisting that Elly stick to Jake's rules and visit only on Sundays. On the other hand, never one to abide by rules herself, she often came up to wander about the yards with the baby on her hip, proudly displaying 'her' boy. With the child in her mother's capable hands, Elly at last settled down to peaceful times at the house. Until now.

She liked the old boss, with his wispy white beard and twinkling eyes, but instead of being the head of the household he didn't seem to count. He never gave any orders to any of the staff inside or outside the house, except Toby, and he treated him more as a companion on his walkabouts picking flowers. The young boss, Mr Morgan, completely ignored him, which Elly thought was rather shocking, but the old man didn't seem to mind.

As for the young boss, Elly was wary of him. He was a pretty feller with pale eyes and shiny hair like corn silk, but he was cold and hard, and he shouted a lot. He never spoke to her directly and Elly was miserably certain he didn't like her.

The missus was a sweet lady. Elly warmed to her as soon as she noticed a baby was coming, and she felt possessive about her, wanting to care for her. But it was difficult. Elly was shy. She had never worked for ladies before. They ran ahead of her all the time, wanting things done before Elly had got around to them. Mae had set her a strict routine, starting with a sweeping of the front veranda and then on through the house making beds and cleaning up as she went, but these two ladies had it all backwards. And what was worse, they'd give her different jobs at the same time.

The sun was rising, so it was time for Elly to begin work. She smiled as she made up her own bunk. Some things had improved. The missus had inspected every inch of the house and was horrified that Elly slept on an old mattress with a blanket. Now she had sheets on her bed like a white person, and they were so nice to sleep on.

And now the dresses. For the first time in her life she had to make a decision on what to wear. The missus had given her bloomers and four new shifts. They were the best dresses she had ever owned and they were all different. The materials and colours were brightly patterned, one with flowers, and two of them had narrow frills at the hem. And, as the missus had said, they all had to be worn with their cord belts. She chose the blue with white squares, and slipped it over her head, pleased that it didn't squash her boobies like the old dresses, then tied the belt, wishing she had a mirror. But later upstairs she could admire her new self.

Her first job was to bring the milk up from the cowshed, which would give her a chance to show the other girls yet another new dress. They were both extra nice to her now, because a birth was not too far off and they all knew that white ladies needed nurse-girls. Elly was in a position to recommend one of them to the missus.

She took the milk up to Tommy, then went inside and, using a tablecloth as the missus had shown her, set the table for four – even though the four never sat together for breakfast. The boss had his first. The old man came in any time, if at all. Miss Langley preferred her breakfast in bed, and the missus did too, sometimes, depending on how she felt. Elly wasn't allowed to sweep too early in the mornings these days because it disturbed them. Miss Langley had yelled at her the first time she'd been woken up by her banging about. At a loose end now, waiting for the boss to get up, she wandered down the back steps and found the old man emerging from the wash house.

'Still smoky,' he said to her, indicating the residue of the palls of smoke that still hung in the air from the burn-offs.

'Yes, boss,' she said. And didn't she know it! Miss Sylvia had been complaining for days, slamming all the doors and windows shut, and wailing about the smell of their clothes again. And the missus too was finding the permanent haze of smoke upsetting.

'How much longer does the burning take?' the Professor asked.

'Till all paddocks get burn,' she told him. 'Plenty more each season, fires go on long way. You want brekkie now?' she added.

He looked at her carefully. 'Would it be too much trouble for me to have my breakfast over in my room?'

'No, boss, I bring a tray.'

'Oh good! I only want tea and toast. I much prefer to be on my own.' Suddenly he stopped to examine a frangipani: 'How beautiful! It's coming into bloom!'

'Plenty more up front,' Elly said. 'All flowering now, nice smell.'
'Really? You must show me. They're so delicate. Much prized back home.'

He followed her along the side of the house until they were level with the front, and Elly pointed out a large tree with the white blooms already peeping from the greenery.

'Marvellous!' the Professor said. 'I can smell that wonderful perfume from here.' He looked down towards the Moreton Bay fig tree. 'Who's down there?'

Elly peered in that direction. 'Looks like one of them Kanakas gone to sleep there,' she said caustically. 'Maybe him drunk. By gee, the boss give him hurry-up, comen near house!'

'You'd better go down and wake him,' the Professor advised. 'Tell him to make off before he gets into trouble.'

'He get plenty trouble if Mike sees him,' Elly said as she marched off. 'I chase the bugger.'

Smiling, the Professor turned back towards his quarters, but he'd only gone a few paces when he heard her shriek: 'Aaahee! Comen back here. This dead feller!'

The Professor sprinted across the uneven ground, surprised at how fast his old legs could move when there was a need. He puffed up to Elly and pushed her away. 'Go back, dear, go back.'

She needed no urging, taking to her heels with alacrity.

Horrified, Langley stared at the bloodied body, slumped sideways as if the poor fellow had been sitting cross-legged before he died. His throat had been slashed. He seemed to have been nursing a bag of his possessions, so, taking a deep breath to combat the rising stench, the Professor brushed at the swarming flies with his hat and gingerly removed the bag.

Was it the odd shape, or the fact that it seemed to contain only one item, or his own insatiable curiosity that caused him to look inside the bag? Langley didn't have time to isolate his reasons. Shocked, he instantly regretted his action, as he stumbled away, gasping for air, palpitations threatening to choke him. He swayed, near to fainting from fright at the gruesome thing confronting him, but summoning up his courage and a small reserve of strength, his hands trembling uncontrollably, he grabbed the bag and ran a few yards to the nearby scrub. With the dreadful object hidden safely away, he returned to the body, looking helplessly about for something with which to cover it.

Since there was nothing he could use, he broke off a large piece of foliage with which to, at least, combat the flies until someone came. Given the distraction of something to do and the removal of that object far more terrifying than the fate of this poor man, he sat on his haunches to study the manner of death, paying attention to the bloodied cane knife lying nearby. But this time he left the scene untouched.

Corby was dressing, bone weary but determined to stay on the job. For

79

the last three days, at Devlin's request, he'd been riding the track between Providence and the sugar mill at Helenslea to keep the drays moving. It had begun as a nine-mile journey each way, but it became longer each time the cane cutters moved further into his estate.

The Kanakas infuriated him. Except for a few experienced cutters they had no sense of time, and to his mind were a mob of slackers, their grinning dark faces a constant irritation. He didn't hold with Devlin's amused acceptance of their lackadaisical ways.

'You get more with pull than push,' the manager advised Corby. 'I've found that too much whip has them working like mad while you're watching, then taking a smoko when you turn your back. We can't be everywhere. That's why we need a foreman; another white man would make a difference.'

'I'll be the judge of that,' Corby snapped. He had noticed too that Devlin spoke pidgin English which most of the Kanakas could understand. It depressed him that he would have to learn that language somehow, since it was a far cry from normal English. Quite unintelligible. With Devlin off overseeing the field work, he was finding it difficult to communicate with the stupid workmen, who would grin and yabber at him and get his instructions all wrong. Deep down he was certain that they really could understand him and were deliberately trying to make a fool of him, so he retaliated with his riding whip, managing to get results that way.

The men in charge of the drays were blockheads, there was no other word for them. Unless he was there on the road with them they only plodded along, stopping to talk with men on returning drays, taking rests whenever they felt like it, as if they had all day to waste.

The track was rough, cutting through dense scrub, and it was so narrow there was confusion when the drays tried to pass, the horses struggling, men shouting and at one stage an inevitable capsize. It also dragged up hills and ran down steep gullies, sometimes across dry, caked creek beds and at others through rocky streams. Ungreased wheels seized up, wheels fell off, harnesses broke – there seemed to be mayhem all along that track and Corby had to deal with it. The air was stifling with dust and smoke, and he shouted at the men until his throat was raw. He got down with his whip, forcing the Kanakas to drag the drays out of difficulties and to go on ahead to remove rocks from the trail and the creek crossings, in order to keep moving.

They were bloody awful days, made worse by the discovery that Helenslea had tram tracks to deliver their cane to the mill in deep wooden bins on wheels, like a miniature railway.

'Why don't we have tram tracks?' he'd asked Devlin.

'Jake was working on that,' he said. 'The plans are in the desk. He just hadn't got around to it.'

'Then I want them built by next season,' Corby stormed. 'Every last inch.'

Most of the workers at the mill were white men and they greeted the new owner of Providence cordially, but they didn't have time to stop and talk to him. He had hoped to meet his neighbour, Edgar Betts, but he was nowhere to be seen.

'He comes and goes,' one of the men said, without enthusiasm, and Corby realised with approval that Betts ran a tight ship. He took his horse around to the trough and lit his pipe, watching the activity, listening to the satisfying drum of the crushers and the swish of the chutes as his harvest went safely on its way. He considered riding on the extra eight miles to visit the Helenslea homestead, if only to take a look at it, but he couldn't afford the time.

One of his drays was standing empty, the Kanakas resting underneath in the shade. This was why he couldn't visit Helenslea, these wasters had to be watched all the time! He slammed his whip on the dray, making them jump, and roared at them to get back to work.

It was an effort now, for him to bend over and pull on his boots, he was so stiff from spending days in the saddle, but he gritted his teeth and dragged at them. They seemed to be two sizes too small.

'Is there anything I can do for you, darling?' Jessie asked, preparing to get up.

'No,' he snapped. 'Go back to sleep. I prefer to take my breakfast in peace and quiet.'

As if to deliberately upset him, a woman's screams rent the air. 'Who the hell is that?' he shouted, stamping his boots into place and walking out on to the veranda in time to see the silly black maid charging down the side of the house.

He flung the bedroom door open and stormed out to the kitchen. 'What's going on?'

Tommy was slicing a large loaf of bread. 'Not me making noise. Dem Abos,' he said with a dismissive nod of his head.

Then Toby was hammering on the back wall. Even in a crisis he would not come further than the open doorway. 'Elly says you got a dead man in the front yard, boss!'

'What?' Corby saw the frightened, tearful girl cringing behind Toby. 'Who's dead?' For one terrible minute he thought his manager had also been murdered, and fear had him rooted to the spot – fear of a repetition of that foul killing, and panic that he couldn't cope without Devlin. Were all the whites here to be killed? One by one? By unknown assailants?

'I go see,' Toby said, running back down the steps. The old blackfellow's action roused Corby. He tore through the house, bumping into Jessie.

'Corby? What is it?' she asked anxiously.

'Stay here,' he ordered. 'Stay in the house. You too,' he added as Sylvia appeared, winding her dressing gown about her.

But it was only a Kanaka. That was some relief, but not enough to stem Corby's angry reaction. 'Bastards!' he snarled. 'Disgusting bloody bastards!'

81

'I'll get something to cover him,' the Professor said.

'No you won't,' Corby said grimly. 'I want him shifted. This is a direct affront to me, to the women, putting him in front of my house. By God, they'll answer this time, the brutes. Toby! Get him out of the way. No. Leave him here. Get my horse. I want Devlin to see this.'

'I'll get a blanket then.' The Professor hurried away, and Toby made to leave too.

'Where are you going?' Corby roared at him, hysteria rising as nausea threatened to overtake him again.

'For your horse, boss,' Toby said.

'Stay here,' Corby ordered, needing to get away. He ran back towards the house, yelling at the quickly gathering mob of Aborigines to disperse, and shouting at the stablehands to saddle his horse.

He rode wildly down the track to the compound, scattering gangs of Kanakas who were tramping to work, shouting for Devlin. Frightened, the workers jumped out of his way, pointing to the west fields.

He found Devlin preparing to fire one of the big acreages. 'Leave that,' he called. 'We've got more bloody trouble. One of your Kanakas has been murdered right at my front door!'

'Oh Jesus!' Devlin turned to his men. 'You go sit down. No fire, you hear me. No fire! You wait.' He gave a piercing whistle and a Kanaka lad came running, leading his horse.

'Who was killed?' he asked Corby.

'How the hell do I know?' Corby snapped.

The two women were standing nervously on the front veranda when Mike and Corby arrived, and practically the whole tribe of blacks from the camp, at least fifty of them, were lined up silently on the perimeter of the clearing.

'I told them to leave,' Corby said angrily, but Mike ignored him, jumping from his horse and striding over to the tree, where the Professor was standing by the body.

'His name is Katabeti,' the manager said as he replaced the blanket. 'He's been here a couple of years. Why would they want to do this to him?'

'Why would they want to kill Perry?' Corby demanded. 'You never found that out! You're responsible for these fellows. You hired them. How many more murders are going to happen here?' He paced up and down, storming at Devlin. 'If you can't find the murderer I insist you get rid of all these Kanakas. I want them all off my property and we'll engage another lot.'

'That's impossible,' Devlin replied. 'The harvest has to go on. There won't be any more hands available until the next ship comes in, and even then . . .'

'Excuse me,' the Professor said quietly. 'This man wasn't murdered.'

'Like hell he wasn't,' Corby said. 'He cut his own throat, did he?'

The Professor nodded. 'That's exactly what he did do. I've examined him carefully and there's no doubt at all. For a start, look at his wrists, they're slashed too. Why would a murderer do that? And look, his knife is right there. Mr Devlin, look at the angle of that cut on his throat, and at the man's right hand, it's covered in blood.'

Corby was listening but he refused to look. 'He would have been trying to stay the knife,' he said. 'So naturally his hands would be bloodied.'

'That's it. Hands,' Langley replied, 'but he'd hardly be fighting off a killer with one hand. The left hand is clean. More or less.'

Devlin squatted down by the body and picked up the knife, tracing its path. 'The Professor's right. This bloke has suicided.'

'Then why would he choose to do so in front of my house?'

'I don't know. A message of some sort. It could be defiance. Any number of reasons. Suicides are not unknown among the Kanakas. They get homesick, depressed or even afraid of getting sick. Katabeti could have been feeling sick lately, they're all working very hard.'

'Do we have to have the police back?' Corby asked.

'No. Not for a Kanaka. They've got their own graveyard here.'

'How sad that they don't seem to count,' Langley said, and Devlin nodded wearily.

'Yes, but that's how it is. I'll still have to report his death, but there won't be any investigations unless a complaint is laid.'

Corby turned on him suspiciously. 'Who would complain?'

'Kanakas can complain if the death is caused by ill-treatment – if they're game to. But we don't have that problem here.' He called to Toby. 'Go and get some of his own people. They'll take him away and attend to the burial.'

When Toby had departed, the Professor looked at Mike. 'Do you think this death is related to the death of Mr Perry?'

'For God's sake, don't complicate things, Langley,' Corby said. 'It's just a suicide. Leave it at that.'

'Coming so close on Perry's murder,' Mike said quietly, 'I feel there is a connection, but I'd only be guessing.'

'And what is your guess?' Langley asked.

'I said leave it!' Corby insisted. 'Your conjectures will only bring the police back. Think of the women. They don't even know that Perry is dead, let alone that he was murdered. They think he left the plantation. You can pass the word about that this unfortunate person suicided while not in his right mind, which also explains why he chose this spot. He didn't know what he was doing. You stay here, Devlin, until they take him away. I have to explain things to my wife. This will be very upsetting for her.'

The Professor stood uncertainly around the other side of the tree as they removed the body. He stepped over the strong, muscular roots of the great tree and picked up some of the mushy yellowing seeds that littered the ground. As he appeared to contemplate the seeds, his mind was on that other thing hidden in the scrub, and what to do about it.

He'd had every intention of telling Corby and Mr Devlin, but Corby had been so upset and angry that he'd decided it wasn't the best time to be adding to his woes. He realised that both men must have known how Mr Perry had died. They'd said murdered, by a knife, and had given no further details, not to him anyway. That had been sensible of them. He didn't need to know the rest, it was too horrible. But now he'd stumbled on the truth and couldn't decide what to do next.

The police had viewed the body, they'd have known too, as would the Kanaka bearers who had brought the body up from the scrub. And so, he mused, human nature being what it was, they'd have told their friends and the news would have spread. It dawned on him then that he was probably the only person who knew about the murder but not how it had been perpetrated, and he found that irritating. Even the blacks would have known; according to Toby the Kanaka population was a constant source of gossip in their camp. They didn't miss much.

So what to do? If he went to Mr Devlin, the manager would be duty-bound to inform the police of the grisly find, which made a connection between the murder and the suicide indisputable.

He shook his head. Corby would be in a terrible rage if the police were recalled, and the manager would come off second best in that argument. The Professor liked Mr Devlin, who had told him to call him Mike, which he would do when he remembered. He wished Corby would unbend a little with his manager instead of keeping him at a distance. But that was Corby. He hated being the new boy, the dunce in the class up against this man's years of experience and learning, even though he needed Devlin's expertise. He sighed. A little humility here on Corby's part would go a long way.

The Professor was aware that Corby regarded him as a silly old fool. And maybe I am, he thought. I never was much good in practical matters. But none of them were able to locate the murderer, and I believe I have.

He walked around the base of the tree and stood looking up at the house. 'It seems to me,' he said, addressing the deserted yard as if it were a classroom, 'that this man chose this spot for a reason. He killed himself right here while he had in his possession something the bosses must have been searching for. No. As he killed himself, he was delivering up to the bosses what it was they wanted. And by doing so he connected himself with the murder. No . . .' The Professor looked up at cumulus clouds drifting across the pale sky, grey shadows carrying a warning of rain.

'The message,' he continued, 'that this man was trying to convey is evident. I believe we have here the murderer who, perhaps in a fit of remorse, or defiance, as Mr Devlin said, is confessing. And what better way than to present the evidence?'

Satisfied with his explanation, he looked about him, wanting to tell someone, to explain the logic of the suicide, but to whom? Would Corby listen, or believe him, or care? The Professor blanched at the thought of incurring Corby's anger. What would be the result? More hysteria on Corby's part and an order to dispose of the object. To whom? Would Corby do it himself? Not likely. Nor could he involve any of the staff without calling attention to the contents of the bag.

The Professor hated trouble. He was so enjoying his time here. He even had a job. Mr Devlin had shown him the long shed where they were sorting setts of cane for replanting. Thousands of cuttings were required and he'd found the process most interesting; in no time he was at the bench himself, examining and sorting, for to him this was a most important stage, the heart of the next harvest. He'd stayed there all day, sharing a bowl of rice and hunks of pineapple with his fellow workers, intrigued by their pidgin talk. And he'd returned the next day to become the shed overseer, appointed by Mr Devlin – Mike – who was glad to have one job fewer on his hands.

So he couldn't stand around all day. He had work to do.

But what about that bag? Corby would not thank him for producing it. Best to keep it quiet.

He dived into the scrub and, gritting his teeth, picked up the dreadful object. He had no implements with which to dig a hole, and to ask for a shovel would create interest, so there was no other way. He began to push his way through the scrub, heading for the river.

It was much further than he had estimated, but having made up his mind, he had to keep going, struggling on through the thick bush for an hour before he came to a track skirting the canefields which he guessed was used by Aborigines. But at last there it was, the wide, velvety river overhung with foliage all along its banks. He pushed through the mangroves, stepping over exposed roots to find a strong foothold, and at last threw the bag out into the deep.

In doing so, he almost fell in himself, and that gave him a fright, so he clambered back, his nerves on edge, to find a resting place after all the exertion.

In the quiet heat of the morning he nodded off and was soon asleep in the soft brush, but nightmares assailed him, violent dreams of bloodied faces and huge terrifying altars.

He awoke with a scream, his clothes soaked in perspiration, feeling himself surrounded by disembodied demons. He staggered to his feet, intending to run from the place, but as he began the long trek back to the house, he patiently examined his dreams and deduced that they were quite normal, caused by the sight of that decaying severed head. 'Enough to send a man mad,' he said to himself as he forged on, not noticing that he'd lost sight of the track.

Hours later, worrying that he might have been travelling in circles, he pushed through to a clearing to search for the sun, but a thick cloud cover had moved across the sky and all he could see above him in the small open patch between the trees was solid luminous grey.

Without his London pals to distract him, and with the house as his only refuge from the physical demands of being the master of Providence, Corby became, like his father, a clock-watcher. He liked to return home by four in the afternoon, at which time he expected a bath to be ready, and clean clothes and tea prepared for him in his room, where he could enjoy the solitude, without interruption, away from the jabber of his labourers. Sometimes he would take a nap, but most days he would just lie on the bed to gather his thoughts on the progress of his investment.

At six o'clock it was time for him to emerge and join the women on the veranda in the cool of the evening. Dinner, he'd decided, should be served at seven thirty on the dot, mainly because he was finding their company rather boring, and their questions – Jessie's especially – irritating. In her eagerness to learn all she could about the plantation, she was becoming quite tiresome. And on this particular evening, after the events of the morning with that fellow cutting his damned throat right on the premises, they'd be sure to badger him with even more questions.

Jessie started it. 'That poor fellow. It was such a shock. Did he have any family? Is there anyone we ought to get in touch with?'

'Devlin's handling the matter. I really don't know.'

'Perhaps we should write our condolences?'

'Don't be ridiculous,' Sylvia said. 'They can't read or write, those people. Why do you suppose he did it, Corby?'

'I've no idea. Surely you can find something pleasant to discuss.'

'Like what?' Sylvia asked. 'We're shut up here all day. We never go anywhere, we never have any visitors. What is there to talk about?'

'There's nothing to stop you going for walks,' he said. 'I wish I had time to enjoy this property.'

'I'd rather ride,' she retorted, 'but where can I go on my own? Jessie can't sit a horse now. And you're always too busy or too tired.'

'Corby has to attend to the plantation, Sylvia, you know that,' Jessie said. 'He's really doing a wonderful job. After the harvest he'll have more time for us. Mr Devlin said that everyone is busy at this time of the year . . .'

Sitting back in his chair, Corby let them talk. He was more interested in the starless black sky. With several acres still uncut, everyone had been watching the bank of clouds that had moved across the valley.

'No dummy run this time,' Devlin had said anxiously. 'The wet is on its way.'

By 'the wet' Corby had presumed he meant the monsoon season, and he was worried about the last of his crops. He needed every penny he could make out of this harvest, bumper year though it might be according to Devlin. As if to echo his thoughts, splotches of rain began to fall on the dry and dusty front yard.

'Marvellous!' Sylvia cried, jumping up. 'Look, Jessie, it's raining! We haven't seen a drop since we came here. I was beginning to wonder if we'd ever see rain again. Doesn't it smell wonderful? It'll clean the air of that choking smell of smoke.'

Corby refilled his whisky glass and glared at Jessie. 'Your sister can be incredibly stupid at times,' he said. 'Or is it that she is just devoid of tact?'

'Now what have I said?' Sylvia challenged him, pushing her dark hair away from her face and lifting it from the nape of her neck to catch the small breeze accompanying the rain.

'Wet weather can ruin the crop,' Jessie explained, looking to Corby to explain further.

Sylvia laughed. 'What? A few spots of rain? I should imagine it would be hardier than that.'

To be truthful, Corby rather agreed with her. The way the fires roared through the cane he doubted that a little night rain would matter, but he resented her attitude. There were times when he thought she was laughing at his endeavours, comparing him with Devlin's matter-of-fact approach. For that matter with Devlin's masculinity. He'd noticed the way she looked at Devlin when he came to the house after dinner to show Jessie how to make daily entries in the journal and to discuss the day's progress with him. He was twice Sylvia's age but she sidled about him like a purring kitten.

He looked at his watch by the lamplight. 'Where's your father? It's dinner time. I refuse to stand about waiting for him night after night.'

As they went into the dining room Jessie sent Elly to find the Professor. 'I'm sorry,' she said. 'He doesn't have much sense of time.'

'Then he'd better learn,' Corby said, placing himself at the top of the table. 'I can't abide delays.'

'Oh, Corby,' Jessie laughed. 'You sound just like the Colonel!'

That was all he needed. By now rain was thundering on the roof, not just a shower but teeming, pelting rain. 'How dare you compare me to my father!' he thundered. 'That man has never done a stroke of bloody work in his life. I'm out there in that bloody wilderness day in and day out, until I'm saddle-sore and worn to a frazzle doing the best I can for your family, and you throw him at me!'

'I'm sorry, dear,' Jessie said. 'I didn't mean it that way.'

'Oh no. You never do! You and your sister idling your time away, sitting here blaming me because your lives are so boring . . .'

Elly interrupted him. 'The old man, he's not home.'

'Then serve,' Corby said coldly.

'Where can he be?' Jessie was worried. 'I'd better have a look for him.'

'Sit down!' Corby said. 'I won't have my schedule turned upside down on his whims. The cook can put up his meal.'

They took their soup in silence, with the rain still pounding down on the shingle roof. Jessie was growing increasingly concerned. 'I'd better look for Father,' she said as Elly placed the steaming corned beef in front of Corby for the carving and went back for the vegetables.

'I told you to sit down,' he instructed, but Jessie had stood up, pushing her chair aside.

'Corby, don't address me like a servant.'

He saw Sylvia give a twitch of a smile, enjoying the confrontation, and that provoked him with the necessity of winning this argument. 'I am not addressing you like a servant,' he sighed. 'I am simply saying that if we are to maintain our standards out here then we should abide by them.' He picked up the carving knife and fork. 'Now, shall I carve?'

'By all means,' she replied. 'While I fetch my father.'

Sylvia's amused silence didn't help his mood as she passed over her plate and helped herself to vegetables and mustard sauce. Without a word, they began to eat, until Jessie came rushing back. 'No one has seen Father all day! Not even Toby!'

Corby was about to tell her to resume her place, that the old man was probably down at that disgusting Aborigine camp which he found so interesting, when the fear suddenly struck him, rearing up like an animal. Was this another victim? Had he believed the Professor's explanation about a suicide this morning only because he'd wanted to?

Had the old man been murdered too? Were they inevitably all in danger from these heathens? What time was it, for God's sake? He consulted his watch. Just after eight and the wretched rain was blanketing the homestead. Surely the old man wouldn't be out on a night like this? Damn him! Where was he?

Corby had never in his life felt so bone weary as he rose from the table, his limbs sluggish as if they were dragging weights. He didn't want to face this, why should he have to? None of these disasters were of his making. Both of the women were now clamouring at him as if he were responsible as he forced himself to stride through the kitchen and talk to Toby.

No, Toby hadn't seen him. The old boss, he'd thought, was working up in the cane shed. That was news to Corby. No one had bothered to tell him that the Professor had been preparing the new cane for planting.

'I go get Mike,' Toby said eventually, and although it went against the grain, Corby had to let him go. Everyone, he admitted to himself sourly, turned to Devlin in a crisis. But eventually he, Corby Morgan, would be the real master and he would brook no interference. He tried to console himself with the thought that the old fool was just sheltering somewhere from the rain, but the fears still hovered.

His appetite gone, he poured himself a whisky and went out to the front of the house to wait for Devlin.

Sylvia joined him. 'Jessie's upset. Tommy's making her a cup of tea. Do you want one?'

'No. Thank you. No.'

'Then do you mind if I have a whisky too?'

'No.'

'I rather like the taste of whisky,' she said. 'As long as it has plenty of water.' She put a hand on his arm. 'Don't be worried,' she whispered.

'It's not the first time he's gone wandering off until all hours. And what could happen to him here? London was a very dangerous place to be wandering about at night.'

'I suppose so,' he said, appreciating her kindness and feeling sorry for her that she was unaware of the very real dangers lurking in Providence. Murderers were afoot, he was certain.

The lamps had been removed and it was dark on the wide veranda enveloped by the steady rain. He walked with her to the far end, feeling the warmth of her and catching the fragrance of that light perfume she wore. 'I still worry,' he said, as she moved closer to him, away from the sweep of rain. 'I really do care what has happened to him,' he went on, but her soft fingers touched his lips.

'Don't, Corby. I know you're just as worried as we are. I'm sorry I tease you. But . . .' he saw that light smile in her eyes, 'it's only something to do. I get so lonely here.'

'I know,' he admitted. 'I do too. Don't you think I miss all my friends, all the good times I used to have, all the company. But we just have to bear up for the time being. I'll make a go of this, you'll see, and then we'll have plenty of good times here.' He put an arm about her to reassure her, and she looked up at him, her sweet young mouth too close, far too close. He kissed her gently, consolingly, but their mouths lingered and grew more passionate, and then he had Sylvia in his arms, wanting her, needing her so much, her lithe, firm body pressed so evenly against his . . . not like Jessie, who was so swollen that lately it had been beyond him to attempt lovemaking, and she didn't seem to mind . . .

'Oh, Corby,' Sylvia breathed, 'Corby.'

He kissed her again with an excitement that he hadn't experienced for a long time. Too long.

But then she pushed him away. 'No, Corby dear. We mustn't. We mustn't.'

She was right. But all he wanted, he thought, was just another minute with her, one more kiss, just a moment longer to hold her in his arms. She persisted and he released her with an awful sense of loss. 'We'd better go inside,' he said bleakly.

She kissed him lightly on the cheek. 'Yes. We surely had, Corby dear.'

As she walked ahead of him into the light she turned back suddenly and looked at him as if in a last yearning farewell, and his heart melted at the beauty of her lovely blue eyes. He'd noticed them before, of course he had, but they'd never been lit for just him like this, and the urge to take her in his arms again was so strong that he had to detour away from her into the parlour.

It had been a bloody awful day! For the first time in all these years Mike was fed up with Providence. 'And all who bloody sail in her,' he muttered savagely as he rode through the rain to the main house.

From early morning he could smell the rain coming, so knowing he

89

was running out of time he'd hustled the labourers out quickly making them grab what food they could on the run. No standing about drinking tea today. He'd ridden hard from field to field, and just when he had them all pointed in the right direction, there was Morgan galloping down the track like a madman!

He should have shut the man up in his house with a couple of brandies, got rid of him while he investigated Katabeti's death, but he'd missed that chance and walked into a situation where Morgan was practically blaming him for all their woes. The bloody ingrate! Thank God for the old Professor and his sharp eyes! Mike admitted to himself that he should have spotted the suicide, but with Morgan cursing at him as they rode back, panicking about another murder, he was conditioned to believing before they reached the scene that someone had cut a Kanaka's throat. A suicide was bad enough, but another murder would have thrown the whole plantation into chaos. 'From the top down,' he said meanly.

Mike hadn't dared mention to Morgan that when one of the Kanakas died, the whole mob observed a day of mourning for their burial rites. One problem at a time. He escorted the men with Katabeti's body up to the compound, where the island women took over, wailing like banshees, and then he went to find Pompey.

He explained what had happened and, with some trepidation, pointed out that since the rain was coming he couldn't spare a work day. Pompey shrugged, and Mike made a silent prayer of thanks that he wasn't dealing with Aborigines, who would never countenance such a suggestion.

'Later,' he said to Pompey, 'when we finish. I'll give them another day off.'

But Pompey shook his head. 'Not the same, boss.'

'What can we do then?' he asked, appealing to Pompey's new-found sense of importance now that he had a horse. 'We have to get the cane in or the master will be very angry. There'll be more punishments.'

Pompey considered this and offered a compromise. 'Katabeti, he a Malaita man. The rest of us keeping working but I reckon Malaita men, no.'

'That's no good,' Mike said. 'I need all hands. You go tell them everyone stays on the job.'

The news of Katabeti's death spread fast and Mike's heart sank as he watched the labourers coming in from the fields to gather sullenly by the long-house.

Pompey was right, these were the Malaita men, which meant at least that fifty Kanakas were still working, but with this mob missing there'd be too many gaps in the system. And there'd be no drays moving. For that matter, he thought angrily, where was bloody Morgan? He was supposed to be in charge of that end of the deal.

He rode over to the Kanakas, expressing his sorrow at Katabeti's death, and apologising that it was not possible to spare them from work

90

on this day. They were obviously prepared for him. Their faces were hard as they massed across the road, muttering angrily. Pompey, he noticed, had backed his horse well away from the confrontation, wanting no part in it.

Kwaika and Sal were in the mob, so Mike appealed to them. 'You Kwaika! You Sal! You don't want trouble. You tell them Malaita men all good fellows. Another time mourning day.'

There was no reaction from them, but others began to tramp forward, menacing the boss with shouts of resentment, brandishing knives and machetes.

Mike knew it was too late for him to back off. If he did he'd lose face with these natives and the whole show would get out of hand. If this mob got away with disobedience it was likely the rest of the Kanakas would down tools too and enjoy the victory. They were a tough lot and it was part of their culture to deride weakness.

As a stone zinged past his head he loaded his rifle and levelled it at the mob. 'Get back to work!' he shouted. 'The next one to throw a stone gets a bloody bullet!'

They showed no inclination to move, so he yelled at them again, lowering the gun with a confidence that he didn't really feel. Then he heard a voice raised above the growl of the mob. At first he thought someone was calling to him, but as the Kanakas fell silent he realised that whoever it was was addressing them in their own language. He stood high on his horse to identify the speaker, and saw that it was young Joseph.

Curious now, Pompey came over to listen.

'What is he saying?' Mike asked him urgently.

Pompey seemed nervous. 'Doan know,' he muttered.

'Of course you bloody know. What is he saying?'

Mike caught the glance that Pompey gave him, rolling his dark eyes against the stark whites as if he were afraid of something, but this time he did reply: 'He says it all right. He says Katabeti wished to die. He doan need the mourning.'

'What?' Mike said, staring at Joseph who was still talking. 'What else is he saying?'

The young native was standing sturdily among his people. His voice was even, and to Mike's ears had no special quality about it, but they were all listening. Intently. Pompey too.

'What's he saying now?' Mike insisted.

'Nothin' much,' Pompey said evasively. He wheeled his horse about and rode away, and Mike was astonished, relieved, to see the men moving back to the fields without so much as a glance at him. It was as if he had become unimportant.

He caught up with Joseph who was walking with Sal, and tapped him on the shoulder with his whip. 'You there. Joseph. You talk good sense to the Malaita men, eh?'

The lad looked embarrassed, and Sal answered for him. 'Joseph bloody good cutter, boss. Good worker!'

They hurried away across the burned fields, and Mike stared after them. He felt he should thank Joseph for his logical solution to the argument, but the young man had made the episode seem of no consequence.

'Well I'll be damned!' Mike said.

For the rest of the day he hadn't had time to think about the events of the morning, but now, riding through the rain to yet another crisis – the missing Professor, who was probably asleep somewhere – he remembered that expression on Pompey's face. That Kanaka was a happy-go-lucky bloke, always busy looking out for himself. Mike had known him for years, but he had never seen that look of fear on Pompey's face before.

Mike hoped that he'd imagined it.

'No, I didn't,' he said as the horse plodded along, taking the dark slippery track carefully. 'I bloody didn't imagine it!' And why did they all suddenly back off when some young kid decided to have his say? What the hell was going on?

As he came in sight of the house he too felt an odd clutch of fear, recalling Pompey's face, remembering Perry. Hadn't it been Joseph that Perry had flogged? And yet he'd have backed a hundred to one that Joseph wasn't trouble. For God's sake, he asked himself, what are you thinking of? Joseph was the one who stopped the trouble. You owe the kid, you silly bugger.

As he rode under a bank of trees he saw Morgan and his wife, obviously thinking they were unobserved, in an embrace on the veranda. Mike smiled, appreciating the normalcy of the little scene after his harrowing day. People, even Morgan, still found time for love. A loneliness drifted over him. He'd been married once, a long time ago. His wife had run off with an army officer while he was at sea. He should have remarried then but he'd never stayed in the one place long enough to think about it . . . and these days even if there were a lady about who might take him on, his career at Providence was not looking all that bright.

Why did Jake have to go and die on him?

He headed for the back door of the homestead, accepting that entering by the front door was no longer his prerogative.

The guest house was a simple building, three bedrooms in a row, with the inevitable long veranda to protect residents from the extremes of sun and rain. A lamp was lit in the Professor's room so Mike went over there, thinking that the call must have been a false alarm and the old gent was safely tucked up in bed. He dismounted and strode along the veranda, shaking water from his hat and his heavy oilcloth cloak, then stopped suddenly at the open doorway.

Seeing her standing there was a physical shock. She was obviously distressed, and one side of her thick brown hair had come unpinned, to drop down in soft loops. It crossed his mind that her hair, damp now and glistening with rain, must be very long.

'Oh, Mr Devlin,' she said. 'You startled me. One can hardly hear oneself think with the noise of the rain.'

'I'm sorry,' he said, bewildered. She couldn't be as startled as he was. She couldn't have come to this room from the front of the house in such a short time. So who was it out there in a clinch with Morgan? There was only one other woman in the house. God Almighty! The sister! What was going on here?

'Don't be sorry,' she was saying. 'I'm so glad you've come. We don't know what to do. There's still no sign of my father, and look, here's his walking stick. He never goes for his hikes without that. Where can he be?'

Mike pulled himself together. 'We'll find him, Mrs Morgan. When did you see him last?'

'This morning, when you were here. Down by the big tree where the poor man died. He was so thrilled at being able to help you in the cane sheds. I thought he'd gone there for the day. I didn't realise he was missing until it was time to call him for dinner.'

'What does Toby say? Has he seen him?'

'No. He's searching for Father now. Some of his Aborigine friends have gone with him. It's so kind of them in this weather.'

'Don't be worrying,' he said. 'The weather doesn't bother them, they'll find him.' He took the Professor's overcoat from a peg behind the door. 'Here, put this around you. You go on back to the house and have a cup of tea. We'll have him back in no time. He's probably sheltering from the rain somewhere.'

He watched her run across to the house but couldn't bring himself to follow her. To face Corby Morgan. What was the man thinking of, with his wife due to bear him a child in a matter of weeks? Was it the age-old story? The pregnant woman not attractive enough now for Corby's pleasure. Surely not! She was a beautiful woman, and blooming in the way many pregnant women did at this time, her whole countenance shining with freshness and life.

The rain was easing; it should be fine again in the morning, just a little hotter and steamier as the summer crept at them. He hadn't been altogether truthful with her. The rain wouldn't bother the blacks but it would impede their search. Obviously Toby had taken some black trackers with him, but they'd only be beating about in the dark. If they found the Professor it would be more good luck than good management.

Where had he been all day? And why? Mike climbed back on his horse and rode back to the Kanaka compound to ask among the various groups if any of them had sighted the Professor during the day. It was too late now to organise a search, but if the old man hadn't appeared by morning, there would have to be a full-scale hunt using every available man. On a property this size, when they had no idea which direction the Professor had taken, it could take days to find him. Mike clung to the belief that the Professor was lost in the bush somewhere, not an unusual occurrence, because he dared not entertain a more sinister solution, but he was worried. Very worried.

He couldn't just go home and sit on his butt, so he picked up a lantern from the long-house. No one had seen the old man and the Kanakas were concerned. They all seemed quite fond of him. Apparently he'd met a lot of them on his travels. As he looked about for someone to carry the lantern for him, he spotted Joseph.

'You want to come with me, Joseph?' he asked, holding out the lantern.

'Yes, boss.' The young man jumped up quickly, eager to help. He took the lantern and stepped out on to the track. 'Which way we go?'

'No point in going into the bush,' Mike said. 'We'll stick to the tracks.'

Together they went endlessly up and down between the fields, the islander leading the way with the lantern and the horseman trotting along behind him. Every so often Mike called out, hoping to locate the Professor, his voice sounding intrusive in the sibilant hiss of the night.

'That's far enough,' Mike said at last. 'We'll try the river roads. Are you getting tired?'

'No, boss,' Joseph said. He was certainly no chatterer; he'd hardly said a word since they'd set off.

Fortunately the river road where they'd found Perry's body was further out. Mike didn't fancy traipsing down there on a dark night with a strange Kanaka. Then he roused himself, shaking off the foolish superstition as they began searching the river tracks closer to the house. They were all dead ends, more or less parallel with each other depending on the curve of the river.

They were well down the second track when they were plunged into darkness.

'Oh cripes!' Mike called. 'Has the lamp gone out?'

'Yes, boss.' Mike heard a shiver in Joseph's voice as he added: 'This place bad medicine.'

'Yeah, well we're going back,' Mike said, thinking that the lad was afraid of the dark.

'No,' Joseph snapped, startling Mike with his sudden sting of authority. Then he yelled something in his own language. For all Mike knew, he was calling to the Professor, but there was no reply and Mike's horse was becoming spooked, twitching nervously. He looked back down the deserted track as the moon moved out from the clouds, and felt he should call out too, but enough was enough. The search would have to wait until morning.

Joseph ran down the road ahead of him towards the river, still calling, making a hell of a racket, his voice sounding weirdly defiant. Mike let him go. 'Enough to wake the dead,' he muttered to himself, and instantly wished he hadn't said that, thinking of the old man. As if in response, he heard a cry from the bush.

'Come back,' he yelled to Joseph. 'Hurry.'

Hitching the horse, he dismounted and waited for Joseph. 'In there. I think we've found him.'

They both waded into the soggy scrub, Joseph following Mike and muttering: 'This a very bad place. This an evil place.'

'Shut up!' Mike growled at him. He couldn't have the Kanaka bolting on him now.

They found the Professor, soaked and covered in mud, sprawled in the long grass.

'Are you all right?' Mike asked, lifting him up, but the old man began babbling incoherently.

'Devils chase him,' Joseph said.

Mike disagreed. 'Rubbish, he's got a fever. Come on, we'll get him out of here. Help me carry him, we'll have to get him on the horse.'

'What the hell was he doing out there?' Morgan demanded. 'Upsetting the whole damned household.'

'I've no idea,' Mike said. 'I've sent one of the blacks to call in Toby and his mates who are still searching the back road — that's the route the Professor usually takes. He must have had some reason to head towards the river.'

'Bloody old fool,' Morgan said. 'I'm convinced he's not all there! It's a wonder he didn't fall in the bloody river.' He set two glasses on the table. 'Care for a brandy?'

'I would indeed,' Mike said, even though he was ill at ease now, having been afforded a too-private glimpse of these people.

Morgan handed him his drink. 'I suppose the old fellow will survive?' he remarked drily.

'I hope so. He's probably caught a chill on top of the shock of being lost out there. When the ladies get him settled down I'd recommend hot milk and a good shot of brandy, that does wonders.' He remembered Joseph, who was still waiting outside, and called to the cook. 'Tommy. That Kanaka boy out there, he helped me find the old man. He's a good feller, take him out some supper.'

The good boy could have gone back to the compound when the white people came rushing to the aid of the old man, but this was his first chance to examine a white man's house, and it intrigued him. Unnoticed in all the fuss he'd circled the house several times, peering through windows at the lamplit rooms, pop-eyed with wonder. To Joseph the bungalow was a mysterious opulent palace; he'd never seen anything like it in his life. Floors were covered in gleaming boards, a protection against fleas, he deduced. The Kanaka bunk-house had rush-mat flooring and was jumping with fleas. Everywhere here were magnificent padded seats, big and small tables, all sorts of delicate ornaments. The beds were a wonder in themselves! One to a room, big beds on legs covered with magnificent cloths! And the smells of the place, so different! Clean, polished smells like newly carved artefacts, luscious kitchen smells, and the delicate smells of the ladies, the white ladies. They had come so close to him when he was lifting down the old man, and now he was dizzy with their perfume, like coming upon new and seductive flowers.

A little dog nuzzled into him as he sat cross-legged in the yard with a good view through the wire door of a display of pretty plates. It was all too much for him to take in, so he sat, spellbound, dreaming of a life like this, despairing, for what could a Kanaka expect? At best a lifetime of cane-cutting, living in a bunk-house with a mob of strangers. At worst, in his case, returning to the island where death lurked at the whim of chiefs. He fondled the dog, feeling desolate that the path he had chosen would deny him the joys of a family.

'This can't be,' he said to himself, realising how naive he'd been in his plan to hide from the cruel island practices in the white world, where, the missionary Pastor Penn had told him, such sacrifices did not exist. It was old Pastor Penn who had taught Talua English, but in the end Pastor Penn had done something wrong, and he too had lost his head. 'There has to be a place for me here,' Joseph whispered.

A white lady came rushing towards him, and Joseph jumped up, afraid that he'd done something wrong.

'Oh!' she cried. 'You've got Tuppy. Thank you.' She looked up at him and smiled. 'I thought I'd lost him again, he's such a naughty dog.'

Then the black girl brought him down some food and a mug of tea. Good tea, hot and sweet without a mess of leaves, and some slices of bread with meat between. He munched hungrily and the girl stared at him. 'My name Eladji. Who are you?'

'Joseph,' he said warily. He'd been warned to keep away from these dark black people; they had powerful magic and they didn't like island people.

But this girl seemed friendly enough. 'I got a baby,' she said proudly, and he nodded.

'Your husband, he work here too?'

'No husband,' she grinned. 'Me, I am top house-girl.'

'You work in there?' he asked, impressed.

'Yes, got nice dresses too.'

He watched as the white lady, carrying the dog, crossed the yard again and mounted the stairs into the kitchen. 'That white missus,' he said. 'She's a good lady.'

'Her!' Elly said. 'She not the missus, she only her sister. Her name Sylbia. And she no good lady.' She poked Joseph in the ribs, giggling. 'She a flirty lady.'

He shook his head. 'I don't know that word.'

Elly laughed. 'She like men. Better you watch out. Big feller like you. Maybe she like you too.'

Joseph too was laughing as he finished his food. This girl with her preposterous comments was very funny, but more than that, she had access to and she understood the white world. She was the most important person he had met in this place. If he could get to talk to her at other times her advice would be invaluable.

Too soon Mr Devlin came out and whistled to him that they were leaving. As he trotted along beside the horse, Joseph plucked up the courage to ask a question: 'When we do the fence job, boss?'

Mr Devlin had said that the fence was to surround the big house, and had put them to splitting logs, but that job had only lasted a day before they were sent back to the canefields.

'Any day now,' Devlin said, 'I'm waiting for the timber. As soon as the harvest's in we'll get on with it.'

Joseph nodded, satisfied that he had made a step in the right direction.

Elly watched them leave. She'd never seen a man as beautiful as Joseph. He was so strong and manly and his skin was a lovely nut-brown colour. She shivered in anticipation. What would it be like to have Joseph make love to her? She never went into the Kanaka camp, so she would have to work out ways of meeting him again.

Chapter Seven

Sylvia couldn't believe it! Visitors! She rushed madly through to her room to change, calling Jessie as she ran. 'Visitors! You see to them while I tidy up!'

'Who?' Jessie cried, jumping up to dispose of her needlework.

'Mrs de Flores and a gentleman,' Sylvia replied before she disappeared.

'Oh dear,' Jessie wailed. She hurried to a mirror, pulled pins from her hair and held them in her lips while she smoothed the front and repinned the rolls, wondering all the time what she would do with these unexpected visitors. Would they be staying for lunch? And what was for lunch? She didn't know. Quite often, on their own, she and Sylvia only had sandwiches. Should she send for Corby? The harvesting had finished weeks ago but he was still kept busy all day. And he had made it plain he didn't like Mrs de Flores any more than she did. But maybe she ought to send for him.

Worrying, Jessie managed a smile and walked out to the front to welcome their first guests. She was shocked to see Mrs de Flores riding astride a flashy black horse like a circus rider.

'Hello, Mrs Morgan,' Mrs de Flores called, waving her hat. 'We took a chance you'd be home.'

Where else would we be? Jessie thought glumly.

Two Aborigine stableboys appeared from nowhere to take the horses, and Mrs de Flores chatted gaily with them as she dismounted as if they were old friends.

Sylvia had never changed her clothes so swiftly in all her life, Jessie noted, as her sister came swanning out to join her at the top of the steps, looking cool and pretty in a full-skirted white cotton dress with a blue sash and fringed blue silk shawl. Jessie felt a frump next to her, but Mrs de Flores, with her suave ways, managed to say the right thing. 'My dear, you look positively blooming. When's the babe due?'

'Not long,' Jessie mumbled, accepting her embrace.

That answer seemed to satisfy Mrs de Flores, who moved quickly on to throw her arms about Sylvia. 'And you look gorgeous too! Country life is agreeing with you. Isn't she lovely, Johnny?'

The gentleman following her up the steps raised his cap and smiled. 'Indeed.' It was a seaman's peaked cap, and his black brass-buttoned jacket told the same story.

'How good of you to call, Mrs de Flores,' Jessie said, rescuing her manners from this onslaught.

'Lita, darling,' she laughed, sweeping them inside with her. 'And you're Jessie, aren't you? This is Johnny King. Captain Johnny King of the good ship *Medusa*. He's taking a little holiday.'

Jessie felt as if she were the guest trailing behind the woman into her own parlour, but it gave her a chance to inspect a local lady's clothes, which could be useful once her figure returned to normal. Lita was wearing a strange riding habit, a black divided skirt (half-mast, Jessie thought, just touching her boots), a tan belt and a plain but expensive-looking white silk shirt (it couldn't be called a blouse). Her sleek black hair, parted in the middle, was drawn back and held in a silver filigree clasp, allowing the thick tresses to fall loosely but tidily down her back, the severe style accentuating her fine profile.

She was talking up a storm with Sylvia, both of them as excited as schoolgirls which gave Jessie time to observe her further. Even in these plain clothes and out here in this wilderness, she had to admit that Lita had style. But her clothes also looked comfortable, and really seemed quite ideal for riding, for a plantation. Jessie was determined that when the baby was born and settled, she wouldn't be sitting about the house. All she knew of Providence was contained in the books and daily journals, she wanted to get out there and see every inch of it for herself. She wondered if Lita would mind recommending a good dressmaker. Jessie now knew that her formal city clothes wouldn't do at all.

'Would you like tea?' she asked.

'We'd kill for a cup of tea,' Lita replied. 'Is Tommy still here?' She spied Elly peering round the door. 'There you are! Haven't you grown! Quite the young lady now. Come here to me.' She gave Elly a hug. 'Now don't dash off on me. Wait a minute.' She produced a box from her pocket and handed it to the maid. 'This is for you. And don't let that mother of yours take them from you!'

Dumbfounded, Elly opened the flat white box to stare down at two coloured glass butterflies.

'They're hair clips,' Lita explained. 'Come here and I'll show you.'

She pushed Elly's black woolly hair back and secured the clips on both sides. 'There now. Don't they look pretty!'

Elly, all smiles, backed shyly from the room. 'I show Tommy.'

'Are you staying for lunch?' Jessie asked.

'If it won't inconvenience you,' said Captain King, managing to get a word in.

'Not at all,' Jessie replied. 'If you'll excuse me, I'll just talk to Tommy.'

She hurried out to the kitchen to find Tommy already busy. 'Miz Lita, she like good tucker,' he said. 'She give me a whack if I serve up crook stuff.'

Jessie frowned. How did Mrs de Flores know this household so well? She must have been very friendly with the two men who lived here before, to take such liberties. Or with one of them. Mr Devlin, perhaps? It occurred to her that this impromptu luncheon might be easier to contain if she were to invite Mr Devlin too. But Corby would never approve. Best not.

'What will we have?' she asked Tommy, not sure what provisions were available at such short notice.

'Vegable soup. Beef pud. Mash tatoes. Cabbage. Apple pie. Aaaah! No apples! Custard pie!' Having rapped out the menu, he raced to the stove to make the tea, dismissing her.

Elly was setting the tray. Jessie turned to her. 'Is Mr Langley home?'

'No, missus. Him bin gone walkabout with Toby.'

Jessie nodded. Her father had survived the fever and been on his feet again, thank God, in a few days, and now his main interest was orchids. He had quite a display in the bush house at the back of his quarters, and was already sending sketches of new varieties to London. He claimed that he could earn money exporting rare orchids, but as long as he was happy, that was all that mattered. Corby had been cross that the Professor seemed to have taken Toby over as his personal servant, but Toby didn't appear to have any specific duties, so the subject was dropped. Besides, as Jessie had pointed out, none of the Aborigines were paid, they just got their keep. It wasn't as if her father were taking anyone from the workforce.

'Elly,' she said, 'since Toby isn't home, could you send someone to find Mr Morgan and tell him we have visitors?'

'Yes, missus.' Elly flew out of the back door to rouse a messenger, not wanting to miss anything that was going on in the house.

When Jessie was settled in the parlour again, Lita changed her tone. She was suddenly serious. 'My dears, I hope you'll forgive us for barging in. I've been down in Brisbane and when I heard the dreadful news I had to come. How terrible for you, so new to the country. What must you think of us? Two murders on your property! It's so ghastly!'

Jessie's heart missed a beat. What was she talking about?

Sylvia gasped. 'What murders? There haven't been any murders here.'

'The Kanaka,' Lita said. 'I was told one of your Kanakas was murdered. Someone cut his throat.'

'Oh God, don't remind us,' Sylvia said. 'It happened right out front there. But he wasn't killed. He committed suicide. It was quite disgusting. We were in shock for days.'

'Really?' Lita said. 'Then what about your foreman, Perry?'

'We never met him,' Sylvia said. 'He left just after we arrived.'

Jessie saw Lita and King exchange glances. She remembered that about the time the foreman departed without a word, without his pay, the police had been here.

'What about Mr Perry?' she asked steadily.

'Oh dear. I think I've put my foot in it,' Lita said. 'What are they doing out there, building a fence?'

100

'Yes,' Sylvia said. 'The outlook is so ugly Corby wants the house completely fenced and a formal garden planted.'

'What a good idea,' King responded quickly. 'It should be very pleasant. It doesn't take long for things to grow here.'

'Excuse me, Lita.' Jessie leaned forward. 'What were you saying about Mr Perry?'

'You mustn't let it bother you,' Lita replied. 'I mean to say, peculiar things happen on the plantations from time to time, but they're perfectly safe.'

'Lita's right,' Captain King said, running a large hand through his thatch of yellow hair. Jessie listened politely as he tried to distract her with stories of amusing events on the various plantations. She didn't take to King. He was in his thirties, with tanned weathered features, and though he was a friendly man, obviously pleased to meet them and now concerned that she and Sylvia might be upset, she felt that he was overdoing the charm, that there was a shabbiness behind his trim façade.

'I'm sure you're right, Captain,' she said, ignoring Sylvia's frowns, 'but what peculiar thing happened on our plantation? With Mr Perry.'

'Oh drat,' Lita said to Johnny. 'They're bound to hear sooner or later.' She turned to Jessie: 'Just don't tell Corby I told you.' Unable to resist sharing the gossip with them, she launched into her story as if they were neighbours entitled to a place on the grapevine, not women directly connected with the tragedy. 'It's common knowledge in town,' she whispered, 'that your foreman was murdered. Surely you met the police when they were out here? The coroner's verdict was murder by person or persons unknown. It was in all the papers.'

'We don't get newspapers out here,' Sylvia said, worried now.

'Of course you do. They come out weekly with the provisions. Mike has probably got them. But Corby would have read them. They were probably doing you a kindness in not mentioning the matter; after all, the rumours about his death are rather horrible.'

'What rumours?' Sylvia asked.

'I think we've heard enough,' Jessie said stiffly, ' and I should appreciate it if the subject isn't mentioned in front of Corby.'

'I'd like to know.' Sylvia appealed to Lita, who smiled and patted her hand. 'They're only rumours. I'll get it out of Mike. Leave it to me.'

Corby's arrival rescued them. He was in high spirits, even pleased to see Lita, and Jessie was happy for him. The poor man deserved a break from the long hard days he put in on the plantation. It was not as if he were born to it. Every night he came in dog tired, but he was still up and about in the early mornings. Jessie was proud of him.

And Lita helped. She congratulated Corby on his crop. 'My father bet you wouldn't make it. He said a new chum like you trying to run a plantation without a couple of white foremen would get into a helluva tangle. Isn't he dreadful?'

There was a slight hiatus in the conversation when she mentioned foremen, and Corby noticed the hesitation, moving quickly to suggest that they should celebrate with some wine for lunch. 'I'm afraid I don't have any champagne,' he apologised. 'I ordered it from the general store but it didn't arrive. The wines they did send are not the best either, I have to say. It's really quite a problem.'

'Leave it to me, Corby,' King said. 'The stores here wouldn't know a vintage from a Saturday night stew. I'll have some decent French wines sent out to you.' He winked. 'And no duty to pay.'

'Good show,' Corby said. 'I'd appreciate that. I must call on your father, Lita, pay my respects.'

'Take a bottle of brandy and you'll be welcome,' she replied. 'Old Edgar's not one for company really. Nor is his lady.'

'I heard Mr Betts was a widower,' Jessie said. 'We didn't know he'd remarried.'

She laughed. 'He hasn't. He's got a black woman. His "housekeeper" is the accepted euphemism. She's quite nice, really, keeps to herself. And it suits me, darlings, so don't look so shocked. I mean, if a white woman got her hands on him, my inheritance would be shot to pieces.'

Sylvia giggled nervously. 'You must have a very nice house there at Helenslea.'

'It's passable,' she said, but King wouldn't have that.

'Hang on, Lita. It's a fine house.'

'For these parts,' she shrugged.

'The best in these parts,' he persisted. 'It's two-storeyed, painted white with black shutters. I've seen houses like that in Hawaii.'

'That's where Edgar got the idea,' Lita said. 'He and my mother went to Hawaii for their honeymoon. He had a picture of his favourite house in his head before he finally built it.'

'And you've been to Hawaii, Captain King?' Sylvia breathed.

'Many times,' he replied.

Jessie was fascinated now by these people who spoke so casually of exotic Pacific Islands as if they were only across the bay, and she began to realise that distance here had to be understood from a different point of view. The capital city of this state was two thousand miles away to the south. Very hard to grasp. She made a mental note to discuss this with her father. Perhaps they could find maps of the continent which would give her a better perspective. After all, she mused, her child would be Australian-born, and as a mother she ought to know these things.

Led by Corby, the company had reverted to talking about cane. He turned to Lita: 'I believe our sugar has gone from the mill to the refinery. What did Mr Betts think of the standard?'

'Oh yes,' she smiled. 'I forgot to tell you. Edgar said it is very high quality, you'll be riding high this season.'

Corby beamed. He poured the wine, toasted the Queen and the ladies, apologised for the scratch lunch which was, nevertheless, enjoyed by all, and exchanged funny stories with Johnny King. The two men got along famously.

'I hope we'll see you at the meeting next week,' he said to Corby.

'What meeting is this?'

'We're forming a Planters and Friends Association to combat the trade union. It'll be the biggest meeting ever held in Cairns, you won't want to miss it.'

'Of course I shall be there, but why is a trade union involved?'

'The so-and-sos,' King said, deferring to the ladies, 'they want Kanakas banned from Queensland.'

'Kanakas?' Corby echoed. 'Why would they want to do that? How will we run our plantations?'

'They want you to employ white men. But it isn't only planters who are up in arms. Ship-owners and masters like myself will be losers too. It's a lucrative business carting Kanakas backwards and forwards from the islands.'

'I don't understand,' Corby said anxiously. 'White men can't work the fields.'

'They say they can,' King said. 'They've formed a trade union council in Brisbane, and one of their first moves is to get rid of the Kanakas. They've got delegates in all the sugar towns stirring up trouble.'

'Surely the Government won't go along with such a proposition.'

'Don't be so sure, they bend with the wind. But we're having a dinner the night before the meeting to welcome the Member of Parliament for Mulgrave. He's coming up from Bundaberg to give us a report. I tell you, if this Pacific Islanders Act goes through he'll be out of a job so fast he'll wonder what struck him.'

Corby was white-faced now. 'What will this Act do?'

'Prohibit the indenture of Kanakas.'

'Good God!' Corby said. 'I'll be ruined.'

Lita tried to cheer him up. 'It won't happen, Corby. It's just a lot of hot air. But you must all come into town. There'll be entertainment as well, a dance after the dinner, picnics during the day, and I believe they're organising a twilight cruise on Trinity Bay. It will be fun.'

'How marvellous,' Sylvia cried. 'We wouldn't miss it for the world.'

The men retired for a further talk on this important matter, and Jessie sat on the veranda while Lita and Sylvia took a stroll. They walked down the road towards the fields, with Sylvia talking excitedly about the visit to town and what clothes she would need. When they turned back, they stopped for a while to watch some Kanakas digging postholes for the fence.

'Who's that?' Lita asked, pointing at a young bare-chested Kanaka who was working with a long-handled spade.

'I don't know,' Sylvia said. 'I'd love to go to that dance, but I wouldn't have a partner.'

'I'll find you one,' Lita said absently, strolling up to the workmen.

103

'What's your name?' she asked the Kanaka.

He stopped, surprised, and muttered: 'Joseph, missus.'

'Well, Joseph. You seem to be a hard worker. We need some fences over at Helenslea. If you do a good job here we might hire you and your team to build some for us too.'

'Yes, missus,' he replied, bewildered, standing very still until they had moved off.

'Isn't he gorgeous?' Lita whispered to Sylvia. 'Did you see those broad shoulders and those muscles? Just divine.'

Embarrassed, Sylvia giggled. 'Oh, Lita, you are awful!'

'Why?' Lita said coolly. 'They're no less of men because they're coloured, and he's quite the most superb specimen I've seen in years.'

'But, Lita, you wouldn't . . .'

'Wouldn't what? I've no idea what you're talking about.' She laughed. 'Now where's Mike? I was disappointed that he didn't join us for lunch. He's such a pet.'

'He's staff,' Sylvia replied. 'He never has meals with us.'

'Really!' Lita's eyes flashed angrily. 'Then I shall have to look for him myself. You go on in, I'll find my horse.'

'I'll get a horse and come with you,' Sylvia offered, but was devastated when Lita snubbed her.

'Don't bother, darling. Since he's only staff I wouldn't want to put you out.'

He recognised the summons. Lita had a piercing whistle that would put a drover to shame. She waved her hat as he rode across the ploughed field to meet her. 'Hello, stranger,' he grinned. 'I heard you were here. What are you doing hanging about with King?'

'A convenience,' she said. 'And you're not interested, so what's a girl to do?'

Mike laughed, jumping down from his horse and offering her his hand. 'How's old Edgar? I haven't had time to get over to see him.'

'He's fine. Still roaring about the place as if none of the foremen know what they're doing. But you look tired. Hasn't Corby replaced Perry?'

'No, and he's not likely to. He thinks he can do the job himself. He tries but it's hit and miss, he hasn't really got the hang of anything yet.'

'What a bore! Oh well, if you get sick of Providence, Edgar would always take you on. He could swap three of his foremen for you.'

'Ah, you're too kind, my love,' he laughed. 'But you know I wouldn't last ten minutes with your old man. We don't see eye to eye on anything. Come and I'll show you my house.'

They led the horses until they came to a cross-track. 'It's up there.' He pointed. 'You can just see my veranda through the trees.'

'How lovely. You must have a splendid view.'

'Well, come up and I'll show you.'

She looked up at the rain clouds re-forming from the coast. 'I'd better

104

not. I have to get away before that lot moves in. I'm not keen on having to stay over. We had lunch with the family. I must say Corby's improved. He's almost human. But the wife's very pukka.'

'Not really. I like her. She's terribly shy but I've been showing her how to manage the books and she's got a far better grasp on the works than he has.'

Lita teased his chin with the flap of her riding whip. 'Don't tell me you fancy her?'

'Good God, no! The lady's pregnant.'

'It's not a terminal disease,' she grinned. 'Did you ever find Perry's head?'

'What?'

'Come on, Mike. You heard me. Everyone knows about it. It's the best horror story they've had for years. You can hush things up on paper but you can't stop people talking. Is it true?'

'Yes. And don't be morbid, asking for the gory details.'

'It's not a case of being morbid,' she said seriously. 'That's why those two women haven't had any visitors. People are too scared to come near Providence. It was the first thing I heard when I got back from Brisbane.'

Mike frowned. 'I'm sorry about that, but what can I do? It's up to Morgan to invite people, and he doesn't seem inclined.'

'Nor does he know, obviously, that it's usual for folks about here to tin-kettle newcomers, to converge on their homes and make them really welcome. That just hasn't happened. And you didn't notice?'

'To tell you the truth, Lita, I didn't. But it's too late now. Come on, I'll walk you back.'

'But you will be a pet and see what you can do, won't you? If these people don't mix they'll get a reputation for being very odd.' She took his arm. 'And you are not to turn into a hermit! Johnny has talked them into coming to town next week, so you must come with them. There are meetings about this labour business but a lot of parties as well.'

'Thanks, Lita. If the boss is going, how can I leave the plantation?'

'Oh damn! I forgot about that.' She stopped. 'Mike, you have to put your foot down. Tell him you need at least two more white men here or you'll quit!'

They walked through the bush separating the fields from the homestead and she saw Mike glance about him with a smile. The green trees sizzled in the afternoon heat, cicadas zinged, the smell of eucalyptus was heavy in the listless air. A brown snake roused itself from sunning on the mud-caked track and slid swiftly away.

Lita understood. Not in a million years would she admit it, but all that time in Europe she'd felt she was travelling under false colours, a displaced person, hungering for just this smell and sound of the bush, yearning for soft Australian voices like Mike's. The clipped and haughty tones of her companions in the northern hemisphere had been a cacophony to her ears at times, too fast in their release, too hard in

105

their presentation. And yet back here, she heard herself imitating them, unable to stop herself, her own voice louder than the slow tenor of the voices that surrounded her. She knew she would never go back there, except maybe for a visit, but what was to become of her here? She had become an unreal exotic flower in a land strewn with exotica. The real thing.

She touched Mike's sleeve. 'Providence,' she said to him, 'is not the end of the world.'

'I know,' he laughed. 'But you can see it from here.' A local joke. He took her hand. 'It would be hard to leave. Bloody hard!'

They watched Lita and King ride away. Sylvia was relieved that on her return to the homestead with Mr Devlin, Lita seemed to have forgotten that she'd snapped at her. Indeed, looking again at the coloured boy, she'd given Sylvia a mischievous blink, almost a wink. Quite outrageous, but Sylvia was thrilled to be included in such a wicked secret.

'I shall definitely be going into town next week,' Corby told Jessie.

'Yes, it's obviously very important to be present at the meetings,' she replied. 'The Kanakas appear to do the work very well. Why would people want to change things?'

'Just for the sake of it, I suppose. Such destructive ideas have to be nipped in the bud. But it will be most interesting to meet fellow planters.'

'I'm sure it will be,' Jessie said.

'I can't wait to get there,' Sylvia enthused.

Corby stared at her. 'It won't be possible for me to take you. Jessie isn't coming, she's not up to the journey on those bone-shaking roads, and I'm certainly not taking the wagon. It's far too slow.'

'But Lita has invited me,' Sylvia wailed. 'I'm entitled to go. I insist on going. I can ride.'

'Out of the question,' Corby said.

'It's a long ride, Sylvia,' Jessie said gently. 'Are you sure you can manage it?'

'I damn well will,' she said, 'otherwise I'll be stuck out here forever.'

'Corby,' Jessie said, 'do take her. Father's here, and the servants. I don't mind staying home, but Sylvia really does need a break and a chance to meet young people. It will be a nice change for her.'

'I'll think about it,' he said as he strode into the house.

'What does that mean?' Sylvia asked her sister.

'He'll take you,' she laughed. 'He just doesn't like being bombarded with demands.'

'Marvellous!' Sylvia cried, throwing her arms about Jessie. 'I'll tell you all about it when we come back. And I'll bring you a present.'

'I'd prefer it if you chased up the man at that general store to see if the pram has arrived. It should have come on the dray with the bassinet.'

'I'll find a pram for you if I have to turn the town upside down,'

Sylvia cried gleefully. 'Now. What to wear? What to take? Oh, I'm so excited!'

Lucas Langley was interested to observe the change in them. 'My goodness,' he said at dinner, 'everyone has plenty to say this evening.'

'A little human contact does make a difference,' Corby replied. 'Gives us something to talk about.'

The Professor sipped his pea soup. 'Human contact, you say? Then what are all those souls out there? I was under the impression that we live among hundreds on our estate.'

'You're being deliberately obtuse, Professor,' Corby sighed. 'You know perfectly well what I meant.'

'Indeed I do. I can't speak for you, Corby, but it is a great disappointment to me that my daughters regard the islanders as mere workhorses, and the Aborigines as untouchables.'

'You're being unfair, Father,' Sylvia said. 'It is not our place to be mixing with those people.'

'And in what bible is that dogma writ?' he asked her. 'Has it never occurred to you to extend a hand of kindness to them?'

'What could we do?' Jessie said. 'We're kept busy here.'

'Oh yes, I see that. Curtains and fripperies have to be made while your workers live in rags. I noticed you were busy yesterday making soap, lavender-scented, for yourselves. You didn't think of sharing it with your sub-human neighbours, most of whom don't have soap.'

'No, we didn't think of it, Father,' Jessie said firmly, 'but if you had mentioned it we should have been only too pleased to make more and distribute it.'

'Jessie,' he said sadly, 'I didn't mean for you to see yourself as the lady of the manor. If you made a genuine effort to get to know these people, to learn who they are — as individuals, not just workers who will make you rich — you'd be richer in a far more positive way.'

Corby threw down his table napkin. 'I've had enough of this! Jessie, tell the girl I shall finish my meal at the table on the veranda.'

As he stalked out, Sylvia turned on her father. 'Why do you have to cause trouble? What's it got to do with you anyway?'

He looked at her sadly. 'Unfortunately it has a lot to do with me. I am a partner in this plantation, and while I am content to accede to Corby's authority on the nuts and bolts of cane-growing, I feel duty-bound to attend to the welfare of these poor souls.'

Jessie's conscience was stirred. 'You make me feel dreadful. I was under the impression, as Sylvia was trying to explain, that we should not interfere. What could we do to help?'

He sighed. 'I suppose I'm being too hard on you. But you are educated women, both of you. I had hoped you'd have more go in you. That you'd see the futility of sitting here doing needlework, concentrating on trivia, when within the perimeter of this estate is a wealth of life experience. Have you bothered to visit the hospital where

107

simple native women are trying to cope with diseases alien to them, like 'flu? Do you care that there is no hospital for the Aborigines, that they have no medical aid whatever?' His face was becoming red and he was puffing with emotion.

'Father, don't upset yourself,' Jessie went round to put an arm about him and kiss him on the cheek. 'If you tell us what we should do, we'd be only too pleased to help. Now eat your dinner.'

But the Professor had lost his appetite. He picked at his meal and took his coffee out to his room. He knew he shouldn't be blaming the girls for their ignorance. No doubt white ladies on other estates had exactly the same detached attitude. Hadn't he gone skimming off in search of botanic specimens before the real weight of his responsibility here began to dawn on him? Followed by the realisation that it would be a Herculean task, and costly, to improve conditions for the natives.

He'd spoken to Mike about the problem and was not comforted to hear that conditions on Providence were a vast improvement on the treatment of Kanakas and blacks on other plantations.

'That does not relieve us of our responsibilities,' he'd said.

'I do the best I can,' Mike said wearily. 'But there's no denying that sickness bowls them over.'

The Professor lit his lamp and closed the door, looking forward to a pleasurable evening.

After his dreadful ordeal he'd been in a feverish state for days, worrying, in his lucid moments, that he might have contracted malaria. Apparently Mike had sent for the doctor, but the gentleman himself was down with a bout of that ailment and was unable to attend. As it turned out, he wasn't needed; the fever passed and the patient recovered. Well, almost. The Professor doubted that a doctor could assist him in dispelling the aftermath of that awful time. He was left with persistent frightful nightmares, gruesome garbled images of dismembered bodies, of crocodiles and a wild raging river. And always he himself was there, caught up in a vortex of evil, screaming for mercy.

In the safety of the day, he dissected the dreams logically in an attempt to cure himself, to convince his brain not to entertain such foolishness. He understood that by connecting himself with violence, and perhaps some dark form of sorcery, he had put too much strain on his mental abilities.

'You are not going mad,' he told himself. 'You were simply not equipped to take on such a task as disposing of that severed head, or even viewing it.' As his family knew, he didn't like upsets of any kind; they made him nervy, unable to refocus his concentration for days. And that experience, he pondered, was far too shattering for me.

He tried visualising the dreams again. Sometimes he saw himself walking doggedly towards a high cliff, filled with trepidation at what lay beyond, and was interested to note that there were no surprises in dreams. Why was he not surprised to be walking to that cliff? Why was he not surprised to find himself in a river, but not wet? And at a myriad of other impossible events.

But his calm study of the dreams, his explanation of the cause, had no effect, and the nightmares came back at him with renewed vigour until Tommy Ling brought him relief.

Tommy was there one night, in his room, shaking him. 'Wake up, boss! You makee lotta noise. You have bad dreams again?'

Gratefully, he clutched at the Chinaman to rescue him from this horror, and when he was fully awake, he apologised. 'I am sorry. Stupid of me. Thank you, I'll be all right now.' But he was still trembling violently and his bed was damp with sweat. He watched as Tommy put some drops from a small bottle into a teaspoon.

'You take this medicine, boss,' he said, and obediently the Professor took the liquid like a baby.

The smell was familiar, but in his dazed state he couldn't identify the liquid. 'What is it?' he asked.

'Make you sleep good. Opium velly kind stuff.' Tommy plumped the pillow and persuaded the Professor to lie back. 'You good now, go sleep. I mind you, no more devils.'

And sleep he did, at last. With fond, gentle dreams that he couldn't recall.

The next afternoon when he took his nap, he treated himself to another teaspoon of the small quantity Tommy had left for him, and again that night. The bad dreams were replaced with delight.

He bought a packet of opium grains from Tommy so that he could make up and administer his own bliss, finding that a teaspoon in the morning was good for him, making him more aware. Now he was taking at least six teaspoons a day. He marvelled at how he'd been able to confront his daughters about the natives without becoming too upset, knowing the opium helped.

Professor Langley knew he was becoming addicted to opium, but he had no qualms about it. He'd read Thomas de Quincey's book, *Confessions of an English Opium Eater,* which outlined the joys of that drug, but he had never before had the opportunity to experiment. Coleridge, too, had been a great one for opium, as were many others. He decided to read for a while, and then indulge.

Until now, Jessie hadn't realised that the activities of the white people were so interesting to the Aborigines, who were now standing about in cheerful groups watching the departure of the boss and 'Missy', together with Toby and two mill hands. It struck her too that they were always cheerful, ready with waves and wide grins as they passed by the house, despite her father's claim that they lived under miserable conditions. Looking over at them she was bemused by their attempts at clothing. None was permitted near the house 'undressed', except the children, who were running about completely bare. The men wore battered old trousers or rough shirts, only just achieving decency, and the women had pulled on shifts, some of old calico, some even made from sugar bags. Jessie guessed that underwear was unknown. She promised herself that she'd have Elly take her to visit the camp soon. Investigating the blacks' camp and the Kanaka hospital would be something positive for her to do with Corby and Sylvia away.

'We'll be off now,' Corby said, leading his horse over to her. 'You look after yourself, Jessie, and get plenty of rest.'

'I'll be fine, darling. But you take care; that old road will be very muddy and slippery.'

He laughed. 'It couldn't be any worse than the tracks around here. I just hope your sister can cope.'

'I'm sure she will; she's been practising riding astride for hours every day, thanks to Lita's example, and she says it's very comfortable, that she feels more in control of the horse with both feet in the stirrups. When I'm well again, I must try it.'

He shook his head. 'I'm not sure that I approve, but Devlin says it's safer for women to ride that way.'

Sylvia was already mounted on the chestnut mare called Prissy, a fine horse that she'd claimed as her own. She was impatient now to be on their way. In case Corby changes his mind, Jessie guessed.

Corby was having a last few words with Mr Devlin. She saw that he was wearing a gun again, and that reminded her of the death of Mr Perry. Ever since the visitors left she'd been trying to muster the courage to ask Corby about that man's death, to get to the bottom of the matter. She still resented looking a ninny in front of Lita and the captain, not knowing that Mr Perry had been murdered. Not being privy to events on their own property. But she never seemed to be able to find the right time to ask him, and as the days passed her resolve diminished. She did know now and what would be the point in confronting Corby? After all, he was probably correct in not wishing to worry her, or Sylvia, who seemed to have forgotten the matter anyway.

She stood with her father and Mr Devlin, waving goodbye until the riders disappeared down the track, then she turned to the manager. 'Mr Devlin, when do the next lot of provisions arrive?'

'In a couple of days, Mrs Morgan, all being well.'

'Who checks them in?'

'I do when I have time, but lately the driver just unloads the dray himself and puts everything in the storeroom. Tommy shifts what he needs to your store and coolroom.'

'I think I ought to take on that job, don't you?'

'By all means, ma'am, if you're up to it.'

'I might miss a few weeks when the baby is born, but I'm quite up to it,' she smiled. 'And by the way, you can let the papers come straight to the house now. I know about Mr Perry. What happened to him, I mean.'

'I hope it didn't upset you.'

'Well,' she said, 'it should have, but it seems so remote, difficult to believe. You don't think it will happen again?'

'No. We still want to know who did it, but it will be hard to catch him. Ted Perry could be cruel; I think his death was an act of revenge. You're not worried about being in the house on your own?'

'Not at all. I'm quite surprised to be so confident. I must have settled in well. Besides, Father is just outside in his room.'

He nodded. 'There isn't anything to worry about, but I'd suggest you tell Elly to put her bunk on the veranda. She won't mind. Then she's handy if you need anything.'

'I'll do that. Thank you, Mr Devlin.'

He tightened the saddle on his horse, prior to leaving. 'And don't forget now, just send one of the blacks if you want me.'

Left alone, she stood on her front veranda watching the three young Kanakas at work on the fence. Mr Devlin had spent quite a bit of time with them, showing them what they had to do, and the posts and support rails had finally been erected. The palings had arrived, drayloads of them, and the Kanaka lads had begun hammering them into place with gusto. After that, a coat of white paint, and the homestead would be fenced in, except for the gates which had yet to be constructed. The half-built fence already made a difference, making the area seem more civilised and not just a house one stumbled on after emerging from the bush.

She decided to have her morning tea outside in the warm breeze. It was rather exciting being left in charge of a plantation, if only as titular head with Mr Devlin nearby.

Chapter Eight

'You were so shy, saying goodbye,
Here in the dark.
Only a glance, full of romance,
And you were gone.
Though my dreams are in vain,
My love will remain,
Strolling again,
Memory Lane with you.'

The song lifted and swelled in the crowded ballroom. Male voices, deep and resonant, harmonised with the sweet voices of the women. The room swayed with the waltz, and Sylvia, in the arms of Captain King, was entranced. Never before had she heard dancers and onlookers join in a community of singing at a ball, and it gave her a wonderful sense of belonging.

'Memory Lane' was such a romantic song, touching the hearts of all these country people, and the spontaneous singing added poignance to a gay and lively evening.

Sylvia was very pleased with the fact that she'd handled the long ride into town without any complaints. Not that she would have dared to complain to Corby, even if she'd been riding a donkey.

They'd been escorted into Cairns by Toby who led a packhorse carrying their bags, and two white men, mill hands from Helenslea. The men talked sugar with Corby most of the way, which gave Sylvia a chance to try to make sense of her surroundings. She'd shuddered when she realised how isolated they were out at Providence, and the long desolate road, hedged in by relentless greenery, didn't help her mood.

When they came to the Chinese market gardens on the outskirts of town they were caught in yet another shower of rain. It had been the same all the way, rain and sun, rain and sun, so that her cloak and hood, drying out in the heat, kept her in a state of steaming damp.

But this time the rain persisted and became heavier as they rode along the Esplanade, and Sylvia's determination began to wilt. She wondered why she had bothered making the effort to come to this horrible place, all grey and drab with men slouching along bent over in the rain like hunchbacks. There was no wind, only this curtain of rain that blotted out the bay and the mountains which were all she could remember of the area.

As they dismounted at the Victoria Hotel, Sylvia's courage deserted her. She was stiff and sore and soaked to the skin, her clothes clinging to her and her skirts already trailing in the mud. She clutched at Corby, whose clothes were also wringing wet. 'I can't go in like this. I look terrible. What will people think?'

He seemed to agree with her. 'We haven't got any choice,' he said grimly through the rain. 'Just hold your head up and don't let anyone think we're bothered. It's an expensive hotel and Captain King has hired us two of the best rooms, so we're not just nobodies off the street.'

The other men went on their way and Toby took the horses, leaving them to negotiate the sodden planks that passed for a footpath.

As they entered the lobby a porter rushed over to take their coats, and people certainly stared, but in a good-humoured, sympathetic manner.

'Nice day for ducks,' a man smiled as he walked by, and no one seemed to care that their boots sloshed and they dripped water across the lobby.

Soon they were whisked to their rooms. Sylvia was delighted. She'd never stayed in an hotel before, only in boarding houses when the Langleys had taken holidays, and this was an adventure in itself. Her room was lovely, in direct contrast to the ugly town, with a good firm carpet, green plush drapes bordering the lace curtains on the windows, a double bed with a white counterpane, plush-covered armchairs, a willow-patterned jug and basin on the washstand, even a small desk and chair. She pressed a button on the wall, not sure if this was the right thing to do, but a maid came running. She scooped up Sylvia's wet clothes, promising to 'fix' them, and left her several towels to 'fix' herself.

'Lunch is over, miss,' she said. 'Twelve to one on the knocker it is. But I can bring you some tea and sandwiches if you like.'

'Thank you,' Sylvia said. 'It's very kind of you.' And then, feeling very sophisticated: 'Would you tell Mr Corby that I'll rest this afternoon. I have to dry my hair and unpack. I'll see him at dinner. By the way, what time is dinner?'

'Six o'clock,' she replied. 'Six to eight. Coffee in the lounge. Where's your luggage?'

'Oh, heavens. Our black servant had it, on the packhorse. Where would he have taken it?'

'Round the back I suppose,' the maid laughed. 'I'll get it up to you.'

Lita woke her at five thirty. 'Come on, sleepyhead. You're missing all the fun. There's a party on downstairs, a gathering of the clans, so to speak. Now, let's see . . . what will you wear?'

Sylvia was out of bed in an instant, sopping water over herself at the basin, undoing the rags in her hair and brushing it until it shone in a gloss of loose dark curls.

'I see you remembered to bring a ball dress,' Lita observed.

113

Sylvia laughed. 'As if I'd forget! When is the ball?'

'Tomorrow night, in the ballroom here, thank God, so we won't have to go out in the rain. What about this one?' She pulled out the pink silk evening dress that Sylvia had worn so often on the ship.

'I don't know,' Sylvia worried. 'It looks so plain now.' She really meant that it looked boring and juvenile beside Lita's low-cut gown of rose taffeta.

'Don't be silly. It's very pretty, the bodice is nice and tight, it gives you a good figure. Hurry up and get dressed, and put your stays on too. No cheating. I'll see you downstairs.'

She was almost out of the door as Sylvia called to her, 'Will someone come for me?'

'Not in this neck of the woods, darling. If you can ride a horse in from Providence you can get yourself down a staircase. This is frontier land, don't expect too much.'

But Lita was wrong. From the minute she descended the stairs, Sylvia was the centre of attention. She didn't care that most of the men wore old-fashioned dinner suits that strained across their chests, that she seemed to have lost height in this company of big bush men, she was just so thrilled that there were so many of them. The ratio of ladies to gentlemen at the party, and later in the dining room, was at least one to ten, which of course made the other ladies genuinely pleased to welcome her.

The dinner party had been a whirl of excitement and new faces, with aspiring beaux pressing in on all sides. Even Corby was enjoying himself in the company of other planters, mainly Edgar Betts, who was an awful old lecher. Lita certainly didn't get her looks from him. He reminded Sylvia of a turkey gobbler with those piercing eyes and his beak of a nose, and his movements were quick and jerky, twitching about him, observing everyone keenly as if he owned this farmyard. Maybe he did, she thought, watching everyone fawning over him. She hadn't given him a chance to paw her a second time with those knotty claw-like hands; she'd drifted over to Johnny King's table and, conveniently, had forgotten to return.

Having done this, though, she'd had to accept Johnny as her partner for the ball the following night, bypassing younger, far more handsome gentlemen.

There wasn't much to do the following day, with all the men at their meeting and the rain coming down like hot soup, so she spent most of the time in her room, lazing about and preparing herself for the ball. From her window she could look out over Trinity Bay, grey and turbulent now, with small ships bobbing out there like corks, and she prayed that the weather would clear; she'd been looking forward to the twilight cruise that Lita had mentioned.

Drat the rain. She felt like a wet sponge, and she despaired as she examined her blue lace ball frock that should be crisp and full but was hanging like a limp rag, even with the help of its whalebone hoops.

As the rain continued, she worried that the ball might be cancelled, but the maid reassured her, and at long last Corby came to escort her downstairs. He looked so elegant, easily the best-dressed gentleman there, and Sylvia knew that with her hair pinned up in thick dark rolls and the lovely dress trailing richly over the carpet she could match him. They made quite an entrance! Several people thought she was his wife, which was quite a giggle. But soon Johnny King claimed her and she had a rush of eager partners for every dance.

It was hard to believe that it was already two in the morning, and they were dancing slowly to 'Goodnight Ladies' in the soft light of dimmed lanterns.

'Have you enjoyed yourself?' Johnny asked her.

'Oh yes, it's been wonderful!'

'That's good. I was worrying that this show might have been a bit rough and ready for you.'

'Not at all.' She smiled at a group of young men who were watching her earnestly, having missed out on partners for the last dance.

Noticing, he grinned down at her. 'You're the belle of the ball, Sylvia, and that makes me the luckiest man in town.'

He was holding her too close now, even though the floor was jam-packed with couples, and she resented his possessive tone, but she couldn't pull away without making a fuss. Dancing had been reduced to a rhythmic romantic sway due to the lack of space, and he pressed against her now, his arms dropping to loop about her shoulders. 'You're so beautiful,' he whispered. 'Lita told me you were but I didn't expect you to bowl me over like this.'

She didn't reply, relieved that the roll of drums signalling 'God Save the Queen' forced him to release her.

As they walked from the floor King had his arm about her, and she saw that Corby was watching. She raised her eyebrows, hinting that the captain's attentions were not appreciated, and he made his way over to them. 'Splendid night, Johnny?'

'You can say that again,' King replied.

'What about a game of cards? The night's still young.'

But King wasn't to be put off so easily. 'Not for me, old chap, but you'll find plenty of starters. I'll look after our young lady.' He took her arm. 'I thought a champagne supper might be in order.'

Sylvia was cross. She'd adore a champagne supper, but not with him. She busied herself in undoing the skirt hooked to her wrist for dancing, and manoeuvred away from him, fluffing it out again. 'Thank you, Johnny, it's a lovely idea. But really, I'm exhausted. Excuse me, I must say goodnight to Lita and the others.'

The two men walked her to her room and then went off jovially for champagne and cards, but Sylvia didn't mind. She was feeling rather hot and limp anyway. And she'd made her mark; everyone who was anyone in the district now knew that there was an attractive single lady living at Providence, and her social life could begin.

She opened the door on to the hotel veranda for a breath of air. The contrary rain had disappeared again, clearing the skies for a shower of stars against the inky blue, and the bay was calm, almost still in this humid atmosphere. She sighed, slipping out of her dress. The bay really was quite a beautiful sight now, glistening as if touched with silver. The heady perfume of tropical plants invaded the air, adding a sweetness to the night, and brazenly, still in the doorway, she began to remove her stays and her slip. She remained there in a voluptuous mood, her breasts bare, creamy and taut. Beautiful breasts, she mused, much better than Lita's, which were smaller and a bit droopy. She'd peeped at them often when she and Lita had shared a cabin.

Not ready to relinquish this euphoria, Sylvia glanced down at Corby's room. What would she do if he suddenly walked from his room on to the veranda? Duck out of sight? Or stand there with her breasts exposed for a few seconds, pretending she hadn't seen him? She felt a tingling of excitement. He'd danced with her. One dance, the duty dance, and they hadn't spoken, but to be in his arms again had been tantalising, and she'd known he felt it too. As a matter of fact, she told herself, that had been the best dance of the night; he was more expert on the floor than the others.

Disappointed that there was no light in his room, nor likely to be for quite a while, she gave up on being the *femme fatale* and turned to more practical matters, such as removing the counterpane and the useless blanket from her bed and turning back the sheet. She took off her drawers, giggling as she remembered that Jessie disapproved of complete undress, and put on her cool nightie.

In no time Sylvia was slumbering peacefully, satisfied that her debut in this strange land had been a success.

As for Corby, his day had been worrying.

He attended the crowded meeting with Edgar Betts and Captain King, paying his membership fee and signing on as a planter, not just as an associate.

The Member for Mulgrave, Bede Hornsby, Esq., chaired the meeting which was held in the Masonic Hall. When he eventually called the room to order, he began by welcoming everyone, especially 'those sugar-growers who have, by their entrepreneurial strength and foresight, pioneered a thriving sugar industry in this great state of ours'.

'Hear, hear!' called Corby, in unison with the other men surrounding him in the crowded hall. Beards, he noticed, seemed to be in vogue, dark, full beards. Few men were clean-shaven except for the very young fellows, and as far as he could see, he seemed to be the only one sporting a moustache. He considered growing a beard and then decided against it. He didn't want to be just one of the mob. Besides, beards made men look old before their years.

'No one knows as well as I do,' Hornsby was saying, 'how important sugar is to the economy of our state, and I have been doing my utmost to support the industry.'

'Like what?' a voice called.

'A great deal, my man. A great deal. But what I say now is: if we all pull together, shoulders to the wheel, there can be no limit to our achievements. Sugar is a staple food, a valuable product not only for the local markets but for export, and I personally have been proud to see us reaching out to the rest of the world . . .'

'Ah, get on with it!' another voice yelled.

'All in good time, sir. I bring you personal greetings from our premier, Samuel Griffiths.'

Edgar Betts lumbered out of his chair. 'I don't want greetings from bloody Griffiths, and I don't want to hear no more about his bloody cast-iron regulations. I want to know what you bastards are up to with this new law.'

'And you will know, Mr Betts. I am here to explain it to you.'

'Bugger explaining,' Betts yelled. 'I don't need it explained to me. I want it chucked out, strangled at birth!'

'Let's hear about it first,' someone else called. 'Give him a fair go!'

'I'd give him a bloody stockwhip,' Betts muttered to Corby as he resumed his seat.

'Thank you,' Hornsby said, loosening his stiff collar and plucking nervously at his bow tie. 'Now, gentlemen, the Bill to be put before the Parliament of Queensland is the Pacific Islanders Act.' He leaned on the podium. 'This Act is in response to public demand. It has long been thought that the use of Kanaka labour is a blot on our society . . .' The growl from the hall was ominous, but he kept on. 'You all know that blackbirding had continued despite Government efforts to stamp out this foul practice. Only last month the captain and crew of the schooner *Hopeful* were arrested for the kidnapping and murder of Kanakas. The *Hopeful* was a slave ship,' he said sternly, 'and you can't deny it.' Then he took a deep breath and made his final statement in a rush, as if afraid he wouldn't be allowed to get it out if he didn't hurry: 'The Pacific Islanders Act will prohibit the indenture of Kanaka labour after the thirty-first of December, eighteen-ninety.'

Uproar! The audience was on its feet in shock, stamping and shouting insults at Hornsby, who had no choice but to stand there until the noise died down. He raised his hands. 'There are two gentlemen here who wish to address you.' He indicated two men who had entered by the side door and who were now making their way across the stage. 'Might I introduce Mr Joe Pollock and Mr Andy Summers.'

Hastily he stepped aside, out of harm's way it would seem, leaving the newcomers to explain their presence to the angry crowd.

Pollock stepped forward, a burly man in worker's clothes, his sleeves rolled up, while his companion, who looked more like a prizefighter than a public speaker, stood by him, brawny arms folded. 'I'm Pollock,' he shouted, in a voice more powerful, more authoritative than that of the politician. 'Some of you know me. Andy here, and me, we're members of the Trade Union Council.'

117

'Who let them in?' angry voices roared, and Betts was on his feet again: 'By Christ, Hornsby, you'll lose your job for this!'

' 'Tis no job, sir,' Hornsby replied haughtily. 'A job's paid!'

Pollock glared belligerently at Betts. 'Siddown, old man. You ought to be ashamed to show your bloody face here. Even your own mates reckon that Kanakas that end up on your plantation have drawn the short straw. God help them!'

His retort drew, if not a chuckle, then close enough from the crowd, at the sight of Edgar being put in his place. Corby, still feeling his way in the town, realised that his neighbour was unpopular. He recalled that Devlin had often made disparaging remarks about Betts, but he had thought nothing of them, regarding Devlin as staff. He was sorry now that he'd come from the hotel with Betts, having been introduced by Lita, and he moved his chair closer to Johnny King on his left.

'I've come here to try to talk some sense into you,' Pollock resumed, ignoring the fact that not one soul there wanted to hear his brand of sense. 'Hornsby's right. Not all, but a lot of the sugar plantations in Queensland are the last bastions of slavery. And whether you blokes like it or not, it's going to stop. And that's the word, mates, from the top. From Queen Victoria herself.'

Corby had been listening carefully. He rose to his feet. 'I am pleased, sir,' he called, 'that you admit not all plantations are on your guilt list. Providence, my plantation, has an excellent reputation, my Kanakas are well treated and we abide by the regulations. It seems to me that by banning all Kanakas, you're throwing out the baby with the bathwater.'

Pollock took in his statement with a pained expression and shook his head slowly as if he were dealing with a dull child. 'Well treated are they, mister? What hours do they work and for what pay? Don't bother to tell me. I know. Let me tell you. They work from dawn to dusk, six days a week. That's the lucky ones!' He glared at Edgar Betts. 'So that works out to about seventy-eight hours a week, and they're paid three pounds a year. That's about twelvepence a week. Did you hear me, mister?' he thundered. 'Twelvepence a week!'

'There's no necessity to shout at me,' Corby said calmly. 'I can hear you quite well. You seem to have forgotten that the Kanakas are aware of the terms and have no objections. Many of them sign on again. They don't need any more money.'

'Ha!' Pollock cried, pointing at Corby. 'Out of his own mouth this planter has come to the crux of the problem.'

Corby sat down with a smile, pleased that he'd been able to contribute reason to the debate, but Pollock now turned on him furiously.

'You!' he raged. 'Sitting there like a smug bridegroom! You're the type that worries us the most. You're dead set on tearing down our standard of living. You'd employ Kanakas for tuppence a day while white men starve for lack of work. No white man can live on that wage, let alone support a family, so you're driving a stake into the hearts of your fellow Queenslanders. And it's not just the sugar industry, it's the

118

tea and cotton plantations too. The only people who've got the brains to resist you, right from the word go, are the Abos. They've got you beat.'

'We're not talking about Abos,' Corby shouted.

'Oh yes we are,' Pollock replied. 'They're smart. They work for nothing and they walk off when it pleases them. You've seen them in action, they'll never be slaves. They'll work if it suits them, or they'll fight you for their land and they'll die, but they won't stoop to what you've made of Kanakas.'

He paused to take out a handkerchief and wipe sweat from his face, but he was such a powerful orator that, despite themselves, his audience waited for him to continue.

'We've learned from them,' Pollock continued. 'The Abos, who owned this land before we turned up, won't be coolies. Have you got that word? Because that's what your Kanakas are . . . coolies!' He jabbed a large hand at them. 'You planters and your hangers-on, you want to build a society here with coolie labour like they've got in China. You want to keep on getting rich on the backs of slaves. Well, you won't get away with it!'

Stung by these insults, several men moved out into the aisles, menacing the speaker, but Summers strode forward, raising ham fists: 'Let him have his say! You want a fight, you'll get it.'

'No need for a fight,' Pollock called. 'Just hear me out.' His voice was quieter now, more persuasive. 'We know that at least sixty thousand Kanakas have arrived in this state over the last few years. That's sixty thousand jobs lost to white men . . .'

A planter pushed forward. 'Bullshit! There aren't any jobs lost; white men can't work the fields.'

'White men will work them.'

The planter laughed. 'You're a dreamer. Haven't you heard the expression "white men's grave"? That's what plantations are in these tropical climates. They'd go down like flies.'

'Try them,' Pollock said defiantly.

'Goodoh, mate. I'll give *you* a job. You can start on my plantation tomorrow. And let's see how long you last.'

'What will you pay me?'

'Ah . . . so this is what it's all about. You're a begrudger. You hate to see us turning a shilling.'

'You haven't answered my question,' Pollock said. 'What will you pay me?'

'What you're worth,' the planter replied. 'A penny a day. You couldn't keep up with a Kanaka.' He turned his back on the speaker. 'Righto, mates. We've found out what we came for. We know what this Bill is about, and we'll fight it. I say we adjourn to the pub and let these blowhards have the floor to themselves.'

'You can't fight the inevitable,' Pollock shouted after them as they began to move out. 'We will have a White Australia policy to keep out Chinese and Kanakas and give our workers a chance to earn a living.

119

They can't compete with coolie wages. We have no choice.'

But the hall had emptied.

All that night, at the ball, Corby had tried to enjoy himself. He had even managed to overlook the rough demeanour of these backwoods characters masquerading as gentlemen and be as pleasant as possible, but anxiety was nagging at him, so when they'd delivered Syliva to her door he sought King's advice.

'That Bill won't be passed, will it?'

'From what I've been hearing today, I reckon it will.'

'Good God! But the planters have raised a fighting fund. I've made a donation to it.'

'Then I think you've done your money,' King said. 'Come on, I'll buy you a drink.'

They made their way to the bar where revellers, including women, were still celebrating. Corby gazed at them morosely but King steered him to a quieter corner. 'What are you drinking?' he asked.

'Brandy,' Corby said and waited impatiently while King stirred the sleepy barman and stopped to talk with some men who were leaving. When he finally returned with their drinks Corby asked him, 'How do you know the Bill will succeed?'

'Because most of the pressure is coming from the south. We don't count for a lot of votes up here, we haven't got the population, and besides, those trade union blokes aren't kidding. They're busy signing up white working men by the hundreds whether they need jobs or not, and the word is out that unless the Bill goes through there could be race riots, even attacks on the plantations.'

'But that's anarchy!'

'Not the way they see it.'

Corby digested this information for a while, and then, as if bowing to the inevitable, took his enquiries a step further. 'So what happens? If the Bill goes through they'll prohibit Kanakas from entering the country after eighteen-ninety?'

'No fear,' King replied. 'From the minute that Bill becomes law, which could happen at the first Parliament session next year, Kanakas are to be phased out, as I understand it.'

'What does that mean?'

'It means,' King said angrily, 'that when their terms are up they'll go home and they can't be replaced. There'll be a race on now to get as many as possible on to the plantations. Planters have been putting out orders for Kanakas all day.'

Corby was shocked. 'I didn't know this.'

'Of course not. The right hand doesn't tell the left hand what it's doing. My ship's on a coastal run down to Sydney at the minute – my first mate's got a master's ticket – but when she comes back I'll be busy. We'll all be sweeping the islands for Kanakas now. I could sell a thousand already.'

'I hope you'll keep me in mind.'

'I'll try but I've got a lot of orders and the price'll go up. If you keep it to yourself I could line you up a mob of Kanakas at the old price in a couple of months.'

'Thank you. I'll take as many as I can get.'

'There's a catch though.' King looked about him to make certain they couldn't be overheard. 'They'll be coming in on the sly. Cheaper that way. You won't have to pay Government fees, just take them straight from the beach to Providence.'

Corby was bewildered. 'Isn't that illegal? And how can we get them past the customs men?'

'Illegal?' King laughed. 'Everyone does it if they're in the know. This lot won't be coming through Cairns. They'll be dropped off at Elbow Bay.'

'What's in it for you?' Corby asked suspiciously.

'Commission, that's all. I daresay Edgar Betts will want a few too, being on your route. He'll make the arrangements with you when the time comes.'

'But how would I get them to Providence?'

'Easy! March them across country, through the bush. Stop worrying, Edgar's an old hand. He'll jump at the chance to bring a mob in so close to home. All you have to do is get them on to Providence and feed them through your place to Edgar's.'

'What ship and who's the captain?'

'You don't need to know that. I trust you and I trust Edgar. You don't have to pay yet because we don't know the exact number he'll be landing, or how you and Edgar will split them up.'

'I want half at least.'

'That's fair. Then you pay me ten pounds a head, and I take my commission, then pay the captain. If I'm at sea, pay the money into my account in the Queensland Bank. What could be simpler?'

'I'll have to think about it.'

'Tomorrow,' King said. 'I'll need your answer tomorrow. I'll have to make the arrangements and I know a dozen planters who'd jump at a chance like this.'

'But none as close as Providence,' Corby said, resisting the pressure.

'No, but I could always redirect the ship to another secluded inlet; there are plenty like Elbow Bay up and down this coast.' He stood up. 'Some mates of mine have just gone down to Heaven Lee's brothel. She's a star turn and so are her girls. Do you want to come with me?'

'Not tonight,' Corby said. 'I have to think about this.'

'There's nothing to worry about, it's a simple, normal operation. Happens all the time.'

'But what about that ship, *Hopeful*? They've been arrested.'

'Hey! Don't put me in that class. Those blokes were South Seas brigands. They deserved what they got.'

When King had left, Corby sat brooding over another brandy, and then another. He lit a cigar. This was too good an opportunity to miss.

121

It was imperative to build up the workforce against inevitable losses as the Kanakas' terms expired, and there would be huge competition for labour now. He couldn't bear to think of how his plantation could survive in the future if they were forced to employ white labour. Apart from the ridiculous idea of having white men struggling in the fields, a penny saved now would offset the obvious extra cost of white labour, which was a nightmare concept in itself.

What he needed now was as many Kanakas as he could get his hands on to get as much extra work done as possible, such as clearing more land, building those tram tracks, fixing the roads through the estate. He began to feel more confident. It seemed to him that it wouldn't take long for everyone to wake up to the fact that white men couldn't survive the work. Eventually they'd have to allow Kanakas back into Queensland, then everything would return to normal. The experiment of white labour would fail.

In the meantime cheaper Kanakas would be a big help.

'Closin', sir,' the barman called to Corby, the last customer. 'Do you want a bottle to take up to your room?'

'No thanks.'

He walked across the deserted lobby and up the carpeted stairs, feeling wide awake and more than interested in King's offer. He was entitled to protect his investment the best way he could. And why should he let those trade union fellows dictate to him how to run his plantation? Those men were pushing planters into slightly illegal enterprises and he, Corby Morgan, didn't intend to be left standing. He'd show them! It was obvious that King was an adventurer, prepared to flout the law, and it would take daring to pull off a scheme like this. Maybe King thought he didn't have the guts. 'Well, King would be wrong,' he murmured as he came to his door. Corby saw himself as a real frontiersman now, a man of action, the brandy firing up his courage.

Sylvia's door was just along the passage, so he took those few extra steps and knocked.

When she carefully opened the door, just a little way, he apologised. 'I'm sorry. I hope I didn't wake you. I thought I'd better check to see if you were all right. Strange place. Lot of strangers about tonight.'

'No, you didn't wake me. Come in. I hoped you might keep some of the champagne for me.'

She was all in white, with her dark hair fluffed out into curls, framing her face. 'You didn't miss anything,' he said. 'We didn't have champagne after all. I hope you enjoyed the evening?'

'Oh yes, it was such fun. But you only danced with me once.'

'Hardly my fault,' he said, touching that glossy hair, smoothing it from her face. 'You were surrounded by gentlemen all the time.'

'So I was, but none of them could dance as well as you. I'd never danced with you before . . .'

'You enjoyed dancing with me?' His arms went around her and he

122

knew that this was what he'd been waiting for all night, though he'd been unwilling to admit it even to himself. Until now.

'Yes,' she whispered, her hands stealing up to his face and slipping gently to clasp behind his neck, bare arms soft against his skin.

'You looked so beautiful tonight, Sylvia,' he murmured, 'I was proud of you.'

She kissed him. 'Corby, I was proud of you. You made all those other men look like farmhands.'

The passion for her was there again, not that it had ever left him, and he lay on the bed with her, kissing and caressing her, gradually removing her nightclothes. But then he stopped. And that took an effort, because he knew in his heart that he was in love with her. He hadn't been able to think of anything but her all week, and he'd almost been hoping to have to leave her behind at Providence, so that he could remove himself from her for a while at least, and allow this madness to pass.

'I'd better go,' he murmured. 'I really ought to go.'

'Why?' she asked, stirring voluptuously beside him.

'Because,' he said, almost angrily, 'you flirt with everyone, Sylvia, and I will not be one of your conquests.'

She sat up, pulling at a sheet to cover herself. 'If you think I'm just flirting with you now, you're a fool, Corby. I think it's the other way around. I love you. It wasn't until last week when you kissed me that I realised how much.'

He took this lovely girl in his arms. 'Tell me again. Tell me you love me.'

'I do,' she whispered, her mouth to his ear. 'And I'm the fool because you'll go back to Jessie and I'll be just the nobody about the place again.'

'It won't be like that,' he told her. 'I promise you. I didn't want this to happen but I love you beyond all reason.'

He left her for a minute to lock the door, then came back to her as her lover.

They watched the dawn come up over Trinity Bay, a glorious dawn shimmering pink and gold on the dazzling waters, the dark ranges beyond still mysterious in the mists.

'What is to become of us?' she asked him, but his only response was to lift her up and carry her back to the bed.

Disloyal though it sounded, Jessie enjoyed that first day.

Even though Corby stayed out on the plantation until late afternoon, she'd always felt restricted in her movements, as if he were at her shoulder, disapproving. Of course he had a right to be concerned for the child, worried that she might tax her strength too much walking about in the heat, but she rarely went far, for the immediate surrounds were immensely interesting. Little wallabies often hopped into the clearing to graze quietly right in front of the house, and one day a large kangaroo had appeared, his tall ears twitching as he stood grandly surveying the scene before he made a leisurely retreat. She hadn't seen a koala yet, so that was a treat in store, but she'd spied a large goanna padding down the track, his head raised and weaving from side to side. Although Elly had told her they were harmless, that encounter had kept her back on her veranda for a couple of days.

And from her veranda, where she liked to sit and sew or write letters home, she had become a bird-watcher. With her father's guidance she was building up a log of Providence birds. There seemed to be no end to the wonderful variety, from the grey honey-eaters to the black and red cockatoos and the myriad of flashy parrots.

The Professor joined her in the dining room. 'I've got a surprise for you, Jessie.'

'Wonderful! What is it?'

'Come outside and see for yourself.'

'All right. Just a minute.' With Sylvia away, Jessie had been given charge of the spaniel and he was already becoming a problem. He was a skittish little thing, full of life, but he was never allowed to run free outside the house in case he collected more ticks or ran off into the bush, so at the minute, Jessie had him tied to the leg of her chair. He had wound his leash round and round the chair leg, placing himself on a tight rein, so Jessie had to bend down to untangle him while Tuppy leapt and pranced at her, trying to lick her face.

'Be still,' she said, 'or you'll strangle yourself, you silly dog.'

Finally she managed to release him but kept him on the lead as she made for the front door, with the dog skidding and straining ahead of her.

The wagon was down by the front steps, with one of the stable boys in the driver's seat, holding the reins.

'Your carriage awaits, madam,' Lucas said with a mock bow.

'Where are we going?' she asked.

'Down to visit the compound. It's too far for you to walk in your condition so we shall ride. By the way, when is my grandchild due?'

'About a month,' she replied absently, wondering about the correctness of taking such an excursion as soon as Corby turned his back.

'Come along,' her father said, 'don't stand about.'

'Oh, I don't know . . .' she faltered. 'I've got to mind the dog.'

'Lock him in your bedroom.'

Lucas wouldn't take no for an answer, so she locked the dog in and was soon in the wagon rolling down the track.

When they emerged from the bush surrounding the homestead it was a surprise to be confronted by a flat landscape, the barriers of high cane removed. Men pushing hand ploughs and other field workers waved to them as they progressed, and Jessie looked about her. 'It is immense,' she said. 'I thought we'd be able to see the river now.'

'No. The river comes from the north-west; the further we go into the plantation the wider the distance from the river.' He seemed to shudder. 'The closest point is by the house, and even then it's a fair distance.'

'I should like to see the river,' she said.

'Some other time. This is the native compound ahead of us.'

A half-dozen women emerged from the long open-sided hut, buxom nut-brown women wrapped in colourful sarongs. They came forward to be introduced by the Professor as the stableboy helped Jessie down. She was intrigued by their stately and dignified carriage, and was suddenly overwhelmed as strong arms hugged her and soft lips kissed her on the cheek, murmuring a welcome like a bevy of loving aunts. Their polished skins had a not-unpleasant oily fragrance as they surrounded her, vitally interested in her pregnancy, even patting her stomach and laughing joyfully. 'Baby soon, missus. You bring 'im baby to us. We mak 'im big fat.'

Rather than taking offence, Jessie found herself laughing with them, their excitement infectious. She was glad Corby wasn't here to frown on such intimacy with the natives, to freeze at the liberties they were taking. He would never understand the female camaraderie of the incident.

The women brought them tea and rice cakes and hovered about them smiling benignly, as one large lady, fingers flying, made a fragrant lei of frangipani blossoms which she duly hung about Jessie's neck with great ceremony and another kiss on the cheek.

'Should we visit the hospital?' Jessie asked her father.

'I wouldn't today. They are so happy to meet you it would be unfortunate to give the impression you are just passing by.'

In all, the visit was a wonderful experience, and Jessie promised to visit them more often so she could learn their names and really get to know such warm sweet people.

She took her nap in the afternoon with the dog slumbering peacefully on the bed beside her. Elly had taken him for a long walk and now, since he normally slept on Sylvia's bed, Tuppy had demanded the same right in Jessie's room and she'd had to agree. At least she knew where he was. Nevertheless she had closed the doors so that he couldn't escape, Sylvia would have a fit if he got lost, so she suffered the airless room with a resigned smile.

Later, the Professor suggested that they should invite Mr Devlin to dine with them, but this time Jessie could not agree. 'I'd be happy to have him here, Father, but it would be childish and unfair to Corby to break his rules. Besides, Mr Devlin would be quite aware of the implications and it could embarrass him.'

Elly brought her breakfast the next morning, then took the dog for a walk and delivered him back to Jessie.

'Couldn't you tie him up outside somewhere?' Jessie asked.

'No, missus,' Elly grinned. 'Him cry too much, Missy never do that.'

'Oh, very well, leave him with me.'

She spent the rest of the morning with the wretched dog trailing along

125

beside her on the leash or tied to chairs once again. Sylvia had obviously become accustomed to minding Tuppy with such care, but it was already beginning to irk Jessie. She considered handing him over to her father, but he was so absent-minded the dog would be missing in no time. He was always scrambling to get outside.

By midday, feeling sorry for Tuppy, she decided to take him for a short stroll before lunch. She walked him out to the veranda, but as she reached for the timber banister so that she could take the steep steps carefully, the dog realised that a walk was on the agenda. With a yelp of excitement, he leapt out over the steps, the leash slipping from Jessie's grip. She went to grab it, lost her balance and went crashing heavily down the steps, head over heels. She heard herself scream, an unnatural sound, and then she landed with a thud, sprawled on the ground.

Her nose was bleeding. It was numb and Jessie wondered if it were broken. Her face, her hands were grazed and stinging. Then Elly was beside her, weeping, trying to lift her up. 'You alri', missus? You alri'?'

Jessie was winded. She couldn't answer but she too was crying, afraid for the child within her, and she couldn't raise the strength to move. She lay with her cheek pressed against the earth, trying to calm herself as people gathered about her. Then a man scooped her up, lifting her firmly and gently to carry her back up the steps as effortlessly as if she were an infant, her head against his bare chest.

She had a ferocious headache now but she was aware that she was being carried through to her bedroom, with Elly running alongside frantically issuing instructions. As he placed her carefully on her bed she murmured her thanks to this kindly man, and looking up saw that it was one of the Kanaka boys employed in fence-building out at the front. In her confused state she thought he had the countenance of an angel, a sorrowful, beautiful angel, and she reached out to him shakily, taking his hand, needing comfort because she was so afraid.

'I go get Mae,' Elly cried, darting away, but the Kanaka stayed with her, making no attempt to remove his hand.

'My baby,' she whispered, soothed by him, not registering that this was a stranger. 'I'll lose my baby.'

He squatted down beside her, talking – or was he chanting? – in his own lyrical language, and Jessie felt mesmerised, calmer. 'Doan be frighten,' he said softly. 'That baby strong feller. He make big life.'

Mae came running. 'Ay eee! Ay eee!' She screeched about Jessie like a disturbed bird. Tommy raced in to peer at her, his pigtail flying, and then rushed away, calling, 'I find Mike.'

'No,' Jessie cried, becoming more aware now, embarrassed to be making such a fool of herself.

The Kanaka boy had slipped away, and the Aborigine girl and the Chinese woman undressed her and bathed the scorching grazes on her face and hands. Her shoulder was badly bruised, as was her hip, but nothing was broken, they told her, as if she didn't know that. No one could tell whether the baby was all right, though. As they fussed over her, brushing her hair and trying to settle her down, Jessie felt that this scene was completely unreal. Surreal. How had it come about, she wondered, as Mae gave her a teaspoon of medicine, that she should find herself being nursed by three such diverse people as this. And then she saw the funny side of it. A brown man had carried her in, handing her over to a black woman and a yellow woman. Benign presences all three. Now Corby seemed to have appeared from nowhere, frowning at her, accusing her of being careless with his child, trying to chase away the brown, the black and the yellow who had now turned into beautiful butterflies, high on the rafters beyond his reach. Jessie giggled. She laughed heartily, and then she slept.

The Professor was sitting by the bed when she awoke. 'How are you feeling? You silly girl, diving off those steps.'

'I don't know. I'm a bit bruised but I'm in one piece.' She felt her stomach. 'Oh God. The baby. I can't feel anything. No movement.' As she spoke she thought she could remember someone telling her not to be frightened, not to worry, but who? Who had that been? Maybe she had dreamed it.

'Should we send for the midwife?' he asked. 'Mr Devlin is outside. He's very worried.'

'No, I don't think it's necessary yet. I don't want to bring the woman out on a false alarm.'

'Are you sure?'

'Yes.' But she wasn't sure. She needed time to think about what had happened to her body. And to pray. And then she felt a familiar nudge. She slid her hand under the covers to reassure the little person moving about inside her, needing the same reassurance herself that he hadn't been injured. 'It's not time yet,' she said to her father. 'I've had a shock. I'll just have to stay here and rest until I'm feeling more confident. Thank Mr Devlin for me, and do apologise to him. Where's the dog?'

'The dog?' Lucas asked. 'I don't know. I'll ask Elly.'

They searched the grounds and eventually Lucas reported back to her that Tuppy was nowhere to be found. 'Don't worry, he'll turn up when he gets hungry, Jessie.'

'Oh dear, I hope so, the poor little thing. Sylvia will be furious if he gets any more ticks on him.'

Mr Devlin came again the following afternoon on a more formal visit, bringing with him a large basket of fruit from 'the ladies'. The basket was made of reeds and lined with leaves, and the fruit was decorated with large tropical blooms.

'How lovely,' Jessie said. 'What a beautiful presentation.'

'Yes, they love colour. And of course the good Lord provides plenty of that here to remind them of their islands. The fruit is grown here, not in the quantity that I'd like but we should improve on that in time.'

Jessie examined the basket. 'It's wonderful! A pineapple, bananas . . . they grow here? I had no idea. And what's this?'

127

'It's a pawpaw. They call it papaya. The leaves are from the pawpaw tree, they're very easy to grow . This smaller fruit is a mango. They're dropping from the trees like hail at the moment. Have you ever tasted one?'

'I've never even heard of them.'

'Then you've a treat in store. They're very sweet.'

'It's so kind of them,' Jessie said. 'Do thank them for me.'

'I'll do that. Now tell me, how are you feeling?'

'Much better, thank you, but Mae insists I stay in bed for a day or so, and one wouldn't dare oppose her. For a little person she can make an awful lot of noise.'

He laughed. 'Are you sure you don't want me to send for the midwife?'

'Goodness, no. But tell me, have they found the dog?'

'Not yet. The blacks have made finding him their latest project, they're making a great to-do about the search.'

Jessie sighed. 'They're all so kind, Mr Devlin. I feel wretched that I've been ignoring them.'

'You shouldn't. One step at a time. It's better to get to know them gradually. Now is there anything I can do for you?'

She looked at him carefully. 'Yes, there is. Elly said a strange thing; she said that if the dog went near the river the crocodiles would get him. Are there crocodiles in that river?'

'Don't let that worry you. They'll find the dog.'

'Mr Devlin, ignorance can be dangerous, and if there are things about Providence I should know, I would like to be told. Now, tell me about the crocodiles.'

'They're bad news,' he said. 'I was surprised when I first saw Miss Langley with her spaniel. Dogs wandering into the swamps or near the rivers . . . well, they don't last long.'

'Good heavens! And are these creatures dangerous to humans?'

'Yes.'

'There you are. Here I was thinking we could have picnics by the river.' She laughed. 'You see, I could have lost a couple of guests. But I'd love to see a crocodile. Is that possible?'

'Of course. And the river really is beautiful, you just need to know the high spots, the bluffs where you can have your picnics out of reach of the crocs.'

'Good. Now that we're on the subject, what else should I know?'

'Can you use a gun?'

'No.'

'Then perhaps you should learn. Some of the snakes here are venomous. I don't know about this, Mrs Morgan, I shouldn't be sitting here worrying you.'

'Indeed you are not. Like the natives, I'm interested in everything about me, especially staying alive. Thank you, Mr Devlin, it's been a most informative talk.'

128

As he took his leave she called out to him: 'If you think of anything else I should know . . .'

He turned back to smile at her. 'I think that'll do for the time being.'

She spent the next two days quietly, being thoroughly spoiled by her staff of three. A pile of newspapers suddenly appeared on the table in the bedroom to keep her occupied and the Professor came up to play cards with her. She hardly missed Corby and Sylvia but was determined to be up and about by the time they came home. Corby had said they'd be away no more than five days.

But that night she woke with grinding pains in her back. It was very late and the house was quiet. She suffered them as long as she could and then struggled out of bed to light the lamp. Instantly Elly, from her bunk on the veranda, was at the door. 'You sick, missus?'

'No. I've just got these awful pains in my back.'

The girl's eyes widened. 'Better I get Mike.'

'No. Not at this hour. I'll wait until the morning and then we'll see.'

The pains increased and the night seemed interminable. As the hours passed Elly became more worried. She brought Mae up to sit with Jessie, and then disappeared, but Mae, in a state of panic, was no help. She flitted about the room like a trapped bird, her only solution to give Jessie cup after cup of tea. 'You drink plenty hot tea, good for you.'

Whether it was or not Jessie didn't much care; it was sweet and it soothed her dry mouth. Then her stomach seemed to convulse and she realised the baby was coming. She'd left it too late for the midwife. 'What I do?' Mae cried as she listened to Jessie's moans.

'I don't know,' Jessie said through clenched teeth. 'Oh God, I don't know.' She clutched at the bedpost for support.

Suddenly Elly was back, bringing with her a burly Aborigine woman who strode into the room laughing excitedly. Jessie could see nothing amusing in the situation and was shocked when this strange black women jerked away the sheets covering her. 'Go away,' she cried. 'Leave me alone.'

'No, missus,' Elly said. 'This my mum. This Broula, she good at getting babies.'

Then Broula was looming over her, smiling down at her as she quickly removed Jessie's clothes, leaving her totally naked before these women, in an agony of embarrassment. The large rough hands explored her stomach, and Broula gave a grunt of delight. 'Baby comen alri'. You be good girl now.'

Elly put a thick cloth between Jessie's teeth, and the mother-to-be, racked with pain, hung on to the bedpost and shut her eyes tight. Let them do their worst, she thought, I'm going to die anyway. And the baby will be born dead. It was that fall. It's all my fault. I should have been more careful.

Elly leaned over her. 'Broula say stop cryin' and make big push, missus. She say you want this baby you gotta help.'

Angrily Jessie spat away the cloth. 'Easy for her to say! This is all wrong!' She was yelling at them, screaming at them. 'It's too early, too soon. Leave me alone!' The more she yelled, the more these crazy women grinned at her: 'Good! Good, missus. Plenty noise!' She was sinking into an abyss. Or were they drifting away from her? They seemed so remote now, so distant, and she wept quietly at her own stupidity for not allowing Mr Devlin to get the midwife to save her baby.

The Professor was standing beside her, holding her hand, trying to comfort her. 'I'm so sorry,' she whispered to him. 'So sorry.'

'What for?' he asked.

There was the crisp smell of fresh linen. The bed was a cool expanse of white, no longer that dark tempest of the night. Dawn light was stealing softly across the room and Broula was standing triumphantly at the foot of the bed holding a small bundle.

'You'd better take your son,' her father said. 'Your midwife is so excited she's likely to make off with him.'

Corby attended more meetings and hounded the shipping agent and Government agents, placing orders for Kanakas while they were still available, but his name was far down the list. Too late he learned that bribes should have accompanied his orders so, in desperation, he sought out Captain King. 'If you are able to get labourers for me, under the lap, so to speak, I'd be obliged.'

'Consider it done. Edgar will let you know in good time. By the way, I've got the wine you wanted. If you fix me up now I'll have it sent out to Providence with your next batch of supplies.'

'Come to the hotel this evening. I'll have the cash.' He hoped he would. With all these other worries he'd forgotten about the bank.

'Pleased to meet you, Mr Morgan.' The genial bank manager was not at all the elderly sober gentleman he'd expected to confront, but a laconic lanky fellow in his mid-twenties, the sole occupant of the single-fronted shop premises that masqueraded as a bank.

'I was wondering how my credit stands,' Corby said stiffly. 'I've had an excellent harvest, Mr . . . er . . .'

'Billingsley. Bob Billingsley. Come in and take the weight off. I've been meaning to come out to see you but you've saved me the trip. How's Mike?'

'He's quite well.' Corby watched nervously as Billingsley riffled through the vellum pages of a heavy ledger and then turned to another book running his finger down the entries. 'These are the sugar returns,' he said. 'I get wind of them first, see. Then I don't have planters fudging on their figures.'

Corby thought that was rather a cheek, but dared not comment.

'Ah. Here we are, Providence! Jolly good. You're doing great! You're well in the black already.'

'How can that be?'

'Jake made the arrangements. Instead of having the cheques sent out to him at Providence they're paid directly into your account here. Otherwise you'd have to send them back to me and mail can get lost.'

Corby was stunned. 'You mean I don't owe anything?'

'I'd say not. Sugar prices are high, keep us all smiling. I'll write you out a statement. I'm a bit behind in those jobs at the minute. How about you pick it up tomorrow?'

'Certainly,' Corby said, bewildered. 'And, er . . .' How should he put this? 'I presume there are more cheques to come?'

'Yes. Is there anything else I can do for you?'

'I'd like to draw some cash.'

'Right!' Billingsley took out some heavy keys and made for a safe in the corner. 'What'll it be? A couple of hundred?'

'Yes. Please.'

The world was a different place. He stepped out into the muddy street, not caring abut the drizzling rain, not caring that the heat seemed to have intensified in the few days he'd been in town, in this drooping scarecrow of a town. He was in the money! He was on his way. And the more land he cleared for crops the more money he'd make.

Jubilant now, he headed for the bar of the Victoria Hotel. The Kanaka problem would sort itself out. That Bill wouldn't get passed, everyone was worrying too much. It was time now for Corby Morgan to enjoy himself.

Sylvia found the rain irritating, but it was still better than sitting at home listening to it drumming against the windows. The bay cruise was cancelled, as was the race meeting. Although this was disappointing, Lita knew everyone, and there seemed to be no end to the luncheons and parties, even on the Sunday. Corby had intended returning to Providence the following day but last night he'd agreed to stay an extra day; they had so little time left.

During the day he went about his own business, practically ignoring her, but it was for the best and made their nights together in her room so much more delicious. Sylvia didn't care if they never went back to Providence. He'd been in a wonderful mood the last few days, and why wouldn't he be? Their lovemaking had become more and more intense and he'd told her over and over how much he loved her.

She was sitting in the hotel lounge with Lita and several other people, reading the paper and waiting for their escorts to take them to a luncheon at someone's home, when a maid told her she was wanted at the front door. She hurried out, wondering who on earth this might be, to find Toby dancing about excitedly. 'Missy, you get the boss and we comen on home.'

'Why? What are you talking about?'

'Mike, he sent a message. You come home quick.'

'Why? What's wrong?'

He gave a wide smile, delighted to be the bearer of the news. 'Missus

131

got a baby! A baby boy! You tell the boss. I wait here?'

She frowned. 'No. You go away. I'll tell him. Go away.'

Reluctantly he moved off and Sylvia stood at the door, thinking about this. It wouldn't be hard to locate Corby, but why should she? He had promised they could stay tonight. If she told him the news he might want to leave straight away. Then again, he might not; he'd miss a night with her. But best not to take any chances. She'd tell him later. When it was too late to leave for Providence.

In the afternoon they went on to a musicale, held in the hall, but it was so awful she and Lita slipped away.

'Let's have tea in your room again,' Sylvia said, but Lita had other plans.

'Not today, darling. I need my room, so don't come barging in whatever you do.'

'Why not?'

'Because I'm entertaining some friends.'

Sylvia was hurt. Wasn't she Lita's friend? But she held her tongue. Instead she stayed glued to Lita's side until the friends arrived, certain that if she remained in place Lita would have no choice but to invite her.

When they finally bowled in, shaking water everywhere and laughing about what a splendid idea it was to stay indoors on such a miserable evening, which Sylvia didn't think was all that funny, there was only Carver Parkes, a handsome blond grazier who had partnered Lita at the ball, and Johnny King. Even though Sylvia had managed to make it clear to Johnny without insulting him that she wasn't interested in his attentions, she was furious to see that he'd brought along a cheap-looking girl who was wearing a black and white striped taffeta and a horrible satin hat, also in black and white. Sylvia hated black and white, it was so gauche, so loud. She looked to Lita, expecting that this person would be well and truly snubbed by her hostess, who was very good at getting rid of people, certain that her place in this small silly party was now assured.

She heard Carver giving an order to one of the hotel staff – champagne, plenty of ice . . . He called to Lita: 'Oysters?'

'Why not?' she laughed. 'I'm feeling peckish. Order the works, darling.'

'Oysters,' he said. 'Opened. And cold chicken. Plenty of it. Put it on my bill but send it up to Mrs de Flores's room.'

Sylvia thought that was truly outrageous fare for tea, but it would be fun; whatever Lita organised was fun. And then Lita was talking to the cheap girl in her usual charming way, as if she were really interested in her, asking where she came from, how she came to be in Cairns, and the girl was answering in an unmistakable Cockney accent, smiling at Johnny King who was holding her hand like a lovesick swain.

'Have we got everything we need?' Lita asked, and that seemed to send them off into peals of laughter. Then, before Sylvia's very eyes, the party of four excused themselves from her company and made for the staircase.

Shocked at their rudeness, Sylvia sat uncomfortably in her chair in the busy foyer, certain that all eyes were on her, on this girl who had just been dumped by her friends. Frantically she looked about for a familiar face, for the young men who had been at her beck and call for days, but none was to be seen.

An elderly woman in a massive black dress adorned only by a glittering diamond brooch rose from a nearby sofa. As she passed Sylvia she looked down at her and sniffed. 'You're wise to avoid that company, my girl. They're no better than they should be.' And she swept on.

Sylvia wondered where Corby was. There was a lot of noise coming from the bar, accompanied by cheers and toasts, but she couldn't look in there, a male domain. Further on was the billiard room, another of his haunts, but also out of bounds to women.

In the end she fled to her room, hoping that someone would come along and take her down to dine. But no one came, not even Corby, on this her last night in town. Thoroughly depressed, she took a nap, waking to darkness in this twilightless land. She sneaked along the passage to the door of Lita's large corner room. She could hear them in there, talking, murmuring. It didn't sound much of a party, but they were still in there, that was the annoying part, without giving her a thought. So damn them! She had her own plans anyway. Corby would come to her.

Rather than call the maid to bring her something to eat and so admit she had no partner while everyone else in the world was dining in company, she crunched on the last of the boiled sweets from a box Johnny King had given her, and dabbed her face with cool witch hazel. Then defiantly, she took off all her clothes and slipped into her frilly pink wrapper. She stood in front of the mirror, admiring the way the wrapper showed all her curves when she pulled it tight. How could those men bother with that cheap girl, and Lita for that matter, when she was here, younger and far better looking.

She lit the lamps, brushed and brushed her hair, sprinkled her bedroom with lavender water, turned down the bed and then pushed the armchair over so that she could sit at the open french doors, looking out into the night.

A heavy tree brushed against the side of the building like a wet cloth. The heat was stifling and there was no breeze at all from the bay to dispel the foul odour of the swamps. Music drifted up from the dining room below, mingling with the voices and laughter of the revellers. She hoped they were all boiling hot and uncomfortable. And she was furious that she'd left that musicale so early with Lita, who, selfishly, had already made her own arrangements. There had been plenty of young people in the hall. Had she stayed, she'd have been available to accept invitations for this evening. Any number of the young gentlemen would have been thrilled to have her company.

Damn Lita! She'd spoiled everything.

What would happen when they got back to Providence? she wondered. Now that she'd proved herself as a horsewoman she'd be doing a lot more riding on the plantation. She'd probably accompany Corby during the day; that would be romantic, riding with him. She could make lovely picnic lunches for him and they could be together in a secret place. Sooner or later he'd have to tell Jessie about them. She might be hurt but that couldn't be helped. Jessie had made her come to Queensland in the first place. She'd practically been thrown at Corby, and he was only human. It wasn't her fault that she was younger and more attractive than her sister. And Jessie had a baby now, that would keep her busy. She'd probably take the child and go back to England. Where would she find a nanny here? Or a school? Father could go with her. The climate really wasn't agreeing with him, it was sending him senile. Ever since that time he'd got lost he'd been behaving quite oddly. She sighed. Jessie would never fit in here anyway. She was the scholarly type, and the people around here were definitely not that way inclined . . .

Curled up in the armchair, Sylvia fell asleep dreaming of a new house at Providence, a two-storeyed white house with black shutters. Her house.

Sylvia awoke with a start. Corby was in his room, banging and clattering about, making enough noise to wake the dead. She ran down the veranda to stop him. The hotel was quiet, closed down for the night, and that fool was drawing attention to them.

'What on earth are you doing?' she cried as he stumbled about his room, throwing off his coat and tie and waistcoat, lurching against the bed, trying to undo his cuff links.

'Where have you been?' he asked her, his speech slurred.

'You're drunk!'

'Of course I'm bloody drunk. I've got a son! Bronte Wilcox Morgan, heir to Providence.'

'How do you know?' She was curious, and afraid he might be angry with her.

'Everyone knows. Someone told someone told someone and they came to tell me. You could have knocked me down with a feather.'

'I still could,' she snapped.

'Bloody good fellows here,' he muttered as he staggered to a chair to take off his shoes. 'I haven't bought a drink all night. Celebratin' Bronte Wilcox Morgan. Give us a hand here, jolly buttons, all too damn small.'

She helped him undress, trying to keep him quiet, and managed to get him over to the bed, where he sat hazily staring at her. 'Give me a kiss.'

Sylvia pulled away. 'No. You're drunk and you smell like methylated spirits.'

'Spirits,' he chortled, 'not methypolated. You smell nice. What's under that wrapper?' He pulled her to him and she struggled to get away, but he held her too tightly.

134

'Let me go,' she said angrily. 'You're so drunk, you're disgusting.'
'And I suppose King was sober, was he?' Corby snarled. 'Where have
you been anyway?'
'I've been in my room.'
'With King, eh? He's been missing all night too. You thought I
wouldn't bloody notice, you little whore!'
Sylvia was so shocked she slapped him hard across the face. Just as
swiftly he slapped her back, sending her reeling. He wrenched the wrap
from her and threw her on to the bed. 'You need a firm hand, my girl,'
he growled.
'I do not,' she cried, kicking at him, but he slapped her again.
'You like a bit of rough stuff, do you? Well, I'll accommodate you and
I'll do a better job than King!'
Her head reeling from the second blow, Sylvia tried to regain her
senses, but Corby had grabbed his riding whip. He lashed her across the
buttocks and she screamed into the pillow, too afraid to cry out, too
embarrassed to summon help.
He bent over her, shaking her, demanding to be told about her, about
what she'd done with King, about Lita. 'Did you know she likes
blackfellers, like her old man?' he snarled. 'Maybe you do too. Would
you like me to get you one?' And then he was on top of her, pounding
her, turning her about as if she were no longer a person but a rag doll,
and the horror of it was that he was enjoying himself. As his rage
diminished he was slobbering over her, kissing her, dragging her face to
his and telling her in a teary, drunken voice how wonderful she was.
'Promise you'll never go with King again,' he said thickly, and she
promised, she promised. Anything to get away from him. But it was still
dark night and he wasn't finished with her.
She heard the clatter of kookaburras heralding the dawn, maniacal
laughter as if the devil himself were mocking her, while beside her
Corby was snoring. Slowly, painfully, she extricated herself from his
sweaty naked body, retrieved her torn pink wrapper and slipped quietly
back to her room.
The lamps had burned down, but in the half-light her room looked so
normal, so neat. Shivering, she poured water into the basin and taking a
flannel tried to wash him from her. She wept as she combed her tangled
dank hair, and as the light came in at last she examined her bruises. Her
face was sore but not marked. Her body was bruised and tender, and
turning about she managed to see in the mirror the welts from the whip
on her back and buttocks.
She climbed into the blessed clean sheets of her own bed, curling up
quietly in an agony of despair. Wondering if this had happened to
Jessie. Knowing somehow it had not. Knowing too that she couldn't tell
anyone what had happened to her. As the weary morning approached,
as the prospect of facing Corby loomed, Sylvia's mood changed, just as
his had. But she was sober. Very sober. And there was time to think.
He would pay for this, she resolved. Oh, how he would pay. If it took

135

her the rest of her life. She felt sick. She was so sore all over it hurt to move, but move she must. Get up, get dressed, pretend to everyone that nothing had happened. Right now she had no answer to the thoughts of revenge that hammered at her aching head, and she didn't feel well enough to entertain them. There'd be time enough. She'd find a way. One of these days Corby would be sorry he ever . . .

He came to her room hale and hearty, knocking at the door. 'Are you dressed? Good! There's an early breakfast ready for us. Quite a troop riding with us this morning, a general exodus one might say.' He kissed her on the cheek as she stood frozen at her door. And then he whispered, 'You're just the sexiest little devil. We had quite a night, didn't we?'

Chapter Nine

Christmas. Christmas Day in the tropics. An adventure in itself. Jessie tucked Bronte back in his basket. He was such a good baby, he only cried when he was hungry, and that was more a lusty yell, the greedy little rascal. She sighed, thinking of his birthday, the pain forgotten, the confusion remembered.

That day Tommy Ling had done a little too much celebrating, earning a noisy scolding from Mae. By teatime the dog had been found and given to Lucas, who promptly lost him again. Sadly, poor Tuppy was never found again. Most likely he'd run foul of a dingo. Hysterics from Sylvia, of course, when she came home to find her pet missing, blaming her sister for not taking better care of him.

Another argument had followed Bronte's arrival. As Mr Devlin explained to Jessie: 'The black women are all vying for the job as the baby's nursemaid.'

'A nursemaid?' Jessie said. 'I hadn't thought of that. Is that usual? I mean, to employ a black girl?'

'My word, yes,' he laughed, and Jessie appreciated this man with his pleasant, easy ways. 'They know that white ladies have nurse-girls for their babies, and they all want the job. They consider it a great honour, not to mention the perks of presents and better tucker.'

'But are they capable? I don't wish to sound stuffy but the black girls I've seen don't seem to be . . . well, house-trained, for want of a better word.'

'They learn quickly,' he said, 'and I think you'd be wise to take one on, she'll guard this little fellow with her life.'

'You seem to have one in mind.'

'Yes, I'd suggest the dairy girl we call Hanna. She's a mate of Elly's and that's important, otherwise you'll have ructions. They can get rough when they fight among themselves. Broula wants the job, of course, but that's out of the question. I'll send her packing.'

'No, wait. I want to thank her. I never thought I'd have a black woman deliver my baby, and I'm extremely grateful to her.'

Jessie mollified the tearful Broula by presenting her with a colourful fringed shawl. Broula was delighted with her gift but before she left she had to establish her seniority. She took hold of the smaller, slimmer Hanna and shook her, shouting at her in their own guttural language.

'What did she say?' Jessie whispered to Mr Devlin.

137

He kept a straight face. 'She's telling Hanna to look after *her* baby or she'll kill her.'

So Hanna, thrilled, joined the household staff. One of the other girls, Kali, forgot her disappointment when Mr Devlin appointed her assistant to Elly to learn housework.

Peace at last. And then Corby and Sylvia were home. Sylvia looked exhausted. Obviously that long ride from the town was too much for her. Something would have to be done about that in future, the journey broken along the way by a few hours' rest somewhere. After all, no one was in that much of a hurry. Except on this momentous occasion. As Corby said, they'd ridden hard to get home to see his son.

Jessie had never seen such a proud father. He scooped up the tiny mite and strode about the house with him, laughing, making great plans for him. 'We're doing well,' he told Jessie triumphantly. 'This very day I'll sit down and write to my father, to tell him that I have a son and that Providence is a hugely successful plantation. I'm glad he didn't come into it now, and I can't wait to pass on the news to Roger. He can blame that wife of his for missing the opportunity of a lifetime.'

He kissed Jessie again. 'You surprised us all. What a great day this is. I'll tell Devlin that he can declare a holiday on Providence when Bronte is christened. And another thing. I can pay your father off now. In cash. Isn't that marvellous!'

Sylvia was sweet with the baby. Afraid to pick him up. 'He's so little!'

'He was a few weeks premature, that's why. But he's well formed and strong. And I've had plenty of advice on how to care for him.'

'From black women!'

'They're women too and they know more about babies than I do. They say I should give him small feeds, often, and see that he gets plenty of sleep, so that's easy enough.' She changed the subject. 'Did you enjoy your visit to town?'

'If you can call it a town. I went to a ball and a few things.'

'And did you meet any nice young gentlemen?'

'Plenty of them. They all said I was the belle of the ball . . .'

'That's wonderful!'

'Yes, but you should have seen them. They were all so gauche, hayseeds mostly. And that awful Captain King seemed to regard me as his own private property. I spent most of the time dodging him.'

'What a pity. Still, it was a change for you to see how the other half lives. After Christmas, when the minister is available, we'll have a christening party for the baby and you can invite anyone you like.'

As things turned out, Sylvia quickly adopted Kali as her personal servant and kept her trailing about with her, an arrangement that obviously suited both of them, since the black girl was mightily proud of her missy.

And now Christmas. Jessie was looking forward to this special day. What a shame Bronte was too little to know about it. But what joyful Christmases they could look forward to in the future, with exciting surprises for the boy. A rocking horse, he must have . . .

She sat quietly in the corner of the room, feeding the baby, dreaming of happy days ahead, half listening to the sizzling sounds of millions of cicadas in the bush surrounding the house, forecasting heat, that ponderous weighty intruder.

There were protocols to be observed on this auspicious day, and so the ladies emerged in their cool white muslins, large hats and shimmering silk parasols to board the buggy.

'Why, Mr Devlin!' Jessie cried. 'You've put a canopy on it. How thoughtful of you.'

'It's my Christmas gift for the family,' he joked. 'Sorry I couldn't wrap it.'

Nursing the baby, Hanna was permitted to sit in state with them. Corby and Devlin rode alongside as Toby slapped the reins and the party set out on their rounds, first to the banks of the lagoon four miles from the house, where thousands of magpie geese swooped and chattered and leggy pink flamingos dipped daintily among rafts of water lilies, and where a large group of Aborigines waited breathlessly for their treat of lemonade, lollies, cake and watermelons.

After a few minutes the mannered pose was forgotten and a free-for-all ensued as they scrambled for their share. Then all interest turned to the baby. Jessie was afraid for him as eager black faces crowded about them, but Broula was there, bullying, shoving, forcing them to stand back, to wait their turn to admire *her* baby.

Sylvia was horrified by the proximity of these dirty, half-naked wretches. She ran back to the buggy out of harm's way to find Corby standing, smoking a cheroot as he watched the proceedings.

'Is this really necessary?' she fumed.

'Devlin seems to think so,' he said. 'And may I say you look charming today.'

'I don't feel it,' she snapped. 'It must be a hundred degrees out here.'

'You've been avoiding me,' he commented calmly.

'No I haven't,' she lied.

'You always have that black girl to heel.'

Sylvia didn't reply. Why was she still attracted to him when she hated him so much? Even now as he leaned languidly against the buggy, his shirt open at the neck, his well-cut breeches tight on his strong legs, she wished she could touch him, feel him against her. He leaned down and whispered to her and her face flamed at his words. She would not dare say things like that, but he seemed to have read her thoughts and she yearned for him. She turned away and walked to the bank to watch the birds lifting and settling in a patterned procession.

From there they travelled down to the Kanaka compound, where the hand-outs were the same. 'We don't dare differentiate,' Devlin said. The welcome was just a warm and a special choir had been assembled to sing island songs to them.

They clapped their appreciation as the concert ended, and once again the baby was on display to clucking women and shyer men.

Jessie called Mr Devlin aside. 'The young man over there. Is his name Joseph?'

'Yes, that's Joseph.'

'I feel terrible,' she said. 'I just remembered. He carried me into the house, he was very kind to me. I didn't thank him. Can I reward him in any way?'

'I already have,' Devlin said. 'I gave him new clothes and he was over the moon. It takes them ages to earn enough to buy a decent shirt.'

'You really do think of everything, don't you?'

'It's practice,' he replied. 'And probably survival. We're heavily outnumbered here, it pays to keep them all on an even keel.'

'I see. I think I'll still have a word with him.' She walked over to Joseph and shook his hand. 'It's nice to see you again. And I want to thank you for your kindness to me.'

He beamed down at her. 'You got good son there, missus. One day I teach him to fish.'

'That would be wonderful,' she replied.

The Professor hadn't bothered riding out to the lagoon. He had promised to come down and help Pompey with the concert and was delighted that it had gone off so well. Ever since that suicide he'd spent more time with the Kanakas, determined to find the truth behind the murder and subsequent suicide, but his surreptitious enquiries and deliberately offhand comments had met a wall of silence. He'd studied the islanders carefully, though. Pompey was the boss, there was no doubt about that, and even though Mike, displeased with him over some other matter, had considered demoting him, in the end he'd sensibly let him be. On the other hand, all of the islanders treated that lad Joseph with special respect, for some reason Lucas was unable to define. They were a mysterious lot for all their seemingly civilised ways, which contrasted strongly with the Aborigine defiance of European standards.

And why wouldn't they be, he asked himself, plucked from a totally heathen environment and its collection of pagan gods? The more he watched Joseph the more he realised that this self-effacing young man possessed some sort of mystic power over his people, a power that, strangely, Pompey didn't seem to object to.

The Professor tried to put the small enclave into some sort of perspective. If, he mused, Pompey could be classed as king, then it was his guess that Joseph was the archbishop. Equal acceptable power.

He had been watching for an opportunity to catch Joseph off guard, and this could be the moment.

'Would you like to ride my horse back, Professor?' Mike asked him.

'No thank you. I always prefer to walk. You people run along. I'll be back shortly.' He was eager now to put his plan into action, the trappings of Christmas taking second place.

'Walk with me,' he said to Joseph. 'The heat is hard on my old bones.'

140

He waited until the buggy and riders were well out of sight before beginning the trek back towards the house, conversing amiably with Joseph. Eventually he said to the Kanaka: 'You like the missus?'

'Yes. Fine lady.'

'Ah yes,' Lucas sighed. 'My daughter, she's a good woman, but badly troubled. She lives in fear.'

'Who would hurt her?' Joseph bridled.

'She is afraid the man who killed Mr Perry will attack her and her baby.'

'That will never happen,' Joseph burst out. 'He is dead!'

'She will be relieved to know that. All along I have thought the man to be Katabeti. Is this true?'

Joseph stopped short and looked ready to bolt, but the Professor took his arm. 'Don't be afraid. This is just between you and me. No one will know we spoke of it. Is it true?'

'I cannot say,' Joseph mumbled.

'Then you cannot tell me it is not true?'

'No.'

The Professor found the truth in Joseph's eyes and nodded. 'If you ever need anything, Joseph, you come to me. I am your friend. And thank you. This is far enough, I can walk the rest of the way on my own. By the way, that's a fine fence you built, it looks very smart.'

The fence. As Joseph retraced his steps he dismissed the other conversation. The old man, he knew, would keep his word. But the fence. He was so proud of it. Often he stole up to stare at its elegant whiteness stretched across the land, to admire his handiwork. One day he would have a fence too. Even a house maybe.

He sang as he strode along. Day by day he was earning a little more respect among these powerful whites, and that was very important, not only for his own welfare but to please Ratasali, who often spoke to him in his dreams these days. The god Ratasali needed to be proud of his son.

There were jokes aplenty over their traditional Christmas dinner, the reversed climate down under the equator being a rich source of conversation and comparison. Mike was just as interested in their stories of a wintry festive season. Mrs Morgan had issued the invitation to him to join the family on Christmas Day, and he had accepted graciously to please her. He was in no doubt that the master would have been aware he'd been invited and was coldly amused by Morgan's greeting. He appeared startled as Mike mounted the front steps. Deliberately: 'Oh! Ah . . . Devlin! Yes, of course. Damned sticky day. Have a drink.'

The Professor, rigged out in his Sunday best with a purple bow tie, made a fuss of seating everyone at the decorated table before assuming the role of wine waiter, and the meal progressed splendidly until the dessert. Tommy's efforts fell apart towards the end, due, Mike guessed,

141

to an overindulgence on the sly of Christmas cheer. The plum pudding, which would have been made some time ago, had survived, but the custard was burned and the brandy sauce was almost neat brandy, served piping hot.

Jessie apologised, while Sylvia ran out to do battle with the giggling drunken cook. The Professor poured more wine and Morgan adopted an attitude of pained silence until Sylvia returned with a jug of cream.

'Madam,' he said to Jessie, 'you can tell your cook that if this happens again he'll be fired on the spot.'

Mike made a mental note to warn Mrs Morgan against such a foolhardy move; they'd never find a cook as good as Tommy in this backwater, and they'd lose Mae too, their laundress and queen of the vegetable garden. But as Morgan turned away for a minute, Jessie gave Mike a quick, mischievous smile, as if to let the manager know that she'd read his thoughts, and even that she'd found the incident quite funny. Mike smiled back and was tempted to raise his glass to her but thought better of it.

Morgan tapped his crystal goblet with a teaspoon. Standing, he addressed the group. 'Ladies and gentlemen, may I wish you all a very happy Christmas.'

There were murmurs and smiles all about as he dug in his pockets. 'Now I have a little surprise,' he said. 'For my lovely wife and the mother of our dear son.' He handed her a soft black velvet package.

'Why, Corby!' she cried. 'What is this?'

'Open it,' he replied proudly, and as she spread out the cloth, she gasped to find a string of pearls.

'They're beautiful,' she said.

'Indeed they are,' he agreed. 'They're real pearls. I was fortunate to obtain them. Someone took me to visit a pearling ship while we were in Cairns, and when I heard about our son I dashed back to find one of the Chinese chappies and managed to buy the pearls from him.' He was just as excited as his wife. They were truly beautiful gems. 'Don't lose them now, Jessie. They'd be worth a fortune in a shop. I struck a good bargain with him. The catch isn't much but you can find a fitting clasp later.'

The pearls were admired by all. 'Hold on a minute,' Morgan said. 'I'm not finished yet. Here is something for my lovely sister-in-law. Happy Christmas, Sylvia.'

She took her gift from its velvet bag, a small opal brooch, and although she thanked him charmingly, her disappointment was evident.

'It's lovely, isn't it, Sylvia?' her sister enthused, examining the brooch, but Mike saw Sylvia glance at her brother-in-law. If looks could have killed, he thought, Morgan would be stiff on the floor by now. Obviously she'd been expecting something to match those pearls.

Morgan seemed not to notice. He picked up two envelopes. 'For you, Mr Devlin. A bonus for your unfailing support of me and of my family.'

As he took the cheque from the envelope, Mike wished he could retract all the nasty thoughts he'd had about his employer, and before he read the cheque he was thanking Morgan profusely. Too late to take back those words, he saw that the amount was two hundred and sixty pounds, exactly the amount Morgan owed him in pack pay. This wasn't the time or place to enquire about it, but he knew the bonus was his own money, and that was the end of it.

Morgan moved on. 'And the Professor. I have the best news for you, sir. I have to thank you for coming to my aid in London and for your faith in this enterprise. I'm sure you never expected to be repaid so soon, but I am glad to do so. Here is two thousand pounds. The loan paid in full.'

There was a silence as Lucas took out his spectacles and studied the cheque. Then he looked at Morgan. 'I think you've made a mistake, Corby. My two thousand pounds wasn't a loan, it was an investment.'

Morgan smiled. 'No, no, no. In borrowing from you I intended my interest in Providence as collateral. Now that I am repaying you in full we can cancel that collateral. You haven't lost a penny.'

The Professor took a gulp of wine and Mike noticed he was trembling. 'I don't want this,' he said, placing the cheque back on the table. 'I bought a half-share in this property and it shall remain mine. I paid my own way out here, and my daughter's, and have contributed what little else I had left to expenses here.'

'Oh, then if you feel you are out of pocket, let me have the figure,' Morgan said magnanimously, 'and I shall make you a refund. I certainly don't want you to lose on the arrangement.'

'I have no intention of losing my share in this plantation,' the Professor replied, and Mike watched the tension build.

'Father's right!' Sylvia cried triumphantly, and it occurred to Mike that Morgan was being paid out for the insignificant gift. Or was it more than that? She and Morgan had been very chummy that night on the veranda.

'I'll thank you to keep out of this,' Morgan snapped. 'It's none of your business.'

'As my daughter, it is her business,' the Professor said staunchly.

'It's all a misunderstanding,' Jessie said quietly. 'There's no need to spoil this lovely day, we'll sort it out another time. We're all family, so there's no problem. Corby, why don't you take Mr Devlin outside where you can enjoy a cigar.'

Morgan slammed cigars, matches, a bottle of port and two glasses on to a tray and stormed ahead of Mike, who followed obediently, wishing he'd stayed home, not wanting any part of their family squabbles. But after a couple of hefty ports Morgan calmed down.

'Silly old fool,' he said to Mike. 'He never gets anything straight. You'd think he'd be grateful to have his money back so quickly.'

From what he'd heard, Mike couldn't see any reason for the Professor to be grateful, any more than he was grateful for his own so-called bonus, but he hung about, listening to Corby and his new plans to

143

extend and upgrade the plantation while they still could with the threat of deportation of all the Kanakas hanging over their heads. For once he agreed with Morgan; they had a lot of work ahead of them.

The house was still. Sylvia took up her shawl and opened her door an inch, closing it again quickly. He was still up, there was a light in the parlour. Good. Jessie had fed the baby and would be well asleep by now.

'I'm sure Corby didn't intend to upset Father today,' Jessie had said. 'So you mustn't take sides, Sylvia. Just let the men sort it out.'

'I don't care what they do,' Sylvia pouted.

'It didn't sound like it.'

'Well, it wasn't fair to speak to Father like that.' She studied the pearls laid out on Jessie's dressing table as if on public display.

'I know. But it was disappointing for Corby. He thought he was being generous to all of us. By the way, the wagon came again yesterday, but still no pram. I wonder when it will get here.'

'He just said he'd send one as soon as possible,' Sylvia lied. She'd forgotten all about the pram. 'Everything has to come by ship, you know.'

'Yes,' Jessie said ruefully. 'Bronte will probably be walking by then. I hope it will be here in time for the christening.'

Sylvia didn't care about the pram; she was far more interested in Corby's gifts. The little opal brooch, probably picked up from a street hawker, was an insult. Another insult. Everyone knew that opals were dug up from the ground somewhere out here and were being peddled in all the shops. And then there was the matter of ownership of Providence. She hadn't thought about it before, but now, thanks to Corby's attempt to slide out of the agreement with her father, it had become very important. She had him now. He still wanted her physically, and he needed her to side with him. After all, when it came down to inheritance, she was entitled to a share, so she would see to it that the Professor stayed firm.

On the other hand, it wouldn't hurt to let Corby think she could be persuaded to see his point of view. She had a weapon now, a very powerful one, and she intended to use it.

She strolled quietly down the passage and turned into the parlour, then, as if surprised to see him, abruptly backed away and walked out into the cool night. As she went down the steps she shivered; he was attractive and he looked so manly sitting there in the big chair, his long legs thrust out . . . He would follow her, she knew he would, for this was too good an opportunity to miss. And a teasing would serve him right, she wouldn't let him touch her.

The gardeners had laid out paths in preparation for lawns and beds in the newly fenced area, and she wandered along one of them, marvelling at the clear starlit sky and feeling not a little sorry for herself that nights like this were made for romance, while all she had was a man who had

144

treated her so badly. Another woman's husband.

'What's the hurry?' he said, falling into step beside her.

'Goodness me, you startled me, Corby.'

'I'm sorry, I didn't mean to. It's a beautiful night, this Christmas night, isn't it?'

'Yes.'

'And you're beautiful too,' he whispered, putting his arm about her waist.

'Don't,' she said, edging free. That took an effort. It was difficult to be rude and standoffish with a man who appreciated her beauty and whose voice was so tender. So different from that drunken ruffian who had attacked her. But he was sober now.

'Did you like the opal?' he said.

'Oh yes, a nice little thing.'

'There's dark blue in it, like your eyes, and a fire that reminded me of you.'

'You don't mean that,' she said. 'You're just trying to flatter me to make up for treating me second best. Those pearls you gave Jessie are superb, but I just get a brooch. You'd look silly if I told them about us.'

He took her hands. 'I thought you'd like the brooch. The setting is gold. If you want pearls I'll get them for you.'

'When?' Sylvia's plan to tease him was fast losing ground. Did he care enough for her to buy her pearls too, and what else would he do for her? For love of her. Her mind was racing. What was the best way to hold him? Should she keep him at a distance, easy enough in this household? Or let him make love to her, become dependent on their lovemaking. She had noticed that he'd been sleeping in the spare room lately, the room between their bedroom and hers, to get more rest. He still put in a long day out on the plantation and Jessie's frequent feeding of the little baby through the night disturbed him. Or so Jessie had said.

'I'll get you pearls when I can,' he was saying. 'You can choose them for yourself. Darling, you know I'd give you the world but for now we have to keep up appearances.'

'I don't see why,' she said. 'I don't think you love me at all. I think you're just using me for your own pleasure. You called me a whore and I hate you for that.'

'I what? Oh my God, Sylvia, if I did I don't recall. I was drunk. You have to forgive me. Maybe I was – maybe we both were – simply enjoying ourselves in Cairns, but not any more. Not me anyway.' For a minute there, she thought with a sense of fright, of a moment lost, he had accepted her rejection as inevitable after having spoken to her so cruelly. He turned away from her and she was surprised to see that he seemed genuinely distraught. Still she refused to reach out to him, to offer him any solace, although she desperately wanted to.

What would Lita do in these circumstances? she asked herself. That woman of the world. And she had her answer. She stood loftily, unforgiving. 'Whore!' she said. 'That's what you called me. And I won't have sex with you any more. You didn't just call me a whore, you treated me like one.'

'Please don't say that, Sylvia. Don't use that word again.'

'I learned it from you,' she taunted.

'If you only knew how hard it has been for me since we came back. To have you here in my house . . . Everything has changed for me . . . I thought I could manage but I can't. I think of you every minute. Your loveliness, you are so sweet, I need you more than anyone in the world.'

He walked over to the tree and stood looking at her with a wry smile. 'I don't suppose it's any use apologising for my behaviour. I'll try to make it up to you. But I want you to know, you might as well, that I do love you. I'm madly in love with you and it's too late to turn back.'

'Then prove it.'

He groaned hopelessly. 'And how do I do that?'

'I'm going to bed, Corby, and I'll be waiting for you between the sheets as I did in town.'

'In the house?' He looked towards the white building where a lamp still glowed in the parlour.

'You know how I loved you,' she said, excitement stirring within her at this clandestine and dangerous proposition. 'If you care enough . . .' She gave a naughty giggle. 'Fortunately I have a double bed too. But if you'd rather not, we'll just forget the whole thing and pretend it never happened. Maybe it's for the best.'

'I can't do that,' he said as he watched her walk towards the house, her white skirt swaying. All the men in town had been raving about the beauty of this girl. Why hadn't he noticed it back in London? Why had Jessie insisted on bringing her to Queensland? Shoving a beauty like that under his nose? And one who was made for, was eager for sex. He wasn't sure that he was in love with Sylvia. What was love anyway? Right now he wasn't even sure that he'd ever loved Jessie. She'd simply struck him as the type who would make a good wife and he supposed he'd been right on that count. But was it enough? Jessie couldn't provide the passion, the uninhibited abandon of her sister.

He stayed out there for a long time, then he went back in and sipped a brandy and smoked a cigar, as if considering this decision. Yet all the time he knew he was not considering, but savouring what had been denied him for long, empty weeks. He was captivated by the bonny girl, he craved her luscious loving. And why shouldn't he! For God's sake, it was mutual. She loved and needed him too. Wasn't she entitled to love? Her father and Jessie had practically relegated her to a spinster life, stuck out here with them, expecting her, a woman like Sylvia, to be content. It was cruel of them.

Corby stubbed out the cigar. What was he worrying about? Sitting here moping as if the Colonel were on his tail, waiting to catch him out in a misdemeanour, waiting to punish him. 'That old bastard,' he told himself, 'has got you brainwashed with his rules and regulations. Why are you still afraid of him? Why did you have to write to him and brag about how well you were doing? Only because he still has a hold on you. But that's all over now. Corby Morgan has grown up. Master of his own house, his own life.' He probably wouldn't bother to write to the old man ever again.

He passed Jessie's door, his own door, and went on to Sylvia.

As Mr Devlin had advised them, there was no need to send out invitations. Everyone in the district knew that Pastor Godfrey had set aside this day to christen the Morgan baby at Providence and people came from all over the district – people who had met Corby in town, or people who simply decided it was time to meet the new family at Providence. Jessie worried as more and more men and women arrived on horseback and the buggies and wagons lined up along the fence stretched right back to the bend in the track.

The women brought gifts for the baby and, fortunately, baskets of food – cold meats, sausages, preserves, scones and cakes. They all greeted Jessie with touching warmth, as if they were old friends.

Tommy Ling had set up long tables on the veranda and covered them with sheets when Jessie ran out of tablecloths, and Mae had decorated them with tropical blooms. He had set out cold chickens and hams, salads and various cold collations, and waiting in the wings were huge bowls of wine trifle. By the time all the ladies had emptied their baskets the tables were groaning with food.

'We'll have enough here for a week,' Jessie whispered to Sylvia.

'Not likely,' Sylvia laughed. 'Our audience has arrived. There won't be any leftovers if they have their say.' And sure enough, there were the Aborigines lined up outside the fence, watching the parade with uninhibited glee and calling cheerfully to friends in the 'white mob'. Way over on the other side crowds of Kanakas had also gathered to watch the fun.

'It's as if we're in the royal enclosure at the races,' Jessie said to Corby as they stood at the top of the steps, surveying the scene.

'Yes,' he laughed. 'and thank God for the fence.' He turned to Pastor Godfrey who had arrived early enough to help them welcome and introduce their guests. 'It's after midday, do you think there'll be any more arrivals, Pastor?'

'I don't think so, Mr Morgan. I've found this is a land of early risers and they don't mind a bit of travelling.'

'You've come a long way yourself,' Corby said. 'I've turned the space under the house into a refreshment kiosk. Would you care to come down and have a cold drink? Lemonade or ginger beer, perhaps?'

'Ginger beer will be the ticket,' the pastor replied, mopping his damp collar. 'It's wretched weather. I'll be glad when the rain really sets in. Be done with it so to speak.'

'But it's February,' Jessie said. 'Surely the worst is over by now?'

'They tell me not, dear lady. The monsoon season must run its course. But then it's a blessing for the crops, isn't it?'

147

'Of course,' Jessie said, grateful that they had a clear day today, at least. 'What time do you want to begin the christening, Pastor?'

'Let's say in half an hour, Mrs Morgan, if that suits you. Before there's too much partying.'

Jessie agreed. She liked Pastor Godfrey, even though he looked more like a hardened farm hand than a man of the cloth, with his ruddy complexion and tufts of red hair. He was a kindly man, with shrewd, intelligent eyes, the sort of person one could really talk to, if only one could find the opportunity. She wished she could talk to him. In private.

She went into her bedroom to find Hanna waiting patiently with the baby, already dressed in his long silk christening robe and gurgling happily in his cot, as if he knew this was a special day for him. He'd already been fawned over by the women as they arrived, and all the attention hadn't bothered him in the least. He had picked up weight steadily and was a contented child – probably spoiled, she mused, thanks to Hanna who insisted on nursing him at the slightest whimper. Luckily he seemed to adore the girl, which was a relief for Jessie who had made a determined effort, since Christmas, to become part of the plantation community, not just the lady in the house.

She had never been much of a rider, by no means as competent as Sylvia, but Toby had found her a quiet horse and she'd ridden round the home paddock every morning until her mount, Tripper, had accepted her and she was confident enough to go further afield. Luckily she hadn't ever mastered riding side-saddle, so it was easier for her than it had been for Sylvia to learn to ride astride. Although Sylvia now denied this, claiming that she had always been able to ride astride.

At first, the baby safely with Hanna, Jessie had taken rides after breakfast with Sylvia, but her sister had become bored with Jessie's constant delays. She liked to stop and talk to whoever they encountered, learning as much as she could in her travels, while Sylvia preferred to exercise her horse. In the end they took their own paths.

Hanna interrupted her thoughts. 'Can I go to looking, missus?'

'Yes,' Jessie said. 'I'll sit in here for a little while.' She knew she should be out there circulating, being the hostess, but it was difficult to face people. She felt they all knew and might feel sorry for her. It was easier to stay here in this room, in her comfortable chair, and if anyone enquired they would think she was feeding the baby.

She was proud, though, that by watching and asking she had learned more about Providence than was to be found in the books. She knew that setts of cane were planted flat on the ground so that the eyes could bud into life; that the cane grew in clumps. She understood the word ratoon now, where after cutting, the planter allowed his cane to shoot again, producing three more crops; that this wonderful crop matured in a year ready for the mill. The whole process fascinated her. She spent hours with the Kanaka women, listening to their stories and songs, and was a frequent visitor to the hospital. Then with Elly she returned to the lagoon time and time again to sit amiably with the Aborigine women, watching them fish. From all of this, ideas were forming as to how she could make life a little easier for all these people . . . She'd love to build a school for the native children who were running wild, and bring in a teacher, but she knew she would have to step carefully. This was Corby's plantation, and Corby was master.

Nevertheless, she was no longer that mushroom growing in the house. She now experienced a marvellous sense of belonging, riding safely about the property, recognised with cheerful waves by the blacks and the Kanakas, and she had come to see Providence as a village. Her village. Her home.

Corby disapproved and said so. 'You're behaving like a gypsy. You should be home with the child.'

'Bronte is in good hands, and I only go out for a few hours at a time. Surely you don't begrudge me that?' Her tone was unusually brusque and she was surprised that he didn't react. Instead he shrugged.

'Oh well, suit yourself.'

And it was this change of attitude – Corby normally insisted on having his own way – that lodged the first seeds of suspicion in her mind. While he might be thrilled about the baby, he seemed to be far less interested in his wife now. Since Bronte was born he had only come to her bed twice – no, three times – and even then returned to his own room afterwards. She'd been blaming herself, feeling that she must have become a dull person – which was another reason why she needed to extend her knowledge of the plantation – when a shocking thought had occurred to her. She tried to put it from her mind. To tell herself that is was unworthy of her to suspect that Sylvia and Corby might be . . . well, becoming too familiar with each other.

Once again, though, she turned the argument on herself. 'You're hard to please, Jessie Morgan. You worried when they were not getting along well, and now that they have settled into a more peaceful relationship, making life easier for you, you complain.'

She began to take more notice of them, realising that Sylvia often caught up with Corby during the day, to ride home with him. Of an evening, as she sat with them, conversations seemed stilted, and once again she worried that she might be imagining it, but when she withdrew to her room to feed the baby, she felt as if they were relieved to have her go. And on those occasions, sitting in here, in this very chair, she was lonelier than she'd ever been in her life, as if she were cut off from the world.

The two girls, Elly and Hanna, were adding to her fears by becoming plainly antagonistic towards Sylvia. While they seemed to go out of their way to treat Jessie and the baby with kindness, they lapsed into a sulky silence whenever Sylvia appeared.

Finally she called them together and asked them: 'Why are you taking this attitude with Missy? I don't think you girls are being very nice to her. What is wrong?'

149

They were embarrassed, scratching their heads, toes turned in – they flatly refused to wear shoes. 'Nuttin', missus. No, nuttin'.'

So the weeks went on, with Jessie becoming more and more nervy about this problem, not daring to offend either Sylvia or Corby by asking them, and not wanting to know if it were true. She would not, she could not, spy on them. As a family they must be spared that indignity. She had probably been isolating herself even further by keeping her eyes blinkered when she was with them, unwilling to stumble across movements or glances that might betray them, keeping her eyes averted, concentrating on everything but them. And if that produced a stiffness in her demeanour, they didn't seem to notice. Nowadays Corby hardly noticed her at all.

But for all her efforts to convince herself that this couldn't be happening, the truth was flung at her in a manner typical of the tempestuous nature of Providence.

The black girls were very loyal, but among themselves there were often rows that came to blows, for each one was fiercely possessive of her own role. Elly had the house, Hanna the baby, and Kali had her own missy. Jessie had heard the argument and had taken no notice until it began to develop into a full-scale brawl. She went to the window to put a stop to it.

'My missy say so,' Kali was screaming at the other two. 'You go way.'

Jessie sighed. She didn't care who said what. 'Stop this minute!' she called from above them, but they were making so much noise, pushing and shoving one another, that they didn't hear her.

'Your missy not boss!' Hanna yelled.

But Kali defied them. 'My missy is boss! My missy new wife. Old wife no good now.'

Shocked, Jessie pulled back from the window, ignoring the howls and screams as Mae set about them with her stick, sending them about their business. She felt trapped. There was no denying the certainty that engulfed her. She sought excuses, for herself, for Corby. He was a good man, there was goodness in him, despite his obdurate and often blustering conduct, and somehow she must have let him down.

Sylvia came rushing in now. 'What are you doing? They're ready for the christening. Come on, hurry up! I'll take the baby.'

'No. Leave him. I'll be out shortly.'

She took off her day dress, tightened her corsets and slipped on the more formal dress she had made for this occasion. It was a beautiful gown of ivory lace with a high stiffened collar and a tight-fitting bodice that showed off her now tiny waist. The skirt smoothed over satin across the front was drawn up in folds to meet the bustle at the back, the fullness trailing inches on to the floor. Studying herself in the mirror, Jessie knew she'd never looked better. The dress, which she had worked on for months, was stunning. She added the gleaming pearls, brushed her hair up and pinned on the wide sweeping hat that she treasured, its brim a nest of cream silk roses.

150

Bronte didn't like wearing hats, but she managed to tie on the little crocheted bonnet that matched his dress, picked him up and sailed out to the veranda, quite deliberately making an entrance, looking out over the gathering crowd.

Her ploy worked. Everyone stopped and stared as she glided down the steps, and she heard women making admiring comments all about her. Even Corby, who was standing with the pastor, smiled and nodded at her, to her, and came forward to take her arm. 'My dear,' he said, and people heard him. 'You do look lovely.'

This was what she wanted. This was what she needed. Her husband taking his rightful place beside her. As the ceremony began, Jessie declared to herself, that was where he would stay. Somehow she had to hold on to her marriage.

Sylvia, the godmother, took the baby, with a warm smile for Corby, and Jessie felt like snatching the child back. Now the blinkers were off, their relationship was obvious, almost blatant. Maybe they wanted her to see, to provoke her into a confrontation. And then what? Did they expect her to stand down, to vacate her position as his wife and mistress of this house? Or simply to accept the situation as it now stood?

No. Sylvia would never leave it at that. She would want more. She was holding the baby over the makeshift font, a large china bowl, and the pastor was giving the blessing. Jessie smiled serenely, hiding her anger and humiliation as she'd been doing for weeks now. Her first reaction had been rage, a determination to accuse her husband and order Sylvia from the house. Even now it was hard to keep control, but she must do so. For the time being anyway. Until she could decide what to do. At all costs she must avoid driving Corby to the brink, into making a decision they might both regret.

She tried hard to concentrate on the prayers but her thoughts were jerky, confused, as her mind raced across a battlefield of calm consideration and active outrage.

The Professor was godfather, and he was so proud, standing there beaming at his grandson. 'I'll have to talk to him,' Jessie said to herself. 'Ask his logical opinion. He'll probably find the subject embarrassing, but he must be able to give me some advice. Maybe I can talk him into taking Sylvia back to England, if only for a holiday.'

Everyone gathered for the hymn, and as the voices were raised in song Jessie gazed at her guests. Lita de Flores was standing in the front, looking very dignified in a grey costume with white silk lapels, and her father beside her was wearing a dark cutaway jacket similar to Corby's. Most of the older women were in their best black outfits, the useful colour, while the younger girls had chosen white blouses with their dark skirts. The mill hands and foremen from Helenslea were present, all spruced up, and the midwife and her husband, and of course, Mr Devlin, standing quietly on the sidelines. Jessie had hardly recognised him, with his dark hair plastered down and that bushy moustache neatly trimmed, and she was surprised to see how well turned out he was in his town clothes. In fact he was handsome – and single. Why didn't Sylvia fancy him? He was only a few years older than Corby. There it was again, the anger in her easily roused by any random thoughts.

But at last it was lunch time, with the focus on their now lavish spread, so Jessie was able to relax, away from the spotlight. She saw Sylvia dashing about playing the hostess with plates, platters and cutlery so she took the opportunity to move among the guests herself, making a point of speaking to everyone, asking questions, taking her time, consolidating her position in this society.

Edgar Betts took Corby aside. 'I wanted to have a word with you about Kanakas. On the quiet.'

Corby looked about him. The house had been invaded by guests and the bar under the house was too rowdy. 'Let's take a stroll,' he said. As they walked he explained his plans to clear the land through to the river and landscape the area to give the house a better aspect.

'You've made a good start,' Edgar said. 'Lita was telling me you'd begun proper fencing. Never got around to it meself. Lita says we should.' He went over and tested the palings on the fence. 'Good job they've done here. My Kanakas couldn't nail a butterbox together. I suppose Mike taught your blokes?'

'Yes.'

'Bloody patient he is with them, I'll give him that. But you have to keep a strong hold on them or they muck up something awful.'

'Don't I know it,' Corby replied. 'I never realised how much it takes to keep them on the job. I never have enough hours in the day.'

'You've got the right idea, Corby. You're the master and the master has got to be out there. These planters that sit on their bums and let the paid help run the show don't know what's going on half the time. Then they wonder why they run into strife. But listen, what about lending me your fencing gang for a couple of weeks? Three of them I believe.'

'Be glad to.' Although he found Betts overbearing and irritating, Corby knew it was important to keep on the right side of their neighbour; the shared mill was of paramount importance.

'Good. Now I hear you've been talking to King.'

'I saw quite a bit of him in town,' Corby said, and Edgar laughed.

'Come on, laddie. Don't be crafty with me. King said a mate of his will pull a mob of Kanakas and land them at Elbow Bay out of reach of the Gov'ment agents. He said you wanted half.'

'We did have some discussions along those lines,' Corby admitted, 'but I wasn't sure that he was serious, or that he could deliver.'

'They'll deliver. Everything that can float is out there scouring the Pacific now.'

Corby hesitated. 'I still don't understand these arrangements. Why would they bring Kanakas in this way? Why the subterfuge when they can sell them just as easily at the wharves? I know we can do better at the cheaper prices, but why would the ships' captains sell their contingent of islanders at the lower price?'

152

'Because their ships aren't registered for human cargo. And if any of the naval ships find them they're impounded and the owners fined.'

'Oh. I see. But are you sure this is a good idea? I mean, would there be any repercussions?'

'Not if we keep it to ourselves. I've picked up a few like this before. Leave it to me. When the time comes we'll collect them ourselves. I'll bring a few of my trusties for backup.'

Edgar's intervention reassured Corby. It was better to share with him than to have to deal with these unsavoury customers on his own. 'How will we account for them though?'

'We don't. Once they're on my plantation I don't account to anyone. Just let them mingle with the rest. No one will come out to try to count them.' He chuckled. 'I give them the same names as dead 'uns or sickies or men that have gone back to the islands, to confuse the issue. McMullen knows the drill. Are you worried about Mike?'

'No,' Corby lied. 'I'm the master of this plantation.'

'Good for you. They all have to know who's boss. He might get a bit cranky but he's no dobber. Mike won't put us in. And he'll have no proof of where we got them, the ship will have sailed. My blokes know that if they want to keep their jobs they mind their own business. I'll let you know when the ship's due. We could get in a spot of fishing at Elbow Bay while we're waiting,' he added easily. 'I like to fish.'

Waiting about with this fellow didn't really appeal to Corby, but he supposed it was all in a good cause, and it would be an opportunity to try his hand at fishing like old Edgar. When he could afford it he'd use foremen and begin to live as a gentleman should. And fishing was a gentleman's pastime.

Sylvia was coming towards them with that bouncing step, so full of life and vivacity, that always tugged at his heart, but Edgar, in his vulgar way, spoiled the moment. 'You're doing well, laddie,' he chortled, 'with the two best-looking women on Trinity Bay in your stable.'

'Yes, they're charming,' Corby replied stiffly.

As for Sylvia, she was enjoying the day. Quite a few of the young men she'd met in town, including Bob Billingsley, the bank manager, were in attendance and paying court to her. She was glad that Captain King was away so that she wouldn't have him pestering her, but it was fun to play up to the others, knowing it upset Corby, who couldn't do a thing about it. He was so deliciously jealous it didn't hurt to let him know that she could have her pick of the others if she wished.

Sylvia believed she understood Corby better than Jessie did. He was possessive. It was his property, his child, his everything, and now she was, decidedly, his woman. She shivered with delight as she stepped between Edgar and Corby to walk back with them. She wanted to take Corby's arm but it was tantalising not to be able to touch him. Worse for him than for her really. He had often said how hard it was for him to sit in the parlour with the family of an evening, with her so close and so desirable. And by the time he did come to her bed late at night, he was practically bursting his britches. Mad for her.

'Jessie knows,' she'd told him, and that had given him a start.

'How? What did she say?'

'What do you care?'

'Darling, I have to care. I have to know. She's the mother of my son. I'm in no position to confront her yet.'

'When will you be?'

'When Bronte is a little older. Are you sure she knows? Tell me what she said.'

'She didn't say anything,' Sylvia pouted. 'You don't sleep with her any more, that should give her a hint. Or do you? If you go back to her bed I'll never forgive you. I'll tell her myself.'

He could always calm her tantrums with his tender lovemaking and his sweet dreams of Providence in the future; of the splendid house he would build one day with a ballroom and colonnades instead of these common verandas. Sylvia coloured in the rest of the picture with her own daydreams of being the lady of the house, entertaining governors and visiting celebrities. She had no wish to return to London where there was so much protocol to be respected in the smallest social interaction; here, that stultifying drawing room parade of minute manners did not exist. And more importantly, in this country she had no competition. None at all. She was no longer up against girls with better pedigrees or more money in a marriage market awash with women. She had written to several of her girlfriends at home telling them of this balmy land where women were in the minority, but she hadn't issued any invitations. Nor did she complain about the heat and the flies and the incessant rain and the isolation. No point in spoiling letters that would have them all green with envy.

The afternoon developed into a jolly party. With the tables cleared away, guests danced on the veranda to brisk music provided by an old man with his accordion and his son who played a merry violin. They sang all the 'home' songs with heartbreaking nostalgia for the British Isles that some had never seen, and they gathered about the beautiful Mrs Morgan with genuine kindness, each woman, high or low, planter's wife or overseer's wife, issuing an invitation to her to visit. Insisting, as they said, that she not let the grass grow.

'They mean it,' Lita said to Jessie. 'Most of these women lead hard lives, they don't get much chance to socialise. And what is really mad about them, is that, despite that, they're still picky about who they ask.'

'You mean I've passed the test,' Jessie smiled.

'And some,' Lita grinned. 'They don't know what to make of me, but they have to put up with me because I was here first. They're not such fools though, Jessie, that they don't recognise class.'

Jessie went to speak but Lita shushed her. 'Let me finish. The word "class" here means an entirely different thing from the English. It's better put in German. They regard you as a *gnädige frau* and you should respond.'

'I'll try,' Jessie said. 'But I'd have to write down who they are and where they live, for heaven's sake.' She was aware that this was the first time Lita had called her 'Jessie', and felt guilty about her first impressions of this woman who had now dropped her cool imperious manner to address her as a neighbour, a friend.

'Mike will sort them out for you,' Lita was saying. 'He'll organise your visits and your transport if you let him. And in time, when you get to know these people, you might find good friends among them.' They were sitting in the far corner of the veranda with the afternoon sun at last retreating, and Lita raised her wine glass. 'Here's to Bronte! Drink up, Jessie!'

Jessie couldn't say when she'd enjoyed a glass of wine so much. It was a white wine, light and refreshing. 'To your health!' she said to Lita, immediately sorry she hadn't responded by using Lita's Christian name, but habit had intervened.

'If ever I have a child,' Lita said to her, 'and the kid has to be christened, I want you to do me a favour.'

'What's that?' Jessie asked.

'Lend me that dress. I have to say it's nothing short of spectacular, darling. I mean, the very thing!'

'You shall have it,' Jessie said, hearing glee in her own voice, from relief or from alcohol she wasn't sure and cared less. Lita had given the lead. It was time she enjoyed herself. A gentleman refilled her glass as he was doing the rounds and her confidence grew. She looked over the party from their vantage point, at men gathered in groups discussing serious matters and at some older women seated in a sundown circle, gossiping, hugging exchanges to themselves. 'It's going well, isn't it?'

'Yes. I'm so pleased for you. It's time you started to brighten up.'

'Are you feeling sorry for me?'

The direct question seemed to throw Lita off balance. 'Me? No! Why should I? Of course not! Maybe I'm feeling sorry for myself. What will become of me, do you think? Should I marry a planter and settle down here. Or go back to Europe? No, that's out, I'm poor with languages. Or to England and be suffered as a colonial?'

Jessie laughed. 'How fortunate you are to have so many choices.'

'Yes, fortunate,' Lita grumbled. 'I suppose so. But I do get bored so easily. Maybe the christening has roused my nesting instinct.' She spied Mike Devlin in the crowd. 'Now, there's a man . . . I'd settle for him if he'd stop treating me like his prodigal sister.'

Jessie was intrigued. 'He's a very nice man. Can I put in a word for you?'

Lita stood up, swinging her long skirts aside, and Jessie suddenly felt that this moody, unhappy woman had swept her aside with them. 'Don't bother. I don't need anyone to plead for me.'

Encouraged by Lita's departure, other women were pleased to have

155

the opportunity to talk with their hostess, to discuss the problems of bringing up babies in an alien environment, to offer their home remedies for croup and quinsy and fevers, and to draw her into the unheralded loyal society of motherhood.

Lita was angry with herself for having revealed too much of her inner self to Jessie. It was stupid to let emotions surface, and damn bad form. And worse, she mused, to have any emotions at all. She'd better slow up on the gin. She'd fortified herself with a few before they drove over to Providence and then switched to the wine, which was remarkably good, so she was feeling a little tipsy.

She saw Sylvia in the centre of a group of young blades, and wandered over to join them, effortlessly diverting their attention from Miss Langley, who was not impressed. A clown at heart, Lita soon had them all laughing at the antics of the emu she called Clarence who had taken up residence near the house at Helenslea. 'Sometimes he thinks he's a chook,' she laughed, 'other times he thinks he's a dog and rounds them all up.'

This led to an exchange of hilarious emu tales until Sylvia managed to get a word in. 'I didn't think you'd be interested in farmyards, Lita,' she said disparagingly.

'Oh, my word I am,' Lita replied with a grin. 'Farmyards can teach us a lot. About manners and rules especially. You should pay attention.' She saw Mike placing chairs in the shade of the fig tree for some older women. 'Excuse me,' she said. 'I must pay my respects to Mr Devlin.'

By four in the afternoon most of the guests had begun to depart, and as Lita was leaving with her father, Sylvia accosted her. 'What did you mean by that sneering remark about farmyards? I took it most unkindly.'

'As it was meant!' Lita snapped. 'What you're up to is definitely against the rules.'

'I don't know what you're talking about.'

'Oh yes you do.'

'You can talk about rules! You're the last one!'

'Maybe so, but I haven't yet stooped to knifing anyone in the back.'

There was a huge array of gifts laid out on the dining room table, from babywear and shawls and embroidered mosquito nets to more solid offerings, and Corby examined them with interest. 'Who gave this?' he asked, holding up an engraved silver cup.

'Mr Devlin,' Jessie said. 'And the men from the mill banded together to buy Bronte the little gold bracelet there with the heart on it. And Mrs Creedy, the storekeeper's wife, gave us this little rocking chair. Isn't it sweet?'

'Very nice,' Corby said. 'In all, quite a successful day. Some of them we could invite again. Did you meet the Cavanaghs from Woollahra plantation? They're about the best of the bunch.'

'Yes. Charming people. Corby, I've been thinking, since Bronte is

156

acquiring things of his own now, we ought to turn that second bedroom into a nursery for him. He won't disturb us there and Hanna can come and go without bothering anyone.' She held her breath. She'd been rehearsing this speech all day. It was now or never, forcing Corby to return to their bedroom.

He didn't appear to hear her, seeming to be more intent on the gifts. He picked up a large blue rattle, replaced it, felt the texture of a small sheepskin rug. 'I'll see about it,' he replied finally, and left the room.

Jessie turned and stared out of the window, seeing nothing. The rebuff had left her in a vacuum. There was a rumble of thunder in the distance, horses neighed, birds screeched, but she just stood there, lacking the capacity to make a move of any sort until Elly came in to clear the table. Later, though, she decided she'd have to talk to her father.

She allowed him to take her on a tour of his thatched bush house which held his collection of rare orchids.

'Look at this one,' he said, indicating a spray of deep purple orchids. 'Isn't he beautiful? I've named him *Caladenia Providence*, and this superb blue one I'll name for Bronte.'

'They are lovely,' she said, following him about as he nipped at intruding green shoots. 'What a pity they don't have a perfume.'

'Not needed. They are attractive enough.'

She supposed they were, but she preferred roses. To her the orchids were showy and rather shallow, but she wouldn't dream of saying such a thing. No, she thought grimly, I've something a lot worse to say to him. She took a deep breath. 'Father, I was wondering if you'd like to go home for a while.'

'Go home? To England? What on earth for? Goodness, you mustn't be worrying about me, I'm having the time of my life here.'

'I want you to take Sylvia home.'

'Why? Isn't she happy here? I thought she'd settled in extremely well. To look at her today one would say the climate agrees with her, she's never looked better. And she's quite a hit with all the young people.'

Jessie couldn't reply, she was trying to find the words. The Professor stopped fiddling with the blooms. 'What's the matter, Jessie? You're unhappy about something.'

Tears were welling in her eyes. 'I hate to have to say this, but I don't know what to do. I believe Sylvia is having an affair with my husband.'

She saw a tinge of pink rush into his cheeks, and he moved away, concentrating on his orchids again. Jessie waited for him to digest this information.

'Are you sure?' he asked from the other end of the humid little sanctuary.

'Almost sure.'

'You haven't approached them about this.'

'No. I can't. I just can't.'

'That's understandable,' he said with a shudder, as if he too wouldn't

157

relish such a conversation. He plumped down on a garden bench. 'Oh dear, dear, dear. Come sit with me for a while.'

Jessie felt that she'd made a mistake, that he didn't want to know about this sordid business. He'd always hated unpleasantness, he wouldn't change. He was too wrapped up in his own world as usual. Nevertheless she obeyed him, from habit, and sat staring dully at his array of gorgeous friends, as he called them.

'I can hardly take the horsewhip to Corby,' he said at length, 'and I wouldn't suggest that you demean yourself by a wifely harangue. In my experience these measures are not known to work.' He patted her hand as if she were a small miserable child. 'It's a conspiracy of nature, of course,' he added. 'Nothing to do with you, except the unhappiness it is causing you. Attraction is the basis of all species, even my orchids, and we didn't invent that, nature did. If you are correct, then they are caught up in this mutual attraction. It's a delicate matter.'

'Indelicate more like it,' Jessie snapped, impatient with his attempts to rationalise their sinful behaviour – although it was useless taking that line with the Professor; he didn't believe in the concept of sin. 'It's cruel and unfair to Bronte and to me.'

'Nothing fair about nature, Jess. Listen to that bird. Do you hear it?'

'Yes.' Often of an evening she'd heard the sad lonely cry of a bird that Elly called a rainbird.

'It's a koel,' Lucas said, 'a native bird, much bigger but with the same traits as our cuckoo. Nature conspires to help him too. He's a lazy fellow, can't be bothered making his own nest, so he has been endowed with a throat that can emit the most dreadful noises when it suits him. He finds a nesting bird and makes this dreadful racket, so that the bird flees in fear. Then he calmly throws out the eggs, settles in a ready-made nest and calls sweetly for a mate.'

'That's horrible,' Jessie said. 'Am I the bird that has to flee?'

'Not unless you wish to. Unless you find the situation intolerable. Then I shall take you, not Sylvia, back to London.'

'You should take her!'

'Would she go? I doubt it. And wouldn't such a suggestion precipitate the kind of confrontation you're trying to avoid?'

'I'm not trying to avoid it.'

'Then why come to me?'

Jessie took a long, cool bath before retiring. She put on a fresh nightdress, brushed out her long hair and lay under the canopy of the net feeling calmer and wondering why. Her father hadn't really given her any advice at all, nor had he laid blame on anyone, except for the caprices of nature, which she was too troubled to accept. But then she heard the solo call of the Koel again and wondered at that poor little bird being frightened off, just by noise. Losing the eggs, the nest, everything.

Suddenly she sat bolt upright in the bed. What was he trying to tell

158

her? That she could lose her child and her home in a conflict with Corby if it came to that? The Professor had offered to take her home, no mention of Bronte. He was a wise old man but too vague at times. Deliberately vague. Jessie nodded, sense dawning. If I place Corby in the position of having to choose, what if I lose? Oh my God!

'No,' she said as she rose early in the morning. 'I won't be frightened off. It's humiliating to have to do this, but I'll fight in my own way. I'm not leaving.' There was always the possibility that Corby might come out and tell her that he preferred Sylvia, a terrifying thought, but she'd deal with it if the time came.

She intercepted Sylvia in the kitchen. 'Thank you for looking after the menus for me, but there's no need any more. I've got the time to do it myself. Now, Tommy, let's see.'

She joined Corby for breakfast every morning and arranged for one of the stableboys to take his lunch out to him. Then she changed her schedule so that she could ride out and meet him of an afternoon. Her efforts were desperate, she knew, and not always appreciated, but Corby didn't complain as he might have done, which gave her heart. Sometimes she thought she saw guilt in him, a better sign than irritation, but he still remained in his own room.

'Perturbations!' Lucas muttered when Jessie had left. 'Always perturbations!' He searched about for his teaspoon and prepared a larger than usual supply of his 'medicine', so as to have some for later.

He shut his bedroom door, and after swallowing the first dose with a grimace, for the taste was unpleasant in the way of all medicines, he sat cross-legged on the floor, waiting for the first wave of wellbeing to swell over him. This was a new practice he'd been following lately. It made him feel giddily Oriental and aided meditation, rather than causing him to sink to sleep, too soon, on the bed. For there were matters to consider.

The opium had now given him the necessary courage to speak of his gruesome find back there in the arms of the suicide, and he felt that he ought to report the truth of the matter to Mike, at least. Proving, as best could be established, that the dead man had murdered Perry. And clearing the other Kanakas who need no longer be punished.

This would result in the bans being lifted, allowing the Kanakas to resume their visits to town on their days off. But this presented another problem. In his dealings with the Kanakas, he'd heard all about the Sunday outings which were discussed with glee. Providence was so far out of town, they crowded on to wagons before dawn to have more time to enjoy themselves, but what was their enjoyment? The whorehouses.

Lucas found it pitiful that these fine men should be debauched by that dunghill of a town, and believed the ban was the best thing that could happen to them. They should be kept isolated from the degrading elements of white society, not from a moralistic point of view, but for the good of their health and mental attitudes.

He smiled, comfortable now. This posture was a definite aid to

159

awareness. Although they had to work hard, Providence was one of the best plantations for the labourers, rather an idyllic setting in fact. Or so the Professor, in his benign state, believed. Having decided what was best for the Kanakas, he moved on to the next vexing question. Jessie's unhappiness. Lucas wished she hadn't confided in him. People should sort out their own affairs.

He remembered the vicar back home, who had turned from his wife and taken up with his housekeeper. Rather a plain woman too, no accounting for tastes. By no means as attractive as Sylvia. One couldn't blame Corby for taking advantage of Sylvia's charms, since she was obviously willing. 'Dear heavens,' he murmured, 'just as well she is, or there'd be hell to pay.'

But with the vicar . . . the wife had made no complaint. Maybe she'd tired of him and welcomed the concubine. So the ménage, though quite a scandal, continued without fuss.

Jessie would not be able to do that. A mild-mannered woman in normal times, she could be firm and quite stubborn when it suited her, and Lucas was afraid that a battle was looming. He wanted no part of it. Monogamy was a foolish concept anyway. He sighed, unable to dismiss his concern for both of his daughters. If Jessie brought the matter to a head, and lost, Corby choosing Sylvia, then she'd forgo her husband and her sister. And this simply did not equate.

He scrambled to his feet and sat down at the table, pushing aside piles of notes and leafy specimens, to write a long rambling discourse about Providence and its inhabitants. Then, deciding that this was an excellent treatise that should be worked on, he took a fresh page and wrote: 'The last will and testament of Lucas Langley', addressing his statement to a Cairns solicitor who had often been mentioned in the *Cairns Post*.

'It would be in poor taste,' he declared solemnly to the empty room, 'to air their differences over Corby's sexual favours.' So he wavered for a while before writing a short instruction. 'Mathematically this does equate,' he murmured. 'If Jessie loses her husband to her sister she should be recompensed.'

He studied the line again, deciding against any explanation. It read: 'To my daughter Jessie I leave my full half-share in the plantation known as Providence. Being of sound mind, this is my direction.'

Carefully he signed and dated the document, placed it in a leather binder and hid it atop his wardrobe for mailing at the earliest opportunity. Then, tired of all this worry, he swallowed another dose of opium and drifted into his more pleasant dream world.

Joseph didn't like Helenslea; their quarters were crowded and fouled and the food was sour rice swill. The Kanakas here didn't dare complain, for fear of the white men who spoke only with whips, so he and his two friends, Paka and Ned, went at their work with even more vigour that they'd shown Mr Devlin. All three were Malaita men, but

Ned had been at Providence for two years and was looking forward to returning home after the winter in this country. One thing Ned had noticed at Helenslea, though, was that the Kanakas were allowed to go into town on the sun day off, while the ban on Providence men remained. They boasted about this to the three newcomers, telling ribald tales of the hours they spent with the Jappie girls, until the Malaita men could hardly bear the frustration. Joseph resolved that, on his return, he would ask Pompey to speak up for the Providence people, to request that the ban be lifted.

He could not divulge his knowledge of Katabeti's crime without implicating himself in the murder, but surely, after all this time, the bosses should give up. They'd never find out for sure who killed Mr Perry, although Pompey said they'd guessed it could have been Katabeti. It wasn't fair to keep punishing everyone.

The young missus here was kind – not the master's black woman, but his daughter. She seemed to be in charge of the fences. They had two jobs, to fence the front garden, a much smaller area than at Providence, and then the orchard, which was bigger but the missus said a white two-rail fence would suffice there to keep animals out. She came every day to oversee the work, just like Mr Devlin, and she often brought them fruit or sandwiches to help fill their empty stomachs. Better still, she never allowed any of the foremen to interfere, chasing them off with a stinging tongue. Joseph and his friends called her 'the bee' because she carried honey for them and a sting for anyone who bothered them. All three were in love with her; they felt sorry for her because she was a widow and had no man, and they fantasised about what it would be like to give her loving because, though white, she had a fine firm body, a strong head of hair and a good full mouth.

One afternoon she complained to Joseph that her fernery, at the edge of the orchard, was becoming too damp underfoot because of blocked drains. 'Could you clear the drains for me, Joseph?'

'Yes, missus,' he said, putting down his spade. They'd often peered in at this strange place when no one was looking, and had seen her sitting in there reading, surrounded by jungle plants that hung in baskets from the roof and lined the walls on ledges. They agreed it was a cool place to rest but wondered why it was necessary when the plants had to be watered every day, plants that could live without that trouble in the bush.

'Not now,' she said. 'You have to get on with your work. Come down when you've finished for the day and I'll show you what to do.'

Of course the other two teased Joseph about being selected to meet with her in such a private place, but he scolded them for their foolishness. He felt a great loyalty towards 'the bee' and was proud to be able to help this lady, even in such a small matter.

At dusk he washed the sweat from his body at the trough and pulled his work clothes on again since he had no others with him, not even one

161

of his sarongs which were in his box at home. As he cut through the orchard he realised that he was now thinking of Providence as home, and that pleased him, giving stability to his new life.

One thing that had intrigued them was that 'the bee' always wore men's clothes and high boots. Now, though, she was standing in the half-light wearing a filmy white dress that seemed to float about her like a cloud, and Joseph was dazzled.

'Come on in,' she called. 'I won't bite you.'

Clutching his spade, he padded in, and, following her instructions, began to dig out a channel by the side wall where the water had collected. The proximity of the woman, even more than the sultry air, caused him to sweat again, but he kept going until she noticed and told him to take off his shirt. Feeling freer then, he set to work again.

Afterwards he wasn't sure how it had happened, or even if it had happened. Maybe he'd dreamed it. Lying in the corner of the shack where he and Paka and Ned were billeted he tried to think it through again.

Her cool hand was on his back, rippling down his back, causing his heart to pound and arousing desire in him. He'd kept working, moving along, praying that she would do that again, just once more; even if it was an accident, the thrill of her touch was enough. But she stepped back.

Then when he crouched to clean out the blocked drain, shovelling mulch out with his hands, she spoke to him. 'You have beautiful shoulders, Joseph.' He couldn't move; his hands covered in mud, he couldn't touch the lovely clean woman as she stroked his shoulders and massaged his tense muscles.

'Do you like that?' she asked with a laughing lilt in her voice, teasing him. He could only nod.

That side of the wall cleared, she gave him a rag to dry his hands and pointed to another patch. 'This is worse,' she said. 'It's banked up outside.'

'I go see,' he said, but she was in front of him. Close. He thought she asked him if he found her pretty, or some words like that – in his confusion he was losing his English. Then she touched his face and told him he was beautiful. He was sure he could remember that, and the dress, like butterfly wings, opening up for him to touch her, to see the ivory whiteness of her. It was too much.

She'd been eager for him, so it was natural what happened between them, a good giving of two strong bodies, but his mind blurred in the heavenly release that he'd needed so much and the unreality of this strange and sudden awakening. He hoped he had done well for her, it was hard to remember, time passed so swiftly. And yet he had missed supper, so it must have been a while.

He told Paka that she'd given him food, so he didn't care about missing supper. Paka teased him, asking what else he got, never suspecting that Joseph could have achieved a white woman, a missus.

162

Joseph left it at that. Not for the world would he spoil such a lovely encounter.

A few days later she asked him back to the fernery, and this time he was more man for her because she had raffia mats laid out and he could exercise more skill to match the obvious pleasure she found in his brown body.

The master had been away, and on his first day back he came out to check on their work. He stood by the fence line to see if it were straight, tested every single picket and finally marched away without a word. The fencing gang was relieved. All the workers on this plantation were afraid of the master, he was known to have a vile temper, and they were warned to keep very quiet when he was about. As for Joseph, he could only wait patiently, hoping the missus, whose name he learned was Lita, would need him again, but if not, then he understood. He would always have good memories of her.

Edgar got wind of it. Edgar, who knew everything that went on at Helenslea, soon picked up on the sly remarks from sly men wishing to ingratiate themselves with the master. Who put up a pretence of not wanting to be 'saying things' about his daughter but were tripping over themselves to be first to spill the beans.

'Can't turn me bloody back!' he roared at Dandy, his woman. 'What's been going on?'

She shook her head. 'I doan know what.'

'I'm talking about me girlie and a bloody Kanaka, and I want the truth out of you.'

Dandy wasn't afraid of him. She'd taken plenty of beltings from him when she was younger, but not no more. She'd learned to fight back and the day she'd wrenched the stick from him and bashed hell out of him, not caring if he did shoot her in the end, was the beginning of her new life. Instead of retaliating, he'd done nothing, and she'd realised the old man was no different from the black men who knew when to back off. After that they'd had plenty of fights, trading blows, smashing things, but over the years he'd become weaker, resorting to shouting and growling at her, because he was a bad-tempered bloke and that couldn't be changed. Out there he might be the big man on his horse but in the house he was no match for her strength and virility. Dandy had won.

'I'm talking to you, big ears!' he shouted, waving his whip at her. 'Has one of them dirty Kanakas been getting at her?'

'No,' she lied, with an arrogant stare. 'Why you listen to them fellers?'

He hesitated, banging the whip on a padded chair, then snarled: 'Where there's smoke there's fire!' and lunged out of the house.

Dandy wrung her hands. She wished Miss Lita was here, but she'd gone to visit Woollahra plantation and wasn't expected back tonight. Miss Lita could stop him. She'd lie, cajole, tease him, get away with anything because she was his 'girlie' and he loved her. He'd been

163

broken-hearted when she went to live over the sea, and mad with excitement when he'd heard the husband had died and she was coming home. He wouldn't do anything to upset her now in case she left him again. Lately he'd been hoping she'd marry Mike Devlin, so that she'd live close, and he'd been muttering that he'd do something about that, but so far he'd been unable to persuade Mike to work at Helenslea.

All Dandy could do was stand there and worry, listening to the master raging at a group of men. She gave a sigh, half a sob. Why was it all right for white men to take black women but not for a white woman to have a black man? Or a brown man? Or even, she smiled wistfully, a fine brown man like Joseph. Miss Lita hadn't said anything – why would she? – but Dandy had seen her making for the fernery just on sunset, and from a side window she'd spotted Joseph, alone, heading in the same direction. His lucky day, she'd thought, and forgotten about it. After all, this wasn't the first time. Before she was married, Lita had fancied another one of the Kanakas, another big handsome island man, and when Edgar found out she'd turned on him spitting fire, denying everything, calling her father a dirty old man. Edgar, for all his bluster, couldn't cope with angry women.

It was a dismal day. Winds heavy with rain slammed against the house and she could smell salt in them. 'Big rains comen,' she commented absently. Rains throughout the summer had been sporadic. Now it was time for the big wet to set in at last, borne on the wings of ocean stirrings, to set the river racing and swell the creeks. There being nothing more to see but grey skies and rain-drenched greenery swaying in the wind, Dandy turned away.

Paka saw the three men riding towards them in the rain, like dark monsters in their oily cloaks and sodden hats, and he was glad that they'd kept working, despite the weather, digging muddy postholes for the second fence. He alerted the others and they looked up cheerfully; they had nothing to fear, no one had complained about their work. They were proud to be known as the fencing gang.

The white men didn't speak, but that was nothing unusual, and Paka watched curiously as one of the foremen unhitched a rope from his saddle, wondering what he intended to do with it. The answer came swiftly, with terrifying accuracy. The rope spun for a second then snaked out at him, hauling him to the ground with a savage jerk, and he was being dragged, bumping and banging, behind the horse as it cantered away in a wide circle. The rider dragged him back to lie bleeding, with the master, still on horseback, towering over him.

Paka was sobbing. The master was shouting at him. It took a while for him to understand the terrible accusations.

'Answer me!' Betts yelled at him. 'Tell me the truth!'

The man who had roped him climbed down from his horse and pulled Paka upright. 'Own up, you bastard!' he snarled, and Paka was pushed

164

closer to the flanks of the master's jumpy horse, afraid he would be trampled.

The master leaned down, his voice an ominous scrape: 'You've been chasing the white missus, haven't you, nigger? Over there in the fernery.'

'No, master,' Paka cried, his eyes wide in shock. 'Never!'

Betts's hand gripped Paka's jaw and jolted his face up. 'Did you touch my daughter?'

'No, no, no!' Paka wept. With his arms held tight by the rope, he feared that this terrible man could break his neck, and he tried to squirm away, but the grip tightened.

'Did you rape her?' The old man had Paka's face so contorted he could only croak his innocence. He did not know that word, and he didn't understand any of this.

Joseph could stand it no longer. He ran forward, pulling Paka aside. 'Leave him!' he shouted. 'I did. It was me.'

Then Ned, who understood more of the language and knew the dreadful import of Joseph's admission, joined them, shouting at the master, tugging at his saddle. 'No, sir! He doan mean to say that, sir! He doan know what you say!'

Edgar's whip slashed across Ned's face and the other men threw him aside, still screaming, still endeavouring to explain until the master took out his revolver. 'Get back, you two niggers,' he said to Paka and Ned, 'and consider yourselves lucky you're not going to swing with him.'

The two foremen were grinning as they bound Joseph, muttering to each other. 'The dirty little bugger, he got to her.'

'And her so bloody high and mighty.'

'Put him in the lockup for now,' Edgar said, wheeling his horse about.

'What about the others?'

'What about them?' he snarled as they led the nigger away. It was bad enough knowing that Lita had been entertaining this pig without involving a couple more. He'd be a laughing stock. It was obvious that there'd only been one, and to save face for himself, and for his daughter, she'd been raped. For all he knew she had. Or seduced. Whatever. It didn't matter. Niggers had to learn to keep their hands off white women. Especially Lita. Goddamn it! Weren't there plenty of white men about to keep her amused? The last time this had happened it had suited him to believe her, and he'd bundled the nigger off the plantation, unable to punish the bastard without creating a scandal. But this time she'd been more blatant. She didn't seem to understand, or care, that as one of only three white women on the plantation, and the only single one, she was constantly under scrutiny. There were eyes everywhere, gossip the heartbeat of the place.

If she needed a man, what was wrong with Mike Devlin? He'd have to up the ante with Devlin. Find out his price. Or he could alter his will, giving Devlin a share, that would throw them together eventually. But since he didn't intend dropping dead like Jake had, it didn't help matters now.

He glanced back at the nigger, who was coming quietly, roped to a horse, not a peep out of him. 'Guilty as all shit,' he said to himself. 'Came right out and said so. Proud of it by the looks of him, marching along head high, like he owned the bloody world. Well, he won't see much more of it.' Rape was a hanging offence and he had two witnesses to the confession. Not that anyone would query him; the Government agent only came out here for his payoff.

Then there was the Englishman at Providence. He'd be short a Kanaka. A replacement would be sent, together with a stern note not to foist sex-crazed niggers on his neighbours. Edgar grinned. That would shut him up. The poor bugger was still feeling his way along, jumping at shadows. The ship carrying the spare Kanakas was due any day, and Morgan was as nervous as a kitten about a simple operation. But now . . . He watched as the nigger was tossed into the lockup, a sturdy little shed with a reinforced door and no windows.

'Wait until all the rest of the niggers are camped down for the night,' he said to his men, 'and meet me back here at nine o'clock. Nobody rapes my daughter and gets away with it.' He considered adding a bit more, detailing the suffering this assault had caused his daughter, but he changed his mind.

'I must be getting soft in the head,' he ruminated as he rode around to the stables. 'I don't have to explain myself to that white trash. They do as they're bloody told. And I've seen them watching Lita. If she wasn't such a fiery bitch, and handy with that little revolver of hers, one of them might have grabbed her by now. And it wouldn't be the fun of playing with brown boys.

'Ah, Jesus!' He shook the rain from his hat and squelched across the yard. 'All I want is a quiet life. Lita's smart and sassy, but why couldn't she have been a son? He could have had all the black velvet he wanted and not a word said. But that Lita . . .'

He sat at the long cedar table on his own as Dandy moved silently about the room. It wasn't her place to sit with him but he liked her to serve his meals, because she knew what he liked, and when. He preferred his milk-boiled onions separate, and butter on his baked potatoes, and, like tonight, his chops crisp, fast-cooked over the fire.

Dandy had nothing to say, and that was why he liked her. White women talked too bloody much. Sometimes Lita fair put him off his food with her yap-yap. Dandy refilled his brandy glass, and he took a long slug, peering down at his pride and joy, the painting of a racehorse that faced him on the far wall.

'Did I ever tell you about that horse?' he asked as she served the boiled pumpkin.

Naturally Dandy didn't reply, she was just there. He had probably told her this before but it didn't matter. 'Zulu,' he said. 'The best bloody horse in the entire world. Won the Melbourne Cup in eighty-one, and there I was within a bloody hand's throw of owning him. I spotted him when he was a colt, damned if I didn't. Would have bought him too but some idiot talked me out of it. But I knew. By Christ I knew! A bloody beautiful horse and a real stayer if ever I saw one. Jesus, when I heard he'd won, I tell you, Dandy, I broke down and bloody cried.'

The nostalgia was too much for him. He pushed his glass over to be topped up. 'No sweets tonight,' he told her. 'I'm feeling my age. I'm not getting any bloody younger, you know. And who's gonna run this place when I'm gone?' The brandy was good, the best Hennessy's, mellowing. Better than bloody junket and apricots.

Edgar leaned back in his chair and took a cigar. 'You needn't worry, you're taken care of. And I'll say this for Lita, she'll abide by it. She never done you no harm and she ain't likely to.'

He chewed his cigar and studied the painting. 'By Jove. To win the Melbourne Cup, that'd be something. I was always known as a good judge of horseflesh. I've got good stock here but nothing like Zulu. Ah Christ! I could have been famous.' Dandy refilled his glass and he liked that; usually she held back, trying to make him slow up, but he could hold his liquor, and anyway, who cared?

Another cigar. She lit it for him and he saw the want in her, the pink tongue running across her blue-red lubra lips. 'You want a cigar?' he teased, waving the box at her, and she nodded. Respectfully.

'Then join me, madam,' he allowed, wiping the succulent brandy from his moist moustache and sucking the nectar from his hand.

Dandy never sat at the table but she drew a chair up beside him, bringing her own brandy. She sighed at the exquisite joy of the cigar and rubbed her warm hand along his thigh in gratitude.

Together they sat, the master and his mistress, drinking the brandy which now was within easy reach on the table, looking reverently at Zulu, which they had done so many times before. Everyone knew that blacks succumbed to booze faster than white men, and before long, Edgar grinned, Dandy was as randy as a she-goat. 'A nanny,' he laughed as she smiled and caressed him, and he sucked on his cigar, a prince among men, wondering where he'd find a white woman so brazen.

The hammering at the back door brought him to his feet, shoving her away.

It was a foreman, Abel Teffler. 'It's well after nine, boss,' he said apologetically. 'Did you want us?'

'Yeah! Yeah, I did! Bloody oath I did,' Edgar said, shaking off the sexual fog that he'd been enjoying. 'What's the time?'

'It's ha' past nine,' Teffler called through the wire screen.

'Hang on a minute,' Edgar replied. He hurried through to the hall to collect his oilskin raincoat but took the time to turn back to Dandy. 'You get into bed. Drink some more brandy and heat yourself up.' He tweaked her jutting breasts, noting for the first time that she was wearing a seductive open shirt with her long black skirt.

167

But Dandy pulled him back. 'Don't go, master. I'm feeling good tonight. You want a son. I give you a son.'

'What are you talking about?' he laughed. 'I don't want no nigger son.'

Still Dandy persisted. 'Don't do this. I beg you, don't do this.'

'Do what?' he said, pulling on his boots, or, rather trying to. It was hard enough to sober up and get the right boot on to the right foot without her whining. Already he had them back to front.

'Miss Lita will never forgive you,' she cried. 'Wait until she comes home.'

But Edgar, empowered now by the brandy and Dandy's unmistakable acceptance of the master as a stallion as virile as Zulu, reaffirmed himself as the boss of Helenslea. 'Get to bed,' he ordered her. 'This won't take long.' Dandy, though, was behaving now as he'd never seen her before. The black girl who had grown into a formidable lubra, taking no shit from no one, was crying, her arms about him, holding him.

'Master, don't go.'

She upset him. As much as looking at Zulu did. Her charcoal face, wet with real tears, had never looked so beautiful. In fact up to this second, Edgar had never seen anything beautiful in the Abo. She was just his. But now he saw the agonised twist of her mouth, the rich velvet of the tearful eyes, and he knew that this was no mute acceptance of what had to be. The woman loved him! He was astonished. And at sixty years of age, given a year or two, Edgar was hugely flattered.

'Master,' she pleaded. 'Tonight you must not go out. There is word among my own people that this Joseph is not what he seems.'

'Ah, Dandy,' he said, still under the spell of this loving woman. Hadn't she given him better love than anyone in his life? He was feeling both maudlin and randy for her. 'You are my girl. Is that what you wanted to hear? Help me with these bloody boots.'

Teffler was rapping on the door again, calling to him.

'His name is Joseph,' Dandy whispered urgently. 'Master, hear me beg. Don't go. He is a magic man. You never must touch him. My people, they hear about those Kanakas. They know.'

Edgar stamped his boots into place. Feeling better now. Shaking off this cloying domesticity. Sobering. 'What's he to you? What do you know about the Kanakas? This bastard is a criminal. Get away from me! You lied today, you could have saved me a lot of trouble. But no. You played dumb. So be dumb. And bloody shut up!'

The world had gone mad. He stood there with his cloak on and his damp hat clamped on his head. With Teffler standing waiting for him out there, a rapist locked in his press, and this women interfering. She was on her knees now, clinging like a bloody leech, making a God-awful fool of herself. He kicked her. 'Jesus, woman! Did Lita put you up to this? This man has pleaded guilty. Can you get it through your black brain that a fucking Kanaka has touched my daughter? Any more

168

than that I don't want to think about.'

Or so he said. The very thought made his brain blaze. And he wasn't the only one. Outside, his manager and his other foremen, and his mill hands, had gathered into a solid group to support the boss, their lanterns glistening in the rain, their horses chuffing impatiently, steam rising from their nostrils.

'Edgar!' Dandy cried. She had never called him that before, and he turned angrily.

'You get ahead of yourself, my girl.'

She ran to the door. 'Look at your dingoes!' she called. 'Your tame dogs. Send them home this night, Edgar! They smell blood and they want to be in at the kill, that's all.'

'You're off your head,' he said. 'I have things to do and those men know I'm right. You, you bloody black bitch, know I'm right too. He took her, didn't he?'

Dandy was past lies. The men were waiting. He was away to lead them, to do what the white rules, not the rules of the dark people or the rules of the Kanakas, said. Their rules gave them the right. She stepped up to him in one last entreaty. 'I am a poor woman, I do not understand your taboos, but I know this. The man you want to punish has the name called Joseph, but that is not his tribe name. Unnerstan' this, master? He is not Joseph, he is somethin' else. Bad magic they say. My people say.'

When they'd led Joseph way, Ned ran down to the pump for a pitcher of water to wash the dirt from Paka's badly grazed skin. Fortunately no bones were broken but he was battered and dizzy, hardly able to grasp what had happened. He tried to struggle to his feet but Ned insisted he rest awhile. 'Be quiet. I have to think.'

'No more work for these bad men,' Paka whispered, and his friend nodded. Talua was in the lockup. The white men meant to hang him but this could not be. They had to get him out. Ned wondered if he could enlist the support of the other islanders, but he knew it would be hopeless; they were already too intimidated by the white master and his henchmen. And it would take too long to go to Mike Devlin for help, he'd need wings to make it in time.

'The men are coming in from the fields,' he said to Paka. 'You stay here and I'll go in with them, then I'll slip away to have a look at the lockup.'

'No,' Paka replied. 'We wait here. It'll be dark soon. If you join the gangs you'll have to hand over our tools, and we will need them.' He sat up, holding his head as if to steady himself. 'I'm all right, don't fuss about me. Quickly now, hide those things in the ditch.' He watched as Ned dropped the spades, crowbars and tomahawk out of sight. 'Good. Now help me up, we must hide there too.'

'But they'll be looking for us if we are not there for the count. If I go I can tell them you are sick.'

169

'No,' Paka said firmly. 'No need. Let them think we've run off.' He glanced scornfully at the house. 'We're only scared niggers to them. Got no belly for a fight, us niggers. They'll be sure we ran like rats. So let them think that.'

Rain swept over them, darkness in its wake, and the night seemed sullen, ominous as the supper bell tolled, summoning Kanakas to the shed. The two men crept through the orchard, skirted the house and stables and made their way through the bush towards the barracks. Ned had the steel crowbar and Paka had grabbed the tomahawk. They moved on again, keeping to the edge of the track that led to the isolated lockup, until they lay in the undergrowth. Stealth was second nature to these men from the islands of Solomon, and they had now become the hunters.

One of the white men lounged against the wall beside the only door, his rifle propped nearby, protected from the now misty rain by the overhang of branches from a large tree.

As they watched he smoked his pipe, taking his time, and later he tapped out the ash and stuck the pipe in his pocket. Then he became impatient. He peered down the track, ambled about, walked a few steps up the track, returned to his post, stamping angrily.

'He's hungry,' Ned said. 'Waiting for someone to bring his supper. We should attack now.'

'No. It might take time to get that door open. If other men come we will be caught, and that's no help to Joseph.' Paka corrected himself. 'To Talua.' He was disconcerted that his voice had sounded different, deeper, more resonant. As if someone else had spoken, not him. It was a voice that was familiar, yet he couldn't place it. But Ned hadn't noticed.

At last another man arrived. 'About time,' the guard said. 'What did you bring me?'

'A billy of soup and some bread.'

'Is that all? Am I supposed to bloody starve, stuck out here?'

'Not my problem,' the newcomer said, and Paka recognised him as offsider to the white cook who maintained a separate kitchen, with better food than the Kanakas ever saw. 'Anyway, what's going on?'

The two men conversed for ages, or so it seemed to the watchers, discussing the charges against the prisoner in a lewd banter.

'And they're really going to hang him?'

'By the neck,' the guard laughed. 'I hope it was worth it.'

As soon as the other man left, the guard picked up his rifle to resume his lonely vigil, muttering to himself about his misfortune in drawing this job on such a gloomy night.

'I'll move around,' Ned told Paka, 'so I can come up behind him. Then you make a noise and get his attention. I have to grab that rifle before he can use it.'

When Ned was well away, Paka rustled the bushes.

The guard jerked about. 'What's that?' He walked out on to the track, his rifle trained in Paka's direction. To keep him interested, Paka

170

snapped a branch and dived further into the undergrowth.

Ned put down the cumbersome crowbar and moved swiftly, not at the man but at the gun, which he snatched and hurled away. To use it would bring more guards in this direction. He chopped at the guard's neck with the back of his hand, sending him staggering, but it didn't quite connect and the big man lunged at him. The two men crashed to the ground, locked in combat as Ned, fighting furiously now, managed to get his hands on his opponent's throat to silence him. Grimly he pinned the guard to the ground, banging his head, trying for a stronger grip. Suddenly a searing pain tore at his abdomen and he realised, too late, that the guard had a knife. He could feel the warm blood spreading on his damp clothes and he tried to hang on, but the grunting man beneath him wrenched the knife free and as Ned rolled away he plunged it into the Kanaka's chest.

Just then Ned saw Paka loom up behind them and thought he was saved as the tomahawk flashed and the guard collapsed. The islander smiled as he slipped back on to the soft wet grass. 'Just in time,' he whispered to his friend. 'I thought . . .' But he could say no more.

Frantically Paka fell to his knees, lifting Ned up, feeling the blood, discovering the knife, trying to help his friend, tears falling on to the still face.

He had to leave Ned. He found the crowbar glistening on the track and ran down to the lockup. 'You in there, Joseph?' he called.

'Yes. Is that you, Paka?'

'We've come to get you out.'

'Go away. They'll punish you too.'

But Paka was busy with the crowbar, jamming it between the door and the jamb, levering timbers away, splintering the sides until eventually he'd forced it open and Talua was free.

'You go now,' he said. 'Run away as fast as you can. It would be best to cross the river, they won't expect you to go that way. No one goes near the river.' He dropped his head humbly. 'Talua is a strong swimmer and the crocodiles will not dare feed on him.'

'I hope so,' Joseph said. 'But you can't stay now. Tell Ned to come too.'

'No. We have made our plans,' Paka lied, 'I am to follow Ned. We are going in another direction. You have to go, you must not delay us.'

Paka watched as the son of Ratasali disappeared into the bush, then he went silently back to Ned. He removed the knife and buried his friend in thick mulch, calling on the gods to take this brave man to their hearts. Calmly he turned to the body of the guard and with two sharp chops of the tomahawk severed his head, as a voice within him growled revenge on the white man who had ordered the death of Talua. His work done, he picked up the rifle and stepped back into the bush.

The riders came down the track, shadowy, menacing figures against the bobbing lanterns, with Edgar Betts in the lead, tall and grim in the saddle. There was no talk, despite the fascination of this ghoulish exercise and the men's admiration of the boss's bold show of power. Later they could tell the tale: 'I was there meself when the boss strung up the nigger. No one crosses old Edgar and gets away with it.'

At the end of the track Betts swung down from his horse with the agility of a young man, and Teffler, carrying the rope, strode beside him. The others followed, nudging each other now in anticipation, some suddenly nervous, unsure about this.

'Where the hell's the guard?' Betts demanded and they peered about them, seeing nothing but blackness beyond the lanterns.

'The bloody door's open,' Teffler yelled, striding forward, lifting up his lantern, and then, 'Holy hell, what's this?' He shrieked and stumbled back. He'd almost walked into the face of the guard. 'The door's gone,' he babbled stupidly, 'and there's a head!'

'A what?' Betts shoved him aside to see for himself the head of one of his men hanging by its long dark hair from a nail over the doorway, mouth yawning open as if screaming at them.

'The bastards!' he said. 'Bloody savages!' Ignoring the head he examined the doorway. 'The door's been busted down. He's had help to get out of here. I'll hang the lot of them for this.'

Men crowded behind him to catch a glimpse of this horror – another story for the taverns and bars of the north – until Teffler gave the order to remove the head and the man slowest to retreat got the job. 'Find his body!' Teffler ordered the others. 'It has to be around here somewhere.' Reluctantly they turned away, only to have that order countermanded by the boss.

'Leave it!' he roared. 'You can get it in the morning. I want those bloody Kanakas found, they couldn't have got far. Teffler, send for the black trackers, and, you lot, spread out. Now get going!'

As they made for their horses Paka's voice stopped them. He sprang out into the clearing to shout at the boss in a voice they were certain could have been heard for miles. Already shaken by the fate of the guard, one of their mates, the men swore for ever after that it was the voice of the devil they heard, loud, rasping, evil.

'Hey, you! White boss! White pig! You never get Talua.'

Stunned, Edgar whirled about. He wasn't given a chance to reply. Paka shot him.

And it didn't matter to Paka that he died too, in a rain of bullets. He was following Ned to glory.

To Joseph, the night was soft, a safe and curious place. A new jungle to explore, lit by familiar phosphorous plants and dancing fireflies. After the dank and musty prison the heady perfume of tropical blooms was sweet relief. He had run across the open fields from the scrub surrounding the Helenslea buildings to distance himself from the men who'd be sure to follow, until he'd come to the gloomy sugar mill, now closed down until the next harvest. Then he'd cut across to the dense

172

virgin forests that bordered the river, pushing quietly through the rain forest. He threw off his boots to negotiate more easily the slippery mulch beneath his feet, the decaying leaves and fallen trees that fed these great forests just as they did at home, and he smiled in a touch of nostalgia, brushing past the trappings of the forest, the great vines that hung from on high, littering the green canopy.

When at last he could hear the river, he rested. He had no fear for himself, knowing that when he crossed the river he could survive in this verdant land just as the Aborigines did. He'd heard many tales at Providence of the fearsome tribes that inhabited that country but he was philosophical about them. They could hardly be any worse than the vicious men who'd wanted to hang him.

And why? That puzzled him. He was not a marauder come to kill or despoil their maidens. The lady had needed him, had invited the pleasure on both occasions, and he could not believe that she would complain or brand him as an attacker. There was too much goodness in her. He had been told that racial prejudice existed in this land just as it did between tribes on the islands, differences that caused wars; and that here the whites regarded themselves as superior and didn't want their race sullied. He had to admit that in a way they were superior – they were clever and resourceful – but physically they were no better. No better than any of the dark skins. And besides, their actions contradicted their rules. Even the master had a black wife. It was difficult to understand but no use trying to work them out. He had broken one of their laws and the punishment was hanging so he was ruined. No chance of finding a good life here now, or of making his way back to the islands, for that matter. If he went down to the port they'd catch him and hang him.

He was anxious about Paka and Ned. What did they mean, they were going in another direction? Not towards the town he hoped. Then it dawned on him! They would make for Providence, for Mr Devlin. They'd done nothing wrong, except break down that door; they could explain and Mr Devlin would protect them. If he could, Joseph worried. The master, Mr Morgan, might send them back. The fence wasn't finished yet. He wondered if he could go to Mr Devlin too, but decided against that idea. He'd caused enough trouble at Providence. When the Malaita men discovered that he was marked for hanging there'd be terrible trouble, all because of this god business. Why had his father allowed his pride to aim at such heights? It seemed to Joseph now that by declaring himself a god, Ratasali had brought all these disasters down upon them. Instead of being welcomed by the gods, he'd been cursed for his cheek. A chief he was, but not a god, and neither was his son.

When the first light filtered through the greenery Joseph was on his way again, travelling far upriver. He knew he could be tracked easily by any bushman and sooner or later he would have to cross the river, so he made his way reluctantly towards the bank to stare at the fast-flowing

173

stream. It was wide and swollen with the rain, torrents tumbling with logs and bracken. Paka might have been convinced that he could cross safely but Joseph wasn't so sure. Although he couldn't see any, right at this minute, he knew there were monsters in this river and he doubted if they'd differentiate between a man and a god. A meal was a meal. He could find a measure of safety if he dragged a fallen log into the water and tried to ride that across, but the current was too strong. The river came from the west and that was his destination, far west to the high land.

To postpone the decision he searched about and found nuts and berries. He raided a honey nest far up a tree and washed the delicious sticky fluid from his face and hands at the water's edge, keeping a wary eye out for crocodiles. He moved further north, hoping to find a narrower stretch or rocky shelves that might help, but if anything the river seemed wider, more of a challenge, and each time he studied the banks he saw them, massive creatures with the girth of horses. They drifted disguised as logs or lay camouflaged among the reeds, apparently snoozing, but he knew they were not.

At a bend in the river he looked down from a granite cliff that had resisted erosion and stood for a while studying the grand view of a magnificent gorge. He figured that he could be halfway across at least before any shore-basking crocodiles spotted him. What about the other side? The river was too wide for him to pick out any of the wily creatures or their well-hidden nests. With his luck, he brooded, he'd probably swim right at one, with no knife, no means of protection. But he might as well get it over with.

It was a spectacular dive from that height, one that he never would have attempted into strange and dangerous waters had he not been desperate. To gain distance, he ran at it, safe in the knowledge that as an expert the dive itself would not harm him, but this was not his deep ocean and there could be rocks waiting to smash him under the surface of those swirling waters.

Despite this he revelled in the exhilaration of the dive, flying from the cliff to knife into the warm waters, fighting immediately to pull up from the depths then battling against the fierce current to stay in control. He was swimming for his life now, not caring any more that he was being hurtled back along the river course. Something banged against him and he lurched away in fear, but it was only a log and he swam on, not making much headway, afraid that he'd land back on the same bank from which he'd come, cursing his stupidity at forgetting that at the bend of the river the current would have to swing that way. Halfway across he realised that he was not as fit as he used to be, thanks to the hard work and poor food, but he kept his legs powering and his arms reaching out doggedly, over and over, on and on, and when he could see, through the raging waters, the welcome far bank he fought for it.

Then, like the branch of a tree caught up in a torrent, the outlying current collected him and flung him at the shore, discarding this piece of flotsam.

Exhausted, coughing up brackish river water laced with mud, so different from the taste of salt water, he hauled himself up the bank and collapsed.

As he lay there, his muscles aching, his strength gone, he thought he heard his father shouting at him, bullying him, ordering him to move on, and so powerful was the voice that Joseph lifted himself up – just in time to see a crocodile coming at him, jaws agape, racing out of the shallows at an incredible pace. In terror he found new strength and hurled himself up the rise, as a man flashed past him, spear raised to send it crunching, snapping into the open jaws. Neither of them waited for the result. Strong arms grabbed Joseph and threw him headlong to safety and they both ran from the river.

Confused, Joseph expected his saviour to be no less than his father, come back to save him, but he looked up to see a naked, grey-haired Aborigine grinning at him. Not Ratasali by any means. This fellow was lean and leathery, his skin coarsened by tribal scars, only his eyes and mouth visible behind a wild, wiry beard.

'Good swim,' the old man chuckled. 'I thought you drown.'

Joseph was surprised. 'You speak English?'

'Kanaka speak English!' The blackfellow mimicked his surprised tone sarcastically. 'This my country,' he added as if this were the explanation. 'Why you tomfool come here?'

Joseph wasn't sure whether he was asking why he'd come to his land or why he'd crossed the river, so he chose the latter, hoping for sympathy. And assistance. 'I worked down there but had trouble. I had to run away.'

'Ah.' The old man thought about this. 'Better you run back. No good here.'

'I can't. They'll hang me.'

'You kill white men too?' His companion seemed pleased about that, ignoring Joseph's denials. 'No good, them white blokes. But people here say Kanakas no good neither.' He stood up to survey the river. 'Old croc he get off, plenty mad. Now my good spear gone. You make more for me, eh?'

Bewildered, Joseph found he had a job, temporary though it might be, working for this old hermit as if he were his woman, not only stripping saplings and honing spears with a rusty knife but catching and skinning small furry animals for food and digging for yams, with his new boss standing by, giving orders.

Joseph learned that the blackfellow, whose name was Rawalla, had once befriended some white men and out of curiosity had allowed himself to be taken downriver by boat to the coastal town. 'The dirty place', he called it. He'd stayed there for a few years before drifting away.

Some time later, as they sat by the small campfire, Joseph raised the

175

question of local tribes. He remembered that Elly's tribe was Yindini and he'd taken it for granted that this man was also. 'The bush people who live up there . . .' he waved his hand towards the mountains, 'they are fierce?'

The old man grinned. Nodded. Licking his lips. 'Eat white men. Chinese men too.' He pinched Joseph merrily. 'Mebbe Kanaka too.'

Rawalla liked to tease Joseph, worry him, so that didn't faze him. 'I am told they are called Irukandji,' he said.

His companion was pleased. 'People speak of them?'

'Yes.'

'That is good they know.' He munched on the haunch of a wallaby that Joseph had caught, skinned and cooked for him, and looked meanly at him. 'I too am Irukandji,' he announced, watching for Joseph's reaction. He slammed his hand on the ground. 'This is Irukandji earth, from the river to the sky above the mountains.'

'It is beautiful country,' Joseph said diplomatically, knowing that his so-called friend could not be trusted. To even the score, he added: 'My people too feast on the flesh of enemies. But we do not eat skinny old men.' He smiled at Rawalla, in the same manner as the old blackfellow, his eyes hard. 'We only take their heads to put in our huts. Sometimes we give them to children to play with.'

The message was clear. Rawalla muttered in his own language and moved away to sulk under his bark gunya.

As the days passed Joseph made a spear to his own design. It was short and stout with sharp barbs on the point, a far more dangerous weapon in close combat that the long throwing spears. And so the two men occupied the camp in an uneasy truce; until he could decide what to do next, Joseph continued to feed the lazy old fellow, buying time. He didn't bother to ask why Rawalla lived alone; there could be any number of reasons – taboos, choice, or he could even be a scout, positioned there to watch for intruders – but whatever the reason, Rawalla was obviously unafraid of his own people; he was not worried that his campfire would give him away. From this point Joseph often saw fires in the hills above him, like stars against the dark night. If they were so obvious, so was this one, but no one bothered them, no tribesmen came down to inspect.

Eventually Joseph was becoming so bored with this lonely life that he questioned Rawalla about the lands to the south. If the Irukandji barred his way to the north and west then he would have to travel south. But Rawalla claimed he knew nothing abut that country. Joseph guessed he was lying, but in time believed he could provoke a response because Rawalla liked to show off his knowledge when he was in a good mood. At least, Joseph comforted himself, he was learning to survive in the bush. He wouldn't starve.

Chapter Ten

Jessie tried to tell herself that she was being patient, even wise, overlooking Corby's infatuation with her sister. She was still hoping that she was misinterpreting all the signs. But she knew in her heart that her motive for not objecting was far from noble. It was sheer cowardice. She quaked at the thought of confronting them, meeting with lies. Or worse, the blatant truth.

'Which would you prefer?' she asked herself with grim humour as she tramped back from the hospital. 'Or maybe that's the question I should ask Corby. Whom do you prefer? You wretched man.'

This morning, despite Mr Devlin's frantic efforts, a man had died of snakebite. He had been in agony but he hadn't made a sound, he'd just lain there, his face contorted with the pain as Jessie sat with him, despairing. She'd never felt so helpless. All she could do was swab him with cool damp cloths, hoping to reduce the fever, while the island women stood by in tears. And then he was dead, in this strange place, far from his home.

She had managed to make some improvements. The hospital now had its own rain water tank and kitchen and a supply of real towels and bandages, but the Kanakas had resisted her suggestion of enclosing the building with walls to keep out vermin.

'They don't like being shut in,' Devlin explained. 'It's hard enough keeping them in here; the concept of a hospital terrifies them. But you do a good job cheering them up, they're very impressed that you come to visit them, it makes them feel safer.'

'Thank you,' Jessie said, grateful for the small compliment. 'I was beginning to wonder if I was any use to them.'

'My word, you are. They're all very fond of you.'

Remembering that conversation now, she was angry with herself. She'd almost retorted: 'I'm glad someone is.'

'You're full of self-pity lately,' she muttered, clinging to her hood as a squall buffeted the trees along the track. 'A man died only an hour ago and you've almost forgotten him, too intent on your own trivial worries.'

She began to pray for him, feeling he was entitled to her attention, and by the time she approached the house her depression had lifted. She should count her blessings, she decided. A healthy child, a good home, and company of sweet people of various interesting races. Should she ask for more?

'Indeed I should. I can,' she argued as she mounted the front steps. 'Enough is enough. And if not, I have to leave.'

But once again, it was not the time. Elly came racing out to meet her, crying hysterically.

Jessie's first thought was for Bronte. 'What's happened? Is the baby all right?'

'Oh yes, missus. Baby good. But Joseph, he in bad at that other place. White men goan kill Joseph!'

Elly had made no secret about being madly in love with Joseph, which at first had amused Jessie. Lately, though, it had become irritating, with the girl mooning about lovesick and miserable in his absence.

She grabbed Jessie's hand. 'You come quick, missus. You stop them devils.'

'Don't be silly,' Jessie said, shaking her off. 'They won't hurt him. Calm down, Elly, you're all mixed up as usual.'

'No,' Elly wept. 'You see the boss out there. Him talking bad stuff with big pfeller from nex' place.'

'Stay here,' Jessie said, to shut her up. 'I'll see about it.'

She hurried through the house to find Corby, and Sylvia, of course, talking to Abel Teffler from Helenslea. 'What's going on?'

'Mr Betts has been murdered!' Sylvia cried. 'Shot dead! There's terrible trouble at Helenslea.'

Jessie was shocked. 'Mr Betts? Who would do such a thing?'

'That Kanaka Joseph and his mates,' Teffler said. 'A bunch of killers, them blokes. We got two of them but the ringleader got away.'

'The ringleader?' Jessie echoed. 'You don't mean Joseph?'

'He's on the run,' Corby said. 'We'll catch him. I feel responsible for this. I let them go over there but I had no idea . . .'

'I don't believe it,' Jessie said staunchly. 'And are you telling me those other two boys, Ned and Paka, are dead?'

'Sure are,' Teffler said, sounding pleased.

'Then what did you do to them? Those three worked by this house for weeks. I got to know them well, they wouldn't hurt a fly.'

'Steady on, Jessie.' Corby was embarrassed that she was accusing Teffler. 'There's more to it.'

Sylvia stepped in. 'There's a lot more. Your nice Kanakas also chopped off the head of one of the Helenslea staff. They attacked a white man, Jessie! Cut off his head and hung it up. We're lucky we weren't murdered in our beds.' She turned to Teffler. 'Did you know the same thing happened here at our place?'

'That I did,' Teffler said. 'They're savages. We're getting up search parties to catch the last one before he attacks anyone else.'

'I'm very sorry about this,' Corby said. 'And I'll be pleased to help in any way I can.'

'We could do with some of your blacks to track him,' Teffler said. 'There ain't none living on Helenslea.'

Jessie turned back to Elly, who was standing nearby. 'Go get Mr Devlin!' The girl was gone in an instant, bare feet flying. 'What about Mrs de Flores?' she asked. 'Is she safe?'

'Yes,' Teffler said. 'She was over at Woollahra plantation. We sent someone to break the news to her last night. She'd be on her way home now.'

'Well, perhaps she can find out the truth,' Jessie said. 'And until we hear more, with all due respect to you, Mr Teffler, none of our blacks can be spared.'

Teffler responded angrily. 'Are you calling me a liar?'

Corby tried to calm him. 'My wife has suffered a shock here, Abel. Please forgive her, she's not accustomed to violence. I'll get Toby to bring us some trackers.'

'You will not!' Jessie said. 'I won't have Joseph hounded like an animal until we hear more about this. He'll probably come back here anyway. Order the gig, Corby, we'll go to Helenslea ourselves. Mrs de Flores is our first priority, she'll be devastated.'

'Oh well, if that's how you feel, I'll be on my way,' Teffler said. 'Other planters'll help, you bet they will.'

Corby was so taken aback at Jessie's stand that he allowed Teffler to leave and then turned on her. 'How dare you make a fool of me like that!'

'Oh, shut up!' she said. 'I never liked that fellow.'

'You're being ridiculous,' Sylvia told her. 'There are four people dead and you don't want to believe it. They ran amok and killed Mr Betts and another man, isn't that enough? We don't want that murdering Kanaka back here. Corby, you ought to tell the men to shoot him on sight.'

Jessie rounded on her angrily. 'You mind your own business. You're here at Providence on borrowed time, so we don't need your opinions.'

'What do you mean, "borrowed time"? I think you ought to lie down. This has been too much for you. Corby and I will go over to see Lita.'

'I mean what I say,' Jessie retorted. 'You are here in my home only at my pleasure, and that's fast running out. You keep your hands off my husband or I'll pack you back to England on the next boat.'

'Just try it!' Sylvia spat at her, but Corby intervened.

'Edgar Betts has been killed, another gruesome murder has taken place and all you two women can do is argue. I'll get a horse and go over there myself.'

'You can't leave us here unprotected!' Sylvia cried. 'Lita is my friend. I should go to her.'

'Definitely not,' Corby said. 'God knows what's going on at Helenslea. You'll stay home.' He slammed his hat back on his head and strode away.

'This is your fault,' Sylvia wailed at Jessie. 'We could be in danger here.'

'We're in no danger from Joseph, none at all. He's the one in danger, and I want to know why.'

Corby handed her the revolver. 'You've learnt how to use this, haven't you?' he said.

'Yes,' Jessie replied, 'but I'm still rather frightened of it.'

'Then just keep it nearby.'

'It's not necessary, I'm not afraid of Joseph.'

'For God's sake, woman!' he said. 'Will you stop arguing and use your common sense. It's not just Joseph. Two of our Kanakas have been killed. How will the rest of them here react? I don't know and I'm damn sure you don't. Unless you think they'll just say "Oh poor show" and forget about it. Find your father, bring him up to the house and stay here. Tell Devlin he is to stay here with you.' He picked up his rifle. 'I'm taking Toby with me. I'll only stay long enough to pay my respects to Lita and get some idea of how this happened. McMullen is the manager of Helenslea but he was in Cairns when the trouble started, so Teffler says. They sent for him last night as well, so I'll talk to him. I presume you'll accept his word.'

Jessie nodded, nervous now. What if Joseph really had run amok?

'Now remember,' Corby said as he made for the door, 'stay in the house. Devlin will know what to do. I'll be back by nightfall.'

'Corby . . .' Jessie called, hesitating.

'Yes?' His voice was crisp. Efficient. That was all.

'Be careful.'

He shrugged, and left.

Jessie stared after him. So there it was. She had spoken up at them, at last, but not in the way she'd intended. Not in any of the ways she'd planned, or rehearsed. And she'd made an utter fool of herself, bringing in personal aggravations at such a time, making them irrelevant. Sylvia's reaction was not unexpected, and strangely, Jessie was relieved that her sister had not denied the relationship. Sylvia didn't seem to matter any more. But from Corby there'd been nothing. Not a flinch, not the bat of an eye, only concentration on the matter in hand, except for his scornful reference to the women bickering.

And of course he was right. What a time to pick. Jessie wondered if she could ever do anything right.

The Professor met Mike at the gate with the news from Helenslea. The manager was, naturally, shocked by the deaths and the sudden explosion of violence, but like Jessie he was keen to know what had triggered such a tragedy. 'I would have bet money on Joseph and his mates,' he said. 'I never figured them as violent. You say they killed one of the white men, and grabbed his rifle and shot Betts?'

'That's right. And two of them were killed but Joseph got away.'

Mike shook his head. 'Betts was a bastard with Kanakas,' he said. 'God knows what he must have done this time to provoke them.

And you say they cut off that bloke's head? God Almighty! Who was he?'

'I don't know. One of the white mill hands, I think.'

Mike's forehead creased with worry. 'I had myself convinced that Katabeti killed Perry by beheading him, but obviously I was wrong. It must have been one of these three. I count Ned out; he's been here a couple of years. This business started with the new intake, and Joseph and Paka were among them. Jesus! How wrong can you get? There'll be hell to pay now. And with Paka dead, that leaves Joseph. We have to catch him.'

Lucas listened anxiously and finally had to speak. 'You were right the first time, Mike. The man who suicided, Katabeti, he did kill Perry.'

'How do you know?'

'Well . . .' the Professor began nervously. 'When I found his body he was holding a bag. And it contained Perry's head.'

'Oh come on, you're imagining this.'

'No. I hid it. I didn't want people to be upset. Too horrible. So I took it down and threw it in the river.'

'Was that when you got lost?'

'Yes. You must understand I was very agitated.'

'Why the hell didn't you tell me?'

'There were other considerations.'

'What bloody considerations?'

'You made a rule that none of the islanders could go into the town until the matter was resolved. Now I listen to the men and I believe that terrible town has a corrupting influence on them. They are better off staying here.'

Mike stared at him, amazed and angry. 'You set yourself up as the guardian of their morals?'

'No. No! Their physical wellbeing. They're simple people, they shouldn't be exposed to the drink and disease evident in those brothels, don't you see?'

'I don't see,' Mike snapped. 'You're the bloody simpleton. Drink and disease and brothels are not confined to this country. Ships have been calling at those islands long before this state was even heard of. When it comes to sex these men, these boys, are not simple; they've had more experience than any pimply white youths would find in a lifetime.'

'But they don't have any experience in curing those diseases.'

'Neither do the white men. For Christ's sake, why can't you see them as human beings? Forget their colour! But that's beside the point now. I don't know what crimes Joseph may have committed, but sure as hell now he'll be blamed for Perry's death as well.'

'I'll give a signed statement to the police, exonerating Joseph from the crime at Providence,' the Professor offered, but Mike wasn't listening.

'Why didn't the boss wait for me?'

'He wants you to stay here and look after the women. He thinks the Kanakas here will be upset when they hear of this.'

181

'And he's dead right,' Mike admitted. 'Upset's not the word I'd use. Is everything all right in the house?'

'Yes. Corby told them to stay in.'

'Good. I'll go back and break this to our Kanakas as best I can.'

'Might I make a suggestion?' the Professor asked.

Mike nodded impatiently. He wasn't impressed by the Professor's interference.

'Joseph,' Lucas said. 'Be very careful when you speak to them of Joseph.'

'I'll be more bloody careful when I tell them Ned and Paka are dead!'

'But Joseph is different. I've been studying them. Pompey is their boss man but I am convinced that Joseph is some sort of priest.'

'A magic man? No. He's too young.'

'That's in the Aborigine world. I've noticed that the Kanakas from the island of Malaita have great respect for Joseph, even reverence.'

Mike recalled the time Joseph had stepped forward and quelled the row over the funeral day, but he made no comment.

Lucas continued. 'I'm not saying he's a witch doctor or a tribal seer, but he has immense status among them. He can't be a chief or he'd have replaced Pompey in the pecking order. He's too humble for that. So that leads me to believe that he's some sort of priest, maybe trained for the role as a child.'

'Well, I don't think it's going to help him now,' Mike shrugged. 'Or me. I have to think of the best way to handle this. There could be trouble, so lock up the house. Keep the women in, and that includes the black girls. I'll go down to the camp first and get some of the Aborigine men to keep an eye on the homestead.'

'Don't you think that's provocative in itself?'

'No, they'll keep out of sight. It's only a precaution, in case of a riot.'

Mike rang the bell calling the Kanakas in from the fields, and sent Pompey to round up the gangs in distant areas. While he was waiting for them all to assemble he opened up the storeroom and loaded a box with tins of tobacco and papers for the makings, telling himself that the Kanakas were entitled to the tobacco now. But he still felt guilty, knowing that this sudden generosity was a deliberate effort to earn goodwill before he broke the bad news to them.

He looked uncertainly at tins of Swallow's biscuits and boiled lollies. 'Ah, what the hell?' he muttered, and grabbed them too. They were a rare treat, all the natives loved them, and if he could sweeten them up then it was worth ignoring his conscience. Dammit! He wished Jake were here. This was a job for the master, not for the deputy. The Kanakas understood rank, they'd jump that much higher for the real boss man. Morgan should have sent Mike to Helenslea . . . But then, Morgan could easily make matters worse. He still saw them as a mob of dunderheads, not realising that they were a remarkable race, making the transition from their remote native lifestyles to a regimented workforce

182

almost overnight. But they were very supportive of each other. Very clannish. 'Don't I know it,' Mike growled. 'That's what I'm up against today.'

Some of the women were watching him, mystified. He called to one of them: 'Hey, Tamba! Will you take these over to the long-house for me?'

Pompey's wife ambled forward. 'For gib away?'

'Yes,' he grinned. 'No more tobacco ban. And these are presents.'

Tamba eyed him carefully. 'Why all men comen in now, boss? What's up?'

Mike deflected the question. 'You be in charge of giving out, eh? You tell all men to wait for me, I won't be long.'

He sprinted down to the toolsheds, where Sal had the job of overseeing the handing over of field implements. There could be no mistakes today. He stood watch himself, hauling in careless men who left lying about spades or hoes, or anything that could be used as a weapon. A lot of them had their own knives, breaking a rule that had been allowed to lapse lately, so he insisted that they be handed over also. This was the best he could do, since short of searching them and creating tension, he didn't expect a clean sweep.

It was an hour before Pompey brought in the last of the labourers, and Mike padlocked the sheds himself, pocketing the keys. At last he was standing before them, sad to see how happy they all seemed with this break in routine, munching on the lollies, smoking grandly.

'The master,' he told them, 'had to go to Helenslea plantation, so he asked me to speak with you. And I'm glad you have all come to listen because I have some good news and some very bad news.'

He explained to them that it had now been proven that Katabeti had killed Mr Perry. As he spoke he made a mental note to see that the Professor did make a statement, notarised, to hand to the police.

That news was met with silence, so he hurried on to tell them that the baccy ban was lifted, and also that the Sunday outings to town were now permitted. That brought a jubilant response. Mike waited, preparing himself for the hard part. He had to explain this to them in pidgin rather than have Pompey translate, for fear that his words might be misinterpreted. It was a delicate situation and he hoped his grasp of that sparse language was up to it.

'I am mourning,' he told them, 'for two friends, your friends who died yesterday.' He had planned to add: 'as a result of an accident', but thought better of it. The truth had to be given to them. 'The master has proclaimed two days, no work, as the funeral days for Paka and Ned, who are dead.' In the stunned silence that followed he felt another prickle of guilt for having put it that way – the holidays first – but they didn't seem to notice. The wailing had begun, women screaming, tearful men clutching at each other in their grief.

'How did this happen?' Pompey shouted at him.

Mike held up his hands to quieten them. 'The master has ridden fast to Helenslea to investigate this terrible thing. I will tell you what I can.

183

As far as I know there was a fight. A big fight.' He had their attention now. 'One of the white mill hands was also killed. And . . .' he paused for the impact of the one piece of information that might soften the blow, 'Mr Betts, the master of Helenslea, is also dead. A bad fight. They say that Paka took the mill hand's rifle and shot Mr Betts dead, right in front of his men. And so they shot back. And that is why Paka was killed.'

As they stood there, open-mouthed, trying to take this in, Mike kept talking. He referred to the holidays again, to the funeral feasts which they would have in honour of the dead. Promising that their bodies would be brought back to Providence for burial. Voices began to emerge. Questions were asked and he answered them as well as he could, admitting that he had no idea, yet, what had caused the fight. Emphasising his own shock at the death of Betts to balance the issue.

Then Sal came forward. 'Where is Talua?'

'Who?'

'Talua, known as Joseph,' Sal called angrily.

'I don't know,' Mike said. 'He is missing.'

'They killed him too,' a man shouted.

'No! No! He ran away. He might come back here. I don't know where he is.'

Now there was trouble. The faces staring at him had become like granite, a wall of grim anger. 'Where is Talua?' a fierce voice shouted, and Mike remembered that theory of the Professor's as he wondered why Joseph was so important to them.

'I have always found Joseph a good man,' he said. 'We must be calm and try to help him.'

'They kill him!' one of the women screamed. 'Jus' like Ned. Jus' like Paka! They kill Talua!'

From this point Mike didn't know what to do. This was when he needed the backup of white men to keep control, with guns if necessary. The Kanakas had turned away from him to confer in angry groups. He could see and hear the rage building so he went among them, consoling, arms about shoulders, patting them, taking hands. 'We will find Joseph,' he was saying. 'I am sorry about Ned and Paka, but they killed the master of Helenslea.'

He told the women to make tea. He sent them to the storehouse for more biscuits. For hams to make more food. For anything they wanted. They could have the lot as far as he was concerned, as long as they kept calm. And he promised that a bullock would be killed for the feasts. Anything to keep them busy.

Eventually he turned to Pompey. 'I have to go up to the house. This is terrible, everyone is upset, but they have to be quiet until I find out more. I'll give you a two-day pass for town if you make sure they behave.'

Pompey looked gloomy. 'Malaita men trouble. Better you find that Joseph bloody quick.'

'Why Joseph?' Mike asked. 'He's still alive, the others are dead. Why are they more upset about Joseph?'

But as usual, Pompey couldn't or wouldn't enlighten him. He shrugged. 'Malaita man. You gib me gun, eh?'

'No. No guns. Just see they don't do anything stupid or the master might have to bring in guns, and then everyone will be in trouble. It's a bad business all round.'

'It's a bad business, Mr Morgan, that I can tell you,' Alf McMullen said, welcoming Corby to Helenslea across the deserted courtyard. 'No work today as a sign of respect to the boss, so I've got all our boys penned in out of the way. Most of the men are out hunting for that other bastard. If they put a bullet in him it'll save us a lot of trouble.'

'And me,' Corby said. 'I don't want the police back at Providence, holding up the work, achieving absolutely nothing. But by Jove, it's still hard to believe that Edgar's dead.'

'Sure is,' McMullen said. 'We're wondering what's going to happen now. New boss, new broom.'

They walked over to the house. Without the wide white-pillared veranda it could have been a flat two-storeyed Georgian house. The black shutters on all windows and doors added a neat touch and a reminder of the tropical storms that were known to rage in this latitude. Constructed of sandstone, the building looked serene, even lethargic against a backdrop of luxuriant palms and larger-than-life greenery. Everything about it seemed overdone, and yet it succeeded, having to compete with massive overfed plants and their flaring blooms. A compromise. Vulgar old Betts had got it right. Corby was astonished, and planned, one day, to copy the design himself.

'Do you want to go in and see Lita?' McMullen asked.

'Yes, but before I do, I need to know exactly what happened. Your man, Teffler, was understandably overwrought, so I'm a trifle confused.'

Did he see McMullen's eyes shift? Look away? Dodging something? Corby wasn't sure, but he listened without interrupting as McMullen gave him much the same story as Teffler's, with a few more details.

'Thank you,' Corby nodded, watching the manager keenly. 'But I still don't know how all this started. What did Joseph do wrong to warrant the lockup in the first place?'

'I wasn't here,' Alf said, his voice too vague. 'Something to do with the fencing job. You know what Edgar was like . . .'

'No, I don't,' Corby said. 'I don't set much store by hearsay.'

'All right then. Edgar goes over to look at the job. He's got a couple of the blokes with him. He gets cranky, and your boy Joseph gives cheek. The other bloke Paka does too. So they give Paka a belt or two but Joseph, he objects, so they slam him in the lockup to cool down.'

'And the other two went to these lengths to get him out?'

'That's right.'

Corby eased himself from one foot to the other. 'Why were they so

185

keen to get him out if he was only there to cool down?'

'Jesus, I don't know! They're all bloody madmen, head-hunters! Everyone knows that. Their blood was up, I suppose. Blood tells.'

'Really,' Corby said drily. 'One more thing. If these two got into an argument with Mr Betts – which seems rather odd from what I've seen of them, and him – are you telling me that the only punishment would have been overnight confinement?'

'Ah . . . no. They'd probably have got a flogging as well.'

'And is that why Mr Betts came back to the lockup with his men after supper? Did he intend to carry out the punishment then? On a wet, stormy night? I had the impression that floggings were carried out publicly as a lesson to the rest.'

McMullen strode forward to the wide stone steps and leaned against the low banister. 'How the hell do I know? One of our blokes is dead, with his head chopped off! Edgar's in there stiff as a board with a bullet in his chest. Ask him what he had in mind. He gave all the orders around here. Anyway, what bloody difference does it make now?'

Corby shrugged. None at all, he supposed.

He followed McMullen inside, surreptitiously admiring the polished floors tamed by expensive rugs, the high ceilings and the spacious parlour. The furniture was another oddity. Spanish. Large comfortable leather chairs and fine black timbers, of what breed he couldn't say, and one wall was lined with books. Had Edgar ever read a book? He doubted it. Further on, through open sliding doors, he spied a long table, once again of Spanish design, with matching high carved chairs and sporting a single silver candelabra that must have cost a mint. Corby was fast readjusting his opinion of Lita. He was mortified that he'd become so accustomed to that bungalow he occupied with his family that he'd had the cheek to have the neighbourhood planters to Bronte's christening with a place like this nearby. He would have to speak to that bank manager and do something about the Providence homestead if he were to have any status in this land at all. If he were to offer hospitality to people of his own class rather than the collection of homebodies that had rolled up to the christening.

He sat in lonely splendour in a magnificant straight-backed armchair while McMullen went off to rouse someone, musing on all these things until a tall Aborigine woman walked in. She was dressed in voluminous black taffeta, which seemed all wrong to Corby, but he jumped to his feet in more of a knee-jerk reaction than protocol because he hadn't expected to see a black woman in the garb of civilisation.

'Mr Morgan,' she said, in a soft, velvety voice, 'Mrs McMullen is with Miss Lita. She asks you wait please.'

'Thank you,' he replied, realising that this must be Betts's woman, his black gin.

'Would you like tea?' she asked. 'Or a drink? Brandy?'

'Yes. Brandy, thank you. Brandy,' he stuttered, wondering what was taking Alf McMullen so long.

186

The woman disappeared, then returned with a silver tray containing a decanter of brandy and two glasses, which – since she did not join him – he recognised as a tactful statement that one did not drink alone. Her movements were fluid, the body supple, quite spectacular in fact. Were she not black she'd be noticed in any society, with her thick hair wound up under a white lace cover, not unlike the fashion worn by the Queen.

'I'm very sorry about the death of Mr Betts,' he said awkwardly, worrying what on earth was the correct thing to say to a black mistress.

'Thank you, Mr Morgan,' she replied stiffly. 'Is Mr Devlin with you?'

'No.'

He saw disappointment, and more, in her face. Worry? The blacks had open faces, one could read them in a glimpse. She was obviously grieving, but then he supposed her status had now shifted considerably.

She left him to pour his own drink. Soon Mrs McMullen, also in black, turned up. 'Oh, Mr Morgan. It's so good of you to come over. You've missed Mr and Mrs Cavanagh, you know, from Woollahra plantation. They were here this morning.'

'They've left already?' Corby said, surprised. 'Had I known I should have brought my wife along.'

Mrs McMullen closed the door behind her like a conspirator. 'It wouldn't do any good. Mrs de Flores didn't want them to stay. She won't see anyone. Only Dandy.'

'Who is Dandy?'

'The black woman,' she whispered. 'His . . . Mr Betts's . . . well his you-know-what. I insisted on seeing Mrs de Flores myself, just in case. One doesn't know who one can trust in these circumstances. I mean to say, leaving Lita in the hands of the gin who masquerades as the lady of the house . . .'

'And how is Mrs de Flores?' Corby interrupted.

'Taking it hard she is. A moody person at the best of times, poor Lita, she's in a real state now.' Mrs McMullen sniffed into a large handkerchief. 'Her way of grieving, I suppose, not mine of course, but it takes all types. She's in a foul temper. Been shouting at everyone, hurling things about. Takes after her old man in that department I have to say. God rest his soul.'

'I'd better talk to her,' Corby said.

'She won't thank you.'

'I didn't come to be thanked.'

The woman sighed. 'It's no use. More polite to keep away at this stage. You see, Lita's a bit under the weather, so to speak. More than a bit, in fact. It pains me to have to tell you this,' she said with a disapproving frown, 'but she's plain drunk. Dreadful in a woman.'

'No worse than in a man,' Corby murmured. He didn't like this person, preferring the steady gaze of the black woman, but she had disappeared.

'Where is Alf?' he asked.

187

'He had things to do,' Mrs McMullen replied. 'My Alf will see that everything is taken care of properly. We have to wait for the doctor to get out here to issue the death certificates, and then try to get some sense out of Lita about the funeral. She's talking wild, says she doesn't want a funeral. No service either. But that could be Dandy's heathen influence. Alf told *her*, in no uncertain terms, to leave Helenslea now and go back to her tribe, wherever it is, to avoid embarrassment, but not her. She just looked through him as if he wasn't there. And him the manager. But that's typical of her, thinks she's . . .'

'What other arrangements have been made?' Corby asked, to put a stop to her chatter.

'The undertaker is bringing out two coffins. In the meantime the bodies are in the cool room.'

Revolted, Corby put his glass down with a jolt. 'What about the bodies of the two Kanakas?'

'They buried them,' she said absently. 'It'd be a crying shame if Mr Betts doesn't have the funeral he deserves, don't you agree?'

Corby stood up. The woman was depressing him, telling him everything and nothing. 'That's up to Mrs de Flores,' he replied. 'When will the police be here?'

'God knows. They'll be out searching for that murdering Kanaka too. We can't have one of them running loose.' She peered at him accusingly, her pallid face so close to his he stepped back. 'We didn't know they were violent, those Kanakas, or we'd never have had them near the place.'

'I didn't know either,' Corby retorted.

'But you've had the same dreadful thing happen at Providence, Mr Morgan. People are saying you're too soft on them devils. You need a man like my Alf to keep them in line.'

'Did he keep them in line here?' Corby snapped.

'No need to take it personally,' she whined. 'No one actually blames you.'

'Good of them,' he said, his voice heavy with sarcasm, but it went over her head.

'Yes, Mr Morgan, people mean well, you know.'

The room, with the shutters closed, was stifling him. He edged out. 'I must be on my way.'

As she escorted him across the wide stone veranda, Corby was pleased to be leaving. There was an air of desolation about the plantation now. Not a soul in sight except Toby who was minding the two horses in the shade of a huge jacaranda tree.

As he set off down the steps, Mrs McMullen called to him: 'We'll let you know when the funeral's going to be.'

'Damned cheek!' he muttered to himself, refusing to acknowledge her by looking back. 'No wonder Lita's drunk with all that's happened and a crow like her for company.'

'We go now, boss?' Toby asked.

188

'Yes.'

'Good. This a creepy place now. Bad joss.'

Corby glanced at him, surprised at the use of the term by a blackfellow. Then he realised that they'd be learning some of their English from Tommy Ling. What a tangle, he mused as he swung on to his horse.

Riding home, he worried about his son. What sort of pidgin would Bronte be speaking, surrounded by blacks, Chinese and Kanakas? They'd have to be very strict with him and insist that he spoke correct English at all times. He'd have a word with Jessie about it. Jessie. He'd heard her warn Sylvia, though he'd pretended that he hadn't. So she knew about them! It was inevitable. Obviously she did not intend to allow the situation to continue, so something would have to be done. Like what?

He nudged the horse into a canter as they reached the main track that wound through Helenslea. Toby's horse kept pace. Corby noticed that the black man rode well, comfortable in the saddle though with a different seat. Like Devlin, these fellows preferred shorter stirrups, hugging the horse with their knees for more control of these rougher beasts, who did, he admitted, have minds of their own. He'd almost been thrown a couple of times by this horse, pulling what Devlin called 'brumby tricks'. He wondered if he could utilise the blacks more by encouraging them to ride. It was a radical idea, but half a dozen extra horsemen on the property would come in handy.

Corby knew he was only thinking along these lines to evade the issue of Jessie. No, not Jessie . . . Sylvia. Would he have to give her up? He groaned, thinking of her. She was an exciting lover, completely uninhibited, moody as hell, sometimes wildly loving, at other times angry with him, which made her even more demanding. He'd tried to put a stop to their affair by remaining resolutely in his own room, but she'd come to him and by God, he'd been glad to have her in his bed.

And Sylvia was always making plans. Eventually Jessie would have to take Bronte back to England, to school, she hoped, and she had some mad idea that they should let Jessie go now so that she would be settled in London to receive Bronte when he was of school age. That was fair, she'd insist, and he let her rattle on. He wasn't at all interested in her opinions. On the subject of Bronte he had another radical plan.

The well-to-do here sent their sons, and sometimes even their daughters, back to England for their schooling, just as the English did in India. The boys were usually escorted on the voyage by friends or family, sent away at the age of seven. The girls went later. Corby himself had been bundled off at that age. A frightened, miserable child, he'd hated the brutish environment from the first day to the last, an eternity later. No son of his would be sentenced to that life. To become estranged from his father as Corby himself was, and shy in the presence of his mother.

No. Bronte would grow up here. He would have a governess, then a tutor, and would remain among people who cared about him. Above all, Providence would be his home, and the management of the plantation would be second nature to him. He'd learn all about it by watching, by being part of Providence, not stumbling along having to rely on others as Corby did. And there was so much land surrounding Providence, any amount of land for expansion. Bronte had a great future here, and he'd grow up strong and healthy in this environment. Jessie would agree with him on that.

But it was Sylvia who wanted to send his son away.

That thought irritated him. In the absence of Jessie, what sort of a mother would Sylvia make for the child? Then again, that question was pointless, since he was damn sure Jessie would never give Bronte up.

In these arguments with himself he always ended up in the same place. No further advanced.

He was depressed as they rode towards the homestead, which looked gloomy too, shut down like a dismal Sunday. That alarmed him. The doors and windows were never closed and now with dusk settling hardly a glimmer of light showed.

Some blackfellows stepped out from the shadows, startling him. 'What the hell's this?' he asked Toby.

He listened anxiously as Toby spoke to them in their own language. 'It alri', boss,' he said at length. 'Them fellers jus' minding your house. Mr Devlin he tell them allasame keep watch.'

'Why?'

'Kanaka men cryin' on dead fellers. Mebbe they play up, boss. Get cranky.'

'Have they been up here?'

'No.'

'That's a relief.' Corby remembered to thank his Aborigine guards and they nodded happily, leaning against their long spears. They seemed to be enjoying the excitement.

'What's going on here?' Corby strode through the kitchen to find Jessie on her knees in the passagway, packing clothes into a small tin trunk.

She looked up. 'Oh! Corby. You're back, I'm so glad. I was beginning to worry about you. How is Lita?'

'She'll survive. What are you doing?'

'I'll need these things in town.'

'In town? Who's going to town?'

Jessie sat back. 'Mr Devlin thinks Sylvia and I and the baby should go into town for the time being. Until everything settles down.'

'Until what settles down? What has happened?'

'Nothing really, but the Kanaka people are very shocked at the deaths of Paka and Ned, and the disappearance of Joseph. Mr Devlin thinks it would be wise for us to go away for a little while in case there's trouble.'

'Mr Devlin thinks! Since when is he running my household? And what's this nonsense about the Kanakas? It's his job to keep them under

190

control, not to come up here worrying women. Put that trunk away.'

Sylvia emerged from her room. 'Corby's right. The trouble isn't here, it's over at Helenslea. Everyone knows the way Betts treated his Kanakas, I don't see why we should be inconvenienced.'

'No one is going anywhere!' Corby said. 'Now, I'm famished. Hospitality over there is lean. Sylvia, go and tell Tommy I want something to eat.'

'What would you like?' she asked. 'It will be dinner time soon.'

'I don't know what he keeps in the larder,' he retorted. 'Just tell him!' He went on through to the parlour to pour himself a whisky, irritated that the room was like an oven with the french doors closed.

Jessie followed him in, and he told her to open the room up. 'Bloody nonsense locking up like that. What did you expect? An army of niggers to come hammering? He's got you in a state of panic.'

She opened the doors but there was no rush of cool air, no change at all from the heavy humidity.

'I'm not panicking,' Jessie said quietly. 'We have a baby in the house, I was just taking precautions.'

'Good God!' The whisky was excellent. He swallowed it at a gulp, poured another one and sank into his comfortable chair, watching her. 'You intrigue me. You're the one who is so friendly with the Kanakas. A veritable angel pottering about in their hospital doing all those good deeds. So why would you be afraid of them? Surely your friends wouldn't turn on you?'

'Don't be facetious, Corby,' she warned. 'They're very upset and confused. Mr Devlin isn't concerned about individual response, he thinks they're becoming angry and he's nervous that there might be a riot.'

'There was no riot at Helenslea. It's the white men who are angry. You don't seem to recall that a planter has been killed. And another white man murdered.'

'Yes I do, and I'm very sorry about that, but Mr Devlin seems to think that we could be the recipients of further consequences unless there's a better explanation of the deaths of the two Kanakas. What did they tell you?'

'No more than we already know. And I couldn't talk to Lita. That dreadful woman Mrs McMullen was hovering about because Lita has taken to the bottle.'

'What?'

'Lita's on a binge. Not receiving today, one might say.'

'And what about Joseph?'

'There are horsemen out searching for him. Posses, they call them. He's guilty, make no mistake about that.'

'Oh God. How awful.' Jessie poured herself a glass of sherry and stood by the door to the veranda, looking out into the night. 'I still want to go to town,' she said at length.

'What the hell for?' he replied angrily. 'You're safe here. If I thought

191

there was any danger I'd agree to take you right away, but there's no need. I keep telling you, two Kanakas and two white men have died. Surely these fellows are not such blockheads that they can't understand that nothing will bring any of them back. What's done is done.'

'Yes,' she admitted. 'Mr Devlin could be overly concerned for us, but I saw his suggestion as a good opportunity to leave for town, with the baby.'

'Why would you do that?'

Tommy rushed in with a plate of ham sandwiches. 'Spoil your dinner, boss,' he complained, handing them over.

'Not a chance,' Corby laughed, setting the plate on a handy table and munching on the hefty slabs. 'Good,' he enthused. 'The pickles are excellent. Does he make them?' he asked Jessie.

'No, I do. Corby, I'm leaving you. The present problems here have given me a good excuse to go without creating talk. For now, anyway.'

'I see,' he said, stalling. 'And where are you going? Back to London? Is there a ship in port, might I ask?'

'You'd like that, wouldn't you? If I just made myself scarce. Your wife.'

'Not with my son I wouldn't. What has brought this on?'

'As if you don't know.'

Just then Sylvia appeared in the doorway. 'Oh good. You're having a sherry. I'll have one too.'

'No you won't,' Jessie snapped. 'Get out. I'm having a private conversation with my husband.'

'Don't talk to *me* like that,' Sylvia retorted. 'I've been putting up with your bad temper all day and I've had enough. I would like a sherry.'

'Here then,' Jessie said, pushing the bottle at her. 'Take the lot. Now go away.' She slammed the door behind Sylvia and closed the double doors into the dining room. 'I said I am leaving you, Corby, and I mean it. She's the reason. Is that plain enough?'

He looked so much at ease Jessie wished she could throw something at him. Strike him! Scream at him! But she was having enough trouble appearing determined, without letting him know how painful was this decision.

'I don't know what you're talking about,' he said, patronising her. 'I think all this drama has thrown you into a spin. You have to get a hold on yourself, Jessie.'

'I will go into town,' she said firmly. 'And stay at an hotel until I can find accommodation for Bronte and me.'

'And who will pay for this?'

'You will. Providence will. If you stop my withdrawals from the bank I shall see a lawyer, and that will create a scandal which I am sure you don't need. But I won't be fleeing back to London, Corby. You won't get rid of me that easily.'

She saw his anger growing, anger at being cornered, but she didn't care any more. She wanted him agitated.

'Who said I wanted to get rid of you? There's no way I'll permit you to take my child out of this country. You're being bloody high-handed, woman. Don't threaten me with talk of scandal, I don't give a donkey's hoof for what these colonial upstarts think of me. Your place is in this house and this is where you stay.'

'Very well, I'll stay on two conditions. Firstly, Sylvia has to leave. I've written to Aunt Daphne, asking her to take her in. She lives in Wimbledon and can do with the company, God help her! And secondly, unless you can . . .' Jessie was losing her impetus. She turned away, appalled at the ultimatum she was offering. Humiliated to have to place it on the table like a cold chop. But she persevered. 'Unless you see your way clear . . . want to . . .' she wavered, 'be my husband again, then there is no point in this conversation.' That wasn't how she'd meant to put it, but having blurted it out, her face felt so red she rushed out on to the veranda.

Corby didn't follow. He sat, infuriating her, sipping his whisky. Until she was forced to return.

'So?' she asked. 'What have you decided?'

'I've decided,' he said softly, 'that I will not have women telling me what I should or should not do. Not you, nor your sister. You have a good life here. As does your father, who contributes nothing to the management of the plantation.'

'My father is half-owner,' Jessie said.

'Which is why, since he is useless, I am paying myself a salary from now on, and charging him rent. He already owes me several hundred pounds.'

Jessie was astonished. 'What for?'

'I don't know and I don't care. Maybe he gives handouts to your precious Kanakas. Or to the blacks down by the lagoon. Whatever. The point is, I'm supporting the lot of you. Do you get my drift?'

'Oh yes,' she said bitterly. 'And I won't be threatened! I'll leave in the morning.'

He sighed. 'Don't be so bloody stupid. Who will escort you? Tomorrow I'm sending Devlin over to Helenslea to keep an eye on developments, so I will have to stay here, won't I? I mean, we can't have the hired help acting up. Someone has to manage the plantation with Devlin throwing the vapours.'

'And what about Sylvia?' Jessie demanded.

'I don't know,' he smiled, in command now. 'Ask her. She's your sister.'

Unable to think of an answer, unable to find a way to respond, Jessie ran from the room, across the veranda and down the steps, to burst into tears.

Elly seemed to appear from nowhere. 'Doan cry, missus,' she said. 'Bad for milk.' The girl put her arms around Jessie and held her close as she wept. 'You be all ri',' she murmured. 'What the boss say about Joseph?'

'He's still missing,' Jessie told her.

'Joseph never come back,' Elly moaned, and Jessie hoped she was right. If he did come home he'd have to face serious charges, since Corby had confirmed Teffler's account of the murders. Even if Joseph and his friends had been provoked, Jessie could no longer defend their murderous reactions. They must have gone berserk, she thought. In which case Joseph could be dangerous now. But in Elly's frame of mind, it was better to say nothing and so avoid upsetting her further.

Mike's report to the boss on his day at Providence brought an angry outburst from Corby, who was still smouldering at Jessie's demands. It seemed to him that everyone was conspiring to cause trouble for him. 'I gave no permission for holidays,' he shouted. 'What right do you have to be making all these decisions when my back is turned?'

'I'm just trying to head off riots,' Devlin said.

'What have they got to riot about? That murderers have been punished? That their men killed a planter and brutally murdered another white man? Have you taken leave of your senses? These men have to be shown that if they behave like savages they'll be treated accordingly. They should be down on their knees praying that they don't suffer a backlash themselves.'

'What sort of a backlash?'

'We have to get tougher with them now. Since you're admitting you can't handle them, I'm bringing on two more foremen as soon as possible. In the meantime, since you've already told them they can have a day off . . .'

'Two days.'

'They can have one day, that's all. And the day is a day of respect for Edgar Betts, not for lunatic Kanakas. I'll tell them that myself.'

'They'll want to bury Ned and Paka. I'll have to get their bodies back.'

'Too late, they've been buried at Helenslea, and a bloody good job that is too. I won't have murderers buried here. Get a grip on yourself, Devlin. You're letting this whole business get out of proportion. And you seem to forget I'm the loser here. I'm losing a day's work. With a workforce this size, that's considerable. Added to which, I've lost three Kanakas. It's all money, and the sooner you wake up to it the better. On top of which, you decided, *you* decided, that the women should go into town. Without so much as a by-your-leave to me.'

'I still think they should go.'

'Well I don't. You can go over to Helenslea tomorrow, since nothing will be achieved here, and find out what's happening about the funeral. I had enough of the place today. After which we get on with our own business. Is that understood?'

'Oh yes. And you'd better get your new foremen quick smart because I'm finished here. When they get here I'm off. I've had enough too.'

'Please yourself,' Corby said, relieved to know he'd soon be rid of Devlin and his high-handed attitudes.

When Devlin had gone off to his own quarters, Corby felt better. This heralded a new start at Providence. He'd be the real master now, with foremen who'd jump at his commands and run the place for profit, not to please Kanaka layabouts.

Mike too was relieved. As he rode through the neighbouring plantation he felt better just leaving Providence for the day, away from Morgan's constant harping. 'He treats me as if I'm a bloody idiot,' he muttered to himself. 'He's lucky I didn't flatten him.' Nevertheless, he was still concerned about Sylvia and Mrs Morgan, and considered asking some of the men at Helenslea if they wanted jobs at Providence. But it would hardly be fair to Lita to pinch some of her staff at a time like this.

He found her in Edgar's office, sorting papers.

'How are you?' he asked gently, kissing her on the cheek.

'I've been better,' she said wearily. 'But I'm glad you've come. It's all a nightmare. I woke up this morning wondering if it was true. But true it is. Edgar's dead. I have to keep telling myself that, because I keep expecting him to come stamping in here wanting to know what I'm doing fishing about in his desk.'

'Have the police been?'

'Yes, Sergeant McBride was here early this morning, condolences and all that. You know, I always expected that one day someone might bat my father over the head, he could be very cruel. But I saw it as a sort of mild retaliation, like trading punches with him, serve him right. And I imagined it as teaching him a lesson, rather funny in fact. I actually looked forward to someone thumping him one day so that I could say: "I told you so." But the one and only time someone retaliated, he left no time for the lesson to be learned. Edgar was shot dead on the spot. It's all over.'

Mike sat quietly and let her talk.

'McMullen's nagging me about the funeral. He says the world will want to come to pay their respects, but, Mike, do I have to do that?'

'What do you want to do?'

'I'd prefer to bury him here without fuss. I couldn't stand half the countryside marching through the house singing the praises of good old Edgar. Most of them hated him anyway. Or they didn't approve of him. Or Dandy. McMullen even had the cheek to tell her to disappear. They're afraid of a scandal at the funeral if she's there.'

'Did she leave?'

'No. She says she'll go when I ask her to. And that won't happen as long as I'm here. She's still an excellent housekeeper.'

'Will you be staying?'

'I don't know yet. Do you want a job? I could do with a good manager now.'

'McMullen knows the ropes,' Mike replied, evading the issue. 'He'll keep the show on the road for you until you decide what to do. Did they find Joseph?'

195

Lita shuffled papers about. 'No. But he won't get far.'

'I could have sworn he was a peaceful bloke. I never thought he'd turn aggressive.'

'Neither did I, but . . .' She shrugged. 'I don't want to talk about it.'

'Fair enough. Do you mind if I take a look about?'

'No. Go ahead. Come back and have some lunch with me.'

He rode down to the lockup, past fields where the Kanakas were already back at work, and walked round the area where Betts and the other men had been killed. The door to the lockup was still hanging loose where it had been jemmied open, but rain had washed away any obvious signs of blood.

'This a bad place,' a voice said, and he turned to find Dandy watching him.

'A very sad place, Dandy. Why did the Kanakas go berserk?'

'I warn him,' she said. 'I tell him that Joseph a magic man but the boss, he doan wanna listen.'

Mike was startled. Here it was again. The Professor had said the same thing. 'Who tells you he's a magic man?'

'The people know. Yindini old men spot him. They say he carry two spirits.'

'Bad spirits?'

She looked at him, correcting him. 'Spirits powerful,' she said firmly, as if this were enough of an explanation.

'Edgar rode down here to the lockup,' Mike said. 'With his men. To punish Joseph?'

She nodded, looking about her nervously.

'What punishment?'

Dandy rolled her eyes. 'Hang him.'

'God Almighty!' Mike exclaimed. 'No one mentioned this. What the hell was he going to hang him for? What did he do, for God's sake?'

She stood tall, her face shut down, expressionless, in the maddening way Aborigines responded when they didn't wish to reply.

'Dandy, you must tell me. Joseph must have done something very bad to rate a hanging. What did he do?'

'I do not say,' she eventually allowed. 'Ask Miss Lita.'

'She can't tell me. She wasn't here. She only knows what I know.'

But for Dandy, that subject was closed. 'Magic man called Joseph,' she said. 'He doan kill no one.'

'I see. And how do you know this?'

'Black men, they see him running. Long time before the gunshot.'

'What were the blackfellows doing on this plantation?'

Dandy smiled. 'Through there, in the bush. Big nut trees, good season. They come in to steal nuts.'

The nuts, of course, Mike remembered. He didn't know the name of the tree; whites in the district just referred to them as Queensland nuts. The wild nuts were the tastiest he'd ever come across, and at this time of the year they'd be dropping by the bucketful.

'You forget,' he argued. 'As I hear it the guard was murdered first. Joseph could have killed him.'

'That man outside. Joseph locked in. How he do that? No. You come see this bush.' She took Mike back to the edge of the track. 'See here, bush all smash up. Men fight. Ned killed. Whitefeller killed. Paka get his gun. Paka let Joseph out. Why can't you see this?' she asked him crossly. He watched as she explained every move, her knowledge of the scrub faultless, scratching at the ground where the decapitation had taken place. Moving on from there, tracing Paka's bloody footprints by turning over damp leaves that still held traces of blood. 'One man, bloody feet, come this way. All blood show this. One man.'

'Joseph could have helped Paka when he got out then.'

'No. No. Black men see him. No blood on him. No. Blood smell bad, he get out and run. That all. Paka wait for boss, look here. This where man wait, squash things, long time.'

'Why didn't Paka run too?'

'Doan know. Maybe he too angry with the boss. They doan like him hang that Joseph.'

Mike didn't know what to think. He'd known Dandy a long time and he trusted her, but why all this secrecy? If old Betts had decided to hang one of the Kanakas, a Providence Kanaka at that, the old bastard, then his men would shut up, he'd see to that. Eventually though the stories got out, rumours . . . that was the way with Edgar. He bribed and bullied and by the time rumour began to sound like fact no one cared. But Edgar was dead. The man he'd intended to hang had got away. Only two crimes had been committed, and both of them by Kanakas. Why the hell, then, were McMullen and Teffler and the rest of them keeping their heads down?

'Why are all the white men keeping quiet about a hanging that didn't even happen?' he asked Dandy.

She looked at him gravely. 'Mebbe they frighten to keep their jobs.'

'But the boss is dead. He can't punish them now.'

Once again she brushed aside the subject. 'More better you find that Joseph boy, he done nothin' wrong.'

'Have they got black trackers after him?'

Dandy's smile was grave. 'No blackfeller track magic man. No bloody fear! Whitefeller gangs riding mad in circles, they doan find him. He cross the river.'

'Into Irukandji country? Oh, cripes, out of the frying pan into the fire. Come back with me, Dandy and we'll talk to the men. I'll fetch back McMullen and the police.'

'No,' she said firmly. 'My husband gone to his Dreaming in this place. I got things to do here. You go.' She stepped over and put her arms about him in a bear hug, as if he were a child who needed solace. 'You a sad man, Mike. No woman.'

Embarrassed, he accepted her warmth and then drew away. 'I'll survive,' he muttered.

'Yes,' she replied, her voice vague. 'After big river comen. You find your home then.' Her feet stamped the ground. 'Your earth. You got no home now, I see this in you. Like too many of my people. This land is my home, so I stay. With the house or with the people. You understand that?'

'Of course.'

'Then you do the same. You find where you belong and the woman will be waiting for you.'

'What woman?' He almost smiled at her but managed to keep a straight face. The blacks were a sentimental lot. He didn't want to hurt her feelings.

'Give me some matches,' she said, returning to the white world for temporary convenience. 'I have to burn all this devil stuff.' She began tearing at the undergrowth where the guard had died, ripping away like a gardener beset with weeds.

'It won't burn, it's too damp,' he commented.

'In there it will.' She pointed at the lockup and he realised that she intended to cleanse the whole area, a part of her homeland that had been defiled. To the blacks every rock, every tree, every skerrick of their earth was precious, and they still did what they could to protect what remained of their homelands. As the Irukandji did to a savage extent on the other side of the river. For a moment he envied them. They knew where they belonged. Where was his home now? And for that matter how the hell had she known he was footloose, having given Morgan notice? Maybe she didn't. She was just feeling sorry for him because he didn't have a woman. After all, she'd lost her man. Her husband. Mike knew that Dandy had meant husband in a tribal sense. Edgar might have been living with her for ten years but he would not have married her. Nor would Dandy have cared. What was a piece of paper to her?

As he made his way back to the house, Mike detoured to question three of the heavily armed overseers. He asked them point-blank if they'd heard mention of a hanging on the night Edgar was killed.

'What's it to you?' a surly fellow asked him.

'They were Providence Kanakas.'

'Then you should have kept them tied up down there, mate, instead of lettin' them loose on us.'

'I asked about a hanging,' he persisted.

'Don't know nothin' about no hanging,' the same man said, sucking on the stub of a cheroot.

'Were you there when the boss was shot? Any of you?'

They all nodded, wheeling their horses to move off.

'What were you doing there? Why did Betts want you there?'

'Orders,' one of them said. 'Teffler said we gotta ride with the boss, so we ride.'

'And you didn't ask why?'

'Nope.'

They exchanged glances, amusement in the steely eyes, and Mike was annoyed, believing they were laughing at him. 'You're bloody liars!'

'Ah, come on, Devlin!' the first man said. 'You look after your patch and we'll look after ours. We got work to do.' With that all three rode off, leaving him even more confused.

Lita was waiting for him. 'I've had word that Pastor Godfrey will be here tomorrow, so that settles it. We'll have the funerals for Father and that other poor man in the morning. Mother's buried out there in the little cemetery too.'

'I didn't know that,' Mike said.

'Oh yes, she's there. We lived in a shack out here while the house was being built, but Mother died of malaria before it was finished.' She sighed. 'So I know every stick and stone of this place. It was my playhouse while it was going up. In fact the plantation was one big park for me to play in, in those days.'

'You weren't lonely?'

'No. There were plenty of black kids then. And I had my horses, and a menagerie of pets. You know it wasn't Father who ordered the blacks off Helenslea, it was my mother. Apparently he fancied the gins even while she was alive, so she lowered the boom on the lot. After her death he was so full of remorse he let the rule stand. Except for Dandy, the old hypocrite.' She took him through to the office again. 'I ought to pack up and leave here now, sell the place, but I can't seem to let go.'

'You don't have to decide right now. Give it time, Lita. This has all been a shock.'

'Yes. You're right.' She straightened up. 'I'm getting maudlin. And I have a God-awful hangover. I drank too much yesterday. I need a pick-me-up now. Have a brandy with me. Brandy and soda with limes is a good cure, I hope.'

'Sounds fine to me.' This wasn't the time to be quizzing her about her father's actions or to be worrying her with Dandy's reconstruction of the crimes. And there was nothing he could do about Joseph until the posses came in. Then he could talk to the sergeant and see about clearing the Kanaka. But if he was on the other side of the river, God help him. Mike was beginning to wonder if there was some way he could contact Joseph, bring him back . . .

'Here we are.' Lita came back with the tray of drinks. 'Lunch will be ready soon. I'm not hungry but I'm sure you are. Help yourself. I'm a bit hazy today, and I've only just remembered, there's a letter here that will interest you.'

'What is it?'

'A letter to my father from someone called Turtle.'

Mike took the page. 'It's not Turtle, it's Tuttle. Nipper Tuttle, a greasy little character who hangs about the wharves, generally up to no good.'

'Well, he's still at it,' Lita commented.

Mike began to read the note and sat back astonished. 'The little bastard, he's a go-between for blackbirders! And cripes, Lita, your father was in cahoots with them! I always figured he might be, but here's proof.'

'He wasn't the only one,' Lita said. 'Read the rest.'

Mike persevered with the childish scrawl, learning that a ship called *Java Lady* would heave to off Elbow Bay on the twentieth of February with a cargo of fifty fine Kanakas. It instructed Betts to be there with his partner, Mr Morgan . . .

'Morgan!' Mike yelped.

. . . to take delivery of the cargo as arranged with Captain King.

'Your mate King,' Mike said. 'He'd have to be mixed up in it somewhere.'

'Everyone has their foibles,' she said, refilling their glasses.

The letter went on to say that the master of the *Java Lady* would expect payment through J. King of five hundred pounds plus a landing fee of twenty pounds.

'Landing fee?' Mike spluttered. 'I can imagine your father paying that. Fat chance! When did this turn up?'

'Yesterday. I opened it. The twentieth is next Sunday, Mike. What happens now?'

'I'll tear a bloody slice off Morgan, that's what will happen. Providence has never dealt with blackbirders and we're not about to start now.'

'Obviously he has other ideas. You're not the boss, you only work for him. But if you're working for me, we could refuse to accept them and he'd be stuck with the lot.'

'It's not that simple. The *Java Lady* is a beat-up old schooner. It used to work the reefs for bêche-de-mer and was lucky to stay afloat then. Her master is the well-known Frenchy Duval who has spent more time in prison than out. He must have decided to cash in on this race for more Kanakas before time runs out, but if he's got them on board I pity them, they'll be packed in like sardines.'

'He must have got them as far as Trinity Bay to let the Turtle fellow know. Why didn't he just unload them there?'

'Because he's not registered to carry Kanakas, and it's my guess he'd be fined for carting so many on a ship that size. Not to mention the fact that the poor buggers were probably all kidnapped.'

'Edgar wasn't fussy,' she said bitterly.

'That's right. Edgar wasn't fussy, nor for that matter is Morgan. He's been whining for weeks about our declining workforce, and I guess he must have been buttering me up for the sudden influx of twenty-five more, out of nowhere. What the hell did he expect me to do? Believe his tale? Not listen to the Kanakas themselves when they come ashore? I've seen blackbirded Kanakas and they're bloody pitiful.'

'But they adjust,' she said quietly, 'if they don't die of yearning.'

He looked at her, surprised. 'I'm sorry, Lita. I didn't know you noticed.'

'Aren't you diplomatic, Mr Devlin? Don't you mean "cared"? I grew up with them. I was here. A lot of them were my own age, still in their teens. One is apt to align oneself more with one's contemporaries than with one's parents, don't you agree? I disliked my father.'

'I'm sorry to hear that,' he said.

'No you're not. You're still being polite. You're always so bloody polite! Is that your training as a bartender? Isn't that where you met Jake? In a bar while you were appeasing drunks, patronising them, putting up with their ravings like you're putting up with me now?' She spilled brandy as she tried to pour more drinks. 'Oh hell. You're the bartender. You fix them!'

Without a word he did just that, slicing the limes with care.

'So tell me, bartender,' she challenged, 'why am I mourning my bloody old man? Why am I so shattered that he has finally kicked the bucket? That a Kanaka finally got the old bastard?'

Lita took a Cuban cigar from Edgar's desk, cut it and lit it. Then, as an afterthought, she handed the box to Mike, who took one in silence.

She stood behind the high desk, leaning against it with her brandy and cigar as if she were at a bar, and for the first time Mike was able to see the resemblance between Lita and her mother from the portrait on the wall at the back. Except that her mother's creamy face and clear-cut features were framed in a cloud of black hair, while Lita's hair, as always, was plastered back into a thick roll.

'Who was your mother?' he asked her, and Lita turned to the portrait.

'A Miss Barnes,' she said. 'Born of the squatter clan based in New South Wales. How do you think Edgar got his start? Rich as sin that lot, but they disapproved of him. Not up to their social standing, you see. So he went after money to beat them at their own game, using every trick in the book. But you know about that, don't you? You didn't approve of him either.'

'Is that why you want a quiet funeral? You don't want her family here?'

'You're so bloody naive, Devlin! I don't want them *not* to come. I won't give them the opportunity to snub him again. Your lunch is ready.'

Because she expected him to, he pretended to enjoy his lunch, while his prickly hostess, pouring glass after glass of claret from a silver-encased decanter, fluctuated between being angry and upset at her father's death. As he listened to her he wondered about her description of himself. Was that how people saw him? As a weak-willed, agreeable yes man? A typical bartender. Was he? When he was working with Jake it hadn't seemed to matter. They had an agreeable relationship. With Morgan . . . well, he'd bucked a few times but on the whole he'd been bending over backwards to keep the peace.

Why? he asked himself.

Because I love Providence. Jake and I put it on the map.

'Not true,' an inner voice replied. An inquisitorial voice, not unlike

Lita's sharp jabs. 'Providence has been slipping away from you. It belongs to Morgan, not you. It's not the same any more. You wouldn't care if you did have to leave, that's why you gave notice. But why didn't you quit then and there? You're still hanging about to please . . . who?'

Mike knew he felt protective towards Mrs Morgan. Protective, that was all. Such a lovely woman. With a rogue husband who was sleeping with her sister. Common knowledge on Providence now, confirmed by Elly and Hanna. The bastard! Mrs Morgan . . . Jessie . . . she didn't deserve to be treated like that. Jessie was everything he'd ever dreamed of in a woman. He often dreamed of her. Sweet, serene, intelligent and softly beautiful. A woman devoid of deceit. Who would never look at him because she was the sort of wife every man wanted.

Mike had been in love with her from the first day he'd seen her on the wharf. At least, he consoled himself, his instincts were in good working order. And sharp-eyed Lita, though fortunately no one else, had become aware of it. Thank God Jessie didn't know. She'd be so embarrassed.

'Darling,' Lita said. 'You're cross with me now. I didn't mean what I said. You're my best friend in the whole world. Tell me you forgive me.'

'There's nothing to forgive,' he said, trying to lift himself from despondency. 'But I have to get going.'

'Why do you have to go? They'll all be back soon. McMullen, Teffler, the police. God, I hope they don't find Joseph. They're so bloody gung-ho, those men. It'll be better if he just disappears.'

Mike was alert. 'I thought you wanted them to catch him.'

'So I did,' she admitted miserably. 'But it doesn't seem to matter any more. I think I'm getting tipsy again.'

'It matters,' he said. 'There's no evidence that he killed anyone.'

'Good. You tell them that. And what will you do about the Kanakas at Elbow Bay?'

'I don't know. If I tell the police, Morgan will be in trouble.'

'So?' she replied. 'Mike, I think I ought to have a siesta, it's so damned hot and muggy. But don't go. Stay over tonight.'

'Lita, I'm sorry, I can't. The Kanakas back home are jumpy, and Morgan is likely to make things worse. I'll be back here first thing in the morning, though. Right now I have to watch out for that posse and call them off. Do I have your authority to tell your staff that the search is off?'

'By all means, I hope you're right about Joseph. He did seem such a nice fellow. Now, if you change your mind and stay . . .' She kissed him on the cheek and drifted out of the room. Still, he thought, in her haze. But knowing Lita, she'd snap out of it soon and have them all jumping to attention around here. Lita de Flores would do just as well as her father as boss of Helenslea if she put her mind to it.

He spent an hour looking over a section of Helenslea where ratoon crops were growing. He studied the new shoots of cane, pleased to see that they were strong and healthy; blights of any kind could spread.

202

Then he met up with Sergeant McBride and McMullen, leading a despondent group of riders.

'No sign of him,' McBride said to Mike.

'You won't find him,' Mike told them. 'The blacks say he's crossed the river.'

They took it for granted that the Providence Aborigines had given Mike that information, so he didn't mention Dandy.

'We ought to go after him,' McMullen said.

'No. Mrs de Flores has called off the search. She wants Helenslea settled down as soon as possible. The funeral is tomorrow.'

'How can it be tomorrow?' McMullen argued. 'That doesn't give anyone time to get here.'

'Her father is dead,' Mike told him, 'and she wants to mourn him in her own way without crowds herding about. The pastor will be here in the morning, so he can set the time. Let all the men know, and the Kanakas can attend, that's enough.' To please McMullen, he added: 'Your wife might like to take part in the service. She could have a word with the pastor. Maybe read a prayer or something.'

'Yeah. I'll tell her,' McMullen said, then turned to dismiss the men.

'One more thing,' Mike said to McBride. 'I'm not convinced that Joseph had anything to do with killing the guard.'

'Like hell he didn't!' McMullen snapped, turning back.

'Hang on,' Mike said. 'Lennie Field was the guard, and he was armed, keeping Joseph in. There were two Kanakas outside. They had to attack him to get Joseph out. But Lennie was a big bloke. If two men jumped him he could lose the rifle but he'd fight. You found one Kanaka dead. I reckon Lennie killed Ned in the fight but he couldn't handle the second bloke, Paka, who finished him off. He had to kill the guard so that he could let Joseph out. And you all saw Paka shoot Edgar Betts. Joseph wasn't there. He'd split.'

'That sounds reasonable,' McBride said, 'but he's still an escapee, not only from the plantation but from the lockup.'

'And that brings me to my next question. Why was he in the lockup? I've heard talk since I've been here about a hanging.' Mike confronted McMullen. 'Did Betts intend to hang Joseph?'

'Not as far as I know,' McMullen replied sourly.

'I think you do know,' Mike said.

'What's it matter now?'

McBride intervened. 'I haven't heard anything about this. Jesus, if any of your blokes were up to that business again, McMullen, with or without Betts, they're bloody liable to prosecution too.'

'No one got hanged,' McMullen said, 'so let's have an end to it. If Devlin's right, all we've got now is a bolting Kanaka, and he's not one of ours. If you want him back, Devlin, you go after him. Me, I'm sick of chasing about the bush.'

'What if you'd found him, though?' Mike asked. 'An innocent man in the hands of a posse? What chance would he have had?'

203

'That's only guesswork, and we didn't find him, Devlin, so quit making such a song and dance. It's only a bloody Kanaka.' McMullen snapped the reins and his horse whirled about to canter down the track towards the stables.

'You're putting me to shame,' McBride said. 'There was such a hue and cry on about the killings and the escaped Kanaka that I didn't take the time to think it through. I thought I'd get the facts from Joseph himself when we caught up with him. Although it did sound pretty clear cut, from what I was told.'

'But they didn't mention the hanging?'

'No. And if I were you I'd shut up about it too.'

'But don't you see? That's why Ned and Paka had to get Joseph out.'

'No reason to murder two men, including their master,' McBride said.

'No, of course not. But why hang the man? What the hell did he do?'

'By God, you're a ferret! Tell you what I'll do. I'll write your man Joseph up as a bolter, that's all. McMullen's right. Make an end to it.'

'Ah no. He's one of my men. Before I take him back I have to know what he did to warrant the noose.'

'And these men want to keep their jobs. Edgar might have been rough on the islanders but he looked after white men. Helenslea is big enough to keep the mill hands on too, when the season ends. And they're building married quarters here now, you know that. The work here isn't seasonal any more, it's steady. The last thing they want to do is aggravate Lita.'

'By talking about a hanging that didn't happen? Why would that upset her?'

'Maybe you can ask her one day,' McBride said. 'I'm damn sure I won't. Now, if you're through?'

'No. One more thing.' Mike explained to McBride what the Professor had done in keeping quiet about Perry's murderer, and the police sergeant laughed. 'Poor old bloke. He's probably right, trying to keep the Kanakas on the straight and narrow, but that's not our problem. I'll lift the ban.'

'I already have,' Mike said. He still had the letter from Nipper Tuttle in his pocket, but decided not to say anything to McBride until he had talked to Corby Morgan.

'Are you staying for the funeral?' he asked McBride.

'Yes. I might as well.'

'Good. I'll see you then. I have to get back. It's no joke trying to explain to my lot that two of their mates are dead and a favourite son, our Joseph, is missing.'

'Yeah? Well, just let them know what happens to Kanakas who attack white men.'

'It's not that simple,' Mike said. None of it was bloody simple, he repeated to himself on the long ride back to Providence. And what would make Edgar mad enough to want to hang a Kanaka? Especially a

204

type like Joseph who didn't even look like a villain. Some of them could be mean as snakes, but not Joseph; he was a fine-looking fellow with a handsome, open face . . .

Lita? The thought jolted him. Had she noticed that? Taken special note of Joseph? Infuriating Edgar? Dandy had more or less said that Lita was involved. That's what McBride wouldn't ask, and the men wouldn't discuss. It could be the answer. I'm not going to ask either, Mike decided. Imagine . . . Excuse me, Lita, but what did you get up to that made your father so angry and resulted in his death? He shuddered. Forget it, Devlin.

Elly was waiting for him at the stables. 'You find Joseph?'

She seemed to have aged years in the last few days. Her eyes were red-rimmed and her face drawn with worry. Mike tried to console her. 'No, he's still missing, but don't worry. They're not looking for him any more. The policeman knows he didn't kill anyone.'

'Stupid polis,' she said fiercely. 'They kill Joseph, I kill them.'

Mike laughed. 'Come on now. Settle down. It's not that bad.'

'You'n me, Mike, we go find him, eh?'

He couldn't tell her that Joseph had crossed the river; she was likely to go after him. 'We can't do that,' he explained. 'Joseph has gone long ways. When I get time I'll bring him back and tell him all is forgiven.' He teased her. 'Maybe you want to marry him then, eh?'

That cheered her. 'You fix that with Joseph? You tell him he needs a good wife.' She clutched his arm. 'And you make Broula say yes too.' It was a tall order all round, but he agreed. If Joseph came back, if he could make Broula agree to the marriage of her daughter to a despised Kanaka, and if the proposed groom were willing, then a wedding on the plantation, with its attendant celebrations, would be the very thing to take everyone's minds from their worries.

Elly walked with him back to the house. 'Trouble in there,' she said loftily, now that her own future was looking brighter. 'Missus doan like being number two wife any more. She plenty mad, then she cry. She tell boss Morgan she quit.'

They were in sight of the house now, and Mike pulled her back. 'What's all this?'

'She did. True. She says she takem baby and goin'. Boss Morgan, he says she not goin' no place.' Elly looked at him curiously. 'Where her tribe, Mike?'

Her question saddened him. How easy it was for white people, himself included, to forget that the Ellys of this world were only a jump away from their tribal state, as were the Kanakas. And to forget to give them the encouragement they deserved for making such a difficult transition. He answered her seriously, with respect. 'The rest of Mrs Morgan's family live a long, long way over the sea, in a very different land. Cold country. Now you run along, I have to see the boss.'

205

He would prefer not to see the boss with that sort of row going on in the house, but it was necessary.

Morgan was settled on the veranda, as usual in the early evening, and Sylvia was with him, but there was no sign of Jessie.

'There you are,' Morgan called jovially. 'I was considering sending out a search party. Help yourself to a drink. You'll be relieved to know the roof didn't fall in here today. I let them have their day off. Had Pompey translate for me to get through to the dunderheads.'

Mike poured himself a stiff whisky and leaned against the veranda rail, making no comment, as Morgan rattled on. 'I gave them a real fire-and-brimstone missionary speech. What they needed.'

Sylvia giggled. 'Corby's been telling me. He really read them the riot act. I think you were overreacting, Mr Devlin. They're as quiet as mice.'

'Oh yes,' Mike said. Noncommittal.

'I told them Paka and Ned had already been buried, so that was that. Shamed them that two more of their mob should commit such dastardly acts. Told them they'd have to work hard now to regain their good reputation which has been ruined by savagery, which can't be countenanced.' As Corby continued his resumé of the sermon, Mike wondered what Pompey would have made of words like 'countenanced', if he had bothered to translate correctly at all. Pompey could be a tricky customer.

'What news of Helenslea?' Sylvia asked. 'How is poor Lita?'

'Lita's fine.'

'Sober?' Morgan asked.

'As a judge,' Mike lied sternly.

'When's the funeral?' Sylvia wanted to know.

'Tomorrow.'

'So soon?' she gasped. 'I don't know if I have a black dress ready. I heard what the women here do. When there's a funeral, if they don't own the funereal black, they simply dye a dress. What a waste of good clothes!'

'There's no need,' Mike told her. 'Mrs de Flores has requested a private funeral, she doesn't want any outsiders.'

Sylvia was insulted. 'I'm not an outsider! Lita is my friend. Of course we must go, Corby.'

'What's the point?' he drawled. 'If she wants to put Betts down with only the hired help for company, then so be it. We'd be out of place. I presume you're invited, Devlin?'

The studied snub was not lost on Mike, who didn't react. He had a better card to play yet. 'Yes. I've known Lita for a long time. She took it for granted I'd walk with her.'

'Oh pooh!' Sylvia said. 'Even a funeral is a good excuse for a day out here. I think she's being quite unfair to Mr Betts. He was just the type to be thrilled by a big turnout.'

'I spoke to Sergeant McBride,' Mike said to Corby. 'There are no

206

charges to be laid against Joseph, except as an absconder.' He made no mention of Dandy or of his own part in the decision. 'They've proved now that he took no part in the murders. The other two attacked the guard and killed Edgar. Apparently they let Joseph out and he bolted. They've called off the search for him.'

'Just as well,' Morgan said. 'Let him go. We don't want him back here.'

'But if he's innocent . . .' Mike began.

'He's guilty of some bloody thing or he wouldn't have been in that lockup in the first place,' Corby retorted.

Ominously, Mike saw himself now in the same category as the Helenslea men, by not challenging that statement. By not wanting to discuss why Joseph had been imprisoned. But they were worrying about their jobs. What did he have to worry about?

Lita. He was protecting Lita now, he knew that. At the expense of Joseph? Or was it? Lita was comfortable with men and she was kind to Kanakas. Had Joseph misunderstood her intentions and made a move on her? Assaulted her? But Lita was candour personified. Surely she would have said something.

'Mr Morgan. Before I go, could I have a word with you in private?'

'In private?' Corby laughed. 'I doubt that any place could be more private than Providence.'

'You don't have to worry about me,' Sylvia tinkled. Interested.

Mike shrugged. 'Very well. It's about the Kanakas you ordered through Captain King. They'll be at Elbow Bay on the *Java Lady* next Sunday.'

Corby sat up. 'By Jove! He did it!' he said enthusiastically. 'I wasn't sure he could pull it off.'

'He has. And you're in a heap of trouble.'

'Why? How do you know this?'

'Betts had a letter from a crook called Tuttle, but he didn't live to read it. The letter says that you and Betts are to take delivery of fifty Kanakas on Sunday. With Betts dead, you'll be expected to take the lot.'

'How much?'

'Ten pounds a head plus landing fees. Five hundred and twenty quid.'

'That's ridiculous. I didn't expect to outlay that much.'

Mike couldn't figure out whether Morgan was a crook or a fool, or both. 'Well, you're in a spot. If you pick them up you're liable for arrest. If you don't, the natives will suffer.'

'I said I'd take half, and that I will. What they do with the rest is not my problem. They can sell them to Mrs de Flores.'

'She doesn't want any part of it.'

'Well then, neither do I,' Corby said. 'Forget the whole thing. I haven't seen any letter. It's nothing to do with me. Just a damn pity to lose them.'

'Mr Morgan,' Mike said, 'do you have any idea what state those poor natives will be in by the time the blackbirders dump them ashore? They'll be sick and near to starving. If they're not sold, they'll be dragged back aboard until a market can be found for them.'

'That shouldn't be difficult.'

'When the ship can't pull into port? Communication with the coast is made through other ships. The *Java Lady* will be running short of provisions by now. Finding another buyer will be difficult at this stage, it will take time. Rather than be caught by navy patrols with a hold full of kidnapped natives, blackbirders have been known to throw them overboard.'

Corby shot to his feet. 'Get out! I don't have to listen to your woeful tales. I didn't invent blackbirding.'

'No, but you are willing to be part of it.'

'Get out, I said.'

Mike confronted him. 'I'll go when I'm good and ready. And if you don't listen to me, McBride will. I'm giving you the chance to sort this out legally.'

Ignoring Morgan's protests, Mike outlined his plan. 'Troopers and the police will meet the blackbirders. They'll be arrested and the Kanakas taken into custody.'

'You're trying to get me arrested, you bastard!'

'No. I'll tell McBride it was a deal organised by Betts.'

'In which case it's nothing to do with me.'

'You don't get off that easy. We'll bring the Kanakas here, and quarter and feed them until we work out what to do with them. Some of them might want to stay once they're here, in which case if you pay their immigration and indenture fees you've got yourself more labourers. The Government will deport the Kanakas who don't want to stay, and at least the poor blokes will get home in one piece.'

'What if they all want to go? This will cost me more than they're worth. And since when are you the law around here?'

'It's my law or McBride's. If I show him that letter you'll be on your way to Cairns to face charges.'

Corby paced along the veranda. 'Give me the letter.'

'Oh no,' Mike lied, enjoying himself. 'It's still at Helenslea. Lita has it.'

'Then let Lita take them. Blame it all on Betts. Leave me out of it.' He turned back. 'If you're doing this just to keep your job, Devlin, then I'll admit I've been rather hasty. And now I come to think of it, I appreciate that you haven't shown that letter to the sergeant. You can have your job back.'

'I'll think about it,' Mike said. 'But I'm not doing it for you. Blackbirding is a filthy trade. The Kanakas are your responsibility.'

'Spare me the lecture, man. Maybe I will get more staff out of this mess. At least I won't have to pay the captain the landing fees. That's a saving.'

'I thought you'd see sense,' Mike said grimly.

'I think it's all very exciting,' Sylvia said.

As soon as he arrived at Helenslea, Mike informed the sergeant that he'd got wind of the blackbirding operation organised by Betts. He left Morgan's name out of it.

'The old villain,' McBride said. 'And I suppose you won't tell me the source of this information. Not that it makes any difference. Sunday, you say? We'll have to move fast. By God, to catch Frenchy Duval! That'll be a feather in my cap.'

'Mr Morgan has agreed to take in the Kanakas until we can question them and find out who they are.'

'Damned good of him. That makes life easier for me. I wouldn't want to put them back on the ship, too risky. And it's a long trek for them back to Cairns. I'll send for some mounted troopers right away. You and Mr Morgan, you want to be in on it?'

'We wouldn't miss it for quids,' Mike grinned.

The funeral was a strange affair. Beyond insisting on the private burial, Lita had allowed Mrs McMullen to take charge of proceedings. Whether or not she regretted that decision, Mike couldn't tell, her face remained impassive behind the dark veil. But for his part, in deference to her, there were times when he had trouble stifling laughter.

After he left McBride he went up to the house to be met by the manager's wife. 'Why! Mr Devlin! Don't you look smart,' she said, adopting a formal patronising tone. 'I said to my Alf he should have city clothes too, but not him. Said he'd never get to wear them, and then along comes a day like this and it's too late. Just like a man. He's sorry now, but I suppose it doesn't matter today with no one given the chance to get here. She's really kept the lid on things.'

'Where's Mrs de Flores?'

'In the parlour. That woman Dandy is in there with her. All dressed up she is too – do you think you can get rid of her? I'm petrified she'll come to the service and embarrass everyone.'

'Who's everyone?' he asked stiffly.

'Well, you know, people will talk, and I've gone to so much trouble to make this a fitting farewell for Mr Betts. It isn't easy arranging two funerals at once. There's protocol to be preserved.'

Mike grinned. 'I'm sure you'll preserve it all quite well.' He sidestepped her and made for the parlour.

Lita looked stunning in a formal black dress, the tight bodice trimmed with fine jet beads and the skirt swept from the front into an elegant bustle. A very large hat, the crown ruched in black satin, balanced the outfit and gave her an imperious air as she stood, head erect, at the far end of the room.

The pastor was talking, shaking hands. Dandy gave him a wan smile. He glanced over at Lita and she nodded, as if his presence were acceptable, and then removed her gaze. She was so cool and remote

Mike felt rebuffed. This wasn't the Lita he knew. This elegant woman was the European version. Mrs de Flores, late of that high society.

'Sherry or tea?' Pastor Godfrey asked him.

'Neither, thanks.' Mike had never tasted sherry in his life.

'I can recommend the sherry,' the pastor urged.

'Righto.' He took the small crystal glass. Lita said nothing. She was deliberately setting herself apart from them. Diamond rings flashed on her fingers as she reached for her gloves, and emerald earrings gleamed under the sweep of her hair. Mike suddenly felt like a country bumpkin in her stylish company, and he was relieved when Mrs McMullen blundered in, trying to look sad. 'Come along now, it's time. Ah, Mrs de Flores, you do look pretty.'

Lita's glance as she dropped the veil over her face would have frozen a forest fire, but the McMullen woman was impervious to any subtleties, too busy with her protocol.

The undertaker from Cairns had done his best. His plumed horses led the rumbling wagon carrying Edgar in his ornate casket, which was covered by showers of frangipani blooms and a lei of purple orchids.

Pastor Godfrey followed, reading from his Bible and glancing skywards every so often as if entreating on Betts's behalf for the rain to hold off.

Lita, imprisoned between her manager and his wife, strode doggedly behind the pastor, so Mike took Dandy's arm to follow them with the police sergeant and the nine or ten white staff of the plantation.

Hearing a crunch behind him, Mike turned back to see a horse draped in black, carting a dray on which rested a cheap coffin. 'Good God,' he muttered to McBride. 'Lennie's bringing up the rear.'

'Poor Lennie,' McBride replied. 'He's still an also-ran.'

Behind Lennie's makeshift hearse came the large Kanaka workforce, swaying happily along, dressed in their Sunday best – oddments of menswear and colourful sarongs.

They all filed up to the cemetery on the hill to bury Edgar beside the plain headstone of Lita's mother, and when the pastor had said his piece and given the blessings he announced that Mrs McMullen would read the chosen text.

She bustled forward, smiling at the pastor in this her moment of glory, then slipped in the mud and fell into the dirt piled up beside the grave. The pastor scrambled to help her up, and finally she was on her feet, her skirt caked from the knees down and her muddy hands grasping a Bible. It took some time to find the page, but she announced one of the Psalms and began to read something about wealth and riches and righteousness, stumbling over the words as she scanned the grimy page.

When at last she had finished she announced that they would sing the hymn 'Amazing Grace', after which the Kanakas would 'give us a rendition of one of their hymns'.

The company managed to get through 'Amazing Grace' and then the

Kanakas burst into song, a full-throated, tub-thumping spiritual, full of vitality and fun. Hands clapped beating time, and Mike had to stop his toe tapping, remembering his place.

McBride nudged him. 'I don't think this was on the programme, somehow.'

Before they were finished the mistress of ceremonies was beckoning everyone to come along to the other grave for the second burial. Lita moved forward, her face impassive.

Back at the house, food and drinks were set out on tables in the courtyard for the guests and white staff, and Lita walked among them, thanking them solemnly, even Mike. Then she left the gathering with the pastor, issuing no invitations to anyone else to join them inside the house.

Mike stayed for a while; he was hungry and the spread had been worth waiting for. He made arrangements with McBride for their Sunday expedition to catch the blackbirder, and talked briefly to some of the men, then decided to leave. If Lita chose to ignore him, not needing his company now, then so be it. He was damned if he'd push in where he wasn't wanted, especially since she was playing the great lady today. He downed another whisky before slipping quietly away to ride home, alone and angry.

When he reached Providence, he found he wasn't the only one in a temper. Morgan was in a fury. He stormed outside when he saw Mike riding towards the stables. 'Those useless damn wretches,' he shouted. 'They haven't done a tap of work all day. They've sat on their bums at the long-house the whole bloody day, refusing to move. This is your fault. You said they could have two days' holiday and no matter what I say they're taking them.'

'It's worth it,' Mike said. 'Tomorrow will be the test.'

'What test?'

'They seem to be very concerned about Joseph.'

'Rot. Another excuse to slack. I won't have it, do you hear me?'

'Yes,' Mike said. He was disappointed with Lita and sick of Morgan's nagging. He should have detoured away from the house and gone straight up to his own place. It was so peaceful up there, he wished he could lock himself in for a week. Which reminded him. Some news for Morgan.

'McBride and some troopers will assemble here tomorrow. We're making Providence the rendezvous spot.'

'Why?'

'Have you forgotten? We're going after the blackbirders on Sunday morning.'

'Not me,' Corby said. 'McBride surely doesn't expect me to be part of this?'

'Yes he does. He's relying on us. We're to come armed.'

Corby's face was white. 'Could this be dangerous?'

'Hell, no,' Mike said.

211

As he climbed the steps to his high house he laughed, feeling a little better now with the prospect of some excitement on Sunday. 'Of course it won't be dangerous,' he said to himself. 'What's dangerous about trying to ambush a crew of desperate seamen and round up wild Kanakas at the same time?' He doubted if they'd be able to grab the wily Frenchy Duval, but they should be able to separate him from his catch, the kidnapped islanders.

When he came to thinking about it, Corby too decided that this expedition could be interesting. Better than the hunt, with real people as the quarry. Something to write home about this time.

He was cleaning his rifle and revolver when Jessie approached. 'I'd like a word with you, Corby. You seem to be avoiding me.'

'Of course I'm avoiding you,' he sighed. 'All I ever hear from you are complaints and ultimatums. What's the latest now that you've run me to ground?'

'Why the sudden interest in these guns?' she asked. 'What's happened now?'

'Nothing yet. On Sunday I'm joining with the police and troopers to catch a gang of pirates at Elbow Bay. McBride and the troopers will be here tomorrow. I've told Sylvia the police sergeant can be billeted with Devlin again. The troopers can stay in the two guest rooms next to your father and use Perry's hut too. Depends on how many turn up. Devlin thinks about six in all. He's arranging for the Kanaka women to feed them.'

'Thank you,' she said, and retreated. Sylvia again. Sylvia doing the organising. Very well, let her. Jessie had wondered what she was up to, fussing about the linen press with Mae.

She went back to her desk. She had enough to do here. She wanted to bring all the books up to date, the cane journals, the pay books . . . It was time to give the labourers their monthly pay of a few shillings each, to check the stores and balance the ledgers. Although Corby wouldn't tell her exactly how much was in the bank, she had a pretty good idea. They received indelible copies from the mill manager of the amount of sugar realised from their cane, and she'd seen most of them. Providence had sold more than two hundred tons of cane, at prices varying from thirty to thirty-five pounds a ton. And they had earned at least two hundred and ten pounds from the sale of molasses.

Jessie studied the invoices she'd listed under maintenance. Bills for fencing timbers, casks for the molasses, stumps and shingles for the new huts that were needed, jute bags, lime, harrows, a new plough, and so on. But the maize was turning into a good paying crop, and they were growing far more than they needed. A bonus here. And what with their own cattle and dairy herd, and vegetables and fruit grown by Mae and the Kanakas, the plantation was practically self-supporting. 'We could do a lot better, though,' she said to herself. 'We should have more crops to keep up a steady income, there's plenty of room for cane and crops.'

As it was, she knew Corby was busy ordering more land to be cleared as soon as possible as insurance against the rainy day when Kanakas were in short supply.

'Well, Jessie,' she said at last, 'we're not making millions but we're well on the way, if we expand, to making a very good living. What a pity you won't be here to see it.'

Chapter Eleven

Saturday morning was no different from any other over the last few months. The night had been hot, with more storms rolling restlessly in from the coast. Mike spared a thought for the *Java Lady* bucketing about there in heavy seas, and for her unwilling passengers, shut down in the hold.

He pulled on his boots and walked out into the grey and misty dawn to whistle up his horse from the small corral. He'd taken his job back, and got a rise out of Morgan at the same time, but what had that achieved? Status quo. Nothing had improved, nor was it likely to. And it was time he stopped mooning about Mrs Morgan. About Jessie. 'You're getting as bad as Elly,' he grinned to himself. Jessie had her own troubles, but she never spoke of them. She only talked to him about the plantation, and although he enjoyed her company he couldn't claim they were intimate in any way. On the other hand, that little rogue of a Sylvia was always flirting with him, especially when Morgan was around, which didn't endear him to the boss either.

'I ought to take that job with Lita and be done with it,' he reflected. 'A much bigger job and better pay.' But her coldness yesterday could spell a change of heart. He might have missed his chance there.

Pompey was waiting for him. 'No go, boss. Malaita men won't work. Other blokes comen out but not them fellers.'

'Oh Christ,' Mike said. 'What a way to start the day. What do they want now? They had their two days off, and the funeral feast. They didn't want me to dig up the bodies of Paka and Ned for fear of bad joss. What else can I do?'

The answer was not unexpected.

'Find Joseph,' Pompey said.

At the long-house, some of the Kanakas were mustering for breakfast. 'You get this lot moving,' Mike said to Pompey. 'I'll shift the others.'

The barracks was a conglomeration of huts, open thatched sleeping pavilions and humpies, since many of the islanders preferred to make their own sleeping arrangements. Usually at this time the area was busy, with good workers on the move and the less enthusiastic straggling about among the trees, but today Mike was met with a sit-down. They were squatting everywhere, dark faces grim, and he guessed this was the same scene that had confronted Morgan yesterday, forcing him to retreat.

He hitched his horse to a tree and strode into the untidy compound littered with debris, tins and old scraps of furniture. Mrs Morgan had complained about this. 'The place looks like a rubbish dump,' she'd said. 'Can't we clean it up?'

'It'd be just as bad again in a couple of days,' he'd told her. 'And it's hard to tell what's garbage and what's treasure. They're scavengers, they prize ownership. The busted chairs, that ratty old horsehair sofa, the rusty horse trough – they're all owned by someone. Kudos,' he'd added with a smile.

But he wasn't smiling now as he took a stand by a battered wagon wheel: 'Righto, you blokes,' he yelled, feigning confidence. 'Chop chop! Time to go!'

As he expected, no one moved, but they were listening. 'Hey, Sal,' he continued. 'You hear this. The police say that Joseph is innocent. Not a bad fellow. Joseph done no killem finish.'

Sal came out of his hut with a grey blanket about his shoulders, looking as bleak as the colourless morn. 'Joseph free?' he asked.

'Yes.' Mike decided to leave the charge of absconding for another time.

An old hand, called Charlie, rose to his feet and walked over to Mike. 'Where is Joseph?'

'I wish I knew,' Mike replied.

Charlie spat at his feet. 'You lie. Whitemen chase Joseph so he cross that damn river. He is in the land of the evil ones.'

'Oh hell!' Mike said under his breath. He might have known the bush telegraph between the natives on both plantations would be working overtime. 'What lie?' he demanded. 'You show me where he is and I'll call him.' He grabbed Charlie by the arm. 'Come on. If you're so bloody smart, you show me.'

The islander wrenched free. 'I can't, I don't know.'

'What did I say then? Didn't I say I wish I knew? It's a big country not some ratty island.' He shoved the Kanaka away. 'You stop stirring or you'll find we've got a lockup too.' Such as it was. They usually locked miscreants and drunks in the harness shed for a day if they were a problem, but it wasn't secure.

Sal intervened. 'Bring Joseph back,' he said flatly.

'How can I bring him back? I told you I wouldn't know where to look.' Apart from which, he said to himself, I haven't got time to take a boat out on the river and sail up and down yelling for a bloody Kanaka, no matter who he is.

He appealed to them to go back to work. He told them that Joseph would find his own way home. And he was tempted, as his anger grew, to shout at them, to demand to know what made Joseph so different from other absconders. They'd never before gone on strike on anyone's behalf. Over the years at least a dozen South Sea Islanders, to give them their official title, had bolted from Providence. Some had been caught, punished and returned. Others, smarter, with a fair command of

215

English, had got as far as Brisbane, where southern planters snapped them up for higher pay, and the authorities allowed them to stay. They joined the growing list of Kanakas who had served their time and slipped the noose of indenture. Men who had drifted into the mainstream and were hired eagerly not only by cane- and cotton-growers but by farmers.

Could Joseph achieve that status? Later, possibly, but right now he was too new. It took a long while for islanders to grasp the scale of the geography of the country, and besides, he was going in the wrong direction, looking at jungle-clad mountains and beyond them endless plains that were being claimed by cattle men. No. Joseph would either have to try to survive in Irukandji country or come back towards the coast.

'There's nothing any of us can do about Joseph,' he shouted. And what's more, he added to himself, Joseph is finished at Providence. I wouldn't touch the bugger again with a forty-foot pole. He's too disruptive. I can't have these clowns going on strike every time someone breathes on their favourite son, damn them.

'So much for your leadership,' a voice said behind him. Corby Morgan, a dark, imposing figure in his leather hat and black raincoat, was sitting astride his horse, watching the proceedings. He pushed his mount forward. 'Who's the head man here?'

'Sal, I suppose,' Mike said.

Morgan pointed with his riding whip. 'You! You're Sal?'

'Yes, master,' Sal admitted, not enjoying his role.

'Right then,' Morgan said, levelling his revolver at him. 'Tell these men to get back to work. There's no excuse for this mutiny. If they don't get off their bums, you're under arrest.'

Sal wilted. In his own language he shouted instructions.

There were muttered exchanges, and Mike, with no choice now but to back the boss, also took out his handgun and loaded it. But still no one moved.

'Tell them,' Morgan shouted, 'that police and troopers will be here this morning. Mounted troopers. And they don't take any bloody nonsense. If you persist in sitting here you are breaking the law!'

The men who understood him began to get to their feet while Sal continued frantically translating, as fast as he could because Morgan kept bellowing at them: 'Troopers will not be as kind as me,' he threatened. 'Anyone who wants to test their guns can sit here and wait.'

With his foot he shoved Sal on his way, then rode among the huts lashing at the bare shoulders of men who didn't move quickly enough. Before long they were all trooping across the home paddock to the long-house.

'Do you think you can take over from here?' he asked Mike.

'No,' Mike said angrily. The bastards, they'd made a bloody fool out of him. Score one up to the boss. But it wasn't over yet. 'They'll take some watching today,' he said. 'I can't be everywhere.'

216

'Get them out then,' Morgan retorted. 'I'll be back as soon as I've had breakfast.'

Even with Mike and the master riding among the gangs, brandishing their whips, the Malaita men worked at a snail's pace, frustrating the bosses and the other islanders until fights broke out between the workers.

Corby raged. No sooner did he put a stop to one fight than another would start somewhere else, and he was tiring, rushing about playing rough-house referee between the two groups of natives. He rode on to the big fenced paddock where ploughing and planting was supposed to be in progress. Instead the plough was overturned and a mob of Kanakas were gathered, arguing furiously.

He leapt from his horse and tramped over to them. 'Get back to work!' he shouted.

'This feller and his mates bugger up,' one of the men called to him, resentful of the trouble the Malaita men were causing.

Corby recognised the culprit as the one called Charlie who'd challenged Devlin earlier. Fed up, he charged over and punched Charlie on the jaw, sending him flying. Apart from skinning his knuckles on a jaw that had felt like a block of granite, Corby was pleased with himself. He'd not had any experience with fisticuffs since leaving school, but he'd just packed quite a wallop. 'Get up!' he shouted at Charlie, ready to go a round with him. 'You're brave enough when my back's turned, let's see how you are man to man!'

But Charlie wasn't having any, and, noticing for the first time the Kanaka's broad shoulders and muscular frame, Corby thought it was just as well.

'Grab him,' he ordered two men, who were happy to oblige. 'Find some rope and tie him up. He's under arrest.'

This didn't suit Charlie's friends, who plunged into the argument, shouting at Corby, shouting at the other islanders, moving forward to protect Charlie. Men came running from the other side of the fence and soon there was a full-scale brawl of about thirty Kanakas in the muddy paddock.

Corby was shouldered aside. He stumbled on the uneven ground, dodging sweaty bodies and flailing fists as he fumbled for his revolver, retreating until he was far enough away to draw his gun and fire two shots.

There was a sudden halt. As he reloaded, they seemed to be unreal figures, like a frieze of a muddied battlefield, and he used the seconds to take control. He closed in on them, searching for Charlie, who was looking worse than the rest, blood dripping from his nose. 'Get out here right now,' he shouted, 'or I'll put a bullet in you.'

With the gun only inches from his bare chest, Charlie threw his hands up and Corby drew him out of the scrum.

'Don't shoot, master,' the islander cried.

Corby grabbed him, twisted him around and put the gun to his head.

217

'I'll count to ten,' he roared, 'and if you're not all back at work by then I'll shoot this mongrel dead.' And he meant it. If this were the only way to restore order then he'd have to shoot, he'd be within his rights. He began to count. Some of the men, obviously not from the island of Malaita, were grinning hopefully as they retreated. The others, petrified, began to run for their lives, or for Charlie's. It didn't matter to Corby, just so long as they got the message.

Pushing Charlie ahead of him, he spotted the man who'd made the original complaint. 'What's your name?'

'Billy, master.'

'Right, Billy. You get another bloke and tie this one up.'

Billy ran to the dray loaded with cane setts and hurried back with ropes to hobble Charlie and tie his hands behind his back.

'Good,' Corby said. 'Now, Billy. You run out and tell them I want this paddock finished today. No tucker for anyone until it does get finished. And if anyone else plays up you come find me and give me their names. Understand?'

'Yes, master,' Billy said. 'Bloody mad them blokes. Joseph, he no god, he just another Kanaka.'

Billy had sped away before Corby, in all the excitement, had time to fully grasp what he said, but he had heard the name Joseph, and as he led his prisoner over to where his horse was waiting and pushed him through the two-rail fence, he questioned Charlie, trying to find an explanation for this madness.

'What is this nonsense about Joseph?' he demanded. 'The man has gone. Can't you understand that? You're not helping him by causing all this trouble. But by God, if he's the cause . . .'

Charlie's eyes rolled in fear. 'Not Joseph, master. Ratasali! He come again, same he come to Katabeti. He come in the night with big thunder.' The man's knees were trembling and he leant on the fence for support. 'He put spell on Ned and Paka too. You know that.'

'I don't know any such bloody thing. Who is Ratasali? I'll have his hide, and yours too before I'm finished.'

But Charlie had said enough. His head drooped and he refused to answer any more questions, remaining passive as Corby led him away. It was a nuisance to have to take the prisoner in himself but it was better than taking any more workers off the job, so Corby hitched his prisoner to his saddle and headed up the track, soon to be met by Devlin.

'I heard shots,' he said. 'What happened?'

'A bloody brawl,' Corby told him. 'And this character started it. Lock him up somewhere, he's under arrest.'

'You're a bloody fool,' Devlin said to Charlie. 'Now you're in real trouble. I don't know what's got into you blokes.'

'I do,' Corby said. 'The ringleader is someone called Ratasali. I want him brought in. Do you know him?'

'Can't say I do,' Mike replied. 'Most of them have been given English

218

names or names close to their island ones, and we don't have a record of their family names.'

'Well, dig him out,' Corby said confidently. 'He'll go for inciting to riot.'

Mike looked about him: 'I can smell smoke.'

'In this weather?' Corby queried. He took out his watch. 'It's only just gone one o'clock but it feels like five. I've been putting up with fights and arguments all morning.'

'So have I,' Mike said. 'They're all behaving like lunatics. No one got hurt, did they?'

'No. I fired over their heads. I had to clout this one, he might be a bit sore for a while. They have to learn, Devlin, and learn fast, that they don't run the show. Make an example of him.' He stopped. 'Look up there! Something is burning!' He threw Charlie's rope to Mike and galloped towards the trail of smoke that was lifting dreamily in the humid air.

Encumbered by the prisoner, Mike could only trot his horse, watching anxiously as smoke furled over the treetops to sink into an ominous banner across the sky.

'Bloody hell!' he exclaimed as they came closer. 'It's the feed barn.'

By the time he arrived the barn was well ablaze and there was pandemonium, with Morgan in among the screaming island women trying to organise a bucket brigade from the creek. Mike left Charlie to his own devices and raced down to hitch his nervous horse to the water wagon to bring up a better supply. Alerted by the smoke, Kanakas came running from all directions to help, and although they managed to keep the fire from spreading to nearby sheds, there was no saving the barn.

'Someone will swing for this!' Corby yelled as they finally gave up and stood back helplessly, watching the barn collapse.

'It could have been combustion,' Mike said. He'd seen haystacks go up like this. But as he strode about the outskirts of the smouldering ruin he knew it was no accident, he could smell fumes, probably kerosene.

'The fire was deliberately lit,' he told Corby. 'From the inside I'd say, to create a furnace like that.' He was already assessing the losses. Their supplies of chaff, pollard, grain, lime, rock salt and other such farm provisions would have to be replaced, not to mention the miscellany of equipment that was housed in a barn this size. And the barn itself, of course. The first priority, with the wet season lingering.

Morgan was storming among the women, who had been the first to notice the fire. 'Anyone see who did this? A reward of ten pounds for the name of man who did this.'

They could only shuffle about, shaking their heads, shocked by the fire and very much afraid of the master's wrath.

Then company arrived, too late to be of any assistance. Sergeant McBride and half a dozen mounted riflemen, on their way into the plantation, had also spotted the fire and had ridden on past the house to investigate.

219

'Damn bad luck, Mr Morgan,' McBride said, surveying the smouldering ruins.

'It's not bad luck,' Corby snapped. 'It's arson. We've been battling a mutiny here for days. Ever since that damn blow-up at Helenslea. Is there anything you can do to pull these mongrels into line?'

'Plenty,' McBride said grimly. 'But first let me introduce you to Lieutenant Scott-Hughes. He's brought his troops for tomorrow's event at Elbow Bay but it looks as if he's got a job here first.'

Corby, relieved to have the law on hand, was very pleased to meet the lieutenant. He was a well-turned-out young Englishman, obviously a gentleman, with a keen eye and an air of authority far exceeding old McBride's stolid meanderings.

The four men held a lengthy discussion in order to acquaint Scott-Hughes with the background to the problems, and it was decided as a start to round up all the Malaita men and make Charlie identify the real troublemaker, the one called Ratasali.

The newly arrived show of strength cowed the Kanakas one and all. To have ten armed white men, including the dreaded police and soldiers, riding through the plantation hauling out Malaita islanders terrified them. It was very clear that insubordination of any sort would be met with swift reprisals.

Corby sighed inwardly at more time-wasting, but it was unavoidable, and hopefully constructive.

Scott-Hughes took over, forcing his prisoners to sit, hands on heads, in a clearing, with troopers guarding them on all sides. Then Charlie was brought forward.

'Identify the man Ratasali!' the lieutenant ordered, but Charlie fell to the ground, screaming, and his compatriots raised such a howl on his behalf that the question was put to them.

'Step forward Ratasali!' Scott-Hughes shouted.

There was no response, so the lieutenant turned to Mike. 'You have a go, Mr Devlin. You know them.'

Mike walked among them, talking to them, warning them of dire punishments, and finally returned. 'They say there's no such person as Ratasali. I think Charlie must have made that up. And I still can't find who lit the barn.'

'That does it then,' McBride said. 'We haven't got any choice. Pull out five men, lieutenant. Any five. We know it wasn't Charlie here, so he's safe for the minute.'

'What happens now?' Corby asked Mike.

'They're going to flog them,' Mike said dispassionately.

The harrowing scene unfolded in a silence that in itself was almost as piercing as a scream. The lieutenant stepped so quietly and so slowly into the clearing to choose the victims that the wait for him to point seemed an eternity, a prolonged agony. They weren't dragged or hauled, he simply summoned them, a delicate hand pointing and beckoning, and they came treading carefully among the bowed heads.

220

Time was stretched as each prisoner, stripped to the waist, had to wait while a suitable tree was located – and for the fifth, a lantern post – so that they could be lashed into place, backs trembling in anticipation.

A burly trooper took off his shirt, preparing for this exertion, and tested a short rawhide whip by flicking it in the air with a powerful arm.

The lieutenant strolled past each prisoner in turn, speaking to each in a whisper. Heads shook. Faces turned to him, appealing, but there was to be no repreive. He pointed to the man strung up to the lantern post, and the trooper moved forward.

The first slash made everyone jump, everyone but the trooper with the whip. A skein of blood appeared on the victim's polished brown skin.

Slash! again. The trooper brought down the whip with such force that the victim screamed in agony. Then he stood back, rubbed the muscles of his arm, flexed it as if to get himself into the rhythm of this business and ran forward to deliver yet another vicious blow. No one had asked how many strokes were to be delivered; they all knew such punishments could range from ten to fifty. Already, the man's back was torn and bloodied.

As the trooper lined up his stroke again, a Kanaka jumped up from the crowd and ran stumbling and screaming to Mike. 'No, boss. No! You make them stop.'

The lieutenant held up his hand, and the trooper waited as Mike twisted the native around, shaking him. 'Who lit the fire, Mantala?'

'Me,' the man wept, clutching at Mike. 'You stop them whippings.'

'You sure?' Mike said. 'How you do this?'

Babbling, Mantala told him how he'd doused some jute bags with kerosene and lit them in the far corner of the barn.

Mike looked up and nodded to the lieutenant, who dismissed the flogger. 'That's a relief,' Scott-Hughes said. 'I was hoping we wouldn't have to go much further, it's a horrible business.' He turned to his men. 'Cut this fellow down and attend to him. Release the others.'

Mantala was taken into custody and it was decided to release Charlie with a warning. 'If there's any more trouble,' Mike told him, 'whether you're mixed up in it or not, you go to jail too. You got it?'

'Just a minute,' Corby called. 'Which one *is* Ratasali? Is he the one the troopers arrested?'

'No. He gone now,' Charlie said.

'What is he talking about?' Corby asked Mike.

'I don't know. He was probably so scared he made up a name. But I'll ask Mantala.'

No further information was forthcoming on the elusive or nonexistent Ratasali, so the matter was dropped.

This time Corby was more gracious with the lawmen. Both McBride and Scott-Hughes were invited to dine at the homestead, but when the sergeant realised that Mike was not included, he declined. 'I'd just as

221

soon have a meal with Devlin up there in his lookout,' he told Corby, 'if you don't mind.'

He expected that Morgan would correct the oversight but instead his apology was accepted.

'By Jesus, he's a hard nut to crack,' he said to Mike. 'Not that I care, I'd rather have a steak and a spud here with you than sit up all lah-di-dah. But you'd think the bugger would find a place at his table for his manager.'

'We don't get on that well,' Mike said. 'I'd rather keep out of his way. Besides he'll be all out tonight to impress Scott-Hughes; cut from the same cloth, that pair.'

'Ah no. For all his dandy ways, Harry's a tough character too. You saw him in action today, he doesn't mess about, gets on with the job. And he's a real nice fellow, believe me.' McBride laughed. 'And he's got all the girls in town swooning over him.'

'How long's he been here?'

'Only about six weeks, sent up from Brisbane to replace Monckton, and he's got them troopers on their toes now. Makes my life a lot easier.'

McBride lit his pipe and stood watching as Mike checked in the Kanakas from the fields. With the troopers still patrolling, they were all subdued as they handed in their tools. Only Pompey seemed pleased with himself, riding at the head of a band of weary workers. He waited until they had filed over to Mike and gone on their way.

'Them blokes,' he said to Mike. 'They want their own gangs. No more mix up with men from that other island.'

'I'll think about it,' Mike replied. 'When you go down, Pompey, tell Tamba I want to see her.'

'What she done?'

'Nothing,' Mike grinned. 'Just tell her.'

'It mightn't be a bad idea to split them up,' McBride commented. 'Some of the planters do that to stop them tramping on one another's taboos.'

'Yes, I know. But there are hundreds of islands. Could get too complicated. What I'm thinking of doing is barring any more boys from Malaita. Cut down on their numbers. If I stay, that is.'

'You're quitting?'

'Yeah, I reckon so. What's the agenda for tomorrow?'

'We'll make for the bay at sun-up and wait for them. You coming?'

'No. Take Morgan. Get him out of my hair. But what about asking Scott-Hughes to leave me one trooper? Preferably the beefy bloke with the whip. They only need to see him riding about to believe there are more in the vicinity, in case they get any more bright ideas.'

'That's a good move. I think he'll go along with it.'

Tamba hurried over to them, wide hips swinging under a tight sarong. 'Whatsa matter, boss?'

'Nothing's the matter. It's Saturday. And we've got five troopers and

222

the sergeant to feed. What about you ladies making us a cookout? Chops and yams on the fire, and some of that good rice you do . . .'

She beamed, flattered. 'I make good chow. Better than the Chinee man. You like sweet fish too?'

'Whatever you say. Lend me ten bob, McBride.'

The sergeant searched his pockets and came up with the coins, which Mike handed to Tamba. 'Special pay,' he winked.

Carefully, she undid part of the knot holding up her sarong, tied the money into it and tucked it back into the deep cleavage of her breasts. 'No more bad fellers, Mr Mike?'

'I hope not,' he said.

'This sounds like a good deal,' McBride said. 'It'll be bad joss for them if you go. They'll miss you.'

'Ah, they forget,' Mike replied, depressed now because his mind was made up. It was goodbye to Providence, and the sooner the better.

Sylvia was mortified. As soon as she'd heard that the handsome officer would be dining with them, she'd rushed in to Tommy to see what was on the menu for this evening.

'Shepherd's pie? You can't serve that to guests!' she cried.

He glared at her. 'My pie good chow! Missus say alri'.' He slammed pots about on the stove. 'Tip-top soup! Gravy! Ginger cabbage! Good pudden!'

'I know,' she said, trying to placate him. 'Your pie is excellent. We'll have that tomorrow, but it is not appropriate to serve to this gentleman. Kill two chickens. Stuff them and bake them. And we'll have baked ham too. Mr Morgan wants a proper dinner for his friend.'

'The boss say chickens?' Tommy stopped the clatter.

'Yes,' she lied, knowing that Corby would agree with her.

The cook's eyes narrowed. He guessed she was lying but he couldn't be certain. 'You get the missus,' he snapped.

'She's too busy,' Sylvia told him. 'Now just get on with it.'

So he did, racing outside in a flurry to call Mae to help him.

The officer, Lieutenant Scott-Hughes, was so handsome and so charming Sylvia was pleased she'd worn her lovely blue silk dress, he couldn't help but comment on it. He was attentive to Jessie, as he should be, but he only had eyes for her. She'd seen the way he looked at her when she first walked into the parlour, making a late entrance, her hair waved back to the crown with long dark curls clustered at the back. A very romantic style, Sylvia thought. She had slipped on a soft whalebone hoop to lend elegance of movement to the full skirt of her dress. The lieutenant could hardly take his eyes from her, she knew, as they chatted in the parlour, and she occasionally rewarded him with a small smile and a brush of her long eyelashes.

At the table, though, everything seemed to go wrong. Corby sat at the head, of course, with Jessie on his right and Harry — he'd said to call him Harry — on his left, hogging the guest's attention right from the start, as if no one else were present, talking to him about England and who they knew. Sylvia, sitting beside Harry, caught little of him but the back of his head, which seemed constantly turned away to answer Corby's questions. She was becoming angrier by the minute, sure that Corby was doing this on purpose.

Jessie, sitting quietly, didn't seem to mind, but Lucas was in a peculiar mood. The couple of sherries they'd had before dinner seemed to have gone to his head. He spilled his soup, dropped his bread roll on the floor and kept up some silly chatter, with Jessie trying to listen to him and Sylvia trying to ignore him.

Their waitress, Elly, was in a mood as dark as her face, probably still carrying on about that murdering Kanaka, Sylvia thought. It was really too bad that she should be allowed to take her frustrations out on the family. And, as it seemed, on Sylvia herself. By God, she thought, when this is over I'll punish her, the wretch.

Twice, while she was serving, Elly had stood on Sylvia's dress with her great flat feet, and when she brought in the chicken, she'd slammed the plate down so hard in front of Sylvia that the gravy had slopped into her lap, though fortunately only on the napkin protecting her skirt.

Then there was the chicken. It looked tasty, the skin crisp and brown, but inside it was almost raw. They all struggled with it for a few minutes until Corby exploded: 'Jessie! What's happened here? We can't expect our guest to eat raw meat. Have it taken away and cooked properly.'

He turned to Harry to apologise as Jessie jumped up and Elly began to collect their plates to return the chicken to the stove. Sylvia was certain she saw Elly grin at her and resolved to take the strap to her at the first opportunity.

Corby poured more wine and then the Professor jumped in with his opinions. 'You flogged one of our boys today?' he asked the lieutenant.

'I'm afraid so,' Harry said.

'Why are you afraid?' Lucas asked. 'I'm sure you didn't feel the cuts.'

'I meant,' Harry said quietly, 'that it was a pity we had to resort to flogging, but fortunately it didn't last long.'

'And you have no conscience at flogging an innocent man?'

'Don't be ridiculous,' Corby exclaimed. 'We had no choice. I'd appreciate it, Lucas, if you'd mind your own business.'

'But it is my business,' Lucas replied. 'Violence begets violence. I'm appalled that my countrymen have to resort to violence to settle difficulties.'

'We can't all be as clever as you,' Corby said. 'And fortunately not as ill mannered.'

'Ill mannered, you say?' Lucas shoved back his chair. 'I regard hypocrisy as a serious breach of decent conduct, sir. You ought to look to yourself.'

Corby sat back. 'Professor, if you find our company untenable then perhaps you might like to retire.'

'I certainly will,' Lucas said. He turned back to Harry. 'Forgive me, sir. I did not mean my comments about the treatment of the South Sea Islanders to be taken personally. I simply attempted to alert you . . .'

Harry smiled and Sylvia thought he had just the sweetest expression. 'To jolt me, Professor,' he corrected, 'into giving these matters more thought. Is that it?'

'Just so, my boy,' Lucas said, and, with a slight lurch towards the sideboard, straightened up and left.

'He's drunk,' Corby sighed. 'Sylvia, I think your father keeps a bottle in his room. Damned if he isn't tipsy most of the time these days.'

Sylvia blushed scarlet. How could Corby say such a thing in front of Harry! It was too humiliating!

Eventually the meal was returned, with Jessie apologising for the burned chicken and reheated vegetables, and Corby dominating the conversation with their guest. Occasionally Harry turned back to address Sylvia but each time Corby drew him away, until at last he invited Harry to join him for port in the parlour, excluding the women.

Jessie didn't seem to mind, going back to the baby and all the other things she seemed to be busy with lately. Sylvia took to her room, furious with Corby. He was jealous of course. Deliberately snubbing her to keep Harry away from her.

'Well, he won't get away with it,' she muttered angrily, and stormed down to Jessie's room. 'Isn't it time we joined the men?'

Jessie, who'd been kneeling by her tin trunk, slammed the lid closed, almost guiltily, Sylvia thought but she didn't have time to wonder about that.

'Leave them be,' Jessie said. 'Corby doesn't often find amenable company. I shouldn't intrude.'

Sylvia was afraid of that. If she did barge in and Corby felt she was intruding he could be very terse, and might embarrass her even further.

Once again, with nowhere else to sit but the dining room, Sylvia returned to her room to wait. She didn't care how long it took. She left the door open to listen for them, and at last heard them retiring. Much earlier than she'd expected. Then she remembered that they had to be up early to go on this pirate-chasing expedition.

As soon as she heard Corby's door close, she slipped out of the house and ran across the yard to Harry's room where the lantern was still burning.

He opened the door when she knocked, surprised to see her.

'I'm sorry to bother you, Harry, but I had to come and apologise for that scene at dinner. It must have been dreadfully embarrassing for you.'

'Of course not,' he said gently. 'You poor girl, have you been sitting worrying about that all evening?'

'Yes,' she admitted. 'I couldn't sleep wondering what on earth you must think of us.' She hugged her shawl about her, a gesture of frailty, and he responded.

'Please, don't be upset, Sylvia. I enjoyed the evening. It is not often I have the honour out here of the company of two charming ladies.'

'Oh, you are kind,' she said. 'I suppose you'll be on your way tomorrow?'

'I shouldn't think so. Depends what happens. If possible I'd like to stay tomorrow night. If you can put up with me.'

'I'd love you to stay,' she said, looking up at him, gazing into that handsome face. She touched his hands lightly. 'I must go in, but do stay if you can.'

'Count on it,' he said, his eyes telling her all she needed to know.

She made her way back to the house with her head full of delicious thoughts. Harry was simply the finest man she'd ever met, and he already had a fondness for her, that was as plain as day. Back inside, she locked her door and lay on her bed thinking of him, savouring those private minutes with him. When Corby tried the handle she didn't move. She'd teach him to demean her in front of company.

Sylvia hardly slept that night, afraid that she'd miss the early parade. She was up at the first sound of movement, hurrying to dress. She patted rosewater on to her face and brushed her hair out, primping it into a slightly dishevelled shape to give herself a sleepy air, while watching Harry's room from the rear window of her bedroom.

As soon as he emerged, impeccably dressed in his uniform and high boots, she trotted down the back steps. 'Good morning, Harry. Did you sleep well?'

'Yes, thank you. You're up early!'

'Oh, heavens, this is the best part of the day. It gets so muggy later.'

'Yes, I suppose so.'

She walked with him to the stables and sat on a high stool to watch as the sleepy-eyed soldiers led their horses out. The whole place was buzzing with activity. Tommy served mugs of billy tea, bread and bacon. Sergeant McBride rode in to join them, and by the time Corby arrived, Sylvia was enjoying this unusual morning tea surrounded by a bevy of uniforms.

'What are you doing here?' he hissed as the men began to move off.

'Enjoying this lovely morning,' she laughed, warm and dry in the stables as the inevitable rain began to fall.

'Bloody rain,' Corby said to Harry. 'Is it ever going to stop?'

'They keep telling me the wet season is over,' Harry said, unpacking his waterproof cape from his saddle pack, 'but I'll believe it when I see it.'

He barked orders to his men and they were soon mounted, ready to leave, their horses stamping, looking forward to the day, eyes bright, unblinking, searching for a hint as to what was ahead.

Watching them, Sylvia wished she could ride with this troop. Her horse Prissy was a match for the other mounts, and she would love to be part of the adventure, to chase landed pirates hell-for-leather along a

226

great wide beach, to shoot them with a revolver as they ran, to wheel about in the shallows . . .

It was Harry who interrupted her fantasies. Harry who kept them all waiting – even Corby, who glared at him, his face as pinched and sour as a dried lemon.

He took her hands to say goodbye, right in front of them all, and Sylvia was thrilled! Harry was his own man, he didn't have to answer to any of them, or care what they thought: 'It has been a pleasure to meet you,' he said. 'Thank you for coming to see us off.'

Magpies sang. Sylvia had heard them before but had never really listened. Now she heard their glorious true notes ringing like carillons all about them.

Corby broke the spell. 'Let's go!' he called, and the horsemen wheeled towards the gate, steel clinking, spurs jingling, the smell of polished leather rich as life.

Harry moved to leave the shelter of the stable, then stopped. 'I suppose,' he said lamely to Sylvia, 'you've been told a million times that you have the most marvellous eyes.'

'No,' she said, walking out into the rain with him. 'Not by anyone that counts.' Then she looked up at him, shocked that she had made such a tactless remark. 'Not until now,' she added.

'That's a good start,' he acknowledged, not bothered that the others had ridden off without him.

Suddenly reality overcame Sylvia's fantasies. This foray wasn't a storybook tale, it was real. He had a revolver strapped to his belt, a rifle by his saddle and a bandolier of cartridges across his chest. And they weren't pirates, they were blackbirders. Sylvia had heard enough to know there was nothing glamorous about these ruffians. Mr Devlin had said they were the scum of the earth, desperate, dangerous men.

She was afraid. Cold fear showed her the dreary day as it was. 'Harry,' she called, 'do be careful.'

'I'm always careful,' he laughed, and then he was gone, riding out through the grey drizzle, a glistening phantom way down there at the end of the track, galloping into the mists.

'Bring him back,' she whispered to a God who had never before had time to listen to her. She always seemed to be at the end of the line when favours were handed out. Miss Second-best. With another woman's husband as a lover. With no real place in this household, or anywhere else.

Sylvia's suspicions were well founded: Jessie did have a guilty secret. As soon as the men left, she put Bronte back to sleep and went into the dining room and ate a good breakfast. She would need the sustenance. Then she called Hanna. 'Where is Miss Sylvia?'

Hanna grinned. 'She up too early. She gone back to bed.'

Jessie nodded. That was convenient. It would save explanations. 'Now listen to me,' she said to Hanna. 'Go and tell Toby to bring around the gig. We're going into town.'

'Me too?' Hanna was astonished.

'Yes. If you want to come with me. Otherwise I'll take Elly.'

'Baby come too?' Hanna, the nursemaid, was cautious.

'Of course baby too.'

'So you mus' tak me.'

'That's what I said. Now go give Toby the message.'

She had the trunk brought out and placed in the gig. A carpet bag for odds and ends. A cloth bag for Hanna's meagre possessions. Some rugs for shelter.

Mae came out to watch, mystified.

Jessie took her aside. 'Mae, I can rely on you. You're the one to keep the house in order. You look after everything.'

'But where you going, missus?'

'Into town, Mae, just for a little holiday.'

The tiny Chinese woman shook her head. 'No, missus. You run away. You must not go. You number one wife. You send her away.' She jerked her head back to the house.

This was the first time the truth of Jessie's situation had come into the open, but now that she'd made her decision, it didn't seem to matter that others were aware.

'I have to go, Mae. It is important to me. You understand.'

Mae's black eyes filled with tears. She understood. But Tommy did not. He raced outside to alert the Professor.

'What are you doing, girl?' Lucas demanded of his daughter.

'I'm leaving,' she said. 'That's obvious.'

'Does Corby know about this?'

'I told him I would leave. He didn't believe me.'

'Shouldn't you wait until he gets back?'

'Until the boss gets back and prevents me, you mean.' She put Hanna and the baby in the gig, becoming agitated because an audience was growing when she'd hoped to slip quietly away. Elly was standing by the gig, looking as if her world had come to an end. Tommy and Mae were engaged in one of their shrill arguments. Several Aborigine stableboys had wandered to the front of the house out of curiosity, and Toby was sitting dutifully, stony-faced in the driver's seat of the gig.

'I must protest,' the Professor said. 'This is not the correct course to take.'

'What is, Father?' Jessie snapped, watching as Hanna took a bag of fruit from Mae.

'This is your home. You cannot leave.'

'Can't I? You watch me.'

'Is there nothing I can say that will dissuade you?'

'Nothing.' She called to Toby. 'Just hold the gig until I'm ready. You won't be coming with me, Toby, you're needed here.'

His reaction complicated her exit even further. He protested. He told her the creeks were up. That she could not drive all that way.

'I can and I will,' she argued. 'You stay home.'

Toby's face was a picture of grief. He didn't understand.

Jessie went over to him. 'Toby. You are a good and kind man. I am very grateful to you for everything you have done for me and for my family. But you have no place with me.'

'Who will look after you, missus?'

'Hanna and I will do just fine. If you come with me the boss will blame you.' She was almost pleading. 'Toby, he will whip you.'

He began to understand what was happening. 'He doan know you going?' His eyes were round with fear.

'No,' she said, her voice flat. 'No, the boss does not know.'

'Gor cripey!' he wailed.

Then Lucas made a decision. 'Hold on a minute, Jessie. Wait for me. If your mind is made up, then I'd better come with you.'

'What for?' she said coldly. 'You've been no help to me, Dadda.' The nickname slipped out. It had been a long time since she'd called him Dadda. Not since her marriage, which seemed aeons ago now. 'What can you do for me now? You had your chance, I came to you when I needed help and all I got was talk. You're all talk, like you were last night.'

'Jessie,' he pleaded, 'I was just trying to work out the best thing to do. Give me time.'

'You've had the time. A decent father would have taken the whip to Sylvia, but not you. One has to see every side of the story. Isn't that your philosophy? Well, you're stuck with it. And with them. I hope you'll all be happy ever after.'

'I'll speak to Corby.'

'Don't talk rot. Corby frightens the wits out of you and you know it. Even when Mother was alive, we had to live with her worry — "Don't upset your father". We were never allowed to upset you, she minded you as if you were a cot-case, or better still a hothouse plant, one of those things you loved more than any of us.'

Mae came to his rescue. 'Oh, missus! You being cruel to your daddy.'

'Cruel? Not to him. He's got a hide like leather, like his books. And inside, the heart of a mouse. Get out of my way, Mae.'

She took the reins from Toby and climbed up beside Hanna. 'Are you ready?'

'Yes, missus.'

'The baby?'

Hanna nodded. Plump little Bronte was sleeping happily in the basket behind them, less bother than anyone else in sight.

As soon as they left, Toby ran helter skelter down through the plantation to find Mike.

The horse trotted briskly down the track to the gate and turned left on the road to Cairns, and Jessie felt marvellous. She'd done it! She was leaving that humiliation, Corby's bullying tactics . . . Whatever lay ahead of her had to be better. She never wanted to see Sylvia or Corby or her father again! As she flicked the horse with the whip to keep a steady pace, she wondered why she had placed them in that order. Probably because that was the way she hated them. No. Not hate, lack of care. She just didn't care about them any more, about any of them or what happened to them. They were past history.

It was still raining, that steady, warm, glue-like drizzle, so once away from Providence she slowed the horse to a deliberate trot on the muddy roads. There was no hurry. It was only about seven o'clock. She drove slowly, avoiding potholes, determined not to be waylaid by carelessness. Miles down the road they had to cross a flooded causeway, but with Hanna leading the horse over the shallow drift, they managed to make it to the other side without mishap. This was the first time Jessie had been to town since they arrived at Trinity Bay, another aspect that kept her cheerful as they spun along the strange road.

'I don't recognise this road at all,' she said to Hanna. 'Are you sure we're going the right way?'

Hanna nodded, the thrill of the journey too important to her to be making mistakes. 'This wet time,' she explained. 'All bush grow big.'

'That's right,' Jessie said, reassured. They'd come out to Providence in the dry season; now the regrowth was back in force, tall trees and palms almost forming a canopy over the road.

They travelled mile after mile and not a soul did they see. At mid-morning Jessie decided that they should take a rest for a half-hour. She was surprised that she felt no qualms at leaving, nor was she worried about what lay ahead. 'You're behaving like a scatterbrain,' she told herself as she fed the horse an apple and tightened the harness. 'This is a serious matter, you should be more concerned.'

But she wasn't. The worst that could happen was that she might be forced to return to Providence. In the meantime she was enjoying herself. Many a time at home she had driven the gig for a day out in the country. This was no different, except for the relentless greenery crowding the track and the absence of other travellers.

When at last they came over the crest of a hill and saw a creek below, Jessie was pleased to see people standing by a small shed. She remembered this place; this was where Mr Devlin had rested his travellers, fresh from the ship.

'Where you goin', missus?' a rough-looking fellow asked as she reined in near the shed. Other men drifted over to stare at her.

'Into Cairns,' she said. 'Can I cross here?'

'Not in that toy you can't,' he laughed. 'Who might you be?'

'I'm Mrs Morgan, from Providence,' she replied with a confidence she didn't feel. There were no women in sight and she was nervous now. 'How can we cross?' she asked him.

'Well now. Come on down from your perch and we'll talk about it, Mrs Morgan from Providence.'

Jessie could see now that the creek was flooded, so there wasn't much point in staying on the gig. She climbed down, accepting his hand, while Hanna took the reins, sitting quietly, warily, watching them.

'Do you want a cup of tea? Or a drink?' he asked her, winking at his mates.

'No thank you. Is there any way of getting across here?'

'There might be and there might not be,' he leered.

'I'm willing to pay,' she said. 'Who's in charge here?'

'You might say I am,' he told her, sticking dirty thumbs in his braces and grinning at her through a tobacco-stained beard. 'Stan Bellard at your service. This here's Halfway Creek and this is my store. Not often we have pretty ladies dropping by without their menfolk. What are you doin' on the trail anyway?'

'That's my business, Mr Bellard. Now, can you get me across or not?'

'Come inside and we'll talk about it,' he said, producing a clay pipe and shoving it in his mouth.

'Just a minute,' Jessie replied, stalling. 'I have my baby with me.' She glanced at the other men, but no one seemed inclined to interfere or help her. She took Bronte's basket from the gig and Hanna drove on to a hitching post. Then, hidden from the men by the high side of the vehicle, she lifted Bronte out of his basket and handed him to his nurse. At the same time she took out the loaded revolver she'd strapped in its holster underneath the basket. She'd only put it there to get it out of the house without anyone noticing, because she was terrified of snakes, having already encountered several at the plantation. Now she knew she might need the gun to defend herself and her son.

'More better we go back, missus,' Hanna said nervously.

'No,' Jessie said. 'There has to be a way to cross.'

With the gun hidden in the pocket of her heavy black skirt banging uncomfortably against her thigh, Jessie marched back to the men. 'Now, Mr Bellard. How do I cross this stream?'

'A stream, is it?' he chortled. 'I'd say it's more'n a river now. Come on inside, missus, it's like to get rainin' again any minute. Bring the bubby in.'

Jessie drew her cloak about her and stormed past him to the other men. 'You there!' she challenged a younger man, counting five of them in all, including the Bellard person. 'Is there any means of crossing here?'

'I dunno,' he said awkwardly. 'You'll have to ask Stan.'

'You're lying!' she said. 'If I don't get across there'll be trouble. Sergeant McBride, Lieutenant Scott-Hughes and his soldiers are following me. They'll be along soon and they won't take kindly to the treatment I'm receiving.'

The lad wilted. 'There's the barge,' he admitted.

'Where?'

'Down that track there.' He pointed. 'Easier to cross before the bend.'

'I was gonna tell her that,' Stan said, backing down now. 'Nothin' wrong with offering a lady a bit of a siddown inside.'

'Thank you,' Jessie said stiffly, 'but I don't have time to socialise. Direct me to the barge, please.'

'No need to get hoity-toity,' Stan grumbled. 'We'll take you.'

Before she could stop them, the men had taken charge of the horse and gig and were leading it down a steep slope behind the store. Jessie prayed as she followed with Hanna and the baby that this was not a ruse, but sure enough, there was the barge resting heavily by the bank.

From this level the creek didn't seem much of a hazard, the water lapping at the banks. It wasn't as wide as she'd expected but it was probably deep in the middle, too deep for a gig to handle.

Two men rode into the muddy water, collected a heavy rope from the barge and plunged ahead, making for the opposite bank, the horses swimming part of the way. Jessie was relieved when she saw them attending to a winch of some sort, obviously preparing to haul the barge over. It was primitive but as effective as a temporary bridge. The horse and gig could be transported in safety.

'Thank you, Mr Bellard,' she said, trying to be polite. 'Now if you'd kindly help me take the horse out of harness we can put the gig aboard first.'

'No rush, missus, give us a go.' He tramped away to help heave the barge into position.

'Us jump on quick,' Hanna said, tugging at Jessie's arm.

'Heavens, no, they have to get the horse settled first,' Jessie told her, but Hanna was frightened.

'Come on, we get away.'

'Don't be silly,' Jessie said. 'Everything's all right now.'

Bellard came back, grinning. 'Don't see no sign of them troopers. Funny they're going to let you cross on your own. Don't seem right to me.'

'Never mind about them,' Jessie snapped. 'Get the gig on to the barge please.' When he didn't move she tried again. 'If it's a matter of money, Mr Bellard, I'd be happy to pay you now.'

As they'd come down the slope Jessie had noticed that this was a very pretty spot, the clearing resembling a picnic area surrounded by flowering gums with red and gold bottlebrush nestling in the shrubbery. Now, though, it had assumed an air of menace. Birds shuffled in the trees, something scuttled in the undergrowth near her and she jumped.

'Don't be nervous,' Bellard said. 'It's safe, the lads'll get you across high and dry in no time. You take your bubby and go on down. We don't want no payment.'

'That's very good of you,' she replied, wondering why he was suddenly so helpful.

'No trouble at all,' he said. 'You go on your way. Leave the gin, we can't have too many on the barge. We'll send her over next trip.'

Jessie stared at him. It dawned on her now why he'd wanted her inside the store with the baby. They wouldn't touch her, they were only

232

trying to separate her from Hanna. From the black girl.

'You'll do no such thing,' she said. 'This girl comes with me.' Clumsily she dragged out the revolver and levelled it at him. 'Tell them to load up. I will be crossing and she's coming with me.'

He burst out laughing. 'What are you gonna do? Shoot me? Shoot the other lads? That won't get you across. Now have a bit of sense. You go first, that's all I ask.'

'No.'

'Righto.' He shrugged. 'Then we got a standoff. If you don't do it our way then you don't go nowheres. We got plenty of time.' He marched away, ignoring the gun trained on him, to join the other two men at the barge.

On the other bank of the creek Jessie could see the two barge-handlers waiting with their horses. Hanna was cringing by her mistress's side. Bronte began to cry and the girl held him tight, hushing him. The gun was heavy. Eventually Jessie had to lower it but she stayed defiantly by Hanna, hoping to wait them out, hoping other travellers would come along, hoping that she could appeal to the better nature of one of these men at least.

Fish plopped in the creek, sudden sounds in the ominous quiet as the two women remained aloof from the insolent louts barring their way.

'She what?' Mike stared at Toby. 'On her own?'

'She took Hanna,' Toby wailed. 'The missus done bolted!'

'Oh Christ! Today of all days.' Then he realised that this had to be the day she'd choose, to be certain that her husband was out of the way. If she were hellbent on dodging him and making off. And that seemed to be what had happened.

But to take on that lonely road without an escort? The woman was mad. Or desperate. Or maybe she didn't realise the dangers. Anything could happen. The road was rough, the creeks would be swamped, she could take a wrong turning — not much difference between roads and tracks out here — and at worst, two women alone were an easy target for renegade blacks. Outlaws were less of a problem, they'd hardly waste their time, but there were some nasty characters roaming the bush, half-baked prospectors who wouldn't know gold if it fell on them. 'You get a horse and go after them, Toby,' he said. 'Stay with them all the way to town.'

'No fear!' Toby wouldn't dare. 'Missus say the boss he get angry allasame I go.'

That was a possibility too. But someone had to go, and how could Mike leave today? The men were all back at work, having been jolted into a new respect for the rules, and Scott-Hughes's trooper was patrolling, but the everyday operations needed an overseer. Kanakas didn't invent work; when they finished a job they sat down for a smoke until they were reassigned.

He sent Toby back to the house and rode down to make sure that a gang had started weeding a ratoon crop that was now in its third year and still looking promising. But as he rode, he worried about Jessie Morgan. Wasn't she more important than crops? And young Hanna? A more naive pair would be hard to find in the outback. And they'd got the baby with them! Good God! He envisaged all sorts of calamities.

'If anything happens to them I'll never forgive myself,' he muttered. 'But what will happen when I do catch up with them? Will she come back with me? She'll have to. I can't spare the time to go on to Cairns.' He set off into the depths of the plantation, searching for the trooper.

'Change of plans,' Mike said. 'I've got to leave the plantation for a while, but I'll be back as soon as possible. Go up to the long-house and find Tamba, she'll give you a feed at lunch time.'

'If it's as good as dinner last night I'll be there with bells on,' the trooper grinned.

'Fine, but in the meantime keep visible.'

At the stables he took out a fresh horse, a big bay that was more suited for the fast track than his own mount, and put the animal to the gallop down a side track to avoid the house and explanations. Sylvia and the Professor must have known Jessie was leaving. Why hadn't they stopped her?

He had no doubt that Jessie's decision to pull out was a refusal to no longer countenance being 'number two wife', as Elly had put it. He couldn't blame her, but she was placing all three of them at risk by making this mad dash through dangerous country. He'd like to punch Morgan right on that supercilious nose – and one day he would. Mike had worried about Jessie but he couldn't interfere, it would only embarrass her. Why hadn't she come to him? He could have arranged safe passage for her to Cairns, to anywhere in the world if she wished. But obviously she was too proud to ask favours of anyone. And it was none of his business. Who was he? Not even a friend of the family, Morgan had made that clear.

Every time he rounded a bend on this winding track he expected to see the gig ahead of him, the women standing by helplessly, halted by some problem with the gig, the harness, or the horse. But there was no sign of them. What would he say to her? Would he ask her what this was all about! Or would he go on pretending, for her sake, that he knew nothing of her marital predicament? Yes, that would be best. Explain to her that this wasn't the best move right now, with the plantation in turmoil and the expected arrival of a mob of kidnapped Kanakas who would have to be sorted out.

Given its head, the horse pounded eagerly down the road. Half-brumby, it was as sure-footed as a goat, and made the most of this run, but smelling water on this hot, humid day it began to slow. When they came to the first creek it drank greedily while Mike studied the tracks. The gig had come through here. That was a relief, at least she was still on the right road. He had been worried that she might have veered off somewhere.

234

He pushed the horse down to the causeway, which was flooded, and looked about him in a panic. Surely they hadn't crossed here? Not possible. The only way to check was to get to the other side, but by now the horse wasn't so eager. Mike had to spur him across the slippery timbers with the waters lapping at his boots. The current wasn't strong because the old creek was simply swelling, allowing flood waters to spread.

They'd made it; the gig tracks were there, ploughing up the rise to continue on course. Mike was angry. How could she risk their lives and the life of that baby by crossing here? Bloody stupid. But surely impossible in a gig? In a heavy dray maybe. The mystery bothered him so much he stood staring, and waiting, fixing his eyes on a half-submerged shrub. Before long the level of the creek had risen even further and the shrub began to sink out of sight.

'Flood waters,' he said. 'Run-off from the river. That's bloody lovely. How can I get them back now?'

Back on the road, Mike Devlin knew that whichever way he went, he too was in trouble now. The creek wasn't too wide, he could cross it on horseback, but what about the women and Bronte? Jessie was well on her way; he ought to turn back, let her go. In the wet season there was always a ferry at Halfway Creek, that was the only major obstacle now.

But having come this far it seemed irresponsible to just chuck it in. Blast her!

He kept going. The road had no set course; it was dominated by the size of the trees that impeded its progress, and it detoured and wound through the bush rather than attacking the native giants, so once again Mike was watching at each turn for the gig, becoming crankier as the miles unfolded.

'I can't believe they've got this bloody far,' he fumed, addressing the horse for want of better company.

At Halfway Creek there was no sign of them. 'Now what am I supposed to do?' he asked himself as he reined in the horse. 'Keep going? Pay that bastard Bellard to get me across, or bloody swim the horse and go after the mistress of Providence with my clothes stinking wet on me?'

He strode into the shed that masqueraded as a store, but there was no one about. Tin bins of flour and tea creaked on the rotten floorboards as he marched in, token grocery lines to cover the real object of this enterprise, a grog shop. Wooden kegs, their funnels chained to the taps, served a dual purpose as a counter, dripping with candle grease. Dirty glass jars, tin mugs, ancient chocolate boxes and a conglomeration of coloured cure-all medicine bottles lined the only shelf behind the counter. Horseshoes, for luck, were nailed on the bare timber walls, and Mike noticed Stan's hat and handgun hanging from a nail by the door.

For some reason that bothered him. He edged behind the casks to Stan's filthy old bunk, his home in this one-room dump that he liked to call a store. Something was wrong here. It occurred to him that Stan might have met a richly deserved fate in this lonely haunt and been robbed, but his striped tin money box was in place under the bunk and it shuffled and jingled comfortably when Mike shook it.

So where was he? Not like Stan to be off guard like this. Not the bastard who'd robbed many a traveller after filling them up with the molasses brew that he passed off as rum. There were other horses outside, maybe they were all down at the barge.

He left the bay and headed down the track on foot. A gig had left its unmistakably clean tracks in the thick clay, and he shook his head as he cut through the scrub, bypassing the terraced track down the steep incline. 'I'll bet she's gone on!'

Then he heard her voice, the English accent easily recognisable. The tone of the voice, though! Distressed? Angry? Mike slowed, moving carefully for a better view before he came tramping out into the open.

'Mr Bellard,' she called to the man slouching near the barge, 'I demand you put us aboard immediately.'

Mike smiled grimly. *Mister* Bellard! That scum. He was ignoring her. And, God Almighty, Jessie had a gun! What was happening here? He surveyed the scene carefully. There were two other men there with guns slung on their hips, and they were a mean-looking pair of roughnecks. It would be dicey to take them both on. He scuttled back up the hill and grabbed his rifle from its pouch, tossing a bandolier of cartridges over his shoulder. Obviously the bastards were playing some sort of game with Jessie and Hanna. It was time to up the ante with a more powerful weapon.

He didn't waste any time. The first shot winged Stan, who spun about screaming, out of the argument. The second shot landed between the other two. 'Drop your guns,' Mike shouted, keeping out of sight. They were running for cover but the next shot stopped them. 'You heard me,' he shouted. 'Drop them now or I'll drop you.'

The weapons were thrown down. He ran past the women to pick up the two handguns and hurl them into the river.

'What did you do that for?' one of the men screamed. 'Those bloody guns cost money.'

'Bad luck,' he retorted and backed towards the women. 'Put that gun away, Jessie,' he said, forgetting that she was still Mrs Morgan to him. 'You're making me nervous.'

'Oh, I'm so pleased to see you,' she said. 'Those dreadful men . . .'

'Don't worry about them now, they've run out of puff. Just get rid of the gun.'

While she ran over to put it in the gig, Mike ordered the men to kneel, their hands on their heads, their backs to him. 'You too,' he said, poking at Stan with the rifle.

'I can't,' Stan screamed. 'I been shot. I'm bleedin' like a stuck pig.'

'Do as you're told,' Mike told him, 'or I'll do a better job at point-

236

blank.' He moved back to Jessie. 'What's going on here?'

When she told him, he didn't seem surprised, listening without comment.

'Don't you care?' she fumed. 'They tried to take Hanna. They should be locked up.'

'How? They've got two mates on the other side there. We wouldn't get very far with them. My problem is what to do with you.'

'I would appreciate it, Mr Devlin, if you could get us across here. Thank you for rescuing us.'

Mike turned to Hanna, who was still hugging the baby. 'Are you all right, missy?'

'Yes, Mr Mike, pretty good allasame.'

'Right. Now, Mrs Morgan, we've got a problem here. You ought to come back with me.'

'I'm not coming back, I'm on my way into Cairns.'

'And putting three lives at risk at the same time,' he said. 'But the creek's up back there, you'd have to ride across. Leave the gig.'

'And then what?' She seemed pleased that the return route was cut off. 'We've only got two horses.'

'We could take Stan's,' he suggested. 'He's in no position to argue.'

'I will not ride with a babe in arms,' she said, 'nor will I leave my effects in the gig for any thief to rifle.'

He hadn't thought she'd agree to that idea. There was really no choice but to keep going. Without consulting Jessie, he went down to the men. 'On your feet. Get the gig and the horse on the barge, and be quick about it.' He had a look at Stan's arm. 'You're lucky, it's only a flesh wound, so quit grizzling and give a hand.'

In no time they had the blinkered horse on the barge and ran the light gig up the makeshift ramp. Then Mike took the women on board.

'Go, and be buggered then,' Stan snarled at Mike. 'I'll remember you, mate.'

'You do that,' Mike said, unimpressed. 'Now, you get on here too.'

'Why me? I gotta go and get a bandage,' Stan wailed.

'Use your shirt. We're all going.' He herded all three men aboard and then cast off. 'I don't think your mates over there would cut us adrift with you lot on our team. Give them the signal to start the haul.'

The barge swung sideways, straightened up then lurched out into the current to begin its slow struggle for the far shore.

'One peep out of you mugs,' Mike warned his captives, 'and you'll swim.'

'I can't swim,' Stan wailed.

'Better still.' Mike was worried about the pair on the bank. It was possible they were armed too. 'Who runs this barge?' he asked the captives. Every year a new man took on the job. There wasn't much in it, just a few bob every day or so for vehicular or bulk transport, and it only lasted for the wet season.

'I do,' replied one of them, a weedy young bloke. 'Stan was just havin'

237

a bit of fun. We didn't mean no harm.'

'Like hell you didn't,' Mike growled. 'Now, you stand up front and you tell your mates over there that everything is under control. You don't want any trouble.'

'Yeah! Right! I'll tell them.' He cringed under the barrel of the rifle. 'You don't need to get so bloody heavy.'

'Yes I do. If you get it right, you'll be paid well. If you muck it up, you go first.'

'Whaddya mean, go first? I dunno what you want, mister.'

'Mister Devlin,' Mike said steadily. 'Stan knows me. He knows I could have taken his ear off if I felt so inclined. But you, you're the skipper. You give the orders and we're near to landing. One wrong move by those blokes at the winch and you get the first bullet. Dead in your back. It'll come out the other side but you'll be past caring.'

The skipper was on his feet, shouting and waving to the winchmen, who toiled with the horses to bring the barge to shore. There was no trouble. The winchmen seemed mildly amused by Stan's whining efforts to bind up his wounded arm.

'Lucky he missed yuh!' a sturdy half-caste Aborigine grinned as he tied up the barge.

'I didn't miss,' Mike said, recognising him. 'What are you doing, Danny, mixing with this lot?'

'Nothin' much else to do, boss,' Danny said.

'That other bloke there,' Mike asked. 'Has he got a gun?'

'Under the winch,' Danny whispered out of the side of his mouth, his eyes on the job fastening the ropes.

'Get it,' he hissed. They weren't out of the woods yet; it was difficult to watch all five men as they brought the horse and gig ashore. He grabbed Hanna. 'Take the missus and the baby up there quick.'

At the same time Danny was shaking his head. 'Not me, boss. They get me when you go.'

If I go, Mike thought. Stan and his mates could bet on it that he'd report them when he got to town, and the troopers would be down on them like a ton of bricks. But his horse was back there. Damn Jessie! Damn Corby Morgan. He hoped that old reprobate Frenchy Duval blew Morgan's head off. Duval was a dyed-in-the-wool treacherous bastard; this lot were schoolkids compared to him, but their malice could not be underestimated. And he didn't have a bloody horse. They knew that. He could see the mean gleam in their eyes as they moved about, obeying him temporarily. It wouldn't take them long to get their mounts and come after him. After the gig.

Elbow Bay wasn't the tropical white beach that Corby had imagined. It was a stinking mangrove swamp, alive with mosquitoes that hummed and swarmed in angry thousands as the posse left their horses and began the trek to the coast, slipping and clambering over cloying tree roots in a muddy tidal wasteland.

238

Corby was appalled. He slammed and switched at the vicious insects, trying to keep up with McBride, Scott-Hughes and their troopers, sinking knee-deep in mud when he slipped from exposed roots. The Professor had said that there was a possibility that mosquitoes carried malaria, and already Corby was feeling feverish in this pestilent hothouse forest. The mangroves glittered and gleamed like malevolent trolls as he stepped gingerly from one writhing root to the next, clinging to their greasy knotted branches. A hellhole this was. A bloody hellhole! Those spongy green leaves dripping about him, overripe, decadent, boasting of slimy life that had no right to exist in this foul atmosphere.

His jacket was ripped, he'd lost his hat and he fought to keep up with the shadows of the other men creeping through this suspended forest, half land, half sea. Below him, things slipped and slithered in the clear green waters. So clear that if you looked at them long enough it was hard to tell the water level from the muddy bed.

He heard the curses of the men ahead of him but it was no consolation; they were paid to do this. His gun-belt caught on those insidious mangrove arms so often, jerking him back, that he was tempted to chuck it away and the gun with it, but the sight of the troopers, struggling with rifles, gave him heart as he bent under the tough branches, travelling hunched over like a hobyah. What was a hobyah anyway? Some frightening tale from his childhood. The hobyahs came creeping creeping creeping . . . Well, he didn't feel like a bloody hobyah. He felt like one of their victims, waiting for them to pounce on him.

When McBride called a halt and they balanced on mangrove roots looking out over a placid blue bay, with no firm ground to call their own, Corby took out his handkerchief and mopped his face and neck, imprisoning a battalion of mosquitoes in one swipe.

'There's no ship,' he said, feigning disappointment, meaning: Let's get the hell out of here.

'Patience,' the lieutenant said, and Corby was reminded of his father. He was glad he'd never joined the army. The only thing keeping him here, his clothes ruined by sweat, his mouth dry as a chip in this watery graveyard, was fast-diminishing pride. The only thing he had in his favour was the right to leave when he felt like it. The troopers suffering with him had no such choice.

'They should have been here by now,' he argued, with no facts to back his claim.

'Not necessarily,' Scott-Hughes remarked.

'This is a shit of a place,' McBride puffed, hanging on to a branch like an overweight orang-utan in a black uniform. Corby almost laughed. He was feeling slightly hysterical and feverish, no doubt going down with malaria, but pleased that someone else was admitting to suffering.

At the southern end of the bay, layers of rock lifted up in uneven slabs towards the headland, so they made for that. 'We'll need you to stand out there to be seen, Corby, and we'll stay out of sight behind you,' the lieutenant said. 'And Gardner,' he turned to one of the troopers, 'you go up on to that promontory and let us know if there are any ships approaching. Take off your jacket in case they spot the uniform.'

Corby climbed out on to the slippery rocks. He was glad to be released from the fetid air into the bracing sea breeze, but he didn't enjoy being exposed like this, even if the bay were deserted. A ship could appear any minute. Obviously the blackbirders' crew would expect someone to be there, but not just one man to collect a mob of natives; there ought to be more.

As if in answer to this, two of the troopers, without their jackets, came up to join him, their trousers conveniently disguised by mud.

'They must know this spot,' one of them said to Corby. 'These rocks make a natural wharf, deep enough to bring a longboat right to the edge. And look here . . .' He found an iron ring hammered into the rock. 'They tie up here easy as you like. I reckon old Edgar has used this place before, bloody rogue he was. But we'll catch them this time.'

'Then they'd better get a move on,' Corby said. 'Because this is tidal. At high tide these rocks will be under water and they'll have to shove into the mangroves.'

'That's a point,' the trooper said. 'They caught the last lot at Mission Beach, grabbed the captain and first mate red-handed with a mob of half-dead Kanakas. We could get lucky too.'

'What happened to them?' Corby asked.

'They were sentenced to hang for murder, but of course the order was changed to life imprisonment.' The trooper spat. 'If they'd murdered white men they'd have swung, but it was only Kanakas! And that after our blokes risked their lives to collar them.'

Corby stared moodily at the cool deep water. He was frying out here, the sun behind grey clouds was still fierce. A swim would be marvellous, to cool off and be clean again in those tempting waves. But he supposed he'd better not mention that idea.

The lookout signalled that no ships were in sight, so they handed around the waterbags and waited. Gradually the tide lifted, forcing them to retreat up the rocky incline, where they hung about, waiting and waiting for interminable hours. They devoured the buns and bacon Tommy had supplied, and peered down at the rocky stretch of coastline south of Elbow Bay that confronted the passage between the landmass and a great reef out there.

'Captain Cook came this way when he discovered Australia,' Sergeant McBride told Corby proudly. 'Came right past here trying to find a way out, past the reefs.'

'And did he?'

'Did he what?'

'Find a way out?'

'Yes. At Lizard Island, another five hundred miles north. He must have been in a panic by then, stuck inside the reef for a couple of thousand miles with the thought that he might have to turn back. A great sailor, that man.'

For Corby that was the most interesting part of the long, dreadful day. Something to tell Bronte when he grew up. For the rest of the time he fretted about the plantation, wondering what was going on there. Hoping Devlin wasn't having any more trouble. It had been well proven that the manager was too soft with the Kanakas.

At last Scott-Hughes made the decision. 'I think we'll have to call it a day. They won't risk coming in at this hour, it'll be dark soon, the sun goes down like a stone in the tropics.'

'Best news I've heard all day,' one of the troopers grumbled, and Corby heartily agreed with him.

As they were leaving, Scott-Hughes took a last look at the warm waters lapping over the rocks. 'It's so tempting,' he said to Corby. 'I've been dying to jump in there all day but I'm scared stiff of sharks.'

Corby shuddered. He'd forgotten about sharks.

They struggled back through the swamps, and when they were finally clear McBride said: 'Bloody nuisance, now we'll have to come back tomorrow.'

'Yes,' replied the lieutenant. Corby made no comment. Wild horses wouldn't drag him back to this hellhole again. He'd send Devlin. Let him put up with the misery since he was so bloody holy about the Kanakas.

His clothes, caked with mud, had dried by the time they rode into Providence, and his boots felt like concrete. He was sunburned, his head ached and he had a monumental thirst. The lantern-lit homestead had never looked so inviting. Home at last.

'Danny,' Mike said, 'why don't you come with me? I'll give you a job at Providence.'

'Doing what?'

'Oh, for Christ's sake! A bloody job and somewhere to live. If you stick with these blokes you'll end up in jail.'

'Righto,' Danny grinned. That was the sad part, Mike thought; Aborigines who lost touch with their tribes became footloose, easily led.

Mike lined up the other four. 'Now sit down again, chaps,' he said, still covering them with the rifle. 'Danny, you go up and tell Mrs Morgan to keep going, we'll catch up. Then come back here.'

'How are you going to catch up walking?' Stan laughed. His friends glared at him. There were two horses grazing nearby.

'Can you swim the creek?' Mike asked Danny when he returned.

'Easy,' Danny said.

'Then go and get my horse. The bay.'

Danny plunged into the creek and Mike turned to the others. 'I'm going to make a deal with you.' He fished the gun from under the winch and hurled it into the water. 'I could tie you all up here and now, you stupid clowns, but it could be a while before anyone finds you.'

241

'Like troopers!' Stan snarled.

'If I left you tied up here, mate, you'd be praying for troopers to turn up. And they wouldn't cross down here anyway. As I said, a deal. I'll leave you loose, but when I go I don't want anyone following me.'

'We won't follow you,' the weedy man from the other side cried, and the others nodded eagerly.

'The hell you won't!' Mike said. He knew that as soon as he turned his back they'd head for the store, collect more weapons, grab their horses and come after him. 'Which is Danny's horse?' he asked.

'The mare,' one of the winchmen said.

'I thought so.' He glanced at the two horses grazing nearby. 'That chestnut, he yours?'

'Yes.'

'He's a beauty,' Mike said. 'What do you want for him?'

'He's not for sale. I've had him since he was a foal. He's as near to full bred as you'll get around these parts.'

'I'd have to agree with you,' Mike said amiably, studying the horse. 'That's why I'm taking him with me.'

'You bloody are not!' The owner of the horse would have attacked Mike there and then but the rifle kept him down.

'I'm taking him with me,' Mike continued, 'and if any of your mates show their noses I'll shoot him.'

'Oh Jesus Christ! You wouldn't! Why take it out on the poor bloody horse?' He was almost in tears.

'It's up to you. This game is over unless you want to keep it up. He'll be all right. I'll leave him with the Chinese . . . you know, the market gardeners with the farms just out of town. You can pick him up there. If he's still alive.'

'He'll be alive,' the winchman said, glaring at the others.

'That woman,' Stan intervened. 'She can't go making any charges. We didn't hurt no one. It's her word against ours. We were just giving her a bit of a tease.'

'And the police wouldn't believe you in a fit,' Mike laughed, watching Danny plough across the creek towards them on his horse. 'But as long as you stay put and behave yourselves, there won't be any charges.'

'You cost us our guns!' Stan argued.

'Shut your face, Stan,' the weedy barge skipper snapped. 'You're the cause of all this bloody trouble, you wanted the gin.'

When Mike and Danny were mounted up, leading the chestnut, the horse's owner called anxiously, 'You'll look after Zulu, won't you, Danny?'

'Sure, mate,' Danny said.

As they topped the rise with a last glance back at the confused men below, Mike looked at the spare horse. 'That's not Zulu,' he said. 'What's that fool talking about?'

'He's Zulu Lad,' Danny told him. 'Bred from Mr Betts's champeen

242

stallion. The bloke's dad used to work at Helenslea, won the foal from Betts in card game. The Lad's gettin' a bit long in the tooth now but he's all Fred's got. You wouldn't hurt him, would you, Mr Devlin?'

'No,' Mike admitted. 'I'd rather shoot Fred. Now get going. We have to catch Mrs Morgan.'

In for a penny, in for a pound, he reflected as he gave a Chinaman a couple of shillings to care for the horse until Fred came to collect him, and headed for the township, he and Danny riding shotgun beside the gig with his employer's wife, son, and maid on board.

'I'm gonna get hell for this,' he told Danny, 'but it's been a long day and I'm not going back tonight. You stable the horse and gig and I'll look after the women.'

The licensee of the Victoria Hotel was pleased to give Jessie his best room, but had no accommodation for her 'nigger' maid until Mike settled the argument by demanding that the girl be given a bunk on the veranda outside Mrs Morgan's room.

'You didn't think of that, did you,' he said to Jessie, 'when you decided to hare off into town?'

'Mr Devlin,' she said, 'I am grateful for your help. But I'm too tired to argue right now. We have to get settled.'

'As you wish,' he shrugged. Porters were taking their luggage upstairs.

'But perhaps you might like to join me at dinner?'

He nodded, irritated. Any port in a storm. She could hardly dine alone. The plantation manager could still be useful.

'Unless you have other arrangements,' she added.

'No. I'll be here at six.'

Jessie smiled at him. 'Don't be cross with me. I feel bad enough already.'

Why was he nervous? Mike strode down the street from the Palace Hotel, stopping to stare at his reflection in a window to make certain his borrowed duds were in order. They were. The publican had done him proud, lending him a complete dinner suit, since, fortunately, his frame was only slightly larger than Mike's. Even the shoes were a good fit and worn enough not to squeak.

Of course Mike had to suffer a ribbing for being a traitor for dining with a lady at the opposition hotel, and the teasing whistles of the barmaids as he walked out past the bar, but he took it all in good part, grateful for the provision of decent clothes.

He ran his hands through his dark curly hair, wishing he'd taken the barber's advice and had a haircut as well as a shave this afternoon, but he'd been in a contrary mood, not wanting to put himself out any more for the wayward wife. Hadn't he gone to enough trouble for her? Especially since she'd taken them for granted, he and Danny, when they caught up with her gig, not realising the problems Mike had faced trying to extricate himself from his four angry prisoners. 'Women!' he

243

muttered. 'As long as their paths are smooth . . .'

But what now? How to get her back to Providence?

While they were waiting for the soup, with Jessie looking a picture in a russet-brown silk dress and a wide dreamy hat swatched in folds of georgette, Mike began to outline his plans, trying hard not to stare at the beautiful woman sitting across from him.

'The only way to get you back is to leave the gig and take a wagon. I can arrange that. I'll also find some men to ride with us since we'll have to stick to the track and we won't be the most popular people at Halfway Creek. They'll come all the way in case . . .'

'Mr Devlin,' she interrupted, 'I'm not going back to Providence.'

'But you can't stay here,' he stammered, avoiding the obvious question of why she'd run off to town in the first place.

'Yes I can,' she replied. 'I've already spoken to Mr Billingsley at the bank and he has promised to find me a suitable house to buy or lease right here in Cairns.' She smiled. 'He was rather confused, wondering what I was up to, but then he saw it all in a flash. It's much cooler on the coast in the summer. He thinks Mr Morgan and I are doing the right thing finding a seaside retreat for the wet season, even if we have come in on the end of it.'

'That'd be right,' Mike said, agreeing politely.

'But you know it's not right, don't you, Mr Devlin? May I call you Mike? I noticed you called me Jessie today.'

'Yes. No. I mean yes,' he replied. Billingsley wasn't the only one confused.

Jessie buttered her bread, turned it over into a sandwich and bit into it. 'I'm starving. I ordered a meal in my room before I came down so that Hanna could eat, and now I'm in the dining room starting again.' She giggled. 'They must think I have a huge appetite. But you, Mike. You don't miss much at Providence. I think you know why I've left my husband.'

'Left?' he echoed dimly, relieved to have the waitress intervene with their soup.'

'Yes,' she said, when the waitress had departed. 'I've left him. Take your soup, or it will go cold.'

The soup was good rich mulligatawny, which he polished off far too soon for comfort, leaving a gap in which he was expected to say something. He looked about him, nodded at a few people, aware that the tongues would have started wagging already at this interesting twosome.

'He's not going to like it,' Mike said at last. 'It's my bet he'll come after you tomorrow. If we meet him on the track, let it sink in that you're on your way home. That should cool things a bit.'

'He may come after Bronte,' she said, 'although that's hardly practical since I'm still feeding him. But he won't come for me.'

'You'd be wrong there. He wouldn't want to lose you.'

'Why not? He's got Sylvia.'

244

There. It was out in the open. She had said it so calmly that it sounded like old news. Mike studied a hunting scene on the wall behind her, making no comment.

'Yes,' Jessie said. 'I thought you knew. I shall make my home here in Cairns. I'll miss Providence but one can hardly stay there under the circumstances. Or I can't anyway, it's just not in my nature.'

Mike eventually found his voice. 'Wouldn't it be better if Sylvia left?'

'I mentioned that but it didn't get me anywhere.'

'You should have insisted,' he growled.

'You think I didn't?'

He nodded. 'I see. I'm sorry, Jessie. But things will work out. When he finds you've left he'll get a shock, and that could be for the best. Make him wake up to himself.'

'It's a bit late for that. I don't care whether he does or not, Mike. I haven't done this to force him to take me back. I know I'm not as attractive as Sylvia, but I won't be put down and picked up again like a possession.'

Mike grinned. 'You're far more attractive than Sylvia. Maybe a few days in town will be good for you. Give you time to think about all this. I can't advise you, but since we're here and in the town's first posh hotel, would you care for some wine?'

'I'd love it,' she said, that sweet smile of hers almost breaking his heart. He wished he could say to her that they ought to keep going. Take the baby, take Hanna, board a ship for Brisbane or Sydney where he'd look after them for the rest of his days. Forget Corby Morgan, he's not good enough for you.

'For a start,' she said, 'I'll just have a holiday here at the hotel. You're right, I will need time to think this through now that I'm away from them. I feel better already, the strain has lifted.'

Until tomorrow, he thought. Until Morgan comes hurtling into town. I ought to stay awhile and keep an eye on her, but I can't intrude unless she asks me to.

No such invitation was forthcoming. They enjoyed a pleasant evening together with no more talk of Providence, discussing everything but the plantation and its inhabitants, and as the clock in the lobby struck nine, Mike escorted Mrs Morgan to the foot of the staircase and wished her good night.

By first light he was riding with Danny back to Providence, travelling cross-country to avoid the gentlemen at Halfway Creek who would shortly be receiving a visit from the law. Mike had made a point of calling in at the Cairns Police Station to report the threats and harassment inflicted on Mrs Morgan and her maid.

The same morning Jessie awoke from a blissful dream, smiling happily until she realised, with a shudder of embarrassment, that the dream had cruelly deceived her.

She turned her thoughts back to walk through the dream again: there she was, back at Providence with Corby, and they seemed to be

245

entertaining a lot of people. Crowds and crowds of people. Corby had his arm linked through hers and was gaily escorting her through the happy gathering. Every so often he stopped to smile at her, to whisper encouragement and give her little hugs, because he was so proud of her and she of him, her lovely husband.

As the crowds of admirers pressed in on them, he put an arm about her, drawing her to him to protect her. When at last they emerged they were both laughing, holding hands, and they moved forward, so much at ease together, to converse with their guests. Some of the faces were familiar, some were not but it didn't matter to the joyful pair, with the result that Corby's next move seemed so natural, not at all out of place. Before them all he took her in his arms and kissed her passionately. 'You're wonderful,' he whispered to her. 'I love you, Jessie.' At that moment, she was so proud.

But as daylight dismissed the shadowy dream, she realised with a shock that the man was not Corby but Mike Devlin.

'Oh good Lord!' she said guiltily, as if someone might have witnessed the dream.

But as she rested, waiting for Bronte to stir, she allowed herself the luxury of the dream yet again. Why wasn't her husband like that, so sweet and gentle, proud of her, supportive instead of constantly rejecting her? Though he kept a respectful distance, Mike was everything that Corby was not: he really seemed to care about her and he treated her like an equal, never insulting her intelligence as Corby did.

Eventually Jessie decided that the dream had probably emanated from Mike's forceful handling of that nasty situation at Halfway Creek, which must have upset her more than she'd thought. It was a silly dream anyway, confusing the two men. Then again – she giggled – she'd certainly enjoyed kissing Mike, even if it were only in a dream.

Now she wished he'd been able to stay in town. When she was with him her troubles with Corby didn't seem so bad. She wondered if she were half in love with Mike Devlin, whatever that might mean. Since he and Corby clashed so much it was obvious he wouldn't stay much longer at the plantation, and the thought of Providence without Mike depressed her.

By this time the dream had slipped back into the night, leaving her feeling bereft and afraid to face the reality of trouble and uncertainty.

When the boss rode in with the officer gentleman, the servants couldn't do enough to accommodate them. Toby disappeared with the horses, promising a good feed for them and a good rub-down. The cook sped out to the back veranda to take the muddy boots and to hand each man a chilled bottle of beer, assuring them that 'plenty tip-top dinner still hot'. He accompanied them across to the outdoor showers by the pepper tree, having checked that the pipe contraption was, this night, in good working order, because the boss could get angry when he was soaped up

246

and the water stopped flowing. Tommy screeched at Mae to bring plenty towels and clean clothes for the gentlemen, which he placed on the wooden table behind the corrugated iron screens.

Then he stood outside, wringing his hands in fear as the two men splashed happily in the showers under the lanterns, laughing like schoolboys, drinking beer, luxuriating in the flow of fresh water that was washing away the mud and sweat of the day.

Tommy handed their dirty clothes to Mae, who rushed away with them, black-slippered feet flying. Soon the strain became too much for Tommy, and he too ran, to take refuge in his kitchen.

'I feel much better now,' Harry said, pulling on his trousers.

'Could you go another bottle of beer?' Corby asked him.

'I certainly could, I was so thirsty that one hardly touched the sides.'

'Good, come on up to the house.'

'Just give me a minute, Corby, I'll make a few notes for my report, and then, duty done, I'll join you.'

'Waste of a bloody day,' Corby said. 'Do you think they'll turn up tomorrow?'

'I've no idea,' Harry said, 'but I have to try again. Can't let an opportunity like this slip away.'

They parted in the yard, reinvigorated, looking forward to a few drinks and the excellent dinner Tommy had promised.

Corby went through the kitchen, bagging two more bottles of beer, and made for the parlour where Sylvia was sitting primly in a white dress, her dark hair pinned up and threaded with pink ribbons. He nodded to her as he went to the sideboard and took out two beer steins. 'You're looking very pretty.'

Without waiting for an answer he slumped into his big armchair. 'I've had the worst day of my life. I've been eaten alive by mosquitoes, sucked on by leeches, squelched through swamps and dehydrated by the most ferocious heat. All to no avail. No sign of the damn blackbirders. No sign of anything except great frogs and watersnakes.'

'Oh, you poor thing,' she said.

They both sat silently until he had recovered enough to ask after Bronte. He never forgot to ask after his son.

'How is he? How is the lad today?'

'I don't know,' she replied in a low voice.

'What do you mean, you don't know? Just because you and Jessie are having a war there's no excuse to ignore the child.'

'I never ignore Bronte,' she said quietly. 'I don't know how he is because he's not here.'

'Where is he then? Don't tell me Jessie's got him down there with the Kanaka women at this hour? Tell Elly to go and fetch her.'

'She can't,' Sylvia said. 'Jessie's not here either. She's gone and taken Bronte.'

Her reply hadn't sunk in. 'What do you mean, she's gone. Gone where?'

'To Cairns, I think.'

He was out of his seat and charging through to Jessie's room. The bed was made, the wide double bed. The bassinet looked bare without its mosquito net and he stood staring down at the wire base, hardly comprehending that the mattress was missing too. His son was gone! Still unable to believe this catastrophe, Corby tore open the little dresser that held the child's things; his clothes and soft toys. It was empty. And Jessie's tin trunk was gone too. He wrenched at a wardrobe door. Quite a few of her clothes still hung there, but there were gaps, and satin-covered hangers swung nervously before him as if penitent at being caught unawares.

'Sylvia!' he roared, but there was no need, she was at the door.

'Where did she go?'

'She took the gig and went to town. She took Hanna with her. And Bronte.'

'I can see that, you idiot. Why didn't you stop her?'

'How could I stop her?' Sylvia sulked. 'I didn't see her go. She left before I woke up.'

'You're lying, you little bitch.' He grabbed her arm. 'You were up at dawn.'

Sylvia pulled away from him. 'Stop it, you're hurting me. I was tired, I went back to bed. Father tried to stop her, he said. He's terribly upset. From what I hear she cursed him, said dreadful things to him and just drove away.'

'Oh my God! She's got Bronte and she's out on the road on her own.'

Sylvia shrugged. 'She'll be well in Cairns by now.'

'How do you know? Anything could happen on that road. If she's put my son in danger I'll kill her.'

'I doubt she's in danger,' his sister-in-law said spitefully. 'Mike Devlin has gone with her.'

Corby's head spun. He felt dizzy as if sunstroke was weighing down on him again. He held the end of the bed for support. 'Are you telling me the truth?'

'Yes. Can I get you a brandy?'

'Stay where you are. You say Devlin has gone too. With her?'

'Yes.'

Corby was confused. Spluttering. 'Wha' . . . what about the p-plantation? I left him in charge. Who's been working as overseer?'

'No one as far as I know. But what could I do? They obviously chose this day because your back was turned.'

For a second there, Corby almost slapped her in his rage, needing to strike out at someone. But he heard Harry coming up the passage, calling: 'Yoo-hoo. Anyone home?'

'In the parlour,' Corby called to him. 'I'll be right with you.'

He closed the bedroom door. 'What time did they leave?'

'About seven o'clock this morning, I think.'

'By Christ, I'll kill them!' He stormed about the bedroom. 'How dare

248

she do this! How dare that snake-in-the-grass make off with my wife and my child! Tell Toby to saddle a fresh horse, I'm going after them.'

'You can't go at this hour, it's too late. You'd be even more at risk on that dark road. Sit down on the bed a minute, I'll get you a brandy.' She dashed outside, relieved to be away from him, and greeted Harry with a warm smile. 'Oh dear, I believe you had a hard day. Do help yourself to a drink, I'll be back in a minute. Corby's not feeling too well.'

Harry was disturbed. 'Isn't he? I thought he handled the day well for a newcomer to the field.'

'Touch of the sun, I think,' she murmured. She hoped Corby would stay unwell and she'd have Harry to herself for the evening.

'You look dreadful,' she said to Corby, handing him a double brandy.

'And why wouldn't I?' he shouted. 'Get Toby. I want to know what happened on the plantation today.'

'Leave it for now,' she said. 'If anything had gone wrong, we'd have heard. That trooper was here. And you know what tittle-tattles the Abos are. As soon as Father heard that Mike Devlin had run off too, he took a horse and rode into the fields. The silly fool, he's exhausted now, he's gone to bed. If there'd been any trouble he'd have said so. Why don't you lie down?'

Corby glared at her. 'Lie down? Are you mad? My manager has run off with my wife and you want me to lie down as if I'm some old dodderer!' He drank the brandy in a gulp and tapped angrily on the bedside table. 'She could have done better than him. I wouldn't have thought it of her to run off with the hired help.'

'He's always had eyes for Jessie,' her sister said. 'I'm surprised you didn't notice. Coming up here with his reports and hanging about her desk with his calf-eyes. Jessie could do no wrong, she was the angel looking after his Kanakas. It was his idea, you know, that she started going down to the compound. Probably so that they could spend more time together.'

'Why didn't you tell me?'

She sniffed. 'Why should you care?'

'Because my child is involved, you bloody fool. Because my wife running away with the manager, the bastard, is a scandal the child will never live down. His mother and the plantation manager! It's disgusting!' Corby sat staring at the floor but Sylvia was anxious to get away.

'You've had a shock, Corby. Just stay and rest awhile.'

'No. I have a guest. We'll say nothing about this to Harry. We'll tell him that Mrs Morgan has retired. And thank God your bloody father is out of the race tonight. I couldn't stand another dose of him. In the morning I'll decide what to do.'

Disappointed, Sylvia followed him into the parlour.

Sergeant McBride heard much the same story. He'd stripped off and plunged into the bustling creek near Mike's eyrie to rid himself of the mangrove stink, then let himself into the house, not perturbed that his host wasn't about. He was probably up at the main house. McBride pulled a singlet and underpants from his swag, washed his shirt and hung it to dry under the house, confident that with a good wring-out it'd be dry by morning. Then he brushed the dry mud from his uniform. It was the best he could do. McBride travelled light.

He lit a lantern and made his way into the house, watching for Mike's pet, Snake, who always gave him a start. Having established that Snake was content to languish, wound about the back steps watching for nocturnal visitors, he made himself at home. In the kitchen cupboard he found a bottle of whisky, opened, fine Irish whisky at that – the lad had good taste – and being a bit on the hungry side, he raided the Coolgardie safe for some cheese and hefty slices of corned beef.

After that he sat on the veranda in the warm velvety night, looking at the occasional stars that glimpsed from dark depths, with his feet up, and the good whisky in his hand.

The trooper they'd left on the plantation broke his reverie. 'No go today, Sarge?' he asked as he tramped up the steps.

'Not a whisper,' McBride said. 'You blokes get fed all right?'

'Yes. Tamba's looking after us. But she says you oughta come down if you want a feed.'

'Don't worry about me,' McBride replied. 'I'll wait for Mike.' He grinned, holding up his glass. 'Amazing how whisky can stave off hunger for a while.'

'You'll have a long wait. Mike's shot through.'

'Where to? Over to Helenslea? What's wrong there now?'

'Nothing's wrong there,' the trooper said. 'I wouldn't mind a drop of that whisky.'

'It's not mine to offer,' McBride growled.

'That doesn't matter. We won't see Mike about here for a while. He's taken off with Morgan's wife.'

'Where'd you get that tale?'

'It's true. He was supposed to be on the job here today but he arranged for me to stay with him to keep an eye on the Kanakas.' He spread his beefy hands wide. 'You coulda knocked me down with a feather when he comes along and says he has to leave the plantation for a while. Some overseer! Then I thought he'd only be an hour or so, but he doesn't come back. So at noon I goes up to Tamba for some lunch and the Kanakas are all abuzz. That's when I heard that Mrs Morgan took the baby and the Abo nurse and left for Cairns.'

'Why would she want to do that?'

The trooper grinned. 'Easy enough to work out, since she left with the gig packed to the ears, and Mike went with her.'

'Mike hasn't gone, his things are all here,' McBride said. 'And you'd better shut your trap on that story, I don't believe a word of it. Mike wouldn't slink off like that, he's not the type.'

'All right.' The trooper shrugged. 'You stick to your guns, but if

250

you want some tucker, Tamba's waiting.'

Corby was drunk. All through the meal he'd been swallowing glass after glass of wine, and then he'd started on the port, keeping up a pretence of gaiety for Harry's benefit.

'You can count me out tomorrow, old chap,' he said, brave enough now, in his cups, to refuse to join them, not caring what they thought of him. And since he couldn't send Devlin in his place he made another suggestion. 'I'll let you have two or three of the Abo boys, Harry, they'll be more help to you than me. And I've never met Duval, so you can pretend to be me, I'll give you some mufti to wear.'

'By all means,' Harry agreed. 'I don't blame you. I wouldn't go back there if it weren't so important.' He waved away the bottle that Corby was proffering. 'No thanks, I've had quite enough to drink.' He turned to Sylvia. 'Now tell me, Miss Langley, how do you like plantation life?'

'It's wonderful,' she smiled, not daring to say anything else with Corby frowning at her. She had intended to tell Harry that she found life here too lonely, a misery in fact, hoping that he'd feel sorry for her and consider rescuing her. 'But I do find the climate trying at this time of the year.'

'Bloody trying if you're sitting in the middle of a swamp,' Corby muttered, reaching for the port. 'Have another drink, Harry.'

'Not for me, thanks. I have to be up early again.'

'That's right,' Sylvia said, taking his side. 'Harry has to be up at dawn, Corby. You can sleep in.'

'How the hell can I sleep in,' he snapped at her, 'when I've got to manage the whole show here on my own?'

Harry didn't appear to catch that slip. He stood up. 'I really must turn in now if you don't mind.'

Sylvia despaired. She had hoped Corby would go to bed first or even fall down drunk, but it was obvious he had no intention of moving, destroying any chance she had of being alone with Harry.

But then Tommy came racing up the passage. 'Rider coming, boss.'

'What rider? At this hour?' Corby had to make two attempts to get out of his chair, staggering towards the door. Harry went to assist him but was pushed away, and Sylvia winced. What must Harry think of them? Last night had been bad enough, but this was worse.

Fortunately it was a trooper with a message for Scott-Hughes, so they all went out to hear what he had to say.

'The *Java Lady* went down, sir,' he began, 'foundered on a reef.'

'Good Lord! Any survivors?'

'Only five that we know of. They were on a raft and were picked up by a passing ship. Lucky they were, no water or provisions. But they were sailors, crew of the *Java Lady* hoping they'd be carried towards the mainland.'

'Was Frenchy Duval among them?' Harry asked hopefully.

'No, sir. That's the bad part. The crewmen are savage on him. He and a couple of his mates grabbed the longboat and rowed off, not giving anyone else a chance. She went down fast, they say, in heavy weather, with breakers smashing over her. These blokes were washed overboard but Frenchy didn't stop to pick anyone up. And the poor bloody Kanakas on board . . . excuse me, miss,' he apologised to Sylvia for his language, but she'd hardly heard. 'About forty of them, they say, they didn't have a chance, shoved down in the hold. They went down with the ship.'

'Oh dear God!' Harry said, shocked. 'That's terrible!'

'Not the first time, sir. Another ship was wrecked a while back up near Cape Tribulation, drowning about sixty Chinese coolies headed for the goldfields. But that Frenchy Duval is a slippery customer, he could be anywhere by now. So we've lost him again.'

'That's true,' Harry said. 'You must be tired. Thank you for bringing us this news.' He turned to Corby. 'Can we offer the trooper a meal?'

Corby waved to Tommy, who was standing by, listening to the drama. The cook nodded eagerly. 'I fetch, pretty quick.'

'What a dreadful thing,' Harry said to Corby, who didn't seem concerned.

'Good news, Harry. You won't have to put in another day in the swamps. Come and have a drink now.'

Sylvia saw Harry's irritation and stepped in. 'I don't think there's anything to celebrate.' But Corby was already stumbling back into the house.

'I shall have to tell McBride and the other men,' Harry said to her.

'Of course,' she replied. 'We'll send Toby down to tell them the morning assembly is cancelled. And when your trooper has been fed, Toby can take him down to their sleeping quarters.'

'Good,' he smiled. 'You're very efficient.'

Sylvia could have sent Elly to find Toby, but she had a better idea. 'Toby sleeps in the stables. If you'd like to bring the lantern, Harry, we'll go and find him.'

Having sent Toby on his way they walked slowly back to the house, where all was quiet now, the yard deserted. Harry hung the lantern back on its hook. 'Do you ever come to town, Sylvia?'

'I've only been there once. It's difficult from here with no one to escort me.'

'What if I came for you?'

'Would you? I couldn't very well criticise the life here in front of my brother-in-law, but I do get so lonely. Not much happens out this way. It's a far cry from the social life I was accustomed to back home.'

'Then we'll have to change that,' he said, taking her hands.

'Oh, that would be so nice of you. I'd better go in now.' Sylvia gave him a soft peck on the cheek, just a friendly peck, but it had the desired effect. Harry took her in his arms and kissed her.

'You're so beautiful,' he whispered. 'I've been wanting to do that ever since I first set eyes on you.'

Sylvia was in heaven with this handsome officer's arms about her. Jessie could have Corby, she'd never bother with him again. He wasn't a patch on this sweet and lovely man.

Harry, ever the gentleman, reluctantly released her and stood watching, entranced, as she went quietly to the door, turning, silhouetted against the soft light, to wave to him.

Inside, she hugged herself with joy. She would have gone to Harry's room with him, had he asked her, but he was a romantic and he would court her beautifully. She locked her door. The affair with Corby was over, she'd never allow him near her again.

But on this night there was no need to lock the door. Corby had passed out in his chair. Later, the faithful Tommy came in and helped his drowsy boss to his room and on to his bed.

Several times warriors of the Big River tribe called in at Rawalla's camp. They were strange men, tall, about Joseph's own height, but of a different shape. They had hard bony shoulders and long lean legs which he thought was probably due to the distances they travelled. From Rawalla's description, Irukandji territory extended for at least a hundred miles north and west, and this section was on the south boundary. A concept that intimidated Joseph, coming from his small island. Rawalla said there was no end to this land, that no matter which way you travelled, except east to the sea, you could never come to the finish.

'That is why,' he said loftily, 'the white men and you Kanaka slaves can never defeat us. You would have to fight tribe after tribe as you advanced over the mountains into the plains and on to the deserts until the end of time.'

At first Joseph was disinclined to believe this boast, but when Rawalla began to reel off the names of tribes he had enountered in his travels, and to speak of others he'd been told about, Joseph had to admit he could be right. In which case what chance would he have pushing on any further? He was safer with the white men, or he would have been until the master of Helenslea came at him in a rage.

He would have liked to speak with the Irukandji warriors but he dare not break protocol. They looked at him with the contempt reserved for slaves, their attitude no different from Malaita tribal practices. It was dangerous for slaves even to look at their masters; they risked having their heads smashed in.

Joseph had come to understand that old Rawalla had placed himself outside the tribal family by breaking totems, probably by spending so much time with the white men, but he was tolerated here by acting as a lookout man, too old to be a scout. And he seemed content, especially now that he had his own slave to hunt and work for him. No doubt he was proud of this new status symbol, cackling, showing him off to the warriors. Joseph knew that he himself was only tolerated in this capacity, otherwise these fierce men would have disposed of him very smartly.

Be remaining humble, keeping his eyes downcast and creeping about to serve Rawalla, he remained safe, but at every opportunity he observed the strangers. They wore their hair in topknots glued into shape with beeswax, and the bones through their noses were familiar, human bones the same as chiefs wore at home. Their faces were striped in white and yellow ochre, and their bodies smeared with emu oil and dried mud, which, as he had learned, having to prepare the same mixture for Rawalla, was intended to ward off mosquitoes. And their weapons intrigued him. They carried barbed spears and boomerangs stuck in their belts; and hidden in the small of their backs, held in place by twine, were tomahawks, the handles upward for swift and easy access.

Joseph admired this innovation – he would love to try that movement himself – and the boomerang fascinated him. He'd seen one of the Irukandji bring down a duck with one, so easily it just seemed to require the flick of a wrist, and then the weapon had come back to drop at the thrower's feet. He'd asked Rawalla to teach him how to throw a boomerang, but the old rogue had refused. Soon after, Rawalla's boomerang had disappeared from the camp, hidden somewhere, Joseph guessed, lest the slave used it on his master.

But as long as he kept the peace, Rawalla had nothing to fear from him, the Kanaka had made that plain. In this new role Joseph was properly respectful, biding his time, making himself useful while he worked out what to do. He worried about Paka and Ned. They would have escaped in the night, there'd been plenty of time before the dawn call, but like him they'd now be outcasts. He wondered where they might have gone and hoped they were still free. Ned had been in this country for years, he would know what to do.

Why then was he still worried about them? At night he had had dreams. He dreamed that his friends were lying in muddy graves, rain pelting down on them, but they were still alive, calling to him. And Ratasali too invaded his dreams, a roaring angry entity, demanding his son rouse himself to action. His father stormed at him, appalled that his son should so demean himself by willingly becoming a slave, but when Joseph tried to explain he had no voice, he was struck dumb in the presence of his father. Then Ratasali would show him his powers. Joseph saw him smite Mr Betts. He saw that master fall from his horse. And he heard voices singing the dear island songs as Mr Betts was lowered into a yawning grave with the Malaita chief standing grinning beside Mrs Lita.

All these things he saw but he dismissed them when the sun came up to rescue him from the nightmares and he went about his daily chores. Knowing he was trapped between the white men and the Big River men, Rawalla allowed him more time to himself as long as he brought back fish or game, so Joseph began to explore the river banks. He ran upstream for miles and miles, regaining his strength after the punishing field labour and poor rations, pushing himself to travel as fast as he could before it was time to begin the race back to the camp. For assuredly Rawalla would signal to his people if he failed to return. Once again he was overcome with admiration for this land and its plentiful food supply. The river was alive with fish. Fat ducks by the thousands were there for the taking. Bush turkeys and their eggs were numerous and the bush produce of fruit and nuts and yams and fat worms were only a few of the edibles that Rawalla, pointing with his stick, had ordered him to collect.

One day when he was fishing he heard the unmistakable roar of waterfalls, so, leaving his catch behind he took a chance and climbed higher, clambering frantically over slippery boulders to find a view.

It was magnificent! A cascade of such power that it took his breath away, thundering and hurtling from the heights, dazzling even in this cloudy light, a massive curtain of white light.

Impelled to see this wonder from the heights, Joseph began to climb again. There was no time to detour. He found footholds, tested and clung to damp trees, swung on to ledges and dug his toes into crevices as he forged higher and higher until at last he was up there, as he felt, with the gods of nature, a part of that Dreaming Rawalla spoke of so often. This was a holy, magical place that would, Joseph knew, bring him good fortune.

He plunged into the tingling waters, drinking the goodness, and then he saw that he'd found an easy way across the river, a place that was free of those dreaded crocodiles. Ahead of him stubborn boulders like great stepping stones littered the river bed, forcing the waters to plough about them, immune to the pressure.

Splashing about at the edge, gurgling in the shallow side torrents, Joseph laughed. That old villain Rawalla. He'd never mentioned the falls. He'd never said that the Big River men could cross any time they wished, which accounted for the stories he'd heard on the plantation of wild blacks coming over the river to kill and steal cattle, to kidnap women, to set fire to crops.

Joseph studied the falls and the depth of the water below, deciding it was too dangerous to try from the heights, but further down he climbed out on to a rocky outcrop, and stood, considering a dive, weighing up his chances. If he could do it he could cut a good half-hour from his return journey.

Just then, two young men, Irukandji warriors, stepped from the molten greenery to stare at him.

Joseph had every respect for their skill with spears and boomerangs. He knew that when he came up from that rock pool far below they could pick him off like a fat fish, so he gestured to them to come out and join him on his high and precarious position.

They edged forward, dropping their weapons, but Joseph knew that

255

those knife-sharp tomahawks were ever present. What a marvellous feint, he thought, hugely impressed, a pity our Malaita men never thought of that one. A man could walk up, seemingly unarmed, arms outstretched, and kill you in a second. But they won't get me. He watched them closely. If one hand went to a shoulder he'd be gone, over the edge.

Joseph desperately wanted to establish contact with someone in the tribe. With another human being, he supposed, someone his own age, as they were. He was sick to death of Rawalla's whines and nags, and his stumps of teeth that required his slave to chop all his food, and the abominable stink of him. He stamped his feet, taking a risk on the shiny rock, and beckoned to them again to come join him.

They started to laugh, the two young men, pushing at each other boisterously to be first to get out there with this madman, and Joseph, rejoicing, laughed too. Planting his toes firmly, he pretended he was about to dive, challenging them, but they held back. There was a game here, and this, he knew, was a game for his life. It was too late for them to attack him up here but if he misjudged he could break his neck down there.

From their reticence he knew that for all their prowess in the bush they didn't know how to dive, so he pointed below and threw his arms wide like a hawk preparing to soar down after prey. He saw the excitement in their faces as they urged him on, and reacted to it from sheer bravado.

A spring took him into the air and far from the cliff to avoid the rocks nestling too close to the base, and as his body skimmed through the spray from the falls he limbered in like an arrow, head tucked in, protected by his shoulders, legs disciplined together to cut a fine stripe through the depths but the muscles relaxed, flexible ready for the impact.

Joseph flew. This was higher than any cliff he'd encountered but so was the thrill of this moment. To be flying through the air with more grace than those rumbling, tumbling waters behind him was a challenge in itself and he was almost disappointed when his hands sliced through the surface of the churning pool below and he shot into the depths, twisting now, turning, trying to break his headlong plunge into deceptive waters that could produce a collision any second. But he came about, arms working like oars, feet pounding, and fought his way up again, up and up, bursting for breath, fighting for air somewhere above him, too far! Was it too far? Oh no! He had to keep going, to fight that narcotic, hypnotic voice that was telling him to stop battling, to rest, to lie back and enjoy the lethargy of this magnificent deep.

But Joseph knew about that trap, that sylvan snare. He'd heard men speak of the tantalising nymphs of the deep who whispered to them to stay, to tarry awhile. He made one last mighty effort and shot suddenly from the surface, gasping for the precious air, treading water, pounding his hands on the turbulent waters about him in a tattoo of triumph to be

256

witnessed by the great falls themselves, for he had beaten them.

He made an effort to continue on in the white waters but they were too swift, too rough, swirling and slamming around jutting rocks as they fell away to the river. He wished he had a canoe that would take him back to the camp in no time, and wondered if Rawalla would let him build one. Probably not.

Further down he collected the fish he'd caught with his net and began the return run, soon becoming aware that he was being followed. Two men were bearing down on him.

With no weapons to defend himself Joseph turned to confront them, holding his hands up, palms forward in peaceful salute. He wasn't surprised to see it was the two warriors from the falls, running as if they were being chased by demons.

The first man stopped, slapped him on the back and in a torrent of guttural sounds and excited gestures made it clear that he was being congratulated on the dive. The young man had the widest grin Joseph had ever seen, his large teeth remarkably white against his black face, and Joseph, relieved, responded, pointing to the camp. 'Rawalla,' he said, to identify himself in case the mood changed.

They nodded impatiently. Obviously they knew that. But they had a new challenge. A race? Was that what they wanted. He pointed to himself and then in the direction of Rawalla's camp, miles downstream, and with all the nodding and pointing and jumping about, it seemed that was what they wanted. Or rather he hoped so. With the challenge of the dive not accepted, they were here now to redeem themselves. He held up the fish he was carrying – he couldn't leave them behind, and they would slow him down. But the spokesman of the pair held up his spear; a warrior wouldn't ditch that either. So the runners were more or less evenly matched.

Without warning, the pair took off and Joseph grabbed his catch and hurtled after them.

They immediately made for the open scrub away from the river bank, leaping over fallen trees and tearing through the bush. Joseph stuck with them, since they were obviously using known foot tracks, but it took a huge effort, they were fast. By the time they came down a rise to a clearing with the river valley spread out before them, Joseph was caught up in the sport. He forged ahead, passing one man, who by the sound of him was tiring, and then went after the other, gaining on him. With a whoop he shot past, racing into more familiar country, watching for landmarks; a wrong turn now could land him up to his shoulders in dense scrub.

He shot by a clump of palms back into the wetlands, not unlike the jungle back home. Joseph was in his element. He knew the way now, this blackfellow had no chance of catching him. Bare feet skimming over the damp and greasy earth, Joseph made for the finishing line which was only about a mile away now, laughing, jubilant. He'd show them what a Malaita man could do.

And then he remembered that he was a slave. A slave who beat one of his masters in any sort of challenge had to be killed to maintain the superiority of the tribe. It was very difficult to think like a slave, but he recalled the contempt of other visitors to Rawalla's camp. Did these tribes have the same laws? If he won, he may not live to boast. Gradually he slowed. When the Aborigine gained on him he put in an extra spurt for appearances' sake, making him work for the lead, and added gasps of tired breath as the winner charged past him.

Puffing, he tossed the fish at Rawalla's feet, nodded meekly to his opponent and threw himself on the ground, exhausted.

Rawalla's first sight of his slave brought a round of abuse, but the warrior silenced him. When the third man came running in, taking his defeat in good part, Joseph was treated with respect. He was invited to sit by the campfire by the young warrior, whose name was Guloram and who obviously held rank in the tribe since Rawalla, with scowling resentment, had to agree to this break in protocol. And worse. After a couple of half-hearted replies to questions, Guloram shouted angrily at Rawalla forcing him to translate a conversation between himself and the stranger.

Joseph was delighted by this man's effort at communication, even if they were motivated only by curiosity; he asked about Joseph's tribe, who they were and where they came from, but gave nothing away about his own people.

In the morning Rawalla kicked Joseph awake with his bony feet, ordering his slave to pack up his squalid belongings.

'Where are you going?' Joseph asked.

'Across the valley into the high country,' Rawalla said gleefully. 'My friend Guloram a very important man.'

'Yes,' Joseph said, careful not to show his own pleasure that he'd be rid of this old wretch and confident that he'd be safe from harm at this campsite now that he'd found a friend in Guloram.

As if to reinforce this opinion, Rawalla, in a happy mood, poked him with his stick. 'Guloram says you a good feller,' he wheezed.

Joseph nodded, packing Rawalla's blanket, cooking pot and other odds and ends into a canvas swag, hurrying because the other two men were waiting and he'd hate them to change their minds and leave Rawalla behind. But then, reluctantly, the old man admitted: 'He says you can come too.'

Startled, Joseph straightened up. 'Oh no!' he said. 'You thank Guloram. You tell him he is very kind but I would rather stay here. Tell him I will not bother anyone.'

Rawalla gave a hoot of laughter, and in between guffaws translated Joseph's reply. As they listened, Guloram and his friend began to laugh too, pointing at Joseph and doubling up in merriment.

'What's so funny?' he asked, bewildered, but Guloram was impatient to be away. He beckoned to them to come along.

'Wait,' Joseph pleaded. 'Why can't I stay? Ask him why.'

'You stupid,' Rawalla said, not bothering to pass on the question. 'You drown here. Flood coming.'

'Oh, flood! I understand.' He grinned, seeing the funny side of it now. 'This bank gets flooded.'

Rawalla spat. 'You doan understand, you bloody fool.' He waved his arms at the river. 'Big flood comen. Drown you here. Drown all them white men there too, allasame finish.'

Guloram shouted at them now, and Rawalla screamed at Joseph to hurry, so he picked up the hefty swag and plodded along behind his master, anxious to know more about this flood. Rawalla was probably exaggerating again, he had some wild tales.

He found his chance en route while the other two went ahead, hunting. Food had to be found. He had noticed they never carried supplies with them, nor did Rawalla hoard food. What they had they ate, tomorrow was another day.

'I think you boast about a flood,' he said. 'I never heard of a flood that size. Only the sea can do that.'

'Rivers just as good,' Rawalla said defensively.

'Not much rain,' Joseph scoffed. 'The wet season is leaving.'

'You bloody fool, you. Big rivers comen from far, far. One fat river feeds next river.' He clapped his hands together. 'Bang! Now two big fat rivers comen. Flood all the land, miles and miles.'

'I don't see any fat river. How do you know?'

'They know,' Rawalla snorted, pointing to the hills. 'My people know, they hear the frogs, they send message rivers comen. Dirty whites all die.'

Joseph walked Rawalla until the old man was exhausted, pushing west as Guloram had indicated. He could have run away sooner but he couldn't give Rawalla the chance to raise the alarm. If his voice couldn't be heard, a smoke signal or another of their bush signals would alert them. It was obvious that none of them would want him to cross the river and warn the hated plantation people. From what he'd picked up in their amused backward glances, they were happy to let nature mount the attack while they pulled back.

It was true that he could hardly conceive of a flood of this magnitude, outside of tidal waves, but everything in this land was so big. Even the plantation. He'd been stunned at the size of that, thinking of the garden plots at home. And then he'd been told of towns down the coast which were not hundreds but thousands of miles apart, which made Rawalla's talk of endless land feasible. He had to get away, to warn his friends.

'Stop!' Rawalla cried. 'I'm tired. I can't walk no more.'

'We must keep going,' Joseph insisted, urging him on until he dropped to the earth.

'Stop!' Rawalla commanded. 'I must rest. You sit and watch for Guloram. And don't go away or he will be angry.'

Soon he was snoring, curled up in the cavernous roots of a fig tree, and Joseph slipped away, making for the falls again.

259

As he journeyed on, silently this time, afraid of attracting attention, he watched the far bank, knowing the dangers ahead but resolved to warn his friends somehow. Would they laugh at him? Would they believe this wild story? Doubts were creeping in. Where is this flood? they would say. If he could get to them.

That was the next problem. He loped through the scrub, keeping away from the blackfellow trails, bent double at times to avoid being spotted by Irukandji scouts, worrying about his chances on the other side. He was not only an absconder but an escaped prisoner, wanted for that crime. Joseph, for days, had tried not to think about Mr Betts's accusations and his terrible rage, but now it was time to face the fact that he must have committed a terrible wrong. Broken a taboo probably.

But Mrs Lita had been willing and had wanted him. It wasn't as if he'd deflowered a virgin. Had he done so he could understand the white men's anger, but Mrs Lita, he knew from the talk on the plantation, had been married and her husband had died. She was a woman without a man and therefore entitled to seek her pleasure, was she not? When he reached the falls he sat down and thought about this and it depressed him. His escape from the white world had been a headlong rush of fear, and now that he was contemplating returning, the fear began to rise again like bile.

Why was he doing this? He felt the presence of Ratasali again, his dominating father, telling him to turn back. He could live here with the dark tribes, make friends with them. 'You've made a good start,' the voice argued. 'Stay with them and in time they will see you are a man among men, a powerful person, and respect you.'

Joseph slapped cold water on to his face to keep his head clear of these grandiose thoughts. They might tolerate him, these black people, but they'd never respect him, he'd grow old, an outcast like Rawalla. And if that were all life had to offer him here, he might as well be back in Malaita.

'Yes,' the voice taunted him, 'where the chiefs, whoever they are, would kill you on sight, for fear you'd have the power to overthrow them.'

He spent a dismal hour, mesmerised by the falls, before he gathered the courage to make the crossing, and then he found himself on the plantation side trying to convince himself not to be a coward and retreat. Paka and Ned had saved him from hanging, he had to find them somehow. First, though, where was he?

If he travelled downriver he would have to pass through other plantations before he came to Helenslea, and Providence, where his friends lived, was further still. If this flood came, villages or habitations on the lower reaches of the river would be more vulnerable to a deluge. This much he did know of such matters. A high tide combined with a flood would be devastating. From Providence, that big river flowed on to the sea. It was the last plantation down that road because no bridge had been built across the river.

Still he hesitated. Surely the white men with all their cleverness knew about these things? And the gentle Yindini tribe down there. But they had no contact with the belligerent Irukandjis, who despised them for bowing to white rule, and it was the Big River tribes who had been given this precious information, this warning. It was too late to go back now anyway. Rawalla would be screaming, telling Guloram that Joseph wasn't to be trusted, wailing at losing his slave, his status symbol.

Joseph grinned. That was the only bright light in his miserably uncertain situation; to be free of his treacherous keeper. A day with Rawalla had seemed like a month, the camaraderie of the canefields was better than that. With no weapons, with no plan, he trudged away from the falls to lose himself in the jungle of greenery that hugged the river and bordered a strange plantation where men on horseback, with guns, were likely to shoot him on sight.

The native, Talua, slunk through the undergrowth wearing only battered half-mast trousers. No god this, just a terrified young South Sea Islander caught between two strange worlds, feeling his way as darkness closed in.

Scott-Hughes was aghast. 'Good Lord! I had no idea. The poor fellow! I didn't see Mrs Morgan last night, of course, but I was given the impression that she'd retired early.'

'Retired's right,' Sergeant McBride grinned. 'Retired right out of the picture.'

'No wonder he was behaving curiously,' reflected the lieutenant. 'I was rather put out with him for his callous attitude towards the shipwreck. He didn't seem at all concerned that the islanders on board suffered a frightful death, but I suppose he was in a state of shock.' He looked about him as gangs of Kanakas hurried past on their way into the fields. 'Everything seems back to normal now, wouldn't you say, Sergeant?'

McBride lifted his cap and scratched his head. 'Yes and no. The Kanakas are behaving so we don't have any more business here. We ought to take the prisoner Mantala, and move out but I'd like to hang about for a few hours.'

'Suits me,' Harry said. 'I don't mind telling you, Sergeant, I'd appreciate the delay.' His eyes twinkled. 'Miss Langley is charming company.'

McBride groaned. He might have known young Harry would fall for that flirty girl. As if there weren't enough trouble here. Where the hell was Mike? If what he'd heard about Morgan and his sister-in-law were true, then Harry was stepping on his host's toes too. But maybe that wasn't a bad thing, give Morgan a run for his money. Pity Mike wasn't here, he'd lay odds on Harry winning the lady. 'Did you see Morgan this morning?' he asked.

'Yes, he was saddled up and riding out when I was on my way over to the house for breakfast. He seemed in good spirits. Not a word about his wife. But then why would he? It's rather embarrassing.'

'That's only the half of it,' McBride said. 'Mike's missing too. He disappeared yesterday.'

'Where did he go?'

'There's a rumour among the Kanakas that he took off with Mrs Morgan . . .'

'Surely not!'

'No, I don't think so either. More like it he heard she'd driven off and that left him no choice but to see she got to town safely. He's got a lot of time for her, and the silly woman has the baby with her, and the nurse. No man could leave them wandering around these parts on their own.'

'Of course,' Harry said. 'At least that will be a relief for Morgan.'

'Don't bank on it,' McBride grinned. 'I reckon his lordship has put two and two together and come up with five.'

'Why do you think Mrs Morgan left?' Harry asked.

'Don't know,' the sergeant lied. 'But for a bloke like Morgan it's handy to lay the blame elsewhere, and I'm betting Mike will cop all the blame. The fact remains that Morgan is on his own here today and he's not the best at handling the Kanakas, to put it mildly, so if you keep your troops patrolling it will give him a big boost.'

'Glad to,' Harry replied.

'I think I'll go up and have a talk with the Professor,' McBride said. 'I'll see if he knows what's going on.'

He found Lucas sitting dejectedly in a canvas chair near his quarters. 'How are you today, Professor?'

'Quite well, thank you, Sergeant.'

'That's good to hear.' McBride always made a point of not remarking when people looked ill, he believed it made them feel worse. And this old chap was no picture of health today. His white hair was lank and unkempt and there were dark circles under his eyes.

'I wanted to talk to you about Mrs Morgan,' McBride said, as gently as he could. 'I believe she has gone to town.'

'That's correct,' Lucas said dimly.

'We won't go into the ins and outs of it, Professor, domestic difficulties aren't my bailiwick, but I do have to keep the peace. How is Mr Morgan taking his wife's absence? I hear he was unaware that she intended to leave.'

The Professor brushed an imagined crumb from his knee. 'Badly, I'm afraid.'

'He didn't see fit to go after his wife?'

'Pride, sir.'

'You saw her leave, the blacks tell me. You didn't think it was necessary for her to have protection on the journey?'

The old man was upset. 'She refused help. I couldn't stop her. Did she arrive safely?'

'I don't know, but Mike left the plantation a few hours later . . .'

He was surprised. 'Mike? Is he with her? That's a relief. I can't tell you how worried I've been.'

McBride studied him. He wanted to ask if Morgan really was angry. Sometimes in a situation like this, when the wife withdrew, the tension eased. Maybe Morgan and Sylvia were pleased she'd gone. But the old man wasn't up to any more questions concerning his daughters, so McBride let him be.

McBride was the first person Mike came across that morning when he rode in with Danny.

'By cripes, am I glad to see you,' the police sergeant exclaimed. 'Did you find Mrs Morgan?'

'Yes. I had to take her all the way into town.' He turned to Danny. 'You ride up to the homestead and find Toby. Tell him to give you a job. I'll find something permanent for you later.'

'What are you doing with that rascal?' McBride asked.

'Giving him a chance. He got me out of strife so I have to make payback.' He went on to explain about finding Jessie in trouble at Halfway Creek. 'I couldn't bring her back even if she'd wanted to. The creeks are up.'

McBride couldn't contain his curiosity: 'Word has it that Morgan's been carrying on with her sister. Is that right?'

'She'd rather not have that voiced around,' Mike said, finding an excuse to dodge the question.

'Come on, man! This isn't exactly an outpost, you've got your storekeepers and mailmen and traffic with the other plantations; a spot of gossip like that, true or not, moves like greased lightning.'

'Then let it,' Mike said angrily. 'It's nothing to do with us. I heard the *Java Lady* went down; that was a bad business.'

'Terrible. And we spent a wasted day in the swamps. No sign of Frenchy Duval?'

'No. But my information was correct, he did have the Kanakas, poor devils. Everything all right here now?'

'Quiet as mice. And if you want a bit more gossip, Harry's got a crush on Miss Sylvia!'

Mike stared at him and then laughed. 'Oh cripes! God help him.'

The sergeant went to find Morgan. 'We'll be on our way, then.'

Corby wheeled his horse. 'Hang on, I'll be right with you.' He galloped down to the end of the track to where the Kanakas were floundering about, having managed to get a dray bogged, with the horse sweating and struggling in the mud.

'Stop!' he yelled, jumping down from his horse. 'Unload the bloody dray, you idiots! You're not going to make the horse suffer for your stupidity.' The dray was loaded with logs from a cleared patch, timber too good for burning that could be sold to the sawmill.

He strode about as they unloaded and then had them stuff thick

263

foliage around the wheels to form a mat over the bog. Eventually the dray was hauled clear. 'Use your own legs in future,' he yelled, 'keep the dray on the track and carry the timber over to it. You understand?'

They nodded and set to work again. Sighing and shaking his head, Corby marched up to his horse that had ambled up the rise overlooking the river. As he remounted he glanced with appreciation at the fast-flowing stream. It was a fine river and quite beautiful, the greenery on either side mirrored in its depths creating another dimension. It crossed his mind that the river seemed swollen, higher up the banks than usual, but with all the rains they'd had . . . He thanked God the wet season was over at long last, miserable bloody weather! And the pleasant winter was in front of them.

'I'll ride back to see you off,' he said to McBride. 'Don't forget Mantala, I don't want him here.'

'No, he's in for a nice long spell in jail. Mike's back, you know.'

'I didn't know,' Corby said stiffly.

'You'll be pleased to hear your wife's safe and sound in town . . .'

'Excuse me.' Corby turned on him fiercely. 'What my wife does is my business, it's no concern of yours.'

'You're a bloody touchy lot here today,' McBride snapped. 'And let me tell you, Mr Morgan, what happens in my territory is my business. Especially when women go running off on their own.'

Corby refused to reply, to be drawn into the subject. If Jessie was, as the sergeant said, safe and sound in town, then so was Bronte. But the bloody cheek of Devlin to come creeping back here after spiriting Jessie away! Probably come back for his pay. Well, he could go hop for that. Corby was glad McBride and the troopers were leaving. He couldn't think with them around, knowing they were curious about Jessie and feeling boxed in by their scrutiny. By God, she'd pay for this, and so would Devlin.

He'd take Jessie back, if he had to, to get his son home, even though she didn't deserve his consideration after this performance. Devlin must have spent the night in town. With her? Leaving his post here, as if that weren't bad enough, and blatantly arriving in Cairns with his boss's wife. At least Corby had been discreet with Sylvia. And it was different for men, for husbands. Men had needs that women couldn't hope to understand. Would Jessie prefer he went to a bordello like the others did? Or worse, take up with gins like old Betts? Corby bet that Devlin had had his share of both. And now it was Jessie Morgan! The mother of his son!

Corby was in a highly nervous state by the time he turned for the homestead with McBride riding silently beside him. On top of his anger and confusion, trying to decide what to do about Jessie, he now had to face Harry. He cursed himself for not bidding McBride goodbye back there. Why had he volunteered to see them off when he had every excuse to remain in the fields. A slight breach of manners was preferable to the scene confronting him now. Harry would want to thank his hostess, he could hardly leave without doing so.

Unless someone had already told him that Jessie had run off! Someone like Devlin, the bastard!

At that moment he came out of his furious rumblings to see Devlin riding towards him. In a reflex action, faced with the man whom he now considered to be the source of all his troubles from the first day at Providence, Corby grabbed his revolver, shouting abuse at this lecher, this mongrel!

McBride's reaction was fast, shouldering Corby aside, but not fast enough. Corby saw Devlin jerk back, lose his grip and crash to the ground. The sergeant grabbed Corby's gun from him and leapt down, running over to Devlin.

The shot must have been heard for miles, it seemed to echo and re-echo. Kanakas appeared from nowhere, creating hysteria as usual, but Corby stayed on his horse, remaining aloof. It didn't take long for troopers to come galloping in, expecting a riot to be under way, and then, inevitably, Lieutenant Scott-Hughes arrived.

Oh well, Corby thought, calm now. Nobody seemed to be concerned with him, they were all too busy milling about the body on the ground, with McBride shouting for them to stand back. 'I was within my rights,' he told himself. 'That man seduced my wife. He has sabotaged my work here from the first day. They'll never convict me, especially in this frontier country where violence is practically a way of life.' Corby had read the local newspapers from cover to cover, at first appalled by that violence, and then intrigued by reports of gunfights right in the main street. 'In fact,' he told himself, 'judging by the stories I've heard in town of men settling their own arguments with the gun, the horsewhip and even the iron stirrup, I will be more admired than condemned. A man who is prepared to defend his home and hearth.'

He was so absorbed in these reflections, where he saw himself as a hero, a man to be reckoned with, not just a new chum, that it took a while for him to realise that Harry was asking him to dismount.

He did so courteously, straightening his shirt with both hands as he walked away, and adjusting his collar. 'I'm sorry,' he said to Harry, 'but really, he left me no choice. A man can take just so much. My wife, you know.'

'Yes,' Harry said quietly. 'Perhaps we'll just wait here a little while.'

'By all means.' Corby knew that Harry would understand. In return he was prepared to be the dignified prisoner. No weeping or wailing from him. They would have to charge him, their duty, but he was certain his friends could be persuaded to allow him to remain at Providence until the case came to trial. He could put up bail and a gentlemen's promise to remain at the plantation under . . . what did they call it? House arrest. That was it. And no gentlemen would convict him . . .

Corby's reflections came to a sudden halt as the crowd about Devlin thinned out. The man was staggering to his feet, holding a bloodied cloth to his temple! Corby stared at him, shocked and disappointed, as reality snapped him back to the facts of this situation. He had attempted to kill a man and failed, and the consequences of this were even worse than if he'd succeeded. He saw Devlin glance at him and knew he'd made an enemy for life, a dangerous enemy. As McBride stormed over to him, Corby tried to think what he'd said to Harry. He couldn't recall, no matter how frantically he tried, because he was too busy trying to think of a way out of this mess. Above all, he had to keep calm.

'Mr Morgan,' the sergeant snapped, 'you're under arrest for attempted murder.'

'I beg your pardon,' Corby replied. 'If anyone is to blame for this accident, sir, you are.'

The sergeant was taken aback. 'What do you mean?'

'I mean, sir,' Corby retorted, 'that it was my intention to bail up that fellow and demand to know why, as manager, he left this plantation at such a critical time.'

'The hell it was!' McBride said.

But Corby continued. 'Had you not shoved me, causing the gun to fire, by accident, Mr Devlin would not have been wounded. I regret that he has been injured but no one could dispute my right to call him to order for his behaviour.' Corby could feel Harry's eyes on him and he prayed that the lieutenant would keep silent. 'As you can see, Sergeant,' he said, 'Mr Devlin is armed too. In circumstances like this when one has to enforce discipline, as you would know, one doesn't confront an armed man without obvious protection.'

Since McBride seemed confused by his rhetoric, Corby gave a wan smile. 'I'm not known as a good shot. Had I fired deliberately, without your interference, I no doubt would have missed at that distance. Really, Sergeant, you ought to take a hold on yourself.'

Whether the ploy had worked or not, Corby couldn't tell because the sergeant stamped back to hand Devlin over to some island women who were fussing over him. Harry made no comment.

Eventually the policeman returned. 'I have to accept your explanation, Mr Morgan, because Mike won't lay charges, but you'd best keep your nose clean from now on, because I'll be watching you. And I'm not altogether sure that you weren't mixed up with Edgar Betts in that Kanaka trade that went wrong. If I ever hear of you having any illegals on this plantation, believe me, mate, you're a goner.'

Sylvia clung to Harry in the seclusion of the drooping acacias by the stables. 'Oh, Harry, I'm so frightened. Has Corby gone mad?'

'No, dear. I think he was just overwrought. Everything will be all right now. It was as he said, an accident. Nothing for you to worry about.'

'I wish I didn't have to stay here.'

'So do I. But your father's here with you. He says there won't be any more trouble.'

266

'More trouble?' she cried. 'This place is jinxed, there's always trouble. When will I ever see you again?'

Harry smiled and kissed her on the forehead. 'Will next week be too soon? I'm due for some leave and I was hoping you might invite me to visit.'

'Invite you? Of course. It will seem like a year. Come sooner if you can. And Harry, we'll have a lovely time, there really is a lot to see here, the lagoon back there is superb.' She was so eager to please him she went a little too far. 'Corby will have settled down by then, he's had a lot of worries, and Jessie will be back. We can all play cards and have picnics and go riding, make a real holiday of your visit.'

'Your sister,' he said. 'Mrs Morgan. I'm sorry to hear they're having difficulties, she is such a sweet person.'

'Oh yes, but she'll get over it. It was just a tiff, you know how married couples are. She'll be back, she's probably terribly lonely in Cairns.'

'I suppose she is,' he said thoughtfully. 'Do you think I ought to call on her? I shouldn't want to intrude but I could hardly ignore the lady. Perhaps I could persuade her to come back with me next week, after she's had this little break.'

Sylvia was dismayed. What if Jessie told him why she'd left? She'd ruin any chance Sylvia had with Harry. He'd be disgusted, she just knew. She was almost in tears as she kissed him goodbye, forced to agree that it would be kind of Harry to visit her sister. As he strode away, looking so handsome and so elegant in his officer's uniform, Sylvia looked forward bleakly to the worst week of her life, wondering if she'd ever see him again after he'd spoken to Jessie.

Mike lay on his bed, his head bandaged and a damp cloth over his eyes, nursing a fearsome headache. The bullet had only grazed his scalp but it had felt like a cannon ball hitting him, so much so that he hadn't noticed the bump when he hit the ground. But his shoulder was reminding him now with a dull ache. Lucky I didn't break any bones in a fall like that, he reflected, and then corrected himself. Broken bones hell! I'm lucky I'm not dead with that maniac shooting at me.

He tried to sleep, to avoid thinking which brought on inevitable reminders of Morgan, anger fuelling the fiery headache. Tamba had stopped fussing at last, and gone on her way, and all he needed now to speed his recovery was peace and quiet. He'd thought his house was quiet, up here away from the clamour of the compound, but the clock was ticking, the mantel clock he'd won at the rifle range shoot-out a couple of years ago. He'd never noticed it ticking before but now it sounded as if they'd put it in a kerosene tin, so loud was that incessant tick-tick-tick.

'Oh, what's the use?' he groaned. 'A whisky'd be a better idea.'

As he bent down to take the bottle from a cupboard, his head swam, but he steadied himself and saw Snake watching him from under the couch, his favourite spot.

'Well, mate,' he said, 'we're on our way this time. Decision's made. Serves me right. A man should have pulled out of here weeks ago. What shall I do with you? The next occupant of this house might not appreciate your company, and I can't take you to town.'

'First sign,' a voice said behind him. 'Talking to yourself.'

'I'm not talking to myself,' he told McBride, who was standing in the doorway. 'Snake here is interested in the next move.'

'And what would that be?' McBride said. 'I'm interested too. I wouldn't like you to start a war with Morgan.'

'It wouldn't be a bloody fair fight,' Mike snapped. 'He'd lose the first round. No, as soon as my head stops pounding I'll be packing up.'

'Do I have your word on that?' the sergeant asked, pouring himself a whisky.

'Sure. I'm heading for town tomorrow. I've got a lot of stuff here but I'll have to leave it until the creeks subside. I don't want my gear stranded in Halfway Creek to end up pickings for Stan Bellard.'

McBride nodded. 'If he's still there after I get my hands on him. We're leaving now. Do you feel well enough to travel with us?'

Mike laughed. 'Don't you trust me?'

'Not a case of not trusting you, I'd just feel easier if I could put a few miles between you and your boss.'

'My ex-boss,' Mike said. 'And I'm not riding anywhere today. My head feels like someone hit it with a bullet. Besides, I need time. I have to pack up and say my goodbyes to everyone, I'm not slinking off.'

'All right then. Is there anything I can do for you before I go?'

'No thanks, I'll be fine.'

'I'll see you in town then.'

Mike watched him leave then turned back into the house. He had intended to start the packing but his headache defeated him, so he retreated to his bed. The snake uncoiled his long, powerful body and slid silently out of the house. Mike watched him sadly. 'Maybe Lita will take you, otherwise I'll have to move you out into the bush and hope you don't find your way back.'

Then he smiled grimly. 'Pity I can't do that with Morgan.'

He would not retaliate, keeping his promise to McBride, but he would tot up his wages and the money Morgan still owed him and he wouldn't leave without it. He'd have to do that tonight, present him with an account and require immediate payment.

Tomorrow he'd head for town and call in at Helenslea on the way. Even if Lita were still playing the *grande dame* he couldn't leave without seeing her.

Late in the afternoon, he strapped on his gun, and rode down to the house, keeping the horse at a walk. His headache had subsided; the whisky had helped. He dismounted in the shelter of trees and slipped quietly on to the veranda, coming up behind Morgan who was in his usual seat, a rifle to hand.

'Waiting for someone, are we?' he asked, and Morgan spun around, fumbling for his gun.

He was too slow and the cane table was in the way. Mike grabbed the rifle and dropped it over the rail.

'Get off my property,' Morgan yelled. 'Get off, I say. You should have learned your lesson by now.'

'Don't bother to apologise,' Mike said sarcastically. 'Why the gun? Were you going to have another go?'

'It was an accident,' Morgan blustered. 'The police accepted that and I have no further need of you here.'

'Of course not, and you don't need your wife either, since you've got her sister as a bedmate. What a rat you are, Morgan!'

The master of Providence jerked up in his chair. 'How dare you! If you carry tales like that with you I'll have the law on you.'

'No need for me to carry tales,' Mike said easily. 'Everyone knows the setup here. It has been common knowledge for quite some time.'

'It's common knowledge that you've been leching after my wife, more like it, and invented the rest to cover your own foul ways. Did you have a good time with her in town last night?'

Mike leaned forward, grabbed Morgan's velvet jacket and shook him. 'Not another word out of you or I'll bust your head. Now get up and go inside. You can pay me my wages and I'll leave.'

Morgan managed to stumble away from him. 'You'll get your wages, I'll send a cheque to the post office.'

'Do it now!' Mike said, pushing him towards the door.

Sylvia was standing in the parlour, listening. She backed into the dining room as the two men stormed past her but made no attempt to interfere.

'Here's my bill,' Mike said, shoving Morgan towards the desk. 'Now write the cheque.'

As expected, when Morgan saw the amount, now well over eight hundred pounds, he yelped in rage. 'I'm not paying this, it's daylight robbery.'

Mike cuffed him across the head and put the gun at his back. 'You own me that money. Write the cheque or I'll give you the hiding you deserve.'

With the cheque in his pocket Mike turned to Sylvia, acknowledging her at last. 'Miss Langley,' he said, with a slight bow, 'I'll be leaving in the morning. I wish you well. Give my regards to your father.'

The Professor took his meal in his room, and Sylvia dined alone with Corby, listening to his rendition of the events of the day. By the time they retired to the parlour he was still complaining.

'I'll stop the damn cheque,' he muttered, but Sylvia was in no mood for his tantrums.

269

'Don't be ridiculous. If you owe the man you'll have to pay him sooner or later. And you're lucky you got off so lightly. So now what will you do? Without any white staff.'

'I've spoken to Harry. He'll find a couple of foremen for me. Nice chap, Harry.'

Sylvia made no comment. 'And what about Jessie?'

'I'll attend to Jessie. All in good time.' He put an arm around her and kissed her fragrant hair. 'Come and be nice to me. I'm tired and depressed, I need consoling.'

'Not now, Corby.' She twisted away but he closed the parlour door, leaning against it and drawing her to him.

'Isn't this what you always wanted, my love? To hell with all of them, we've got the place to ourselves now. I've been thinking of you all day.' He was kissing her and fumbling with the buttons on her blouse, but she resisted.

'Let me go, Corby!' she said angrily. 'I'm tired too with all this worry about you shooting someone.'

'You're never that tired,' he laughed. 'And you're looking just wonderful lately. You can't believe the number of nights I've sat here with Jessie in the room, burning up to touch you, and now I can.'

'No!' she said, adamant now, but he pushed her over to the wide settee, kissing her, nuzzling her.

'Don't be difficult, let me have my wish, I've always wanted to make love to you right here in the parlour. You have too, tell me you haven't?'

It was true. Sylvia recalled the many times she'd caught his eye, deliberately brushed near him, run her fingers over him when no one was looking, wanting him, teasing him. But it was different now. The only man she wanted was Harry, but she dare not let Corby know. He was a spoiler. With one word to Harry he could ruin everything, more so than Jessie. She could always deny Jessie's accusations. Sylvia was suddenly and desperately afraid of Corby. While he undressed her, even to her stockings, taking rough delight in this abandonment in Jessie's parlour, she vowed to elope with Harry before Corby had a chance to say a word. And while he made love to her, becoming more and more passionate, she wished that Mike Devlin had fired back.

She drank the wine he pressed on her, glass after glass, and she closed her eyes, pretending this was Harry, that she was making love to Harry.

'That's better, my love,' he murmured. 'I knew you wouldn't turn away your Corby, and I'll never let you go. I promise I'll never give you up, not for anyone.'

'And Jessie?' she whispered, hoping he was just boasting.

'Ah yes, Jessie! She threatened me. She said if I didn't support her in town she'd create a scandal, she'd tell people why she left. But she hasn't got that weapon any more. According to Devlin, people know that you and I are lovers, and so what? When I come to think of it, there's nothing new under the sun.'

Sylvia was shocked, and began collecting her clothes, but Corby continued. 'Jessie has a choice. I will support her financially if she hands over Bronte. If she won't do that then she can come back here with him and live in the other house.'

'What other house?'

'Devlin's place, of course. Have you seen it? I had a look inside a while back, it's very comfortable. Too good for staff. So you see, I've got it all worked out.'

Sylvia was ready to retort that Jessie wouldn't agree to any of it, but she changed her mind. Better not to argue with him now. But was Jessie still in love with him? Hadn't she issued the ultimatum, that her sister had to go, not her. That dash for town was only her way of bringing matters to a head. Forcing the issue. Well, she needn't have bothered, because her sister was leaving and as far as Sylvia was concerned they could both live happily ever after.

'Come to bed, my love,' Corby said, 'in my bed. In the master's bedroom where we belong.'

'No,' she said. 'I really am tired now and we both need our sleep.'

'Very well,' he sighed, happy to oblige. 'You're just not accustomed to our new life yet. Sleep tight, my love.'

When she was rid of him, Sylvia sat down to write a letter to Jessie. In it she asked her sister's forgiveness for any unpleasantness between them, admitting to nothing. She told Jessie about her hopes for Harry and begged her to retain the dignity of the family by not mentioning to him any of the goings-on. Then she played her trump card. She announced that she would be leaving Providence and that Corby wanted his wife back. 'Although he is rather cross now,' she wrote, 'and will probably come up with all sorts of mad plans, he is missing you dreadfully. He was so distraught, thinking you had left him for Mike Devlin, he almost killed the man. Believe me, he loves you, Jessie, you must not leave him.'

Sylvia had hoped to hand the letter to Mike Devlin but she found when she arose that he had already left the plantation, so she paid Toby an extravagant ten shillings to ride into town, find Mrs Morgan and deliver the letter to her himself. That done, she took to her bed again, sniffing heartily on smelling salts to make her eyes run, complaining that she had influenza. There would be no more nights like last night, because she would demand that her father move into the house to protect her reputation. And she really was exhausted. She slept the day away.

He found Lita looking very businesslike in a white shirt and jodhpurs, her black hair braided into a thick plait, supervising the paymaster in the outer office.

'Be with you in a tick,' she called, waving to him, obviously glad to see him. Then she turned back to the table where the shillings were being counted out for the Kanakas and larger amounts set aside for the white staff.

Mike had shown Jessie how to keep track of Kanaka pay, which they signed for with a cross, lined up in the compound after work. It was the paybooks that enabled planters to ascertain when the islanders were due for repatriation, so they were important records. He presumed that Sylvia Langley would have to take over that job now to keep the Providence books in order.

But why was he thinking about that? Not his worry any more. In a couple of weeks' time he'd take a dray out there, collect his belongings and be off. Forget about the place.

He grinned, watching Lita. A chip off the old block already! She was turning pages, questioning, pointing, placing her signature at the bottom of each page so that no one could ring in extra darkies and pocket the cash, a trick often practised by paymasters.

'I've come to say goodbye,' he told her when she finally emerged, tucking the keys of the safe into her pocket. 'I'm on my way to town.'

'No you're not,' she said. 'You'll stay awhile. I heard that bastard shot you. Let me see.'

'It's nothing,' he said as she examined the graze. 'He only gave me a headache.'

'And a bald strip,' she laughed. 'I don't think hair will grow along that line again.'

'I can survive that,' he said. 'Now, how have you been?'

'I'm fine. I'm glad you came, I wanted to apologise to you.'

'What for?'

'Don't pretend, Mike. I wasn't too polite the last time you were here. At my father's funeral.'

'You're entitled. It wouldn't have been your best day.'

They strolled along the neat paved paths that led from the administration buildings through lawns and gardens towards the main house. Mike looked about him with envy. He and Jake had always pictured Providence landscaped like this one day, taking the lead from old Edgar, but they'd never had the time or the spare workers.

'I found out what my father was up to on the night he died,' Lita said. 'Did you know about it?'

'That he was going to hang Joseph? Yes.'

'You should have told me,' she said bleakly. 'I had to get it from that bitch Mrs McMullen. She was plodding about the house the night before the funeral like a Greek wailing woman and I knew she was busting to tell me something. I had to ask, fool that I am! She dragged it out like a cat with a dead mouse, and laid it at my feet.'

'Well . . . that was your dad. He was a fiery old character. You weren't here to cool him down, Lita. What's done is done.'

She stopped to stare at him. 'You really don't know, do you? I don't give a damn about the rest of them but I knew you were coming to the funeral and I couldn't face you.'

'Me? Why the hell not?'

'Guilt, I suppose. Good old guilt. I haven't experienced that since I was a kid and swiped his best cigars. When did you appoint yourself my conscience anyway?'

Mike laughed and put an arm about her. 'Come on now. You're getting maudlin. What do you have to be guilty about?'

'Try being the cause of your father's death.'

'That's crazy, Lita. Stop this. Let's go up to the house and you can make me one of those fancy drinks of yours. I'm on holidays now. I've quit Providence for good.'

'Not before time,' she said, and followed him into the house.

Sooner or later, she worried, as she squeezed a lime into a long drink of brandy and soda, I'll have to tell him. Only because it won't go away, he'll hear the gossip eventually. But I need a few more drinks to pluck up the courage.

On the day of the funeral, with all those knowing, mean faces surrounding her, she'd used her best clothes and a cold demeanour as armour, to ward off the accusations that she knew they were levelling at her. No. To hide her guilt as well, with Mrs McMullen's words ringing in her ears.

'Of course I wouldn't believe a word of it, Mrs de Flores. You can count on me. But you know the way the men talk. I'm only passing this on to you out of friendship, but they're saying that Edgar went out that night to hang the Kanaka.'

'Hang him? What the hell for?' Even as she'd asked the question Lita's heart had sunk. She could still see the sharp glitter in that woman's eyes as she pounced, the revenge of a have-not against the uppity mistress of Helenslea, the age-old jealousy of class.

'They're saying,' she'd tittered, 'that you had – well – dealings, to put it nicely, with the Kanaka Joseph. Not your fault of course. That he forced himself on you and that's why Edgar had to act like he did. No one would blame him, would they? But I've been wondering – and I'd never tell a soul – is it true?'

Lita was shattered. Her father and three other men were dead, and poor sweet Joseph was on the run, marked for life. How had her father found out? Someone must have seen them. Edgar had never given her any indication. No. That would be Edgar. He'd waited until she'd left the plantation to exact punishment on the man. Never on his daughter. But he had! On himself and on her, and he'd left her with this awful guilt.

'Mrs McMullen,' she'd said, 'would you excuse me? I find gossip the most boring of conversations.'

Could she tell Mike the truth of it? One day, maybe, but not now. Her courage had deserted her.

'Mike,' she said as she carried in the tray of drinks, 'I'm glad you've finally left Providence. I can't carry on here, really I can't. I don't want to be tied down to this place. And I intend to sack McMullen and his bitch of a wife as soon as possible. I want you to take over Helenslea. You can't refuse me now, I won't allow it.'

273

The river rumbled along beside him like a fierce animal, its banks rising stealthily. At this rate, Joseph reflected, the people living nearby would have plenty of time to retreat, but Rawalla's jubilant claim that a deluge would engulf the land still nagged at him. It was the way he'd said it, as if a mighty torrent would come down swiftly, not just edging into the lowlands.

Doubts still assailed him as he pushed on past those strange plantations into territory that was part of Helenslea, to watch men, some of whom he recognised, at work in the fields. Not knowing friend from foe among these Kanakas, he stayed low until sundown, waiting for them to head back to their quarters, then he moved on again until the lights of the big house came into view. This was the home of that ugly master, the man who had tried to kill him. He half expected to hear the voice of Ratasali railing at him now, but it was silent. Probably there was enough rage in his own heart to suffice. Rage at the man who had failed to kill him, but had humiliated him and his friends, and ruined his life. Turned him into an outcast. He should be made to suffer, that Mr Betts, to be punished for his vicious ways. What sort of a man was Talua that he'd slink away into the night with his tormentor so close?

He broke a stout sapling from a tree, trimmed it into a handy weapon size and stripped it, feeling its weight with satisfaction. As he moved closer he saw that the house was wide open. If he could just spot that old man he might be able to get to him – there were no guards – and give him a thrashing. What matter if the white men came after him? He was already in trouble and he intended to give himself up at Providence; he had to, in order to raise the alarm about the river. He hoped they would believe him. At least the Malaita men would listen to him and would run to safety, because they had faith in him. As for the rest . . . did it matter? Suddenly he thought of Elly, the sweet darkie girl who cared for him, and the missus and the baby, and Mr Devlin. They did matter, and his other friends on the plantation. He had to hurry, get this over with, and then he'd run, over to the mill and down the track he knew so well through the fields of Providence.

As he crept closer to the house he saw Mrs Lita sitting on that big veranda with someone else. He couldn't distinguish the other figure from this distance because there were no lamps lit outside. This Joseph understood, lamps brought hordes of insects at night, it was more sensible to sit in the dark.

This glimpse of her was almost enough to turn him away from his mission. She was a kind and lonely lady, and an attack on her father would cause her grief, but these were matters for men. Honour demanded that he retaliate. In his efforts to move into a better position to watch for Mr Betts, he stood on one of those small furry animals that lived in these forests, impossible beings unlike anything he'd ever seen before. It screeched and crashed away from him and he dived frantically into the undergrowth, cursing his stupidity, waiting to see if there was any reaction from the house.

'What was that?' Lita said to Mike, but he was already out of his chair.

'Keep talking,' he said as he drew back into the house, raced down the passage, and, pushing aside the carpet runner, dropped through a trapdoor to the cellar.

'It's probably a false alarm,' he told himself, 'a dingo on the prowl, but I'd better make sure, what with one thing and another lately.' He could hear Lita talking to no one, overdoing it a bit, he grinned. She sounded like a town spruiker. Since he wasn't armed, he opted for the element of surprise by charging straight into the shrubbery, only to collide with the intruder who must have decided to retreat, having given himself away.

A Kanaka! Mike felt the bare torso as they both stumbled. He grabbed the man, shouting at him to create confusion as the hackles rose on the back of his neck. His first thought was for Lita. Was she to be yet another target? Was this the only one creeping about. And why hadn't he brought his gun? Stupid!

Fortunately, having been caught, there was no fight in the man so Mike bundled him out into the open, still unable to identify him in the gloom. Then the Kanaka turned on him: 'Mr Devlin. It's me, Joseph!'

Flabbergasted, Mike stared at him. 'Who?'

'Joseph, boss.'

They had him inside in the parlour, his big frame covered only with muddied trousers, but instead of cringing, as Mike had expected, he stood tall, defiant. A new Joseph, not the eager-to-please lad he'd known at Providence. The boy had grown up fast. And he kept watching the door as if waiting for someone else to enter.

He gave Lita a polite bow, his hands on his chest in the islander mark of respect, and faced his boss.

'What were you doing out there?'

'I must go home,' Joseph said, unwilling to admit the truth. If Mr Betts walked in the door now he'd have a chance at him, take them all by surprise. He had only intended to give the old man a beating but that wouldn't be possible now, it was too late. One blow across his windpipe would shut that raucous voice up for a long time. If not for good.

'This isn't home,' Mr Devlin snapped.

'Food, I need food.'

'I'll get him some,' Mrs Lita volunteered, but Mr Devlin stopped her.

'He doesn't need food. Look at him, he's in better nick than when he left Providence.'

'He could still be hungry,' she argued, and Joseph picked up on that.

'Yes, hungry,' he said.

The lady left the room to get him some food and Mr Devlin told him to sit down.

'No, boss, I stand,' Joseph said, watching for his prey.

'Stand then,' Mr Devlin said, 'but get away from that door. I can't have you bolting again, Joseph. I want to talk to you.'

When Mr Devlin told him what had happened Joseph wept. He was glad the lady did not return to see him in this state. Paka and Ned had not run free, they were dead. Mr Betts was dead, killed by Paka, but Joseph would not weep for him. The guard was dead, killed by his friends in their battle to release him. Good loyal friends who had died for him. No, not for him, for that cursed god, the son of Ratasali. The true gods had punished him as they had his father for daring to speak for them.

They talked for a long time. Mr Devlin wanted to know where he had been, and although the boss was keenly interested in his short stay with the Irukandji people, Joseph mentioned none by name. He owed them that. Eventually Joseph came to the story of the big rivers but was nervous of mentioning it because it sounded foolish in this solid house of the white men with all their wisdom.

'You're not in any trouble any more, Joseph,' Mr Devlin said kindly, 'but I don't think you ought to go back to Providence. Things have changed. I'll be managing this plantation now, you'd better stay here.'

'I must go, boss,' Joseph said frantically 'I have to warn them of the big flood.'

'What big flood?'

'Bush people say flood comen.'

Mike sat back as if he'd been struck. When had he last checked the river levels? Weeks ago. The rising creeks should have given him the hint. With rainfall declining, creeks shouldn't rise unless there was a build-up somewhere else. 'You know your trouble,' he told himself as he paced outside to stare into the darkness, 'you've been too busy looking after everything but your own job.' He turned back to Joseph. 'Is the river up?'

'Yes, boss, gettin' strong.'

'We've had low-level floods before,' Mike worried. 'And a couple of flash floods, but they don't do much damage, we don't plant too close.' He was trying to convince himself that this was nothing new but he recalled a remark of Jake's when they'd trekked inland, following the river. 'This old river, she's been a beauty in her day, look at the terrain. We're not following her banks – this sandy soil is still part of the watercourse, grown over now in this climate. I wouldn't like to be around when she gets up full steam.'

'Ancient history,' Mike had remarked, more interested in searching for the tasty shellfish, crabs and lobbies that they'd been feasting on in their travels. But once installed at Providence both men had kept a wary eye on their river.

'What exactly did they say? Those bush blacks?' he asked Joseph, who tried to explain, admitting he'd had a translator who wasn't too reliable. But he was definite in recalling that they'd predicted a big flood.

'If their camp was by the river, naturally they'd move out,' Mike said. 'They might have shifted to avoid the overflow.'

Joseph tried harder. On his island they had streams running down

276

from the hills to the sea. It was difficult for him to grasp the concept of big rivers linking arms like brothers and surging onward as in an ever-growing army. It sounded to him more like legend than fact. But there were the tides; high tides would aggravate. That part he spoke of with more confidence.

Mike, anxious now, was searching his memory. When had he heard of this before? Or read about it? Where rivers from the north had combined thanks to the massive rainfall in the tropics and had cut a swathe of floods for hundreds of miles inland. And what had caught his eye? Sometimes the flood waters took weeks to hit the southern pasturelands. In the past the stations and towns had been forewarned; not that there was much they could do, the floods were devastating.

If he accepted this news, then they could be right in the path of one of these monster floods now; this *was* the north. They wouldn't have to wait weeks. He grabbed Joseph's arm. 'When? Did they say how long this would take? How much time we've got?'

But Joseph shook his head. 'No, boss. You think this true?'

'It could be, and I'd better get a move on. Even if it's only a light flash flood we'd better get ready.'

Lita called to him from the office. 'If you're finished with Joseph, Dandy has a meal ready for him in the kitchen.'

Dandy! He hurried Joseph through to the kitchen. 'Grab yourself some food quick, we haven't got time to hang about. And you, Dandy, what did you say to me about the big river? I distinctly remember you saying something about after the big river comes. What big river?'

She moved leisurely across the wide stone floor to hand Joseph some buns stoked with hunks of cold meat. 'Magic men say river time comen,' she replied vaguely, and smiled at him. 'Good spirits wait for you then.'

'Never mind about that. What do your weather men say about the river? They're talking about a flood, aren't they? When? The river's rising by the sound of things. Do we get a flood, and when?'

'I don't know,' she shrugged, unconcerned. 'He has gone. No black people here. No one to ask.' She pointed at Joseph. 'You got your own magic man. Ask him.'

'This is not my land,' Joseph said quietly, speaking only to Dandy. 'I have no magic.'

'It is in you!' she flung at him.

'No! You are wrong. I want nothing of that.'

Mike intervened. 'Oh Christ, I haven't got time for this.'

Dandy watched the island man follow Mike out of the kitchen, hurriedly munching on the buns. She took a handful of dried leaves from the old dilly bag that she rarely used now and scattered them in the doorway to ward off evil spirits. 'You have put down the bad magic,' she said, 'but your son will pick it up. It is in the blood. Better that one die at his mother's breast.'

'I think we're in for a flood,' Mike told Lita. 'I'm going to ring the fire

277

bell and get the men up here. You'd better change out of that dress. I want you to move to high ground.'

'Now?'

'Right now.'

'But the house is built high, Mike. We've had floods before, they never come up this far.'

'I know, but I've got a nasty feeling about this.'

'Oh come on, have a drink. You've just got the willies. I think Joseph gave you a fright.'

Irritated, he left but Lita reached out to Joseph. 'Don't go. I wanted to say how sorry I am about everything. I didn't know what my father was up to. I'll make it up to you one day.'

Embarrassed, he stood stiffly, feeling out of place in this fine house. The clanging of a big bell covered his muttered reply, which was only sound anyway because he didn't know what to say.

'Do you forgive me?' she asked him, and astonished, Joseph nodded. 'You are a great lady. You should not ask this of me.'

'Yes I should. You learn to keep your head up, Joseph, and be strong. Don't let anyone bully you, you'll get respect that way. Even from white men.' She heard Mike returning. 'And tell me, Joseph,' she asked in a different tone. 'Where have you been hiding?'

'Over the river,' he replied bewildered, then Mr Devlin was back, telling her to get a move on, calling to Dandy, buckling on his gun and jacket, while outside, men were running.

It was easier to shift logs, Mike reflected, than this lot. After a heated argument with McMullen, interrupted when they sighted Joseph, which required an explanation in itself, Mike finally managed to get the grumbling Helenslea staff into motion. For once, he appreciated Mrs McMullen. She, at least, heeded him, terrified at the thought of a big flood, and she turned on her husband with a round of abuse that would have done a bullocky proud.

'All right! All right!' he said, to stop her, and began ordering the men to warn the Kanakas, to shift the horses and stock, to head for the higher ground known as Home Hill. 'If you're wrong, Devlin,' he snorted, 'I'll break your bloody neck.'

'If I'm wrong I'll buy you a drink,' Mike said. 'You'll have to look after things here. I'm going to Providence.'

'I want some Kanakas to pack my house,' Mrs McMullen shrilled.

'There isn't time,' McMullen retorted, and Mike pulled him aside.

'What do you mean, there isn't time?'

McMullen glared at him. 'I don't have to take your word. I sent a couple of blokes down with lanterns to take a gander at the river. They're just back. They say she's rising fast. By dawn it'll probably settle but we might as well move up a bit. In the daylight we'll have a better idea.'

'Have you sent someone to alert Woollahra plantation?'

278

'Of course I have. There's no need for you to hang about. We'll look after Mrs de Flores.'

Ever practical, Lita was in the kitchen, stuffing supplies into a bag. 'Just in case we get hungry,' she laughed. 'I never did like goanna meat.'

'McMullen's bringing your horses around,' he told the two women. 'Whatever you do, Lita, don't try to get to town. Just stay put until McMullen says it's safe to come back down.' He kissed her on the cheek. 'I have to go.'

'Where are you going?'

'To Providence.'

'What for? You don't owe Morgan a thing. And if the river is rising the Kanakas will know.'

'They may not, and he won't know what to do.'

Lita scowled. 'You mean *she* won't know what to do. You've got to run after her, haven't you?'

'You've forgotten,' he grinned. 'Mrs Morgan is in town. Now behave yourself. I'll see you later.'

There was no orderly retreat on Helenslea plantation. Men were running everywhere, shouting and arguing, bumping about with lanterns trying to round up startled cattle and horses. Mike got to the stables in time to rescue his own mount and grab one for Joseph.

'Can you ride?' he asked him.

'No, boss, no good at that.'

'Well it's time you learned.' He saddled both horses and hoisted the unwilling Kanaka aboard a bony grey. 'Stick your feet in the stirrups and hang on to the reins. Let's go.'

He headed for the mill with Joseph bumping along beside him, and followed the familiar track towards Providence, travelling only as fast as the darkness and the unsteady rider with him would allow. When he heard the sudden clatter of kookaburras he breathed a sigh of relief. Half an hour to dawn. Those birds were never wrong. This track was well away from the river, so he had no inkling of its progress, nor could he spare the time to investigate.

The eastern sky was billowing yellow as they cantered into the compound. Some of the Kanakas were already moving about. They stopped to stare at the two strange figures emerging from the gloom, and then there was a shout of joy. Not only was Mr Devlin back, but Joseph was with him!

'Don't panic them,' Mike told Joseph. 'Just move everyone to high ground quietly.'

But it wasn't as easy as he'd expected. Precious time was lost in the wild enthusiasm at finding Joseph among them again. Each man, each woman, seemed to find it necessary to greet him personally despite Mike's orders. But eventually, with Pompey's help, the women with their children were hurried away, the horses released and the compound evacuated.

'Get back on your horse,' he said to Joseph. 'I'm going to the house, you go down and make certain the blacks are on the move. They camp by the river, they'll have shifted ground by now but I want them right up out of the way.'

They'd only gone a hundred yards from the compound when Joseph sniffed the air. He looked about him frantically and the horses too began to prance nervously. Mike could smell it then, an overpowering thickness in the air, the stench of foul mud, as if they were in the swamps. He heard the roar and it terrified him. They couldn't go on. 'Up the hill!' he shouted at Joseph and plunged his horse into the scrub heading away from the river. The islander had lost control of his horse. He could only hang on as the frightened animal, smelling danger, careered after the other horse crashing through the bush, panting as it scrambled up one of the low hills that were scattered about the big estate. Hills that had resisted the elements from their granite cores, honed down to mounds of their former selves, and forested by greedy jungle. They now formed part of the undulating coastal plain, no longer a part of the foothills of the Great Dividing Range cut adrift by the ravages of that river. To the sugar planters they were a waste of precious land, but to the new breed of banana growers coming into the area they were ideal for their creeping crops. Now the orphaned hills had become havens, as all along the river course men and animals scrambled to safety.

Trees snapped and swung into the current, the river bed, undisturbed for years, convulsed, releasing rocks and snags into the surging torrent that swept debris before it in its headlong rush to the sea. The crystal-green river had turned into a mile-wide muddy turbulence, a belligerent, destructive force let loose on the land.

From their homestead built high on the hill overlooking their vast plantation, the owners of Woollahra could only watch in despair as the river plundered their crops, leaving them isolated on high ground.

The river trespassed boldly on the next plantation, Helenslea, with no regard for the years of labour man had endured in this ferocious climate to cultivate crops. It reached out as far as it could to ravage even more of the precious fields, the golden fields, as they were known in man-money terms. It routed savagely through the Hawaiian-style mansion that had belonged to Edgar Betts; unable to dislodge it from its stone foundations, it dumped foul mud and debris throughout and pulsed on.

The homestead at Providence was easier prey. The bungalow shook and shuddered as the waters coursed onwards. Even though Jake had built it a good six feet from ground level, for coolness not protection against floods – for who would have thought the river could belly out like this? – water was streaming now into the basement.

With the smiling wickedness of nature the sun shone on the raging inland sea. It beamed and twinkled that morning on the blue waters of Trinity Bay as a muddy surge spewed from mangrove swamps south of Cape Grafton into the pristine sea, telltale evidence of turmoil.

280

Faithful Toby had found the missus at the hotel and delivered the letter from Miss Langley, and Jessie had told him to rest, it was too late to make the return journey, she'd give him a reply to take back in the morning.

Delighted to have the opportunity to spend time in the town, and with ten shillings, a fortune, in his pocket, Toby wandered away to find his friends, Yindini people who still clung to their tribal lands by the bay despite the encroachment and the devastating influence of the whitefellers.

As for Jessie, she decided to sleep on her reply. Sylvia's pleading letter was true to form; she'd found a new beau in Harry Scott-Hughes, and that was fine, but how long would it last? Sylvia was apt to have crushes on any new men who crossed her path, but they never lasted. There had been several on the ship, then Mike Devlin, and the young bank manager Mr Billingsley and Lord knows how many others in town. But the only one who had lasted was Corby. Whose doing was that? Sylvia's or his? Proximity maybe.

Sylvia had apologised, carefully, for the 'unpleasantness' at Providence. Jessie gave a hollow laugh. She obviously didn't find sleeping with her sister's husband unpleasant, only the fact that she'd been caught and that that information could, and would, upset her latest conquest. And it would serve her right.

But Sylvia was cunning. She was offering her sister a carrot. Say nothing and you can have your husband back. The damned cheek of her! It was not for Sylvia to offer to relinquish her husband. Jessie's husband. It was up to Corby to make the break. Jessie knew she would take him back. Corby was impulsive and temperamental, and, yes, selfish but he was her husband. Other women had come through these miserable affairs and managed to overlook them to stabilise the family structure. She was no prude. Even though it was shocking to have her sister involved, to have to cope with that rotten disloyalty, Jessie understood men more than Corby thought. It seemed to her that they were more vulnerable than women, more easily titillated. When her son grew up she would talk to him about this, teach him restraint. In the meantime there was her husband, who had not exercised restraint. If he apologised, if he could find the means to talk about these things with her and be truthful, they could yet find common ground to recommence the marriage. A faint hope, though, she reflected.

But she would not reply to Sylvia. She would not allow her to intrude any more. She had left Corby and it was up to him now to declare that he wanted his wife back, as a wife. For all her plans and propositions, Jessie still wondered if he were sleeping with Sylvia now that the coast was clear and she was out of the way. She decided that there would definitely be no answer to Sylvia's letter. Let her worry for a change.

In the morning she went to Smith's Allgoods Emporium around the corner from the hotel to search for a pram. The owner seemed to know who she was right away, so Jessie guessed she was already the subject of gossip in this small community. He sat her at the counter on a tall chair and emerged from the cluttered interior hauling an ancient cane pram which, he assured her, was the latest thing. Not that Jessie cared whether it was the latest or the oldest, as long as it had wheels and Bronte could be transferred from the sling that Hanna carried to his own little vehicle. She bought the pram and several other items, including a small sheepskin rug, which the storekeeper pressed on her.

'But, Mr Smith, isn't it rather hot to put that over a child?'

'Not over, dear lady, under. It will keep the baby cool in summer and warm in winter.'

She was pushing the pram back when she met Lieutenant Scott-Hughes.

'Why, Mrs Morgan! How nice to see you again. And how is your baby?'

Before she could stop him he peered into the pram which held not a child but parcels.

'I'm not really mad,' she laughed. 'I've just bought the pram.'

Harry was laughing too. 'That's a relief. I thought it strange that you'd bury a child under the shopping. Here, let me take it.'

The sight of a gentleman pushing a pram brought stares and some comical remarks from passers-by, but he took it in good part and hauled it up the stairs to her room where Hanna was waiting with Bronte. The girl was so excited by this splendid contraption that she wanted to put her charge into it right away.

'No,' Jessie said, 'get some soap and water from the maid and give it a good clean first, it's too dusty to use yet.' She turned to Harry. 'Thank you, Lieutenant, that's very kind of you.'

'What about joining me downstairs for some morning tea?' he asked.

Jessie hesitated, and then smiled. 'I'd be glad to.' She hoped that Corby would hear she'd been seen in the town with not one but two charming escorts. And besides, it was nice to have company. She had no intention of hiding in her room during this enforced holiday.

He made no comment about her sudden departure from Providence and Jessie appreciated his tact. Instead he told her of the long wasted day in the swamps and how much he had enjoyed his visit to the plantation, despite the barn fire and his necessary disciplinary action. All too soon he came to Sylvia. 'I found Miss Langley charming,' he said gallantly. 'It must run in the family. Your father must be proud to have two such lovely daughters.'

'Thank you,' Jessie murmured.

'I'm hoping to ask Professor Langley for permission to court Miss Langley,' he said. 'Do you think you could put in a good word for me, Mrs Morgan? I'm due for promotion to captain shortly and I have a small private income as well. I'd be able to take good care of her.'

He was so earnest, so anxious to do the right thing that Jessie felt sorry for him. She assured him he had her support, and was relieved when a waitress came to tell her a 'blackfeller' was waiting outside for her.

'Oh heavens!' she said. 'I forgot about Toby. I really must go.'

Having seen Harry off the premises, after promising she'd call on him if she needed anything, Jessie sent Toby on his way and decided to take Hanna and Bronte for their first walk with the baby carriage.

'Looks like I'll never get a go with the pram,' she laughed as they strolled along the Esplanade, with the nurse grasping the pram as if it might run away on her with its precious cargo.

The outing was wonderful, a real tonic. For the first time Jessie had a chance to enjoy the scenery, the colourful trees and the strange mix of people who ambled about. No one in this new port seemed to be in a hurry; women nodded to her, men doffed hats as they passed by and she felt very much at home. They stopped to peer in shop windows, to watch bullock teams clomping through the streets, to look at everyone and everything. 'I'm a real country bumpkin now,' she said to Hanna, who didn't know what she meant. 'It's so long since I've seen a town that this village is like a big city to me. It's marvellous.'

The baby gurgled and smiled his approval of these perambulations, unfazed by the bumps and dips in the street, and his mother sighed contentedly. She bought two glasses of raspberry cordial and they sat on a bench outside the shop watching the world go by. She was intrigued by the number of craggy-faced horsemen riding out of town, looking like peddlers with so much equipment strapped to their saddles. Miners, she guessed, heading for the goldfields somewhere out there. What a thrill it must be to find gold, she mused, to just reach out for it. No wonder so many people were caught up in the gold fever. Every paper she picked up reported new gold strikes. This ancient land must be riddled with it.

That reminded her to buy a newspaper on the way back to the hotel, but as she approached the offices of the *Cairns Post* she saw men gathering outside, so she stood back shyly, waiting for them to disperse.

The crowd grew, women had joined them and horsemen reined in curiously. Jessie could see the agitation and she became uneasy with a premonition of trouble.

'Stay here,' she said to Hanna and hurried up to ask a gentleman what was wrong.

'Floods,' he said. 'They reckon a big flood has hit Woollahra plantation, madam.'

'Woollahra?' she echoed. 'Would it affect Helenslea and Providence?'

'Couldn't miss. They'd be right in the path too.' He stopped to stare at her. 'Excuse me, aren't you Mrs Morgan?'

'Yes,' she said numbly.

'Good heavens! Forgive me. I'm Bede Hornsby, Member of Parliament. Now don't be upsetting yourself. Floods and droughts, they're all one in this country, we get over them. Where are you staying?'

Jessie felt dizzy with fear. He had said a big flood. 'The hotel,' she replied. 'The Victoria.'

'Then I'll escort you there.'

He ushered them, with the pram, back to the hotel. 'Look on the bright side,' he was saying. 'You couldn't have picked a better time to come to town with the babe.'

'Are they in danger out there?' she asked.

'No, no, of course not. Goodness me, no, don't you be worrying your pretty head!'

He was lying and she knew it. 'Mr Hornsby, when will we have news of Providence? I am worried.'

'Leave it to me. As soon as I hear I'll let you know. Now I must rush, we have to organise rescue parties.'

Rescue parties! Jessie stood helplessly, watching the sudden change in the atmosphere of the town as the residents were galvanised into action, people were running, horsemen galloped past with excited dogs yapping behind them, and a group of dazed Kanakas milled on to the road, asking questions of anyone who would stop to heed them.

'Baby's dinner time,' Hanna reminded Jessie, being single-minded about her duties, and Jessie nodded.

The hotel proprietor barred her way. 'Mrs Morgan, I've been meaning to speak to you. Blacks can't use this entrance. Would you send the girl around the back, please.'

'Don't talk rubbish!' Jessie snapped. 'Get out of my way.'

He leapt aside to avoid being run down by the spindly wheels of the pram as Jessie swept passed him, dragging Hanna with her. She shoved the pram across the lobby, lifted out the baby, sent Hanna up ahead of her and called to the proprietor to carry the pram upstairs. 'Immediately!' she added, and stood back, as, red-faced, he performed the duty.

'Thank you,' she said, at the top of the stairs. 'Now I should like lunch for two sent up to my room. And if you upset me again I shall move to another hotel.'

'I didn't mean to upset you, Mrs Morgan,' he began but Jessie cut him short.

'Good. I'll consider the matter closed.'

She felt a little better. The argument had released some tension but she was still anxious, unable to envisage a flood or its impact on everyone at home, or on the plantation itself. She asked Hanna about floods but gained little information. The Aborigine girl wasn't concerned. 'Water come, people move,' she shrugged.

'But the house? Would it come as far as the house?'

Hanna's eyes were round as she considered this. 'That make allasame big mess, missus.'

'The house is away from the river, though.'

'Yeah,' Hanna conceded, to please her.

The waters were swirling around them, grasping, unwilling to give them up but they made it ashore. From habit, in times of trouble in the bush, Mike had looped ropes to his saddle and grabbed a tomahawk and hunting knife from the shed, tossing another heavy coil of rope to Joseph. Now they might need them.

They rode through a canefield, watching the ever-widening river engulfing the young crop, not caring that the horses were trampling plants underfoot, a crime on normal days, heading south until they were abreast of the rear of the homestead.

'Oh Christ!' Mike groaned, staring across the muddy torrent, looking beyond the bedraggled branches of trees and the bloated animals that swept past. It was a strange sight. The house stood alone in the distance, half submerged, but none of the outbuildings were visible. The dairy, the stables and the barns, even the guest house where the Professor lived, all had disappeared, swallowed by deep flood waters.

'Look, boss!' Joseph was tugging at his arm. He pointed to a horse struggling in the torrent.

Mike looked about frantically. This land had been cleared, there wasn't a tree near enough to help. He looped the rope and threw the other end to Joseph. 'Dig your heels in and hang on.'

He plunged into the water, swimming out towards the horse, which had sighted him. It made a big effort, gallantly turning across the current to meet him. Mike lassoed the animal as they were both swung about in the heaving waters, afraid that his rescue attempt was too frail to cope, but he saw the horse jerk as the rope went taut and it began to move to the bank. As he swam back he was astonished at the strength of the Kanaka who was, inch by inch, hauling the animal to the banks. He hit solid ground at the same time as the horse and, waist-deep, pushed the frightened animal to shore. It careered ahead of him, shuddering to a stop. Joseph was laughing, leaping about, petting the horse. 'Got him, boss,' he yelled triumphantly.

'You sure did,' Mike said, throwing off his muddy shirt. 'I reckon you earned him. He's yours. Let him go, we'll catch him again later.'

He peered again at the Providence homestead and over at the hill, noticing that his own house up there in an island of greenery was secure but completely cut off. He doubted if any of the Kanakas had sought refuge there since they'd all been ordered to the same safe ground as he and Joseph were on.

'People in that house,' Joseph said, pointing.

'Where? I can't see.' He strained his eyes, hoping Joseph was wrong, hoping that Morgan would have got his family out at the first sign of the river rising. Surely on his rounds he must have noticed. And Toby, who was always alert, Toby would have told him.

But Toby wasn't there, he was away on his mission for the young missus. It was Broula, no respecter of doors, who had come barging into the house in the middle of the night to shout that the river comen and to claim her daughter, the mother of her beloved grandson.

Elly raced upstairs to shush her before she woke the master, but it was too late.

Corby lit his lamp and, clad only in pyjama pants, strode out into the

285

passageway. 'What's the meaning of this uproar? Get that woman out of my house.' He was appalled. Broula smelled of sweat and that revolting fat the Aborigine smeared on herself, and she was wearing only a grubby lap-lap, her big tits swaying.

In her anxiety Broula had lost her English. She yelled at him in her own language and, ashamed, poor Elly tried to explain.

'She says river up, boss. We gotta go.'

'What's she talking about? The wet season is nearly over, we haven't had rain for the best part of a week and even that wasn't much. She's drunk. Get her out of my house!'

At Sylvia's urging, the Professor had moved into the second bedroom. He emerged, hearing the racket, at the same time as his daughter, but he seemed confused, still half asleep, asking if it were morning.

Sylvia was frightened. She turned to Elly. 'What is she saying? What does she mean about the river?'

'Flood, missus! Broula says flood comen, cross the heart true.'

'Did you hear that, Corby?' Sylvia shrieked. 'We'll be drowned!'

'Don't be ridiculous. We're a long way from the river and well above the level. I won't have this hysteria. I'll look at the situation in the morning. Calm yourself. There's nothing we can do at this hour, it's as dark as pitch out there. Where's Toby?'

'Toby gone,' Elly said, looking to Sylvia who said nothing in their black servant's defence.

'Marvellous!' Corby fumed. 'If that idiot is ever around when he's needed I'll give him a week off! Sylvia, get these women out of here, I need my rest.'

Broula had a grip like a vise on Elly's hand and began dragging her out. 'No, missus,' she called to Sylvia. 'Doan stay. You bring the boss. Bring your dadda too.'

But Corby was adamant. 'God spare me crazy women! Put your father to bed, Sylvia. If there is any problem I shall attend to it in the morning.' When she hesitated he took hold of her and pointed out over the front veranda. 'The river is down there, woman! We are up here! Surely even you can grasp that! I will not be panicked by these natives.' Then he softened, and took her hand as Broula, disgusted, muttering he knew not what, cuffed Elly and led her away. 'Don't fret, my darling,' he told her, kissing her soft cheek.

'But, Corby, what if she's right? What if there is a flood?'

'Then we pray it doesn't happen. I need every acre of crops out there, Sylvia. Forget the blacks, they'll just move away from the lagoon. I can't move my canefields. I won't sleep a bloody wink tonight worrying about them. Come and keep me company, I just need my arms about you, my love.'

On their way down the steps from the house the two Aborigine women met Tommy and Mae. 'What here happenin'?' Tommy demanded.

'Broula say flood comen,' Elly told them.

'Wha'?' Tommy shrieked.

Mae was all for going back to get the young missus and her venerable father, but Tommy had much the same attitude as Broula. He slapped his wife, demanding obedience, and the two Chinese fled with the dark people across the yard where the Aborigine stablehands were already releasing the horses.

Sylvia lay in the comfort and solace of Corby's strong arms. He'd made no attempt to make love to her. He was true to his word, he just needed her with him and she understood, she reciprocated, curling into the curve of his body as naturally as if she belonged there. He was breathing quietly, steadily, clasping her to him in a gentle protective embrace, and she wondered about Harry. Could he make love to her as well as Corby did? With the same suavity, the same passion? She doubted it. Corby was an experienced lover, she guessed, well before he came to Jessie. His moods in themselves were a thrill, sometimes hard and demanding, other times so loving and sentimental she melted and dissolved at his touch.

But there was another worry. A strange feeling. Elly had referred to the Professor as her dadda. Her dadda. And that had resurrected old yearnings. As a child she'd always called him Dadda, she'd loved him dearly. But he'd never taken much notice of her. Jessie was the bright one. In his eyes she could never measure up to Jessie's intelligence, she was just an afterthought in the Langley household. Why worry about that now, though? she asked herself as she nestled closer to the warmth of Corby Morgan. Except that he seemed so frail now, poor old Dadda.

In the morning the crash shook the house like a thunderbolt and Corby was out of bed in an instant, shocked at what he saw.

'What was that?' Sylvia, a sheet wrapped about her, was clutching the bedpost.

'Get up! Quick!' he said. 'The river's flooding.'

'But what was the bang? I thought the house was going to collapse.'

'The surge of the water,' he said, dragging on work trousers and a shirt, and, by habit, picking up his boots, which he quickly tossed aside.

'Lucas!' he shouted, barging into the Professor's room. 'Get up quick. The river's in flood.'

'What time is it?' the old man said groggily.

'What the hell does it matter? Get up!'

The sun lifting from the east gave the ugly waters a yellowish tinge as he stared from the front of the house at where the river ought to have been. But now only half of the long garden fence was visible, collecting debris, and beyond it the rough scrub he'd hoped to clear one day was swaying restlessly, branches swishing miserably in their watery surroundings. He stood wondering what he could retrieve from under the house, mesmerised by the glint of the waters for a few minutes, then he dropped down a few steps to peer through the trellis, only to be faced by a grey shuffling gloom.

287

And then it hit him! The crops! Oh God, no! He ran through to the back of the house, trying to remember how far the eastern fields were from the river, and gave a groan of despair as he saw the water running freely, flooding the outbuildings and the house paddocks.

He tested the depth of the water, cursing that it was nearly two feet deep here at the back, the house being built on a slight slope. There was nothing for it. They'd simply have to wade out.

Sylvia panicked. 'I'm not stepping into that water. It's filthy. They all know we're here. We'll have to stay put until they bring a boat for us.'

'What boat?' he said angrily. 'Who's got a bloody boat? Come with me and I'll lift you across.'

Her father was just as difficult. 'My greenhouse,' he wailed. 'It'll be ruined, and all my notes are in my room there, they'll be washed away.'

'It hasn't occurred to you, I suppose,' Corby said savagely, 'that my crops, your livelihood, are also being ruined.'

'Where will you carry me to?' Sylvia said to him. 'I can't see dry ground from here, Corby. We'll have to wait.'

Annoyed with them, furious with himself for not listening to that black woman, he was just about to insist that they wade out right away without any more arguments when he happened to glance down at the back steps. He could have sworn the water had only been up to the third step, but now it was up to the fourth, in that short time. He grabbed a broom from the kitchen and with the handle gauged the depth. For the first time, he realised this wasn't an overflow; there was a heavy current placing pressure on his wooden gauge. The water was at least three feet deep and rising.

'Looks like we'll have to wait,' he told the Professor, 'until the flood levels out.'

All three of them began to watch now as the waters rose swiftly and began to seep through the floorboards. They lifted trunks and carpet runners and mats, piling them on the beds and on the tables, emptying the bottom of wardrobes as they found themselves paddling in the house.

Sylvia climbed on to a bed. 'What if it doesn't stop, Corby?' she asked him breathlessly. 'Will we drown?'

He put an arm about her. 'No, don't be frightened. Someone will come for us.'

'But the house is filling up. It's nearly up to the bed now, and there's no one out there.'

'Stay here,' he said.

There were tears in his eyes as he saw the stables and sheds disintegrate and the guest house shudder and succumb. Ruination was all about him. At least Jessie and his son were safe. He thanked the Lord, convinced now that divine intervention had sped them to safety, and thought sadly of that little boy he probably wouldn't see grow to manhood. Because although he wasn't admitting it, he knew that he and the Professor and Sylvia were in mortal danger.

288

Corby wasn't one for maudlin recriminations. The cards fell where they fell. He dismissed a fleeting thought that he was being punished for his affair with Sylvia, that the Lord was also exacting revenge. He was above such trivialities, too mentally stable to cringe. While his life deeds didn't flash before him, as was said happened in such times of crisis, Corby now felt that it had all been too easy, this swift climb to success. Even when Billingsley, the bank manager, had told him that Providence was doing well, he'd felt the luck was too good to be true. That something would go wrong for the likes of Corby Morgan.

And as the waters rose, he fumed. To survive this and emerge ruined was like putting the lot on a winning horse to find it disqualified. Ah yes, that had happened to him. Sent him broke that time at Ascot, to have to begin yet again. His inheritance had lifted him from bankruptcy and given him Providence, but now that was gone too. He laughed. Why should he be surprised? Some people had all the luck, but he was a dead-set bad risk. Funny how things worked out.

But right now he had responsibilities. Sylvia and the Professor. He had to do something about them. They were huddling together on Jessie's big double bed, silent, fearful, like ghosts at his wake.

He searched the house, wondering what would float. Given a chance he could set them adrift. The dining room table? It was already knee-deep in water. Drenched, determined, he began manoeuvring it on its side out of the back door.

Sylvia, looking so lovely and forlorn in her wet skirts, came to help him. 'What are you doing?' she asked as she pushed and shoved.

'It might make a raft,' he said, 'but at worst it will take us to the roof.'

'The roof?' she screamed. 'Are you mad?' She ran to a window as if there might be some explanation for this impossible suggestion.

'We'd have to be out of our depth to do that,' she whispered, fearfully. 'I couldn't cope, neither could Dadda.'

'Didn't I tell you I'm a good swimmer?' he said. 'One of my few accomplishments. Trust me. Now then,' he went on, with the table beached on the porch, 'we wait, dear heart, and when our Ark floats, we float with it. Don't you think you ought to take off that heavy top skirt? This is no time to be ladylike.'

She dropped the skirt and stepped aside in her cambric slip, too frightened not to obey, and they both took to staring inland, hoping for some sign of life.

'See that tree over there,' Corby said, pointing to the fig drooping with loya vines. 'I've noticed it before. The one behind your father's greenhouse. It's as big as the other one in the front garden.'

Sylvia nodded. She'd always hated that massive tree, the one that had harboured the man who'd killed himself.

'I think we'd be safer there,' Corby said. 'Why don't we try for it?'

'How?' She cringed away from him, crying.

Corby pretended not to notice. He thought he felt the house sway, the floor seemed to shift. 'Stay with your father. I'll investigate.'

Hanging on to the rough stair rail he lowered himself into the water and was instantly swung away as easily as that broom handle. The surge of the waters was still too strong to contemplate such a plan. He might make it on his own but not hauling a non-swimmer, even if he could keep her calm. And the old man? He'd be too heavy. And he'd never hold the table as a raft, it would desert him in seconds. There had been a couple of surges but now the water was inching up, hardly discernible but on the rise nevertheless, creeping up on them like an evil presence, taking its time, sure of its prey.

Corby was frightened now, he didn't mind admitting this to himself. It would be a slow, ugly wait for the inevitable hysteria, and the rest that didn't bear thinking about. Why didn't he just try for that tree? Not now, a little later when things got bad. He was tempted but he knew he couldn't do it. He couldn't leave them. And he laughed again. Here's a man who hasn't got the courage to desert!

He squelched about the house, tearing up sheets to make a sort of rope; if the bloody table wouldn't work as a raft, it could lift them to the roof if need be. But he had to make sure it was well and truly moored or it would float away on him.

'That's right,' he told himself as he worked. 'It's a mad idea, but it's something to do.' Somewhere, sometime, he'd seen pictures of people caught in devastating floods perched on rooftops, and had wondered how they'd got there. 'I think you're about to find out, Morgan Junior,' he muttered, 'but there'll be plenty of treading water in the meantime as far as I can see.'

He also hung a sheet outside the back window; it felt as if he were surrendering to the river, but it might signal that there were occupants in the stranded house. Then he poured himself a stiff brandy, placing other bottles on a high shelf. 'We might as well save something,' he muttered, wondering who might come for them. Surely word had spread? Rescue teams would come from the town, they'd bring boats. But how long would it take? A day? Would this house, shifting on its stumps, last that long? He doubted it. Climbing to the roof, then, was only a hypothetical scenario, they could be ditched long before then.

The water was up to his knees. He brought his two terrified charges wading out to the kitchen on the pretence that they were to watch for signs of life out back, but he wanted them near him in case they had to jump for it. Unless help came, the whole thing was hopeless. He wondered why he bothered, and swallowed another brandy. It had never tasted so good.

Mike Devlin knew they were in a desperate situation. The Kanakas kept a little old dinghy, down on the river road, that they used for fishing, but where would it be now?

'It's a raft or the fishing boat,' he said to Joseph, 'if we're to get them out, and both will take time. Can you make a raft?'

Joseph was stunned. Of course he could make a raft, but he needed days for the sap and wax to make it waterproof. These matters required very special attention. 'Too slow, boss,' he said.

'I don't care how slow it is,' Mike snapped, knowing he was being unreasonable. 'There's the tomahawk, get up there in the bush and start cutting saplings. I'm going to find the dinghy. One way or another we have to get over there.'

He whistled his horse and headed for the road, which was above water level, galloping along hoping to find some of the Kanakas to help him in his search. Instead he came across a mob of blacks squatting aimlessly in the scrub by the side of the road. And Elly was with them.

'Thank God,' he said to her. 'I'm glad you're safe.'

Her mother pushed forward. 'Silly feller boss allasame back dere, with number two wife and the old man.'

'Where are Tommy and Mae?' he asked Elly, who explained that they'd decided to try to walk to town.

'We need a boat to get them out of the house,' he told Elly. 'You tell all the people I need their help. We have to search the banks and see if we can find the dinghy boat. You understand?'

'Yes, boss,' she said, and began shouting at her people, who came running, concern on their faces. But Broula was arguing with them, bloody Broula who could never mind her own business.

'What's she saying?' Mike demanded.

Elly was embarrassed. She hung her head. 'She say Kanaka boat no good, boss. She say big river chew him up.'

Still astride his horse, Mike was yelling at Broula. 'For God's sake, shut up! The boat is just adrift somewhere, you stupid bitch. We have to find it. We've got plenty of people to search, tell them to get the Kanakas looking too.'

Arrogantly she heaved back to him, her wide hips swaying, at odds and yet in rhythm with her dark breasts. She spat tobacco juice before she spoke. 'Kanaka boat, you nebber find dat. Boys bring up my boat.'

'What boat?' he asked Elly, and then he remembered Broula's pride and joy, her dugout! The rough canoe carved out of a log that she used for fishing on the lagoon.

He jumped down from the horse. 'You brought it with you?'

'They brung it,' she said imperiously, pointing at some of her male relations. 'Ribber doan get my boat.'

Sure enough, three weary young blackfellows were carrying her treasure from the bush. It was only a primitive craft but it had been carefully treated and it would seat three people. Mike almost laughed; if it would carry Broula, who had to be hitting thirteen stone, it would carry anyone.

He threw his arms about her. 'Broula, my love, you're a bloody treasure.'

'Worth a quid,' she said, unimpressed.

'With paddles?' he bargained, and she nodded, waving up a spindly

291

old bloke with a grey hairy chest who solemnly delivered the paddles. Many Aboriginal societies were matriarchal, and obviously Broula, by right or by force, had command here.

'Done,' he said. 'Let's go.'

They followed him, all these innocents with scarce a rag between them, men, women and scampering children, tribal people, more interested than anxious because, except for Broula and Elly, and the little children, few understood that there was a problem. To them, flood, fire and drought were an integral part of the Dreaming, not to be feared.

Mike heard their exclamations of delight as they approached the shores of the wide and fascinating new lake that had formed across their river, and Joseph, hauling saplings across the field from the bush, stared.

'Forget about that,' Mike called to him. 'We've got a boat.'

A boat? Joseph peered at this thing the black men dumped on the shore. He remembered his father's magnificent war canoe that he had helped to carve and construct, and the superb rafts he'd made to carry fruit and produce between the islands. Surely the boss wouldn't risk his life in that bulky old log without a single sign to the gods as protection against the elements? He examined it with the practised eye of a professor. Sitting space had been carved out and some effort had been made to seal it, but . . .

Mike hurled ropes into the dugout as the dark men placed it carefully in the water, holding it against the wash. Then he called Joseph. He was strong, he could take the front paddle, but the islander didn't seem too impressed. 'That thing sink!' he said.

'No it won't,' Mike said, and then deliberately: 'Will it, Elly?'

Her face was a picture of joy at the return of her hero. She hardly heard Mike's question but her presence stimulated Joseph into action. He couldn't appear to be a coward with his friend watching.

With enthusiastic cheers the tribal men shoved the log into the deep and Mike and Joseph began paddling furiously towards the homestead. Mike nodded, satisfied. The strange craft was difficult to keep upright at first but the strong, sure hand of the Kanaka soon had it under control, and Mike, sitting behind him, dipped his paddle, keeping his strokes in unison with his leader.

Even with their determined efforts they made slow progress across the choppy waters, but Joseph guided them skilfully, avoiding submerged buildings and heading for the first solid landmark of a massive fig tree.

While Joseph steadied their boat, Mike threw a rope about the tree, leaving it dangling in the water as a safety precaution on the return journey with heavier loads. He could see them now, Morgan, Sylvia and the Professor, and he called to them to hang on as they pushed away from the tree for the last leg, with waters swirling moodily about the house, well over the back steps by now.

'I have to say you're a welcome sight,' Morgan called, and Mike grinned, puffing with exertion because it was difficult to line up by the house.

Morgan tossed a rope made of knotted sheets and Joseph caught it expertly, dragging them closer. 'We can only take one at a time,' Mike shouted. 'Will you help Sylvia out?'

She was eager to get to them, but was panicky and very frightened. She clutched Morgan as he took her into the deep water covering the back steps to lift her into the boat. As he was struggling with her, the house lurched. Mike saw the Professor's anxious face above them. 'We have to hurry,' he muttered, not explaining the reason, for Sylvia's benefit. Morgan, treading water, shoved his sister-in-law unceremoniously at Mike, who hauled her aboard, almost overturning their boat.

With Sylvia, dishevelled and upset, sitting almost in Mike's lap, they headed back. He had considered dropping her off in the safety of the tree to save time, but decided against it. After that effort, getting her out and in again could put them all in the drink. So, paddling hard now, they made for the shore.

'Lucas,' Corby said, 'we have to get away from the house. It could be swept off its blocks any minute and then it will disintegrate.' He stared at the old man, who seemed completely dazed. 'Do you understand what I'm saying? It won't be hard. We just go into the water now, and all you have to do is let yourself float and I'll fetch you across to that tree. There's a rope on it now, we'll be safe there.'

But the Professor pulled away, stumbled, and fell backwards into the water which was already nearly two feet deep in the kitchen.

Corby stood him up again as the house shuddered and cracked. It sounded as if a wall had split but Corby didn't have time to investigate. 'Come on,' he insisted. 'I won't let you sink.'

'No! No!' the Professor screamed, his eyes wild. 'That's the river out there. It's full of crocodiles and they're waiting for me.' He began to babble incoherently. His face was flushed red and he was feverish, and no matter how Corby tried he couldn't make him listen, nor could he calm him. He was now forced to support the old man whose legs were buckling under him and he used that as an excuse to edge him out. But Lucas seemed to grasp what was happening and he began to fight Corby off.

'Stop, you bloody old fool,' Corby shouted, floundering. 'Stop or I'll leave you here. We'll be in the bloody river whichever way it goes.' It occurred to him that he ought to punch the man, knock him out; he'd be easier to drag across the water that way, maybe. But then again, maybe not, he'd be a dead weight. Anyway, not being an expert in the art he wasn't sure that a punch would do any more than cause the Professor damage.

Exhausted with the struggle he took the last course available to him; he grabbed Lucas about the waist and started to drag him bodily out of the house. 'You're going in the water whether you like it or not,' he gritted. As he battled he heard a large crash, and the unmistakable sound of smashed glass told him that a wall had given way in the front of the house and part of the roof had caved in. He looked up, his fears confirmed, to see a wide gap in the roof above him.

Lucas gave one last jerk and then fell. Despairing, Corby was down in the water again, trying to hold him up when he realised that the old man was suffering a seizure of some sort. His eyes were blank and his whole body was shaking uncontrollably.

'Oh God! Not now!' Corby groaned, craning up to watch for his rescuers, hearing only the rustle of the waters and the ominous crack and creak of the doomed house.

At one stage, hanging on to his father-in-law, Corby began to worry that Devlin might not come back. That they'd met with an accident. That they might not bother with two grown men, having rescued the woman. That Devlin, in an act of revenge, might find an excuse not to return. He was chilled to the bones, his limbs stiff from this awkward crouch, trying to support the Professor with water lapping about them. Occasionally the old man wheezed and moaned, and his eyes glinted life, but he seemed totally unaware of their predicament.

Devlin's piercing whistle startled Corby. 'I need help!' he shouted. 'Langley's collapsed! And so will I any minute,' he muttered to Lucas. 'I'm half drowned my bloody self.'

Devlin slipped out of his crazy boat and Corby felt a jab of the irritation that this man always caused him. Surely he could have done better than that apology for a canoe?

The former manager swam the few yards to the submerged veranda. 'Jesus!' he said. 'That's all we need. How bad is he?'

'I don't know. Give me a hand to get up, I'm as stiff as a board.' It had been hard enough lifting Sylvia, who'd had to be prised loose from Corby, but this time they were trying to be gentle with Lucas, holding his head up as they lifted him.

Corby heard the cries of birds, a strangely familiar sound, but not the screech and cackle of the usual Providence bird population. That was just before the floor disappeared from under him, before he went down like a stone into the black depths in a surging tide of lumber.

In that split second as he saw Morgan go without a sound, as if he'd stepped into a deep hole, Mike dived away from the house, dragging Lucas with him.

Joseph was working. He slashed the soggy mooring sheet with his knife to prevent his boat being hauled away with the disintegrating building, and plunged his paddle into the water to right the boat. No need for talk, they both knew what they had to do. He was beginning to understand this craft now. He swung it about so that Mr Devlin, who was supporting the old man as he fought against the current, could grab hold, and then he began paddling furiously for that tree, for the anchor of the rope.

'Can you see Morgan?' Mike asked as he clambered into the rolling boat, dragging Lucas after him.

'No.'

The lower branches of the trees were submerged so they were able to wedge the boat into a firm position as they scanned the waters down river.

'There!' Joseph was pointing but Mike couldn't see anything except for the shattered debris of the house riding the surface of the river in merry escape.

Before he could stop him, Joseph jammed his knife into his belt, threw his paddle to Mike and dived into the murky stream.

Where was the surface? Having been rolled, tumbled and battered into this darkness, Corby was struggling for air, disoriented, tormented that he might be moving deeper, going the wrong way, down instead of up. Then suddenly he bobbed into light, gasping for air. He was being swept along in this raging sea and when he tried to swim, to battle for his life, pain shot across his back. He couldn't recall being hurt but something had given him an almighty whack. Trying to tread water, to save his strength, was impossible; he kept slipping under and, despite the pain, having to fight to stay afloat.

A tree branch sped by, and he tried to grab it, then a sheet of corrugated iron sliced dangerously past him. Bobbing about in the current, weakening by the minute, Corby saw floating debris and struck out for it but he couldn't reach it, defeated by the current.

This was Providence, this alien sea, his Providence. And his grave. He could see those green mountains in the distance. Clear now, no mists hiding them because the sun was out. It was hot on his face. The skies above him were an azure blue. The wet season was over. Planters would be setting to work. He heard those birds again. Seagulls, of course, he should have known that, but he was so tired. And he'd swallowed a lot of this foul-tasting water. He thought he heard someone shout and wished he didn't feel so sick; if he had to drown he ought to be allowed to go down peacefully, not retching like this.

A spark of hope shook him from his reveries. A log was floating nearby. If he could grasp that, he could stay afloat and let it deliver him where it may. As he struck out for it he distinctly heard someone scream: 'No!' But by then it was too late.

As he pounded through the water Joseph had kept his eyes firmly on his master, watching him disappear and come up again out there. Now he was closing fast.

'No!' he screamed. He'd seen that old man crocodile slithering through the water, disguised as a drifting log and he'd been terrified, praying to the gods to keep the monster heading downstream. It didn't seem to have noticed the man in the water with all this disruption of its normal habitats, until the man himself lunged towards it, straight at those jaws.

295

Joseph dived with every inch of his strength, his legs pounding as he shot under water to slash the monster's long white belly with his knife.

The water was rich with blood as the crocodile reared up, dragging the man with him. Then the beast fell away, releasing his would-be victim. At once Joseph was swimming, riding the tide, edging closer to the shore all the time, clasping the limp body of the master to him.

People were in the water, screaming, crying, taking the master from him, helping him up on to the sweet-smelling grass. He lay there for a while, feeling the sun on his back restoring his strength, listening to the wailing of the black people, and he felt sure the master was dead. Miserably he climbed to his feet.

The big fat woman, Elly's mother, was snatching scraps of cloth from the others, even Elly's dress, using every available rag to bind the master. Joseph, watching in horror, realised that the master was still alive but that his arm was missing, leaving only a bloodied stump covered by all those rags. Then the woman was shouting at her men, running with them as they picked up the master to carry him away.

Mike had lost sight of Joseph. Whether the Kanaka had caught up with Morgan or not, there was no way he could swim back against the high tide which was now retreating out to sea, having met the floodwaters head on. Mike guessed that had been the final blow to the house.

But now what to do? Lucas, cramped in the dugout, was barely breathing. They couldn't stay here; the old man needed a doctor. Mike studied the currents. If he took advantage of the tide and manoeuvred carefully, it would be easier for a lone man than the direct route they'd taken before, forging straight across to the house and back. Whatever, he'd have to make the effort. Looking anxiously at the Professor, he said quietly: 'Hold on, mate, I'll do the best I can.'

The dugout spun almost out of control as he left the sanctuary of the tree but Mike squatted down and bent to the paddle, making every stroke count. Down and across and downstream again they went until some of the tribal men from the lagoon swam out to help, dragging the boat ashore, shouting and pointing like madmen.

When they'd hauled him to land, he managed to calm them long enough to hear that the boss had been attacked by a crocodile. And then Joseph came running.

True to his word, Bede Hornsby brought Jessie news of the flood-stricken river properties.

'Is it bad?' she asked him anxiously.

'Not that good,' he allowed. 'But let me hasten to say there has been no loss of life among the families living out there. Difficult to sort out the Kanakas, they're scattered all over the countryside.'

Jessie was tempted to remark that Kanakas were family people too, but let it pass for now.

'A couple of the young mill hands from Helenslea are still missing,' he added, 'white men. There's a search on for them now but I daresay they'll turn up. Young blokes, you know, they take risks . . .'

'What sort of risks?' Jessie still couldn't envisage the flood. She was relieved that everyone at home was safe, in which case why were the Kanakas scattered?

'Word has it they were looters. They went back to see what they could scavenge from the Helenslea homestead. Rich pickings for looters in Edgar Betts's house, but a dangerous things to do.'

'Why?'

'The house had to be evacuated and just in time. The flood went right through it.'

'Oh no! How terrible! Mr Hornsby, what about our house?'

'Ah yes,' he said. 'You'd better sit down, Mrs Morgan. I'm sorry, but it's gone.'

Jessie remained standing. 'What do you mean, "gone"?'

'Be a good girl now, sit down here.' He insisted she retreat to the plush armchair before he would continue. 'I've asked them to bring you up a good strong cup of tea. It should be here any minute. The riders coming in are saying that the Providence homestead was swept away in the flood. Wrecked, I'm afraid.'

'Oh my God! I thought you said everyone was safe.'

'And so they are. Mike Devlin's in charge, he's a reliable fellow.'

'Where's my husband?'

'They're bringing him in, Mrs Morgan. He had an accident. I'm not sure of the extent of his injuries,' Hornsby lied. The news was all over town, but one thing at a time.

'How are they bringing him in? How badly is he injured? Someone must know.'

'The doctor will know. He's out there. They're bringing Mr Morgan to hospital in a wagon. It will take time but he's in good hands, so you mustn't be worrying. I'm afraid, too, that it was all rather a shock for your father and he's not the best.'

'No, I suppose not,' she said, stunned. 'And my sister, Miss Langley. Where is she?'

'She's fine. Everything that can be done is being done to help, Mrs Morgan. The townspeople have rallied, they've sent out wagonloads of supplies and clothes, and longboats for ferrying stranded souls to safety. Now, here's your tea.'

A maid came in with the tray, staring wide-eyed at Mrs Morgan, curious to observe her reactions. Hornsby ushered the girl out before she could speak.

'Is there anyone you'd like to see?' he asked the planter's wife.

'I don't know. I can't think. Oh, perhaps you could find Lieutenant Scott-Hughes for me?'

'I'm sorry, the troopers were the first to be ordered out there, and the doctor went with them in case he was needed. Would you like my wife to come and sit with you, Mrs Morgan?'

'Thank you, you're very kind, but it's not necessary.' She shuddered, trying to come to terms with all this terrible news. 'I'll wait at the hospital.'

'It's too soon, my dear. You'd be better to rest here. They won't be in until late this afternoon.'

When he left, Jessie sat gazing out over the tranquil bay. It didn't seem possible that such devastation had taken place behind this façade of normality. There were so many things she should have asked Mr Hornsby. Corby, what had happened to him? He obviously couldn't ride into town; had he broken his leg in a fall from a horse? And her father? It was no wonder he'd had a bad turn, caught up in all that mayhem at his age.

She poured the tea, not noticing that the staff had made a special effort to please her by producing their best teapot and china set, and adding freshly baked scones with blackberry jam and clotted cream. Hanna ate them while Jessie prepared for a long, anxious day.

Sylvia threw herself into his arms, aware that she looked like a drowned duck, that her petticoat and vest were still damp and clinging to her, barely covered by the blanket someone had wrapped about her, but also appreciating that in this distressed state she made an appealing picture.

'Sylvia, my poor dear girl, what an ordeal!' Harry held her to him, gallantly uninhibited by the curious glances of his men as they trotted down the road, and Sylvia was so proud. She wept; for herself, for the loss of their home and everything she owned, including her lovely clothes, and from sheer exhaustion.

'I've been looking for you,' he said. 'I was so worried. I must have ridden past this spot hours ago and missed you. Are you all right?'

She peered about her, horrified to find she'd been resting, crouched under a tree in the middle of a blacks' camp, with half-naked natives wandering about a smoky fire.

'No,' she whimpered, 'I'm not all right, Harry. Where am I? Where are Elly and Broula? They brought me here. Elly's my maid, she should have stayed with me. I must have fallen asleep.' She clung to him. 'Oh, Harry, you've no idea what I've been through, stranded in the house, actually wading in water in the house with the river rising all the time. I thought we'd drown.'

'There now, not to worry, you're safe now. I'll take you into town myself.'

'Town?' she shrieked. 'I can't go into town looking like this.'

'No one will see you,' he soothed.

'Where's my father? And Corby? Where are they? It's all Corby's fault, you know. Broula warned him about the flood, but would he listen? Oh no, not him. I wanted to leave, Harry,' she wept, 'but he made me stay.' Never would she forgive Corby for putting her through this. She should have gone to town with Jessie, who'd be sitting up in state in a town hotel with every luxury while her sister was here, destitute.

'Corby and Professor Langley have just been . . .' Harry corrected himself; she didn't need any more shocks right now. 'They've gone ahead into town. In a wagon,' he conceded.

'Without even waiting for me? That's typical, nobody cares about me.'

'I care,' he said, kissing her gently. 'Why not come with me?'

She allowed herself to be led barefoot out to the road. 'Everything in the house is ruined,' she told him. 'It won't be habitable any more. Even upstairs the water was up to my waist. I hate to think what it will look like when the flood goes down. What will become of us, Harry?'

He held her hand as he led her over to his horse. 'What if I put you up behind me?' he asked her. 'Do you think you could ride with me?'

She looked down at her bedraggled underwear. 'I'm a sight. What if someone sees me?'

'Anyone who sees you will be too busy thanking the Lord that you're safe to be noticing what you're wearing, dear.' He took off his smart red tunic. 'Here now. Give me that old blanket and put this on.'

Harry smiled. The tunic swam on her, but it made her look even more attractive, with her tangled black hair hanging down over the well-padded shoulders. And with her arms about his waist, she rode well, expertly in fact, taking the movement of the horse for granted, so he was able to add a little speed, with her trusting face nestled into his back and her little bare feet tucked by his legs.

Sooner or later she'd have to find out about her father and Corby, but not yet. The doctor had grave doubts as to whether either of them would survive; there wasn't much he could do for the Professor. Harry and his men had ridden hard to the flood area, in company with Dr Muller, a dedicated fellow if ever there was one. Muller was a German immigrant who had only recently arrived in Cairns, and although he'd heard good reports of him, this was the first occasion that Harry had met him. He'd been immensely relieved that Muller had volunteered to accompany his troop.

On the long ride out he'd learned that Muller, a heavily built blond man, about forty years old, had been a surgeon in the Prussian army, but had eventually been sickened by the wastage of young men. 'Terrible things I saw,' he told Harry. 'Unnecessary amputations by butchers calling themselves surgeons. Sadistic bastards who use the military, yours, mine, the French and all the others, to further their evil careers. Even with my qualifications I was too junior in rank to beat them. I could only patch up their mistakes. I had a nervous breakdown and when I felt well enough I deserted. Does that shock you? A military man?'

'No,' Harry said. 'I saw much the same thing in India. I too am an immigrant. My old army pals rag me that I'm no more than a policeman in this country that has never seen war except for the clashes with the Aborigines. But I've had my fill of cannon.'

When they were waiting their turn to ford the Halfway Creek, Franz Muller smiled at Harry. 'Here I want to see babies born and care for them through their lives, is this too much to ask?'

'I don't think so,' Harry replied.

When they were confronted with poor Corby Morgan, barely conscious, his handsome face grey and his eyes staring mad, with the bundle of blood-stained rags where his right arm should have been, Harry turned to Dr Muller, unable to speak. Here was another patch-up job that would tax the German doctor's capabilities and Corby's ability to live through the shock.

Now he took Sylvia on past the entrance to Helenslea plantation where hundreds of South Sea Islanders were congregated, and left two of his troopers in charge, promising that food supplies were on the way. He directed his men to patrol the road, bringing all stragglers to this point, no matter which plantation they called home. He had been ordered by Bede Hornsby to keep them out of town; it was too small to cope with an influx of Kanakas running loose in the streets.

'Where are we going?' Sylvia asked him as he turned off the main road.

'Woollahra plantation,' he said. 'That homestead is intact, they'll look after you there.'

'I thought you were taking me to town,' she complained.

'And I will, but I have to find decent transport for you. I want you to stay with Mrs Cavanagh for a while, she'll look after you. As soon as I can I'll escort you to town myself.'

But Sylvia was becoming agitated. 'Stop, Harry! What will Mrs Cavanagh think of me? I can't go to her door in this state.'

'We're nearly there,' he said. 'Bear up. We can't double all the way to Cairns and I've a lot to do before I'll be able to leave.'

Mrs Cavanagh, a stern, practical woman, took no notice of Sylvia's embarrassed apologies. 'Come on inside, missy. We've got a house full but there's always room for one more. What you need is a good scrub-up and a bit of shuteye. Thank you, Lieutenant, it was very sensible of you to bring her here. None of the men are about but my daughters are in the kitchen making sandwiches. You take yourself off there and I'll attend to this one.'

Irritated, but too intimidated by her hostess to argue, Sylvia found herself plonked in a bath, while Mrs Cavanagh with hands of cast iron, soaped and washed her hair. 'Stop fussing, missy,' she said. 'You've got lovely hair, we have to get rid of all that mud then you'll be right as pie. I heard you had a bad time of it.'

'Yes,' Sylvia sobbed, eyes stinging from the soap.

'It's all over now. And don't you be worrying about your father and Corby. They're in good hands. They'll be taken straight through to hospital, plenty of helpers all along the way.'

300

Sylvia grabbed a towel to defend her eyes from the dipper of water being poured over her head. 'What's wrong with them? Harry said they got out. Mike went back for them.'

'Oh!' Mrs Cavanagh stopped. 'Come on, hop out now. Here are the towels, you can dry yourself and put on this dressing gown. I'll be back in a minute.' She grabbed Harry's tunic and disappeared, but was back soon to hurry Sylvia to a bedroom, a large, cool room with the shades drawn. 'We'll dry your hair and comb it out and then you can have a sleep, missy, you must be tired out.'

Sylvia was feeling more in control now. In fact she wasn't a scrap tired. 'What's wrong with them?' she pressed.

'You just sit down while I dry your hair. Your father had a heart attack. No use beating about the bush, he's not too good, dear. And Corby, well it's hard to say. He met with a bad accident and lost his arm.'

Sylvia was sitting in front of the mirror, staring at Mrs Cavanagh, dazed. 'No one told me,' she stammered.

'Fair enough. I'm telling you now. The doctor is travelling with them so there's nothing you can do. Except worry, I suppose.'

'Corby?' she said. 'How did that happen? It couldn't have.'

'I'm afraid it did. But Mike Devlin nursed him, nursed them both with the help of some gins, until the doctor arrived. Muller is a surgeon, missy, an experienced man. I'm told he stitched Corby's arm in a field operation, so we can hope for the best.'

'Thank you for telling me,' Sylvia whispered. 'Mrs Cavanagh, I'll have to get to town as soon as possible.'

'Of course you will. First thing in the morning.' As gently as she could she raked the large comb through Sylvia's hair. 'There now, you're looking fine again. You'd better lie down.'

This time Sylvia agreed. She was too stunned to think. She just lay there, her mind a blank, until Harry came in.

'I hope you'll forgive me,' he said, taking her hand. 'I thought it best not to be handing you the bad news until you were on solid ground.'

She nodded. 'Yes, I understand. Harry, how did such an awful thing happen to Corby?'

'Well,' he said carefully, 'the house collapsed in the flood.'

'Collapsed? You mean it's gone?'

'I'm afraid so, washed away.'

'Oh my God! And my father was still in there?'

'I believe they pulled him out just in time, but it was all too much for him.'

'Oh Lord, yes. It was bad enough for me trying to struggle into that little boat, I got bruised with them dragging at me. And coming across that filthy water I was certain we'd tip over every inch of the way. My heart was in my mouth the whole time.'

He kissed her. 'A terrible ordeal for you, you've been very brave. Now you ought to try to sleep. Mrs Cavanagh is putting me up here tonight so I'll pop in on you when I come back. Now promise me you'll rest.'

'Yes,' she said meekly, 'I promise.'

The bed was so comfortable she did sleep and awoke to find one of the Cavanagh girls standing by the wardrobe.

'I hope I didn't wake you,' she said. 'Remember me? I'm Betsy.'

'Yes,' Sylvia said. She'd met Betsy, a gawky girl with fair plaits wrapped about her head, at Bronte's christening.

'I think I'll get up,' Sylvia said. 'Do you have any clothes I could borrow?'

'Of course. I'm just looking for something for you. The maid has washed and ironed your underlinen, so let's see.' She took out a plaid cotton skirt. 'Here you are, and a nice blouse to go with it.'

The blouse was plain white, more like a shirt, and the skirt looked like a tablecloth, Sylvia thought, but she made no comment. She thanked Betsy for the white stockings she handed to her, and tried on brown button-up boots, disappointed to find they fitted so she could hardly exchange them. Betsy was talking about the flood and the devastation of the crops and what a hard time everyone would have now, and Sylvia sat patiently, hugging a dressing gown, until the other girl took the hint, leaving the room to allow the guest to dress.

A sense of dread had descended on Sylvia as she pulled on the clothes. If the plantation were ruined, as Betsy said, and the house gone, where would they live now? And with Corby and her father both in hospital what would become of them? She would have to find Jessie in town and stay with her. Jessie had clothes, some clothes at least. 'But I've got nothing!' she wailed as she saw herself in these awful hand-me-downs. And Harry would know she was destitute; would he want her now without even a wardrobe, let alone a dowry? There was no point in looking to Corby any more, he'd hardly be able to support himself. If he survived. Losing an arm was a terrible thing, the pain must have been frightful. Poor Corby. She tried not to think about it. After all, if he'd listened to Broula it wouldn't have happened and her father's heart attack would have been avoided too. Still, nothing could have prevented the flood and the terrible mess they were all in now.

She combed her hair, primping it into ringlets about her face. Somehow she'd have to try to look nice for Harry; he was being wonderful, caring for her in these pitiful circumstances, but that sort of sympathy didn't last. Soon the floods would go down and everyone would resume their normal lives. 'But we won't be able to do that,' she told herself. 'We'll be just plain poor, Jessie and me, with a baby and two sick men on our hands. It won't do. I'll have to speed things up.'

As she prepared to present herself to the family, Sylvia found a bottle of lavender water and liberally sprinkled her arms and throat. An exciting thought came into her head: I'll never be able to afford a decent wedding now, what if I could persuade Harry to elope with me? That

302

would be the perfect solution! She would throw herself on his mercy, weep a little, tell him she had nowhere to go. He'd have to do the right thing and look after her.

In a better mood now, she walked through the big house, surprised to see a crowd assembled in the long parlour.

'There you are!' Betsy cried, taking her arm. 'Are you feeling better?'

'Yes thank you. Where did all these people come from?'

'They're refugees too. We've got them bunked down everywhere. But you needn't worry, you can stay in my room. I'll sleep in my sister's bed. Top and toe. It's quite fun. Several of the farmers and their families are here and the people from Helenslea, but you know most of them. Do you want to come out to the veranda before it gets dark, Miss Langley? You can see the flood from there.'

Sylvia shuddered but followed Betsy across the room, acknowledging kindly smiles. What she saw outside startled her. A great ochre-coloured lake had spread across the land, with only patches of green hilltops and bunched treetops like shrubs dotting the surface.

'Oh my God!' she cried, reeling back with a little more fervour than she actually felt. She had a part to play now, misfortune would be her trump card.

'Are you all right?' Betsy cried. 'You're not going to faint, are you?'

'No. It was just the shock. I've never seen anything like that in my life. And to think I was out in the middle of it.'

A woman took her arm. 'You poor girl. Come inside and sit down. Betsy, get her a cup of tea.'

'A brandy would be a better idea,' a familiar voice drawled. 'You get it for her, Mrs McMullen.'

'Oh Lita,' Sylvia said weakly, 'how marvellous to see you. I was so worried about you. What a terrible thing to happen to you on top of your father's death. I'm so sorry.'

'These things are sent to try us.' Lita shrugged and Sylvia noticed crankily that her friend still managed to look elegant, even in these circumstances, not a hair out of place. She was wearing a black riding outfit with an open-necked shirt, hardly the correct attire for the parlour at this hour, but it didn't seem to bother her.

'I heard about your dad,' Lita said, dismissing the bearer of Sylvia's brandy. 'And Corby, and I'm bloody sorry, darling. Here, drink this. It'll do you the world of good.'

'They're not any worse, are they?' Sylvia asked, alarmed.

'Not as far as I know. No news is good news in these situations.'

'That's a relief,' Sylvia said, swallowing the brandy. 'You know we've lost the house?'

'Yes, but they'll rebuild. My place will be a mountain of mud. Our best bet is to go to town and stay out of the way until everything's cleaned up.'

'They can't clean up the Providence house,' Sylvia said. 'I've got nowhere to go. You can afford to stay in town. Where can I stay?'

303

'Stop worrying,' Lita said. 'We'll work something out. Oh, there's Mike.' She waved to him as he walked into the parlour. Sylvia was delighted to see Harry coming in behind Mike, but Lita nudged her. 'Who's that?' she asked urgently, admiration in her voice. 'The officer? What a divine creature! Excuse me, Sylvia, I must meet this one.'

Furiously, Sylvia stood watching as Lita made a beeline for the two men, kissing Mike on the cheek and then turning her full attention on Harry, who was smiling at her with that sweet, affectionate smile that Sylvia had been sure was reserved for her alone.

Lita took his arm.

Betsy collared Sylvia. 'There are so many people here, we're having an eat-out this evening. Dad's cooking a side of beef on the spit. Do you know Mr and Mrs McMullen?'

She threaded Sylvia through the crowd again, this time introducing her to everyone. Over at the door, the two men, and Lita, were talking to Mrs Cavanagh.

Sylvia accepted a glass of sherry wine, and drank it down, standing herself in Harry's line of vision, but he still hadn't noticed her. She was determined not to go fawning after him like Lita. Why should she demean herself? Harry was her beau.

'This brandy's jolly good,' the awful McMullen woman said to her. 'Would you like another?'

'Do you think I should?'

'Why not, dearie? Little enough to cheer us up. I'll have one with you. After all, it's free.'

Disgusted, but not enough to refuse the brandy, Sylvia took her glass and turned back to see that they'd left the parlour. All four of them! Harry hadn't even bothered to come in to talk to her. Caught up in Lita's clutches.

As she craned her neck to see where they'd gone to, she stepped back and became entangled, stumbling, in the feet of older women seated on the couch. Laughing, Alf McMullen rescued her. 'You'd better slow up on the brandy!'

'Rubbish!' she snapped. 'They shouldn't have their feet sticking out to trip people.'

Angered by his insolence, Sylvia edged around groups of people, making for the door. Once outside, she saw that Lita was still with Mike and Harry, the three of them talking as if no one else existed.

Harry had his back to her. 'Would it be possible to move your house further inland, Lita?' he was saying.

'Not a chance,' she replied. 'It's too solidly built.'

'Not like the poor Providence house,' Sylvia interjected angrily.

Harry turned, surprised. 'Why, Sylvia! You're up! And you're looking so well. I thought you'd sleep the clock around.'

'You mean you thought I was out of the way!'

'Why no!' Harry blinked, confused.

'He thought you were still resting, Sylvia,' Lita said.

'And you didn't bother to tell him I was in there.'

'Why should I?' she laughed. 'I didn't know you knew Harry.'

'Well I do,' Sylvia scowled, incensed by the possessive note in Lita's voice, jealous of the rapport that was already established between them. 'He's a friend of mine. And how are your friends, Mrs de Flores? How is Captain King?'

'As far as I know he's quite well, thank you.'

Feeling that she was winning this battle, Sylvia smiled. 'Mrs de Flores has some quite notorious friends. Don't you?'

'I guess so,' Lita replied evenly. 'Makes life interesting. But then you like to keep within the family!'

There was no mistaking the thrust of Lita's remark, and Sylvia felt chilled as the colour drained from her face. Befuddled now, she was trying to think up an adequate response when Mike Devlin intervened. 'They're serving dinner. I'm starving. Let's eat, Sylvia.'

Well meaning, he took her arm, steadying her, but that meant leaving Harry with Lita and she couldn't allow that. She pushed Mike away and lurched towards Harry, stumbling again, realising, for the first time, that she'd had too much to drink. She felt dizzy.

It was Lita who took charge, spiriting her away from the thatched breezeway beside the house where trestle tables were set for the guests, through a shrubbery to the rear of the house. She held on to Sylvia under cover of the darkness while she retched and wept, and doubled up again. In no time she was back in that room, lying on the bed, a cold compress on her head. 'I feel terrible,' she moaned.

'I'm not surprised,' Lita said. 'You need some padding in your stomach.'

'No. I couldn't eat a thing. I just want to be left alone.'

'You'll have to eat or you'll feel ten times worse when you wake up.'

'What was that all about?' Harry asked Mike.

'Too many drinks on an empty stomach, I'd say.'

'Of course. Poor Sylvia. It's been a long, dreadful day for her. I really did think she'd still be resting. They should have kept her in bed, it's a shame.'

'She'll survive. Come on, that sizzling meat smells too good for us just to be standing here.'

They joined the others for bowls of hot soup and platters of beef with charcoal-cooked potatoes. Mike added chunks of pineapple to the meat and Harry decided he might as well too. 'First time I've come across meat served with fruit,' he commented, 'but it's jolly good.'

'I think we learned it from the Kanakas,' Mike replied. 'When they cook for me I get mangoes, bananas, papayas, all sorts of fruit on my plate with the meat. I'm used to it now.'

'It's not hard. I must say, I'm enjoying this meal.' To prove a point both men lined up for seconds as Jack Cavanagh carved juicy ribs for them on a well-worn chopping block.

305

Lita found a place next to Mike. They were discussing the various problems confronting the plantations now, and Harry, concentrating on his meal, didn't intrude.

'When the water subsides we'll have to split the labour,' Lita said. 'What if we put McMullen in charge of cleaning up the homestead area and their own house, while you take over the plantation as a whole. If you want, I'll keep McMullen on as your deputy. It's up to you, but I think we'll need every hand we can get for a while.'

'Yes,' Mike nodded. 'I wanted to talk to you about that. Lita, I'm sorry. I'll give you all the help I can but I have to stay at Providence.'

'What? You can't! I need you. You don't owe them anything.'

He shook his head. 'That's not the point. They're in trouble, Lita, you know that. Someone has to take control of Providence.'

'Then let them get someone else. You don't think Corby Morgan will thank you, he'll probably put another bullet in you.'

'No he won't.'

She stared moodily at her plate. 'You're not doing this to help Corby Morgan,' she said. 'It's her, isn't it? You can't bring yourself to leave her. You never intended to leave Providence, or you would have gone months ago.'

She was angry and Harry tried not to listen, but the conversation made him nervous. Was Mike keen on Sylvia? Coming after that other acrimonious conversation between the two women, he wondered what was really going on at Providence. He should have paid more attention. Mike and Sylvia, both single, living on the plantation with no other single people about; it was reasonable to suppose that they might be mutually attracted. And Lita wanted Mike. Not only as her manager either, that was obvious. Harry worried now that by paying court to Sylvia he could be trespassing on Mike's ground. Was that what Lita had meant when she'd said that Sylvia preferred to stay within the family? Of course . . . the family of Providence. The small clique of whites living there. Mike would be regarded as one of the family, being the only other white man on the property.

He excused himself to find his hostess, Mrs Cavanagh. After congratulating her on serving such a fine dinner, he asked if he might impose on their hospitality for a few more days. She had mentioned that transport would be arranged to take Sylvia and another lady to town tomorrow, and he had intended to ride with them to accompany Sylvia. But it might be wiser to withdraw from that association for a little while. Until he understood exactly what was going on. He was still very fond of Sylvia, extremely fond of her, but a strategic retreat for the time being could be in order. And anyway, he had only intended to take Sylvia to town and then return to the problems out here. It really was for the best if he stayed to help keep order and begin the mopping-up process.

Sylvia awoke depressed, not so much that she'd made a scene – she considered she'd been provoked – or that she'd been sick. That wasn't her fault either. She'd needed food, not drink. And it was Lita who'd foisted drink on her when she hadn't eaten all day. Lita, playing the Good Samaritan then, in front of Harry, pretending to care for her, when all she'd done was shunt her off to the bedroom and send the maid in with bread and cheese. None of that had any bearing on her miserable awakening. She was upset because she'd missed spending the whole evening with Harry. And worse, had left him to Lita. There were so many people about it had been like a party, even with all the woes, and she'd missed it.

She hurried to dress, buttoning on the boots as Mrs Cavanagh came in. 'Oh good, Sylvia. I'm pleased to see you're up. Now you have a solid breakfast before you go, you've a long day ahead. Mrs Battersby and her two children will be travelling with you, since their house is under water too. Her husband and some other gentlemen will be escorting you.'

'Lieutenant Scott-Hughes has kindly volunteered to ride to town with me, Mrs Cavanagh, so there's no need to worry about me.'

Mrs Cavanagh frowned. 'I don't know anything about that. The lieutenant's a busy man, he rode out on his duties early this morning. But Mrs Battersby will look after you. They'll take the trap as far as the ferry at Halfway Creek and our man can bring it back.'

Stalling, Sylvia looked doubtful. 'But how will we get to town from there?'

'The townspeople have it all organised from that point. You stay with Mrs Battersby, she'll know what to do. And, Sylvia, do give my regards to your family, you must be desperate to see them.' She handed Sylvia a long serge cloak. 'Here, my dear. I want you to have this. It's new, it hasn't been worn. You'll need something until you get yourself sorted out.'

'Thank you,' Sylvia said. 'It's very nice. I'll return it when I can.'

'No need. Wear it in good health.'

When the woman finally left, Sylvia sat staring at the cloak. It was very nice, and very expensive, about as full as they made them. In navy, lined with blue silk. But it made her feel like a charity case. Was this to be her lot from now on?

And Harry? Sylvia fought back tears. He had promised, and now he'd gone off without a word. Angrily she pulled on the cloak, relieved that at least it hid the ugly skirt, if not the boots. 'I bet Lita's gone with him,' she muttered at herself in the mirror.

Sure enough, when she went down to the dining room where a few older people were still lingering over breakfast, she found that Lita and Mike Devlin had ridden out with the early birds. And with Harry.

Chapter Twelve

The hospital consisted of two workers' cottages linked together by a covered walkway. It was presided over by a stout woman of Italian descent, Matron Ridolfi. Jessie was there hours before they were brought in, sitting stiffly in a cane chair by the main entrance. She'd received several messages, instigated by Bede Hornsby, each one assuring her that the patients were on their way, but as the hours passed she began to think the worst. Had Corby or her father succumbed? Was that the hold-up? One man had told her that Sylvia was safe but she had no idea of her whereabouts.

The first time the matron had spoken to her, wondering who she was waiting for, Jessie had thrown the volatile woman into a panic. 'Two more patients you say? Where can I put them? We are full up now. Dr Briggs brought in three more with the fever this morning.'

'You must find room,' Jessie urged. 'My husband and my father, I'm nearly out of my mind with worry. Dr Muller is bringing them. He will expect beds.'

'Dr Muller?' the matron said. 'He's coming back with them? They must be bad. I'll see to it.'

Her response plunged Jessie into despair, but she appreciated the resultant activity. Three women, hospital maids in grey dresses and mobcaps, bustled about, lugging patients from room to room, dragging mattresses and upending beds, to get them through doorways, until Jessie could stand it no longer. She went in search of the matron. 'I feel so useless, is there anything I can do to help?'

The matron dumped a pile of linen on a thin mattress. 'We can always do with an extra hand, madam. Can you use an iron?'

'Yes.'

'Then come with me.'

In no time Jessie found herself in a steamy kitchen, working through a mountain of clothes and linen with the heavy flatiron. It was hot work, since the kitchen table was only a few feet from the stove, but she persevered, pressing coarse nightdresses and pyjamas for the patients and sprinkling water on the heavily starched bed linen. 'Someone's gone mad with the starch,' she muttered to herself as she threw her weight into the job, trying to make a decent showing.

At intervals she stood by the stove, waiting for the iron to reheat, stirring the stews that were simmering in their large pots, keeping herself occupied. She found a rack and hung the damp linen to dry in neat folds by the fire after it had been ironed. The women came and went, carrying out various duties, taking her for granted. One of them called to her, 'Could you make the tea, luv? She's runnin' us off our bleedin' feet.'

She found a teapot and cups and saucers, and poured for them, feeling like a canteen worker but appreciating their gratitude as they hurriedly slurped their tea, not stopping to sit.

When Matron came in Jessie was back at her ironing job. 'Would you like a cup of tea?' she asked.

'Not yet. Why don't you give it a rest now?'

'I don't mind. I'll keep going.'

'I think you'd better sit down, Mrs Morgan.'

Carefully Jessie placed the iron in its rack beside the stove. 'What is it, Matron? What's wrong?'

'Come and sit over here.' The matron pushed forward a square kitchen chair and Jessie stared at it as if it were proffering not comfort but fear.

'Have you had news?'

'Yes,' Matron said. 'Now I want you to sit down and we'll have a bit of a talk.'

Jessie moved obediently to the chair. It was hard and oddly cold in the hot room.

'You're going to have to be brave,' the Matron began, and Jessie waited for the blow. 'Your father. Would that be Mr Langley?'

'Yes?'

'Ah. Well I'm very sorry to have to tell you, dear, that he didn't make it. He had another attack on the way in and it was too much for him. But he died very quietly, Mrs Morgan, he was unconscious. He just slipped away. We could say a prayer for him.'

Stunned, tears coursing down her face, Jessie tried to join in as the woman recited the Our Father.

'How do you know?' she whispered when the prayer was over.

'They're here,' Matron said. 'They came in a little while ago, that's why we thought it best to keep you busy out here.'

'And my husband? Where is he?'

'The doctor's with him now.'

Jessie tried to get up but the matron kept her seated. 'You can see him soon, he's over the other side. He's been through a lot but he's strong.'

'The accident?' she cried. 'What happened to him?'

As Jessie tried to concentrate, she found herself seeing the face in front of her in detail. The woman was olive-skinned, her dark hair streaked with grey; her eyebrows were dark and her eyes dark too, dark brown. Her lips were very red, the lips that were forming the words. 'I'm sorry, he's lost his right arm. But it's not the end of the world, the doctor says he ought to survive.'

'How?' Jessie was weeping. 'How in God's name did that happen?'

309

The matron took a deep breath. 'You're best to hear it from me,' she said, 'so I can keep an eye on you. It was a crocodile, Mrs Morgan. A crocodile.'

Her face seemed to recede, to fade back into the distance and then come at Jessie with a roar, larger than life. Grotesque. Horrible. Jessie was choking, gasping for breath, but strong hands held her and the familiar fumes of smelling salts berated her, bringing everything back into perspective.

'That's better,' Matron was saying. 'You'll have to bear up. Your nurse-girl is outside with your baby. She was getting worried about you, so she came for a walk. And what a beautiful baby he is, everyone's fussing over him. I think he likes attention, that one.'

'Yes,' Jessie said. 'I'm all right now. Can I see my husband?'

'I think so. He is aware he has lost the arm but I'm not sure he realises what happened, so we'll have to take him carefully. That's a shock in itself. And he's lost a lot of blood. We have to build him up now, get him well again.'

They had given Corby a room to himself, which Jessie appreciated because he looked so grey and drawn. She shuddered; there were scratch marks covered in some dark ointment on his face and neck, and they looked to her like the marks of claws, but she made no comment in case he could hear. She talked quietly with the German doctor for a while and then steeled herself for the next ordeal.

Strangely, Lucas in death looked better than Corby alive, and that frightened her. He seemed so serene, at rest. Jessie kissed him and sat alone with him, allowing her grief to flow in a welter of tears. As the weeping subsided, a new determination took hold. It was up to her now to reshape their lives. She'd met an elderly lady who was also staying at the hotel, a woman who said she'd been through several floods. 'You just start again,' she'd advised an anxious Jessie. 'In a couple of weeks you'd never know a flood had come and gone.'

'But our house has gone too,' Jessie groaned.

'So you build another one, above flood level this time.'

'With what?'

'My dear, Providence is still there. It will provide. And the Government is offering subsidies to sugar planters these days to encourage expansion. We need the exports. Talk to your bank manager.'

Bank manager? What about a manager at Providence. She had to contact Mike Devlin and beg him to stay on. Offer him more pay, anything he wanted, including the white foremen he'd been asking for. She knew Corby would be furious, but it couldn't be helped, their future was at stake and Mike was the only man she could turn to now.

But she didn't need to find Mike. When she finally went back to the hotel with Hanna and the baby she was handed a message from him, advising her that Sylvia was at Woollahra plantation and would be travelling to Cairns the following day, and that he would be at Providence for as long as he was needed.

'Oh, thank God!' she whispered. 'You dear, loyal friend.'

Corby was screaming. He was threshing about in a cave as black as pitch, trying to run from a monster with gaping jaws and claws of steel, but his legs wouldn't work, they were like rubber, and the monster was eating him! Eating him alive. He could hear the crunch of bones.

A man was there, pulling him away, fighting off the monsters, and he called out to him to save him. 'Father!' he shouted. 'Father!'

'He's not here, Mr Morgan,' the woman was saying, but she had a lantern and he struggled towards it, towards the light, lashing out at the creature, trying to free himself from its grasp.

And then he awoke, mid-scream, panting with fear, wet with perspiration. It had only been a nightmare. An awful, terrifying nightmare. He tried to sit up but he couldn't move. He was tied down, tied to a bed. New fears surfaced. 'Get these things off me!' he shouted. 'Cut me loose!'

'In a minute,' the woman said, mopping his face with a cool cloth. 'You've been having bad dreams, Mr Morgan. I didn't want you to fall out of bed. It's nearly sunrise now.'

'Where am I?'

'In Cairns Hospital.' She held his head up. 'Drink this, it's only water.'

He drank greedily. It was like a draught of nectar, sparkling cool and clean, washing away the foul taste in his mouth.

'Better now?'

'Yes.' Corby rested, exhausted from his struggles, taking in the small plain room and the faint rustle of lace at the window.

'How long have I been here?'

'Three days,' Matron replied. Each morning he asked the same question as he recovered from that dream in which, she guessed, he was reliving the attack. She was ready for him this time when he began to scream that his arm was gone. He had quite a temper, this man, and it was best to keep him tied down until his mind was clear again.

'Shush now,' she said, 'or you'll wake up the whole town. It's a lovely day dawning out there. When you're feeling better you can sit out in the sun.'

'I've lost my arm,' he said at length. A statement at last, not the panicky screams that followed the nightmares.

'Yes, Mr Morgan. That's true. But you're a fit man, you're recovering well.' Physically anyway, she reflected; mentally you're not too good yet.

'I got washed away in that flood,' he told her. 'The house collapsed. But I can't remember anything after that.'

'Don't try, you've got enough to do. We have to give you a good wash, then you must try to have some porridge. Do you like porridge?'

He nodded absently.

'Good. We'll try that. Then the doctor will be here.'

'My wife? Where's my wife?'

'She'll be here too. She's been here every day with your beautiful son. You're a popular man, everyone in town has been asking after you.'

'In Cairns,' he muttered as if this were enough to digest. The matron kept chatting to him as she untied him, now that he was back in the land of the living again. Dr Muller had decided that he would talk with the patient today, tell him exactly what had happened in an attempt to combat the nightmares. A wise man, that German, she mused, hoping he would stay in Cairns. Dr Briggs was good with fever patients and general illnesses but he wasn't much of a surgeon, even she knew that. Matron Ridolfi had never had any formal training. She'd graduated over the years from a hospital cleaner to an aide until it was taken for granted in the Brisbane hospital that she was a nurse. And then, two years ago, when her husband died, she'd applied for this job as matron on the off chance she might succeed. It had been the surprise of her life to receive the letter approving her application.

It didn't bother her when she learned later that she'd been the only applicant. Maria Ridolfi knew she was good at her job and she didn't mind the heat. She'd become fond of this little town, and the hospital, although the board policy of not taking patients who couldn't pay angered her. They had surplus in the bank and could well afford public patients but they were a mean lot, those men. Matron hoped one day to get some women on the board. Someone sensible like that Mrs Morgan.

Mrs Morgan wasn't feeling too sensible. She was desperately worried but maintained an air of quiet confidence as she attended to all her responsibilities. Sylvia, a bundle of woe, who was more interested in the absence of Harry than in Jessie's problems, was staying at the hotel now. They'd already had one argument since Jessie had refused to allow her to go to the store on her own and purchase her new wardrobe.

'You can have the bare necessities and two dresses,' Jessie told her. 'We can't afford anything else right now. And I'll come with you to pay for them.'

'To make sure I buy the cheapest available, you mean,' Sylvia snapped. 'It's not fair. I need decent clothes, two dresses won't do.'

'They'll have to do. I've spoken to the bank manager and he's agreed to grant us a loan, but we have to very careful. Most of the loan has to be invested in improvements to Providence so that we can attract a Government subsidy. We can get pound for pound on the money we spend at Providence so we'll be able to rebuild the house and barns and keep going.'

Sylvia sighed. 'I don't know what you're worrying about. I should have gone to the bank. Bob Billingsley would have given me whatever money we needed.'

'Keep in mind it has to be paid back,' Jessie said tersely. 'And the bills

312

we're incurring here. Not to mention the hospital and funeral expenses. And the doctor. They all add up.'

Bob Billingsley was indeed keen on Sylvia; he'd asked about her as soon as Jessie entered his office and she was pleased she hadn't told her sister about the visit. She didn't need distractions or Sylvia's interference. But Bob had been kind and very helpful. He'd arranged the private funeral for her because she hadn't felt up to coping with strangers. Another contentious issue with Sylvia, who had wept, claiming that Professor Langley deserved better than the pitiful little graveside service.

'He was an atheist!' Jessie reminded her. 'He would turn in his coffin if we had a church service. And it's the practice here to invite the mourners back for refreshments. I can't invite people back to an hotel. Please try to co-operate, Sylvia, I'm doing the best I can.'

Billingsley attended, though, to escort the ladies, together with Dr Muller, and the presence of a suitor mollified Sylvia, who wept, hanging on Bob's arms as if Harry had ceased to exist. And Corby? No mention had been made between them of Sylvia's affair with Corby, but Jessie hadn't forgotten. She would deal with that later. Corby was still too weak and too depressed to have anyone worrying him, so Jessie took him day by day. He was always pleased to see Bronte but had no wish to talk to anyone. Jessie spent as much time as possible sitting with him, helping him with meals, doing whatever she could to make him comfortable.

'I'm going to the hospital,' she told Sylvia.

'At this hour? It's too early.'

'You can come along later if you wish.'

'I'll see,' Sylvia sulked.

Good, Jessie thought. Today she had another appointment with Billingsley, which she would keep on the way to the hospital.

He ushered her in, with a glance over her shoulder for her sister, then got down to business. 'Everything is in order, Mrs Morgan. I'll need Corby's signature, and yours, of course. This is a cruel thing to say, but if poor Corby is having trouble writing with his left hand, his cross will do.'

'Yes,' Jessie said miserably. 'That's another hurdle, Bob. He's not taking this too well. In his present state he seems to think losing an arm is the end of the world. It's difficult to cheer him up.'

'That's understandable, but he's very lucky to have survived such an awful attack.'

'I know, but I wouldn't dare say that to him right now.'

Bob passed her the papers. 'If you could sign and take them to Corby for his signature, then everything is arranged. You'll have your loan.'

'Just a minute,' Jessie said. 'Why am I signing?'

'As half-owner of Providence.'

'But I'm not.'

'Haven't you seen the will? Your father's will?'

313

'No.'

'Good Lord. Look here, I'm very sorry. That Mr Rimgate, he's a hound.'

'Who is he?'

'He was the town lawyer, but like so many others he headed for greener pastures.'

Jessie seemed completely bewildered so Bob sat back and explained. 'There's a gold town north of here, Port Douglas. It's booming. Word has it that it will overtake Cairns and we'll end up a ghost town, so a lot of businesses are moving up. It's only about twenty miles up the coast.'

'And Mr Rimgate has gone too?'

'Yes. So has the Bank of New South Wales, but our Queensland National Bank is hanging on. I keep telling them the sugar planters will keep Cairns on its feet when the gold rush is over up there, but it's a battle, I tell you. Even the Court of Petty Sessions is being moved from here. And the pubs, they're abandoning us.'

Obviously the situation was a worry for him, so Jessie sat patiently as he warmed to his subject. Was this to be yet another blow to Providence? she wondered, as the implications dawned on her. If the port of Cairns were closed down and this township foundered they'd be so much further from the supplies and amenities of civilisation, and freight costs would rocket. Overnight leave for staff would be out of the question too, making it all the more difficult to retain their labour force.

'Surely a town like this wouldn't shut down,' she said wearily.

'It's on the cards,' he replied. 'That's why I'm giving the farmers and planters around here all the encouragement I can. I believe the move to Port Douglas is ill advised. But with the gold coming in by the cartload that place is booming. There are already thirty pubs in its one main street.' He shook his head. 'Incredible! But I mustn't bore you with my opinions. Getting back to your late father's will, Mr Rimgate sent it over to me before he left. I thought he would have read it to you but apparently he couldn't be bothered. He just took off.'

'I didn't know Father had made a will. How did Mr Rimgate get hold of it?'

'Your father mailed it to him. It's still in the envelope.' He fished in a drawer. 'Is that Professor Langley's handwriting?'

Jessie looked at the neat flowing writing, fighting back tears. 'Yes.'

'Well then, Mrs Morgan. If you read this letter you'll see that he left his share in the plantation to you.'

'To me? Not to both of us?' Jessie scanned the page, but it was quite clear and deliberate. She owned half of Providence.

'I daresay Sylvia will be disappointed,' Bob commented tersely, and Jessie nodded, not daring to speak. Sylvia would be more than disappointed, she'd be outraged. And her friend Bob Billingsley was far from impressed.

'I'd better sign those papers,' Jessie said at length.

She placed them in her handbag and escaped with a sigh of relief.

314

Walking quickly towards the hospital, she decided there was no point in guessing why her father had cut Sylvia out of his will, although possibly he was expressing disapproval of her relationship with Corby. Then again, he could have been ensuring that the title remained in Corby's family since he had instigated the project. Jessie shrugged. Whatever. She was now part-owner of Providence. It was about time something came her way.

She found her husband slumped in a chair in his room, too despondent to acknowledge her presence.

'The doctor said you're coming along well,' she said cheerfully. 'You can leave the hospital soon.'

'To go where?' he said dully.

'I thought to stay at the hotel for a while until Dr Muller says you're well enough to go home.'

'Where's home?'

'Providence, of course.' Mike Devlin was due in town. She'd have to talk to him about temporary accommodation. It wouldn't take long for the men to build them a hut, somewhere to live for the time being. Jessie was so determined to get back to Providence as soon as possible she was prepared to put up with any inconvenience until the new house was built.

'I'm not going back there,' he said.

'Of course you are. It's your plantation. The floods are all over and we only lost the crops in the west fields. All the rest are intact. We can rebuild the house. I just had a thought. What we should do is design the house now, and build a few rooms for immediate occupation, then add to it as we please. That way we'll end up with a really beautiful house, the one you always wanted.'

'Are you deaf?' he shouted. 'I'm not going back. I'm selling up. I've had enough of that place.'

'Oh, Corby dear, you mustn't say that. Think of Bronte. You've said so often the plantation will be his one day.'

'You fool of a woman! Leave Bronte out of this. Try thinking of me for a change.'

Jessie changed the subject to calm him, but that afternoon she tried again to talk to him about Providence. It was no use, he simply flew into a rage.

They couldn't afford to be wasting time. They needed to utilise the loan now. As soon as Mike arrived she'd ask him to buy all the provisions necessary and whatever else was needed. And he'd have to order building materials, not only for the new house and barn but to repair damage to other buildings – whatever was required. She wasn't sure how much new construction was needed but if they employed two carpenters to start work right away, with as many Kanakas as they needed to assist them as labourers, surely it wouldn't be long before the plantation was back to normal. Or even better, she mused, with new

315

buildings rather than the old ones that had just been thrown up in a haphazard manner as they were needed.

This time, she thought, excitement lifting her spirits, we'll have a plan, not only for the house but for a more orderly arrangement of the buildings, allowing room for landscaping and recreation areas for the workers. Providence will be a show place. There and then Jessie decided to start work on the plans tonight. She would design it all herself, and if Corby wouldn't listen, she'd seek Mike's advice.

But unless Corby signed the papers it was no use making plans, and she hadn't dared mention the loan yet. She had to persuade him to return to Providence first. Or did she? Corby need only sign with a cross. With her signature underneath no one would query who had made that cross. It would be an easy thing to do, to mark the documents with an X and be done with it.

When she handed them to Bob Billingsley he noted the mark where Corby's signature should have been and smiled ruefully. 'Poor old Corby. He'll have his left hand behaving soon enough if he practises.' And that was all he had to say. He stamped the loan agreement and was in a mood to chat, but Jessie, the forger, practically scuttled out of his office, her face burning.

'What are you doing?' Sylvia asked her that night, peering over Jessie's shoulder at the drawings she was working on with pencil and rubber.

'Designs for the new house.'

'What do you know about designing a house?'

'Nothing, but I've got a fair idea of what I want and where it will be situated, enough to instruct a builder.'

'Is this a house at Providence?'

'Of course.'

'Why bother? Corby says we're not going back.'

Deliberately Jessie put the pencil down. 'I wanted to talk to you about that. Corby will be returning to Providence. I know my husband better than you do; he won't let go when he comes to his senses. As soon as he realises the plantation is operating again he'll be back. But, Sylvia, you won't. I don't want you living at Providence any more.'

'Oh really? And where am I supposed to live?'

'You can stay in Cairns, find lodgings here, or go back to England. I'll provide you with a monthly allowance and your passage money if you wish, but there is no longer a place for you at Providence.'

'Corby will have something to say about that.'

'My husband will have no say in the matter.'

'Is that so? And where will you get the money to support me?'

'That's my business.' Until Sylvia remembered to ask what had become of the Professor's share of the plantation, Jessie had no intention of enlightening her. In any case it didn't matter, the will was legal even without a witness because it was written in his unmistakable handwriting and in sensible clear terms. Rimgate had taken the time to

316

countersign it. Billingsley had mentioned that in these outback districts wills did not necessarily have to be witnessed as long as the intention was clear.

Fuming, Sylvia paced the room. 'I won't have you telling me what to do!' she stormed.

'I'm not telling you what to do, I'm just saying you are no longer welcome in my home.'

Her sister banged the door as she left and Jessie went back to her sketches, unmoved.

'Mike Devlin is in town. Do you want to see him?' Jessie asked Corby.

'I don't want to see anyone.'

'Very well. I'll tell him you're not up to it. He's working at Providence again, Corby, and is prepared to stay on.'

'That should please you.'

'It does, and I don't need spiteful remarks like that. He has also offered to move out of his house and let us live there until we have our own place again.'

'You can live there. I'm not going back, can't you get that through your head?'

Jessie tried to interest him. She talked about the plans for the new house. She told him about the two new workmen who were on their way. Matron Ridolfi had mentioned her nephews, who had migrated from Italy and were looking for work, hoping Jessie would be able to place them.

'They worked on sugar beet farms in their own country,' Jessie told Corby. 'I don't know if that has much to do with cane farming but they must have some knowledge of the industry so I agreed to take them on. And Mike Devlin said if they're any good he'll promote them to foremen. He says Italians make good farmers, they're diligent and they work hard.'

But Corby closed his eyes and turned away.

'Are you listening to me?' she asked. 'It's still your plantation. I'm doing my best until you're well enough to see to everything yourself.'

'Do what you like,' he muttered, 'only stop bothering me. If you've got somewhere to live now why don't you go and live there?'

'Without you?'

He jerked his head back to glare at her: 'You seem to have forgotten that you left me, madam. Deliberately choosing a time that would cause me the most embarrassment. And with my manager in tow. You book yourself into the most expensive hotel in town, ride out our suffering in luxury – which you are still doing, running up bills – and then you gape when I say to go home.'

Jessie was shocked at his attack. She had hoped that all this trouble would bring them closer together and that they could go home together and start again. She had even boasted of such to Sylvia. 'I know my husband . . .' she'd said. The words echoed bleakly now.

317

'Corby,' she said gently, 'I'm sorry about everything. We've both made mistakes. I'd never do anything to hurt you, I was just reacting . . .'

'Tell that to your father!' he snapped. 'They tell me he wanted to go to town with you that day, but would you take him? No, not you! Tearing off into the countryside like a madwoman, knowing Devlin would follow. You didn't want your father along, did you? He'd get in the way. But if you'd taken him he'd still be alive today!'

White-faced, Jessie pushed her chair away from the bed and stood up, barely able to speak. 'You terrible man!' she sobbed and ran out of the room, blundering into Matron.

'Ah! Mrs Morgan! Good news. I had a telegram from my nephews in Brisbane. They come to Cairns on the next ship.'

'That's good,' Jessie managed to say. 'Excuse me, I must rush.'

The patient felt better. For months he'd had to put up with her cloying disapproval followed by accusations. Let's see how she likes being on the receiving end, he thought. He was bored with the perfect wife, the lady of Providence loved by all. Sylvia was worth two of her. When Sylvia came to visit she didn't harangue him with all this talk of Providence and what had to be done now; she fussed and petted and amused him. But of course Sylvia had experienced the flood, the danger. Jessie hadn't, she had no idea.

It was a terrible thing to be mutilated like this, and yet in all directions he was met with cheerfulness, as if he'd merely lost a toe. Jessie offended him marching in here with her plans for Providence when he'd told her again and again he wasn't going back. She couldn't get that through her thick head. The very thought of Providence filled him with dread. It wasn't necessary for the nurse to tie him down at night any more, but the dreams were still bad and they were always of Providence. It was as if that place hadn't finished with him yet.

A woman brought him tea and cake, offering to help him, but he swung his legs over the side of the bed and waved her away. He resented being treated like a baby. And he had things to think about. The main thing being that bloody plantation.

Let Devlin take over and clean the place up. Fine. Make it easier to sell. And they could employ Matron's relations if they wanted to. He couldn't care less.

As for Jessie moving into the manager's house, that was no big deal. Devlin could hardly offer less, and it would be a safe home for his wife and son and the nurse-girl, cheaper than an hotel . . . while he went about the business of selling the plantation. As soon as he got out of this place where he had become a showpiece, an exhibit: 'The bloke who got bit by a croc.'

He'd been appalled to hear visitors and patients out there talking about him, and fumed when ignorant passers-by stuck their heads in to peer at him with their 'G'days' and 'How're you doing, mate?' He'd

318

taken to pretending to be asleep. With nothing else to do he'd listened to conversations emanating from the passageways and the veranda beyond his room. The main topic was gold. They talked about the money pouring into a town just north of here called Port Douglas, up what they called the Bump Road.

Corby was fascinated. Gold! What he wouldn't do to be in on that. He heard one fellow say that he'd come across a reef so much aglitter with gold it had looked like a jeweller's window, and the envy he felt was almost a physical pain. Why hadn't he heard about this before he bought the plantation? The money would have been better spent mounting an expedition to any one of these rich goldfields. Instant wealth! Oh Jesus, it was all about him. A man could weep to have missed such opportunities.

And it was too late now. A man with one arm couldn't hope to compete with the diggers unless . . . He was uncommonly polite when one of those very diggers marched into his room.

'Heard you had a bit of bad luck, mate!' the man said to Corby, as if he'd known him all his life.

'I'll survive,' Corby said. 'I hear you did well on the goldfields.'

'Yeah, that's right. And we were having a fine old time in Port Douglas until my mate broke his leg in three places and I had to bring him down here. Hey, listen, would you like a drink?'

'I'd give my eyeteeth for a bloody drink,' Corby told his new friend, who soon produced a bottle of the best Scotch whisky.

Corby considered the time spent with 'Nugget' Yates the most instructive he'd had in years, and he was in a benign mood when Nugget got up to take his leave.

'For a planter,' Nugget said through his dark bushy beard, 'you're not a bad bloke. You ought to come and see us in Port Douglas. She's a lovely town, not all stinking swamps like this, got the longest main street you ever did see, with a port on one side and a miles-long pretty beach on t'other. It's a darlin' place.'

Corby learned that Nugget and his friends found gold, then pulled back to rip-roaring Port Douglas to spend it, and went back for more. 'Easy come easy go,' Nugget had laughed, 'but we're havin' one helluva time.'

'Would you do me a favour?' Corby asked him. 'I haven't managed to write legibly yet. Would you call on Bob Billingsley at the Queensland National Bank and tell him I want to see him.'

'Consider it done.'

'Tell him to come at night, it's quieter here then.'

What Corby really meant was that no respectable women walked the streets of Cairns at night without escorts, so he could talk to Billingsley without Jessie's interference.

His discussion with the bank manager produced some surprises for Corby which hardened him even more against Jessie. He remained calm, though.

'Port Douglas,' he said to Bob. 'I want to invest there.'

'In what?'

'In hotels.'

Billingsley laughed. 'You've got enough on your plate with Providence. The loan will put you back on your feet.'

'Ah yes, the loan.' What loan? The cheery wife had only talked about a Government subsidy. How had she talked this oaf into giving them a loan?

'I suppose it will,' he'd replied without batting an eye. After all, any money she got out of the bank was in his interests. And when he sold Providence this reckless moneylender might or might not be paid.

'Sylvia was disappointed at the will,' Bob said. 'Have you seen her today?'

'No, I haven't. Are we talking about the Professor's will? I'm afraid everyone here treats me as if I've lost my wits as well. I get fed information by the spoonful.'

'He left his share to Jessie,' Bob said, and Corby too caught his note of irritation, although it didn't bother him.

'That's understandable,' he replied easily. 'Jessie is my wife. By leaving it to her he was placing both women in my capable hands. Surely you wouldn't expect him to leave his share to Kew Gardens?'

'No, of course not. But Sylvia might dispute it.'

That gave Corby a jolt. All of Providence was now in his hands. There was no way in the world that he would allow Sylvia to be dragging out her share and selling it to the first bidder. He laughed. 'Bob, take a look in the bottom of that wardrobe. A friend dropped me in a bottle of Scotch. We ought to take a nip while Matron is otherwise engaged.'

The two men took surreptitious swigs at the whisky bottle as Corby led Billingsley on to a conversation about gold and Port Douglas.

'Had I thought about it earlier,' he said, 'but not being terribly aware at the time I'd rather have taken out a loan to invest in Port Douglas than Providence.'

'What the hell for? Providence is a good bet.'

'For anyone else, yes,' Corby said sadly, 'but not for me. I still have nightmares, you know.'

'Yes, I heard.' Bob shuddered. 'By cripes, Corby, you've pulled up well.'

'No I haven't. I can only tell you this, Bob. In confidence. I can't go back there. If you'd been attacked by one of those monsters would you jump in the same river?'

'Not in a fit.'

'Then I wish someone would tell my family that. I need new investments somewhere else.'

'But you've already got the mortgage on Providence.'

'Yes,' Corby admitted. His interfering wife had done this. How much was the bloody loan?

Billingsley made an interesting suggestion. 'A hotel in Port Douglas isn't a bad idea, Corby. I've got a good one on my books right now. The licensee has drunk himself to a standstill. He'd sell out now for what he owes the bank, a song. I wouldn't mind buying it myself if I had someone to run it.'

Corby grinned. 'I hope you're not looking at me. I can run a hotel but as the owner, not for anyone else.'

'But what if we had a partnership? I can't be seen to be buying out one of my own customers, I'd lose my job. But there are good pickings with the big spenders in that town.'

Corby pretended to be considering this. The man was a crook! But on the other hand who would want to be working in a bank all his life? He supposed the art of a good manager was to know when to grasp the nettle. As he did. They discussed the purchase of the hotel using Billingsley's cash and a second mortgage on Providence.

'It was my thought to buy not one hotel, but several,' Corby said blandly, and Billingsley agreed.

'The licensees of those pubs are hopeless, they forget they have to repay the banks. As soon as I spot another one falling down on payments I'll lower the boom and we'll pick that one up too. But you have to keep my name out of it. You run the show, I'll stay in the background.'

'Sounds more sane than fighting the elements and natives on a plantation,' Corby said.

'Maybe,' his new partner replied. 'But two things, Mr Morgan. Firstly, run a good pub and don't cheat them or they'll give you hell. And secondly, I don't trust that town. Within eighteen months when the town is really booming we sell everything and get out.'

Corby blinked. 'Why? I keep hearing that Port Douglas will wipe out Cairns.'

'So keep agreeing,' the shrewd bank manager replied. 'My money's on Cairns. Trust me. Gold towns go bust. Sugar towns survive. I don't know about you, but you'll be wise to follow. Every quid I make out of our Port Douglas hotels will go to buying up abandoned or relinquished property right here in the main streets of Cairns. If you take on our pubs and run them well, we'll form a company and make a killing. And as you say, an easier living than relying on the elements.'

The moon was up and there was just a scud of cloud across the starry sky as Billingsley headed for his lodgings with a skip in his step. He'd been looking out for a respectable partner for some time; he didn't need any of the fly-by-nights or dodgy characters who lived in this town, nor could he trust any of the tradesmen or shopkeepers to keep their mouths shut. Corby Morgan was ideal. He didn't mind bending the rules, he was hungry to make a fast quid, and best of all no one would dare question that arrogant bugger as to how he could afford to branch out into the hotel business. And, although he didn't know it, he was

321

carrying a load of goodwill in the district as the man who fought off a croc and had the amputation to prove it. Customers would come for miles to get a look at him.

Billingsley had observed too that Englishmen were good bets as innkeepers. They didn't get involved with the customers and they stayed on the right side of the bar. Morgan might be a bit toffy for the roughnecks of Port Douglas but that couldn't be helped; he had an air of authority to keep the lads in order and he'd have the sympathy vote to ease him into the job.

'I'll go up myself to settle him in,' the bank manager said to himself as he stepped into a bar for a nightcap before heading to his lodgings. He had every excuse to visit Port Douglas with his own central management still leaning heavily in that direction.

Sitting quietly in a corner away from the mob, Billingsley conjured up names from his bank ledgers, the names of vulnerable hotel proprietors in Port Douglas . . . There was quite a list. Of course Morgan himself was vulnerable, with two mortgages, but Bob knew the man was safe in his hands. The object was to make both of them rich. And besides, he grinned into his brandy, I wouldn't take on that bloke. He'd crucify me. Morgan had already made it clear that he was the boss in this enterprise. And that was fair enough, Billingsley needed to be the most silent of silent partners until he'd made enough to quit the bank.

A second mortgage on Providence. That was interesting. He understood Corby's reluctance to return to the plantation, but there was more to it. He had seen this gradual parting of the ways before and he'd lay odds that Mr and Mrs Morgan were separating. Here she was moving back to rebuild the sugar farm, while he was heading off in the other direction. Plain as the nose on your face, and the best of news for a young entrepreneur like himself.

And Miss Langley. She was gorgeous and very sweet but his interest had waned when he read that will. She had no prospects at all, and to him prospects meant dowry. One day he'd be a rich man, but to be very rich a man needed to marry a rich woman, like one of those squatters' daughters. He had been stunned, ferreting through accounts in Brisbane, to see the extent of their wealth. They had millions earned from the wool clips. Bloody millions! Until his plans had converged on enlisting the necessary partner, Bob had been willing to court someone like Miss Langley from the planter class, but now he was setting his sights higher. With real money to back him he could move into the status class, the cream.

'Why, Mr Billingsley!' a woman said, sitting down beside him. 'Fancy seeing you here at this hour!'

He sighed, irritated by this interruption to his dreams. He couldn't think of her name but she worked at the hospital and lived at his boarding house.

'I'm just leaving,' he murmured.

'So am I. Called in for a pint to settle me nerves. It's been a long day. Saw you at the hospital tonight, visiting Mr Morgan.'

'He's one of my customers.'

'I'm sure he is. Poor man. We didn't think he'd make it, you know, when he first come in, but he's pulling up something grand. And have you met his wife? Mrs Morgan?'

Bob nodded, finishing his brandy, preparing to escape.

'Ah, there's a lovely woman if ever there was one. But I don't go much on her sister.' She nudged him. 'There's talk around the hospital that there's more to her than meets the eye.'

'Like what?' he said dully as he pushed his glass aside.

'They reckon she's more popular with Mr Morgan than his wife. A real scandal it is. His missus comes in and gets the edge of his tongue, but when Miss Flibberty turns up he's all smiles. Mavis says they bill and coo in there like a couple of doves.'

'I was about to buy another drink,' he said. 'Would you join me?'

'You're a prince,' she smiled, 'a real gentleman, I always said.'

'You're very kind,' Jessie said to Mike, 'but I don't think it would be a good idea to visit Corby right now. He's still coming to terms with the loss of his arm and isn't taking kindly to visitors.'

'But he does know I'm back at Providence?'

'Oh yes, he's pleased, he's really very grateful to you.'

I'll bet he is, Mike thought.

'Are you sure you don't mind us invading your house?' she asked.

He shook his head. 'No. I'll be happier to have you there rather than in a camp, especially with the baby. I'll pitch a tent near the site of the old barn. We'll rebuild that first for the stores and feed and I'll move in there until we get organised again. It won't take long.'

'I'd like you to have a look at these sketches,' she said shyly. 'They're of the new house. Very amateurish I'm afraid, but do you think a builder could make sense of them?'

He smiled, studying the pages. 'You have been busy. What is this darkened section?'

'I thought we could build those rooms first.'

'Good idea,' he nodded. 'What are these two wings?'

'Perhaps we could put the living areas in the centre, with that wing for family bedrooms and the other for guest rooms.'

'It looks fine to me. The details would have to be worked out depending on the lie of the land, and we'll try to face the house into the morning rather than the afternoon sun. We made that mistake before; that's why your house was so hot. Now you've got a chance to rectify it. Yes, this should work, I don't see why not.'

'Oh marvellous!' she breathed. 'I can't wait now to see it get started. When are you going home?'

'The day after tomorrow. I should have found everything I need by then. I want to get back as soon as possible. The Kanakas have been enjoying a great old holiday, time I put them back to work again.'

'Do you mind if we come with you?'

He was surprised. 'So soon? Is Corby well enough to travel?'

She shifted uneasily in her chair. They were alone in the hotel lounge at this early hour but Jessie felt claustrophobic, as if the room were crowded and all eyes were fastened on her. She coughed nervously. 'Corby's not coming,' she managed to say.

'Oh, right! I thought it was too soon for him. I really do feel sorry for him, Jessie. When he gets out of the hospital he'll have to learn to handle a horse all over again, and a thousand other things, not easy for a man like him. But are you sure you're ready to leave?'

'Hanna's homesick,' she said lamely.

Mike laughed. 'Sorry about her. Tell her there are plenty of jobs waiting back home, that'll put her off.'

Jessie picked up her plans. They were precious now, something to hang on to. 'No, I want to leave Cairns.'

'Why? Is there anything wrong?'

She sighed. 'I suppose you'll have to know sooner or later. Corby's not coming back to Providence. He refuses to return.'

'But that's stupid, he'll have to come back sooner or later. It's only a stage, hell get over it.'

'No he won't, he's threatening to sell.'

'I see. That puts a different light on things.' He looked at her, confused. 'But what about your plans? No need to spend on a place like that for strangers; a bungalow will do, as long as there's a residence of some sort.'

She wished he'd stop being so logical, providing answers for ideal situations, because her situation was far from ideal. Close to tears, Jessie straightened up. 'Mike. He can't sell, I won't let him. My father left me his half-share in the plantation, thank God, and I will not sell.'

He did not comment, sitting quietly, giving her time to compose herself.

'So if you can manage it,' she said, 'I'd like you to take Bronte and me and Hanna back to Providence. Sylvia won't be coming either.' She laughed with a tinge of hysteria. 'I played right into their hands. I told Sylvia I didn't want her living with us any more, and now I have to leave them both here.'

'Then why don't you stay in town a little while longer. Give Corby a chance to get his priorities in order. Once he sees that Providence is back to normal he'll come round.'

Jessie shivered. 'You don't understand, Mike. I don't want him to come round. I want him to keep away. I was prepared to forgive him for other things, but now he has become just . . . terrible. This time it's nothing to do with Sylvia. He can be very cruel.' She dug in her handbag for her handkerchief and brushed at her eyes. 'Let's not talk about it any more. I've made my decision. Providence stays in the family. I'm prepared to increase your salary and let you have the

324

foremen you need, if you don't mind working for the planter's wife.'

Sylvia was frantic. 'You can't leave in the morning. What about Corby? What shall I tell him?'

'He knows I'm leaving. Here's twenty pounds. I'd advise you to find cheaper lodgings.'

'You're leaving me here unchaperoned?'

'I've never known a chaperon to have any effect on your behaviour. Why should you worry now?'

Sylvia grabbed the money and pushed it into a drawer. 'You think you're smart. Bob Billingsley told me how you seized Father's share of the plantation, stealing my inheritance.'

'Don't lie. Billingsley didn't say any such thing. Not in that tone anyway. But Father did leave me his share and I have no qualms about accepting it. Had you respected my home and my marriage I would automatically have shared with you, Father would have known that.'

'What a weak excuse!'

'It's not an excuse, it's a reason. And if I were you I'd watch Mr Billingsley. He's not the country boy you think he is. He's a very shrewd man.'

'Oh really? Now you're an expert on bank managers. What about plantation managers? And you going off with Mike Devlin? Everyone knows he's always had a crush on you.'

'Who is everyone, Sylvia? I wish you'd stop exaggerating.'

'Lita! She told me,' Sylvia lied. She was pleased to see a tinge of pink on her sister's face. At least that barb had hit home. 'I think you're dreadful. How could you embarrass Corby like this? Your name will be mud in this town, leaving your sick husband in hospital and running off to live with the help.'

'Oh, shut up! I'm not interested in what the town thinks, or you or Corby for that matter. I'm hanging on to that plantation, it will be my home and my son's. You set your cap at Corby, now you can have him. I'll never forgive you or him for your appalling behaviour.'

'It wasn't my fault.' Sylvia cringed at the fury in Jessie's voice. 'He came to my bedroom.'

'Spare me the details. My life was a misery out there, knowing what was going on but afraid to speak in case I'd misjudged you. What a fool I was! Tell me this, does Corby love you?'

'He says he does.'

Jessie's anger seemed to leave her. She sat down on the edge of Sylvia's bed with a puff of skirts. 'What a way we've come! I needed to know that. When you see Corby tomorrow you tell him that under no circumstances will I sell Providence. I'll fight him in the courts if necessary.'

'Don't be ridiculous. You can't run a plantation.'

'You wouldn't say that to Lita.'

'You're not Lita.'

'We'll see about that. I'm tired, Sylvia. I have to be up early. I'm going to bed.'

'What about me?' Sylvia cried. 'What should I do?'

Jessie picked up her shawl. 'I was a starry-eyed bride but I've grown up. Corby is not the husband I hoped for and I'm not the wife for him. Not any more. He can see Bronte whenever he wishes – he does love the child, I know – but apart from that I don't care what he does. And I guess that includes you. If he doesn't support you, I will, in memory of our dear parents.'

'You are so hard, Jessie,' Sylvia wept.

'I learned from you. We'll be leaving at sunup.'

She didn't go down to see them off. She scrambled out to the veranda in her dressing gown, beset by the screeches of parrots that magnified the headache brought on by a sleepless night.

Down below, a small convoy was gathering in the early light outside the hotel. Scavenging dogs and goats slunk along the street, ragged Aborigines stumbled by carrying children, a riderless horse cantered along the Esplanade, and behind all this the sun sent gorgeous plumes across Trinity Bay, the place she'd never wanted to come to in the first place but which was now her nemesis.

Jessie was travelling royally this time, she noted crossly, with Devlin at her beck and call. She watched as he handed her into a heavy covered German wagon with the ever-present Hanna and the baby. A man was driving the wagon, and he sat patiently reining in the two horses, ready for Devlin's signal. Riders leading packhorses trotted along to join them and a team of six horses clattered around the corner hauling a lorry packed with goods hidden under canvas. No one looked up. In the jingle of harness and the snorts of the animals and the jovial shouts of the men it seemed a festive commencement to the day, and Sylvia felt like a ghost at a feast, unnoticed, inconsequential. And then they were gone, turning about by the wharves, heading inland.

She wished she could cry, but there were no tears. She ought to laugh. She'd won. Jessie was walking away from Corby. Unbelievable! And too easy. But did she want to be stuck with Corby? He was still married and very temperamental, one day loving and attentive, the following so cool and dismissive she'd wonder if he even remembered she existed. Not like Harry. He was such a gentleman.

Weighing up the merits of both men, Sylvia decided to send a note to Harry at the barracks, hoping he was in town. She really did care for him. Corby was just . . . well, there. Not a reliable prospect for a single girl. Quite unsuitable, in fact.

She composed the note with care, pretending that Harry's early departure from Woollahra plantation had all been part of his important duties, congratulating him on the assistance given to flood-bound families by his troopers, as mentioned in the newspaper, and hoping he'd find time to renew their acquaintance so that she could thank him

326

personally for his assistance to her in such trying circumstances.

Having sent the note off with one of the hotel lads, she decided with nothing better to do, that she might as well visit Corby.

He was in fine spirits. Sylvia was surprised to find him pacing about his room, waiting for her. 'Where have you been? I have some errands for you.'

'At the hotel,' she sulked. 'On my own. You do know that Jessie has gone back to Providence, with Mike Devlin?'

'Yes, yes, I know all about that.'

'She told me to tell you that under no circumstances will she sell Providence since she now owns my father's share.'

That shook him, but only for a minute. 'It may not be a bad thing,' he said thoughtfully. 'If Devlin gets the plantation on its feet, earning again, then I'm still entitled to my share of the profits without lifting a finger. Nothing wrong with that. Now I want you to go to the store. I need clothes, here's a list. And I want writing implements since I have to teach myself to write all over again. And send up a barber.'

'Is that all?' she asked crankily.

Corby laughed. 'For the time being. Hurry up, then you can come back and help me with my lunch, I can't even cut the damned meat yet.'

The note was handed to Harry as he left for a meeting with the police magistrate and the newly elected town councillors to present his report and conclude the organisation of flood relief. He'd only been in town for two days and had been hoping to see Sylvia; she'd hardly been out of his thoughts all this time, but he couldn't bring himself to barge in on her. Even now he was still concerned about her relationship with Mike Devlin. Several times he'd been tempted to enquire, but he felt it would be rather crude to be asking questions about the private life of any young lady.

All of his reservations took flight when he read her note. It was such a delight to hear from her. Perhaps he had misunderstood what Lita had said, or perhaps she was mistaken. After all, there was the matter of Corby taking a pot shot at Mike. Would a brother-in-law be so protective of Sylvia? Hardly? No, he'd simply been angry with Mrs Morgan for leaving and had taken it out on Mike, who was only trying to help.

For that matter, Harry resolved, he would be better served to call on Corby Morgan first and commiserate with him, the poor fellow. Offer assistance. When Morgan left the hospital and was well enough, Harry could take him through his paces to accustom him to riding single-handed. This evening, though, he would make a proper response to Sylvia's note by inviting her to tea on the morrow, having done his duty by the patient first.

At the close of the meeting, Lieutenant Scott-Hughes was presented with a silver hip flask as a token of the town's esteem, and when he left he promised to deliver the kind regards of all present to the patient, Mr Morgan.

By the time Sylvia returned with the writing materials, having instructed the draper to deliver his new clothes, Corby was waiting impatiently. 'Did you forget the barber?'

'No. He'll be along this evening when he closes his shop.'

'Good, now clear that table and give me the pencil. I suppose I shall have to start with pothooks. It's a damn shame, I had an excellent writing style.'

Sylvia shifted the washbasin and jug. 'Is it true you're not going back to Providence?'

'Quite true. I intend to buy a hotel, several hotels in fact. In Port Douglas.'

'Where's that?'

'North of Cairns. I hear it is a most picturesque town.'

'And then what will you do?'

'What do you mean, what will I do?' he grinned, teasing a curl of her hair. 'I shall manage my hotels, of course.'

'But you don't know anything about hotels.'

'Nonsense, I'm quite a connoisseur, the lessons cost me a pretty penny. I'm shortly to become mine host of the Golden Nugget Hotel in said town.'

'It sounds revolting,' she sniffed. 'And what about me? Am I to be left here alone?'

'Not at all, you can come with me.'

He felt her resistance as she unwrapped the pencils, pen and ink and writing sheets on the table. 'Unless you want to go out to Providence.'

'You know she doesn't want me out there,' Sylvia muttered.

'Well then, you're free to do as you please. There's no need to stay lost and lonely in Cairns, nothing to hold you here.'

As he spoke Corby was facing the window. He saw an army officer dismount at the front gate only yards away and realised with a shock that it was Harry Scott-Hughes, who must be on his way to this very room. He moved his bulk across the window, cutting off Sylvia's view, remembering that she had been smitten with the lieutenant, and that from what he'd observed it was mutual. Was this why she wanted to stay in Cairns? What had been going on behind his back? He was damned if he'd let a pipsqueak like Harry get under his guard, nice fellow though he might be.

He took Sylvia's hand and drew her to him. 'Did I tell you you're looking beautiful?' he whispered.

'Even in these cheap clothes?' she smiled, appreciating the compliment.

He put his good arm about her, as skilfully as ever, he was pleased to note, and held her tight. 'Don't I deserve a kiss? Or am I too sad a creature for you now?'

'Oh no, Corby, of course not,' she said, responding to his kisses as she always did.

'You're just as gorgeous as ever,' he murmured. 'How can I resist you?'

Her arms went about his neck and, locked in their passionate embrace, Corby watched the doorway.

The lieutenant opened the gate and addressed a woman who was settling an old gentleman into a chair in the narrow garden. He spoke softly, as one should, he assumed, in the confines of hospital grounds. 'Mr Morgan? Where might I find Mr Morgan?'

'Go in the front door,' she replied, matching his muted tone, 'first door on the left. It's open, you can go right in.'

Harry obeyed, wondering if he should have brought a gift. A book to read, perhaps, or one of those country life newspapers. Next time, he promised himself, I'll do the right thing. Harry had a large collection of books, boxes full in fact. He began to summon up several of the titles as he made for the door, so that Corby could make a selection. Hospitals were such dull places.

He peered in the door, wondering if he should knock, but the bed was empty. He was about to turn away when he heard movement in the room. Ah! Our patient is up, he deducted cheerfully, that's good news, and he strode into the room.

Shock held him rooted to the spot when he should have run, boots riveted to the coir-matting floor covering.

Sylvia! He saw her mass of gleaming black hair, the curves of her lovely body blending with Corby Morgan, her pretty hand touching his head. She was kissing Corby as she'd kissed him, and he was appalled.

'I do beg your pardon,' he stammered, edging away, his legs like putty.

Morgan saw him first. Calmly, he set Sylvia aside. 'Why, Harry, my dear fellow, how wonderful to see you! Do come in! We were just . . . er well, never mind. You know Sylvia, of course.'

'If you don't mind,' Harry said, retreating, 'I'll call back at a more convenient time.'

He was stumbling backwards, feeling like a fool, and then he managed to straighten up, walking stiffly, almost blindly towards the glare of the day.

Sylvia came running after him. 'Harry, don't go. You don't understand. Please don't go. Let me explain.'

He opened the gate and placed it between them, a permanent barrier. 'Miss Langley, it was unforgivable of me to intrude on you like that, please accept my apology.'

That night Sylvia wept into her pillow. She'd lost Harry. It was nobody's fault, just awful timing and something that could never be explained to a fine man like Harry. One day, she told herself, I'll find him again. He did love me, I know he did.

Two weeks later she was travelling north with Corby, glad to be leaving Cairns. She couldn't bear for Harry to see her with him. Corby was madly happy. Over and over he told her how much he loved her, that they were destined to be together, that he'd be very rich and give her everything she'd ever wanted in the world, and Sylvia listened dully, heartbroken at the shame of being seen by Harry in Corby's arms. For the last few days, Corby had taken a separate room at the Victoria Hotel but he'd hugged her when they were alone. 'There'll be no need for such delicacy in Port Douglas,' he said. 'We can be together there, we'll take the best room in the house. It's a wild mining town, no one will have the slightest interest in our affairs, not in the midst of a gold rush.'

She looked at the white sandy beach and the startling blue of the waters that lapped the shore beside the road on their northern progress. It was beautiful, better than any vistas she'd ever seen or even heard about, with not a soul to spoil the pristine sands with a footprint.

'Magnificent, isn't it?' Corby said enthusiastically, slowing the horse to admire the view. He'd purchased a fine new gig with leather upholstery, and had allowed Sylvia to buy whatever she could find in decent apparel in Cairns. And as a surprise, he'd presented her with a long string of pearls.

The sky was another ocean of blue. The world, their future, was indeed fine on this lovely day, and yet she felt cheated.

'Am I to be just your mistress in this place?' she asked suddenly.

'Good Lord! I told you there's no need to worry, darling, in frontier land like this. But if it makes you feel better I'll introduce you as Mrs Morgan.'

330

Chapter Thirteen

When Jessie came back from her morning inspection of the new Kanaka barracks and hospital, she found Lita sitting on the bottom step of her house, her horse tethered nearby.

'About bloody time, darling,' Lita said. 'I've been sitting here dry as a bone for ages.'

'Why didn't you go inside?'

'Not on your life. I'm terrified of Mike's snake.'

'Oh, Snake! He's not here, Mike took him down to the camp. I just couldn't handle sharing this place with a snake. But, Lita, how wonderful to see you! How are you?'

The two women climbed the tall steps to Mike's former home.

'Just fine. You seem to have settled in well. My house has been cleaned up but it still smells of mould and there's a high-water mark on the walls. I'll have to have the whole place renovated when I can find some workers. How have you been making out? Labourers short here too?'

'Yes. The union men followed the flood like a pestilence, telling the Kanakas they are entitled to better pay, and even though we've applied for more Kanakas we haven't seen one.'

'That's because they're better paid down south, and agents are steering them out of Government control into jobs as farmhands anywhere and everywhere. We're losing them, Jessie, we have to face it. The glory days are over.'

'Oh well, we'll work it out. Would you like a cup of tea?'

'Love one. Where's the help?'

'They're all about somewhere. Elly and Tommy and Mae. We're not as formal as we used to be; they've got their own quarters and their own jobs. I only expect them at dinner time. And if my guess is right, Hanna's asleep in there with Bronte. Excuse me.'

She peeped into the second bedroom and came back smiling. 'They're both fast asleep. Sometimes I wonder who owns that child.'

Lita wandered about the small house. 'I've never been up here before. It's quite grand, isn't it? Like an eagle's nest.'

'A godsend for me.'

'I guess so. And what news of Corby?'

Jessie shrugged. 'I've no idea.'

'Are you interested?'

'Not particularly.'

331

'Oh, come on.' Lita took off her riding gloves. 'You're dying to know. He owns not one but two hotels in Port Douglas, which I hear are minting money. And there's a lady with him.'

'Sylvia?'

'My dear, I hope you're not going to throw a screaming fit, but the lady is known as Mrs Morgan.'

'Bully for her.'

'You don't care?'

Jessie opened a biscuit tin. 'Oh no. It's empty! How on earth do you keep the black girls away from the biscuits? I no sooner open a tin than the lot have mysteriously disappeared.'

'A Chubb safe would be a good idea,' Lita commented. 'So how are you? Pining after Corby?'

'No, I'm too busy now.'

'But do you still care?' Lita persisted.

'No, it's over. He pushed me too far. I do miss him occasionally. I think when you love a man it's hard to get out of the habit.'

'True,' Lita said, taking a thin dark cigarette from a silver case and lighting it with a wax match. 'But what if he comes back?'

'I don't want him back!' Jessie cried. 'Don't wish that on me. He's a wretch of a man, I could never trust him again.'

'Who can you trust?' Lita remarked. 'Since we've made the effort to visit, do you think you could call Mike in from his labours. Let's have a lunch party, we've brought the wine.'

'Of course,' Jessie said. 'I'll send for Tommy, he'll be thrilled, he's always been your ardent fan. But who's with you?'

'Johnny King,' Lita replied. 'One and the same. And take that face off. I know you disapprove of him, but Johnny's all right. We get along well together.'

'Lita, I'm so sorry. I didn't mean to be rude. Any friend of yours is a friend of mine. Of course he's welcome. Where is he?'

'Down in the fields annoying Mike, I'd say.'

'Oh. Yes. But before they come up, I wanted to ask you. Are you selling? Rumours are flying about.'

'Not on your life,' Lita grinned. 'I'm not one to kill the golden goose. You and I, Jessie, the female planters, will scandalise the whole bloody district. We'll work together. That mill needs upgrading, we can swap staff when needed. We'll show them.'

The big black kettle was boiling dry but Jessie forgot about the tea. She slumped into a chair beside Lita. 'I can't tell you how relieved I am. I've been worried sick about a co-operative mill with new owners. Mike said your plantation is big enough not to bother about us, and we're too small to make a Providence mill payable.'

'So stop worrying. I heard Corby was selling. I haven't forgotten he nearly killed Mike. You tell that rat of a husband of yours that if he tries to sell Providence, my mill is closed off to him. Savvy? Without my mill, Providence is dead.'

332

They were laughing, the two women. They rescued the kettle. They made tea. They roused Hanna to find the other servants. They brought the baby out and gurgled with him, watching him scud across the floor in a wobbly crawl. They put down pillows and cushions to slow his progress and then they were tossing the pillows about the tiny living room, hurling them at the rafters, bouncing them off the unsealed walls, whirling about in stockinged feet, these two ladies, graduates of staid boarding schools, behaving like the worst pupils as if it were break-up day, yelling at each other and collapsing in a merry heap.

'Who cares about Corby Morgan?' Jessie puffed.

'Why don't you buy the land south of here and expand?' Lita called.

'Why don't we share the mill hands?' Jessie laughed.

'Why don't we just have a party?' Lita added, hugging a pillow.

'I'll have to tidy up first,' Jessie said, collecting bolts of material. 'I've been making shifts for the Aborigine women, they'd all gone back to nature. What with one thing and another I've never been so busy, but it's fun. When Corby was here I used to creep about almost apologising for living. I can't believe I was that stupid.'

'You weren't stupid; you had a role to play, you were just the planter's wife. Now you're the planter. It makes a world of difference. Even when I marry Johnny I'm not going back to being just a piece of furniture about the place as I was with Edgar. He never even liked me coming into his office.'

But Jessie was staring at her. 'What did you say? You're getting married? To Johnny King?'

Lita bridled defensively. 'Yes. We get along well. He won't try to run my life. We're sailing to Hawaii for our honeymoon and then we'll be back to live happily ever after at Helenslea.' She laughed. 'When we're there. We intend to summer in Europe every so often.'

Jessie hugged her. 'Forgive me, I got such a surprise. I wish you every happiness.'

But then Hanna was back with 'the troops', as Lita called them, and soon Tommy was installed in the kitchen, trilling orders in his singsong voice to Mae and Elly to bring him 'vegables' and more rice while he headed off with a tomahawk.

'I think we're having chicken,' Jessie told Lita. 'I used to be shocked to see him chopping up raw chickens when to my mind they should always be roasted, but he does make a tasty meal.'

She noticed that Elly was wearing her new 'Sunday' dress, a floral cotton that Jessie had made for her, with short sleeves and a belt. It was much grander than her everyday shifts, but Jessie assumed it had been brought out in honour of the visitors.

Since Jessie's new abode didn't run to a dining room they picnicked in a sunny spot by the creek, toasting the engaged couple with the wine they'd thoughtfully provided. It was a happy occasion; they all had plenty to talk about, from tales of the flood to future plans for the plantations, though the men were rather subdued. Johnny King, Jessie observed, was quieter than usual, very solicitous of Lita, and he had the grace to look a trifle embarrassed when the conversation turned to the subject of Kanakas, or rather the problem of finding more islanders.

Jessie stepped in quickly to change the subject but Mike wouldn't let it pass. 'I hope you're done with blackbirding!' he said to King.

'I was never a blackbirder!' King retorted.

'But you run with them,' Mike growled.

'Ah, let up! Half the time the native chiefs are selling their own men. Anyway the whole business is on the way out.'

'Do you intend to stay at sea, Captain?' Jessie asked him.

'No. I reckon I've used up eight lives out there by now, what with reefs and pirates and native attacks.'

'And I want my husband with me,' Lita smiled. 'He'll have enough to do at Helenslea.' She saw Elly hovering nearby. 'Does she want something?'

Jessie looked up. 'What is it, Elly?'

The girl hung her head. 'Him pfeller want speak with Mike.'

'What feller?' Mike asked.

'Joseph pfeller.' She pointed down the hill.

'What does he want?'

Elly giggled, shaking her head, and Mike shrugged. 'All right. Tell him to wait.'

As she scuttled away Mike turned to Lita. 'That reminds me. I wanted to talk to you about Joseph. He's a good bloke but I can't keep him here. There's something odd about him. I get the feeling he's more in command here than I am. Not that he's pushy or a troublemaker. I'd just feel happier if I could move him out. Would you take him on at Helenslea?'

'Hang on,' King said. 'Isn't he the one who caused all the ruckus at Helenslea? Lita's father was killed because of him. We don't want him!'

'He wasn't to blame for Father's death,' Lita said quietly. 'I'd like to help, Mike, but we really couldn't.'

'Joseph stays here,' Jessie said. 'I'm surprised at you, Mike. He came back to warn us about the flood. He went with you to rescue my family and he saved Corby's life. He should have a medal for bravery. For heaven's sake, he fought off that crocodile and you want to get rid of him. He'll always be blamed for Edgar's death. I'm sorry, Lita, you heard Johnny then. That boy will always have a bad reputation, no one else will take him on.'

'But, Jessie,' Mike said. 'You don't understand. This is something else. Your father tried to fathom it, he said Joseph was some sort of magic man.'

'What rot!' she snapped. 'Are you telling me you're superstitious?'

'I'm not, but the Kanakas are. He's got some hold on them.' He stood up. 'I can understand how you feel, Jessie, and you're right, but the problem remains. I'll go down and have a talk with him.'

'I'll come with you,' King said.

334

When they'd left, Lita turned to Jessie. 'If Mike says he can't stay here, I wouldn't insist, you'll only make matters worse.'

'But it's so unfair.'

'I know. We both owe Joseph. We all do. If the men can't work something out, then maybe we can. I was thinking, what we ought to do . . .' And she outlined her plan.

'Would it be permitted?' Jessie asked her.

'My dear! Who's to tell us we can't?'

They dropped down the hill beside the high-set house to the sloping horse paddock, a small area Mike had fenced to shelter his own mounts.

Joseph was standing by the gate, looking spruce in a clean shirt and trousers and a coloured bandanna round his head. 'Good God!' Mike said. 'He's all dressed up, on a work day! Maybe our lad's leaving us,' he added hopefully.

But Johnny stared. 'Is this your Joseph? Jesus, man! Why didn't you tell me he was here?' He sprinted ahead and clapped the islander on the shoulders. 'How are you, lad? I hear you've been up to all sorts of capers!'

Joseph was all smiles. 'G'day, Captain! You lookin' pretty good!'

Mike stared as Johnny sparred playfully with the Kanaka, ducking and weaving, fists up, pretending to punch him in the midriff. 'Watch your guard there, son!' he told Joseph. 'I'll have to teach you better than this!' Laughing, he straightened his jacket and drew back. 'My oath, it's good to see you.'

'You know him?' Mike said.

'Course I bloody know him! How come you gave him a sissy name like Joseph? This is Talua, number one son of the great chief Ratasali. Strong man of the Malaitas.'

Mike had been dealing with Kanakas long enough to know that island chiefs didn't release or trade their sons, especially a fine-looking specimen like Joseph. 'Well, what's he doing here?' he asked, suspicious of King's story, thinking the wine had made him overenthusiastic.

'There was trouble on the beach, I got speared and Talua got me back to my ship and we set sail fast. I was pretty crook on that voyage. Hey, Talua, you could have gone back. Did you stay on board or come on another boat?'

'I stay,' he replied. 'No going back no more, too much killing.'

'God Almighty, I didn't know that. We had a mob of Kanakas on board and so we made fast for Cairns. He must have passed as just another black face.'

Mike was still suspicious. 'And what was the trouble? Blackbirding?'

'You listen to me, Devlin,' King said angrily. 'We're going to be neighbours so for Christ's sake quit with the holy Joe business. I wasn't blackbirding. You tell him, Talua.'

'No, boss. Captain King good mates with my father. Trouble start in

335

family business. Ratasali got wild, kill a Malaita man and guns start banging.'

'It was bloody mayhem!' King added. 'I got caught in the middle of a spear fight and my men, thinking I was being attacked, opened fire. And then this bloody great war canoe came from nowhere! By Jesus, that was a time! But if it hadn't been for Talua here, I'd have been feeding the fishes long ago.' He put his arm about Joseph's shoulders. 'You know his father was a god!' he grinned. 'Old Ratasali, he was one tough character. He told me that very day that he'd been elevated to the status of god in his islands and that no one would dare cross him.'

'And is he still there?' Mike asked.

'No.' King looked sadly at Joseph. 'I'm sorry, son, you know it was a mistake, don't you?'

Joseph nodded.

'My men shot his father, they thought they were protecting me. That was when I had to run for it. But none of them survived, Ratasali's war canoe got them all.'

'Jesus!' Mike said. 'I'll be bloody glad myself when the Kanaka trade ends. I'm sick of hearing this stuff.'

King was still caught up in the excitement of the occasion. 'Ratasali won in the end. He won out in the god stakes. Last time I went back to Malaita they were still paying homage to his altars. Now that he's dead, he's a more powerful god than ever. And so would you be,' he said to Talua, 'if you went back.' King seemed highly amused. 'Ratasali was a cunning bloke, he established the succession by making this one, our mate Talua, a god too. You ask any of the Malaita people. They know.'

'Oh cripes!' Mike said, but Joseph was pulling away from them.

'No,' he shouted. 'No god. This all bad stuff. I don't want no god.' He pleaded with Mike. 'You plenty strong boss. You make them stop. I am not a god, I am only a man. You tell them, Captain, I left behind the badness when I swam with you.' He wept. 'Ratasali was not a god, he was a cruel killing man, killing white men, island people, sacrifices, always more and more. Babies thrown to sharks, bodies eaten, heads collected . . .' He rounded angrily on Johnny King. 'You come too often he kill you too. Why not? Good people, white man and lady, missionaries, they taught me the English and when they finish, Ratasali killed them. That was a big feast.' The horror was evident on his face as he shouted at them. 'I won't never go back to his beach!'

As he stumbled away from them Elly came flying down the track. She threw herself at Mike, pummelling him. 'What you do to Joseph? Why you make him cry?'

'Get her off me!' Mike called to King as he tried to push her away.

King only laughed. 'By God, you've got a way with women, Devlin.'

Eventually, holding Elly firmly by the wrists, Mike managed to quieten her. 'Joseph's all right,' he said. 'What's the matter with you?'

'Why you say no?' she sulked.

'No to what?'

Elly glared at him, reminding him of her mother Broula in a dark mood. 'Me and Joseph. Getting married.'

'Good God! Is that what he was waiting for? Hey, Joseph, is that right? You want to marry this young lady?'

Joseph recovered quickly. 'Yes, boss,' he said proudly. 'Me and Eladji,' using her correct name.

'Why didn't you say so?' Mike smiled, shaking his hand.

At Mike's request, Pastor Godfrey officiated at the wedding.

'He wants to stay in this country,' Mike explained, 'and an official record of the marriage will clinch it for him. And to establish himself as a permanent resident I've advised him to take a surname.'

'They usually choose a family name from their islands, his father's name, for instance.'

'No, he has unhappy memories. He wants to retain the Christian name of Joseph and choose an Australian surname.'

The Pastor laughed. 'What will he have? Smith or Brown?'

'Oh no, he's very impressed by big falls he saw upriver, so Elly gave him their word for falls. Biboora. I'm guessing at the spelling but that's how it sounds.'

A great feast was held in the reconstructed long-house, attended by all the residents of Providence, Lita and Captain King, and, of course, Pastor Godfrey.

It was a gorgeous occasion with the islanders in their sarongs and the Aborigines clad in lap-laps, adorned with paint and feathers. Not to be outdone, Tommy wore a black satin pyjama suit under a long silk coat embroidered with peacocks, while his wife was elegant in a beautiful cheongsam. But all eyes were on the bride.

Determined to do her best for the girl, with Mae's help Jessie had produced a long flowing dress which the island women insisted was called a muu-muu, made from a length of flowered cotton and banded around the neckline with white satin. The other women had braided Elly's hair and wound fresh flowers through it in a long delicate operation that had bored the impatient bride but impressed everyone else.

There were no tables in the long-house; the guests sat on mats, cross-legged before rows of bowls and platters set out on green strips of palm and banana leaves interspersed with huge tropical blooms. Outside some of the island women fussed over two pigs roasting on a spit, and huge pots of rice.

It was a feast long remembered at Providence.

When it was all over, Mr and Mrs Joseph Biboora were invited by the white people to a small private ceremony, where Captain King presented the groom with some papers wrapped in a light leather folder.

Mystified, Joseph opened the folder.

'Can you read?' King asked him.

'No, boss.'

337

'Then you'll have to learn. This is called a deed. And it says that you are the proud owners of twenty acres of land between Helenslea and Providence.'

Both Joseph and Elly stared at the pages, bewildered.

'It's true,' Mike said. 'We all agreed that you deserve land of your own. It was more Helenslea than Providence but Lita won't miss it, she's got plenty.'

'You can grow cane there,' Lita told him, 'or market vegetables, whatever you like.'

'My own place?' Joseph could hardly contain his excitement. 'And this says so?'

'Yes,' Jessie said. 'You mustn't lose it. I'll keep it in our safe for you if you like.'

Reverently, Joseph handed the papers to her. 'Yes, you mind.' He was overcome with emotion but he managed to thank them, and then he added: 'Today I am very proud. This wife and that paper make me a home now, and we make you proud of us.'

Towards evening, after all the excitement, Jessie and Mike walked to the site of her new house where clearing had already begun. 'I thought a round carriageway in front would be a good idea,' Mike commented.

'It would take up a lot of room,' she cautioned.

'No more than a turning area would take. A horse and carriage can't go backwards.'

'Of course not,' she said, watching as he paced out a possible driveway. He'd been rather distant lately and this was her chance to talk to him without interruption. 'You're upset about Lita marrying Captain King,' she said when he returned. 'You're very fond of her, aren't you?'

'Yes,' he said absently and Jessie sighed. She had been, as usual, rehearsing this conversation for a while now. She still found it difficult to approach intimate matters.

Oh well, she thought, here goes. If I don't ask now I never will. 'How fond?'

He came over to her. 'Of Lita? I'm very fond of Lita. She's an old friend. A good friend.' A gust of wind almost dislodged her hat and he straightened it for her, standing close. 'For a minute there I thought you were asking how fond I am of you.'

She gave an embarrassed laugh. 'I suppose I'm a friend too now, though not an old friend.'

'You're more than that, Jessie, and you know it. All this wedding talk has been making me feel I've been left at the post. Although I have to admit I wasn't too pleased to hear Lita was marrying Johnny King. I don't trust him.'

'He's her choice.'

'But, Jessie, he's an adventurer. A dissolute fellow. He's been knocking around the Pacific for years.'

'And Lita doesn't know that? I think he's ready to settle down, and

Lita needs a bit of excitement in her life. Perhaps they've come to a compromise.'

'He'll ruin her.'

'He'll have to get up early. You underestimate your friend.'

Mike laughed. 'I guess I do. Maybe King should make the best of it while it lasts.'

She took his arm to balance herself on the uneven ground. 'Yes, I had that impression. Lita's not one to be put upon, I rather think her reaction would be swift.'

Jessie realised, with a sense of wonder, that she was now strolling arm in arm with him as if it were the most natural thing in the world, but then Mike stopped, to face her. 'Will you divorce Corby?'

'I can't.'

'There are new laws these days. Women have the right to sue for divorce.'

'I know, but I'd have to cite my sister and I couldn't do that.'

'Maybe he'll divorce you.'

'Not as long as we share ownership of the plantation.'

Mike nodded glumly. 'And there's the boy. He wouldn't want to lose Bronte.'

'That wouldn't be an issue,' she said. 'Corby's all talk about his son but it's only talk. He's not a family man and he never will be. He's too self-centred. He knows I'll take good care of Bronte and that I'd never deny him his father. As usual,' she shrugged, 'my husband holds all the cards. He can do as he pleases.'

'It's not all that bad,' Mike said. He took her hands. 'Jessie, let me look after you and Bronte. I have to tell you this, I love you. I've loved you from the first day I saw you standing on the wharf in Cairns. I felt then that I'd been waiting for you all my life.'

Having made that speech, he seemed to lose his nerve, backing away. 'I'm sorry if I've embarrassed you, I just wanted you to know how things stand. But I don't want you to worry. I'd never take advantage of you . . .'

As he was speaking, his voice reduced to almost a whisper, Jessie felt a marvellous sense of joy. That he should be in love with her was more than she could have hoped for because she'd never regarded herself as being particularly attractive, and losing her husband to Sylvia had sapped her confidence. And yet here was this man whose integrity she'd long admired, whose friendship she'd come to value, telling her he loved her! Didn't he know how much she'd longed for him to put his arms round her, to hold her close?

Mike interrupted her thoughts. 'We'd better go now.'

'No,' she smiled. 'Not yet. I was just thinking what a lovely man you are.' She kissed him on the cheek. 'Tell me again you love me because I'm so much in love with you I need reassuring.'

'Oh I love you, Jessie, never fear about that. I'll always love you.' She was in his arms, he was kissing her passionately and to Jessie it seemed that a long journey had come to an end.

'If we can work this out,' he said eventually, 'would you marry me?'

'My dear, of course I would, but I can't think that far ahead; Corby will always be there.'

They stood on the ridge watching the sunset and even though she was aware there were difficult times ahead she was comforted by his presence. It was wonderful not to be alone any more, to have someone to stand by her, especially a man like Mike Devlin.

The sun, brassy yellow now, its power spent, was slipping swiftly, like a huge coin, into the heart of the purple mountains. A kookaburra broke the silence with a long hollow hoot calling his family to rest and two lorikeets fled across the sky.

'I often watch those parrots returning home at night,' Jessie commented. 'They always seem to travel in pairs.'

'Very sensible of them,' Mike said, giving her a hug. 'I was thinking . . . what if I buy out Corby?'

'Could you?'

'I think so. I could raise the finance, but would he go for it?'

'He'd set a high price,' she warned, 'but I think he would. It's not just the work and the worry that have turned him off the plantation, although that played its part. The flood affected him badly, he didn't anticipate having to fight elements beyond his control, but the crocodile attack has taken its toll. He suffered dreadful nightmares after that and may still do so, for all I know. In the hospital we had to tie him down.'

'I didn't know that.'

'But you can understand it?'

'I sure can,' Mike said with a shudder.

'Well, that's the real reason why he won't come back to Providence. He lost his arm. He's had enough of Providence, he hates the place.'

'That's fair enough. I can't say that I blame him. But I ought to make him an offer before the mood wears off.'

'And while Sylvia's still in favour,' Jessie added. And then she laughed. 'Although he won't find her too easy to hoodwink. I think he's met his match there.'

'It doesn't bother you?'

'Not any more,' she said firmly. 'And since we're building a house up here we ought to plan it as *our* home. People will talk but I'm certain they're already talking about us being out here together.'

'You can be sure of that. But if you can't get a divorce, Jess, would you be happy living with me?'

'We don't have a choice, Mike, and I won't allow Corby to ruin my life. I don't want to lose you.'

He kissed her. 'No chance of that.'

Providence was peaceful at last. The Kanakas, though short-handed, were working well and Mike and Jessie were kept busy with their respective responsibilities. Jessie had never been so happy. Bronte was a strong, healthy baby, and Jessie was teaching Hanna the rudiments of sewing, though with difficulty. Tommy and Mae were thrilled that in place of their old sleepout, that had been washed away with the other buildings, they were to have decent quarters at the rear of the new house that the carpenters were already building.

They rarely saw Broula and 'her' child now; she was too busy, Jessie heard, giving orders to her new son-in-law at his farm, but Toby and the stableboys were never far away.

Mike built a cairn with metal plaques on the site of the old house commemorating his mate Jake and Jessie's father, Professor Langley.

But the best time of the day, to Jessie, was near dusk when Mike came home to their little house on the hill. When they sat together in the quiet of the evenings listening to the birds settle, the bell-like sounds of strange birds, the closing hoots of kookaburras and the lonely song of koels, nests found, calling to mates. Mike knew them all and took pleasure in identifying them. They always had so much to talk about, when they weren't making love, but Jessie felt that this special time with him, as they both relaxed before dinner, cut off from the outside world, was a form of love-making in itself. A union that she had never experienced before.

Lita's wedding had been a quiet affair, much to Johnny's chagrin, but Lita had produced the excuse that she was still in mourning, which he'd had to accept. Mike gave her away and Jessie was her matron of honour. Jessie didn't have to ask why it was such a small wedding group, with only a few of the groom's friends present; she knew Lita. The bride wasn't the slightest bit interested in becoming a member of the community. To her, Helenslea was all-important; it had to be run efficiently to make money. She saw no reason why she should entertain any of the locals.

'I'm not interested in them,' she told Jessie, 'so why should they be interested in me?'

Jessie thought that was hilarious. Because Lita had withdrawn from all contact with other people in the district except her immediate friends, she had become known as a 'mysterious' rich woman, and wild tales about the orgies at Helenslea spread far and wide. Fortunately, Jessie pondered, Captain King, having a reputation of his own, was oblivious to public opinion, because there was a disgraceful story circulating about Lita and Joseph which she had been quick to scotch. Appalling the stories people would invent! Jessie didn't even mention it to Mike.

But Johnny King had heard the story in a bar in town, as he and Lita were preparing to depart on their honeymoon.

'What's this about you and Joseph?' he asked his wife, in their Cairns hotel room.

'Darling,' she said, 'how many tales have you told me about black velvet? The last time I was aboard your ship you had the curviest South Sea Islander in your cabin I've ever seen. Did I complain?'

341

'Ah yes,' he sighed. 'Her name was Bella. What a treat she was. I wonder what became of her? You should have stayed, she was something else.' He grinned. 'Maybe we ought to invite Joseph over for a little party when we get home.'

'No, leave him alone. Dandy still swears he's a magic man.' Lita shuddered. 'After what you've told me about his father, I want him to stay on his side of the fence.'

'Since when were you superstitious, my sweet? Keep in mind he saved my life. And Corby's. Though I bet Devlin wishes he'd left him to the croc.'

'And four men died at Helenslea, and two at Providence. I know Joseph's a good man, but good and evil – both sides of the coin – do you think they're fellow travellers?'

Captain Johnny King took her arm. 'I don't worry about things like that. Let's go down to the dining room; our send-off party will be under way by now.'

Jessie loved mail days, all the more because they were so inconsistent, sometimes a week apart, sometimes three weeks. The mail contractor also brought newspapers and magazines, providing them with enough reading matter to last for days. She rarely received personal mail, but this time there were two addressed to her. The first was from Lita, still on her honeymoon in Hawaii, and the second, which Jessie set aside, was from Sylvia. Her heart pounded when she recognised her sister's handwriting, and as she read Lita's lively account of the voyage in the SS *Oregon*, which they'd boarded in Sydney, she kept glancing at Sylvia's letter, not wanting to open it. She even thought of tearing it up while it still hid its contents. One of her father's favourite words came to mind: 'Perturbations!' That, she thought, was relevant now. Any communication from Sylvia was bound to create problems and Jessie resented the intrusion.

Lita was having a wonderful time in Hawaii. Johnny's friends were most hospitable, and they entertained in the grand style, with balls and receptions and excursions almost every day. The scenery, Jessie read, dawdling over the pages with yet another glance at that irritating envelope, was magnificent, and many of the palatial houses had ocean views. Lita had visited several cane plantations and was bringing home new varieties of cane that would be suitable for the Queensland climate.

Jessie read the letter several times, dwelling on the description of the value and reliability of the new canes as if, by being businesslike, paying attention to this section, she was telling Sylvia that she didn't have time for her and whatever she had to say. But in the end, she grudgingly opened the envelope and took out the single page.

Dear Jessie,
It is my fondest hope that you and Bronte are in good health. Corby owns three hotels in Port Douglas now and we are kept

342

very busy. This town is very pretty in the daytime but a raucous madhouse at night, so I stay upstairs in my quarters out of the way. Corby is coping well with the loss of his arm and is quite a celebrity here. The rough crowds that jam his hotels don't bother him, he says the gold miners all have plenty of money and they should be allowed to spend it however they wish.

Jessie put down the letter impatiently. 'What's the point of all this?' she asked as if her sister were in the room. 'Am I supposed to be impressed? Or are you just crowing that you're living with my husband?' With an effort she returned to the letter:

There is a matter of urgency before me at present and I seek your co-operation. After all, you wilfully left Corby in that hospital, making it plain to him that you did not wish him to join you at Providence, so I cannot see that you have anything to argue about. It now happens that I am with child and I am extremely worried. Quite frantic, in fact. Corby says he would marry me but is sure you would oppose a divorce. If you do so it would be cruel and selfish of you. Many important people come through here, judges and magistrates even, and I was speaking with a kind gentleman of the courts who advised me that a quiet divorce could be arranged if you don't cause any trouble.

Jessie was laughing as she turned to the second page.

I implore you to give this your urgent attention in the interest of my child.
    I remain,
    Your loving sister,
    Sylvia.

'What a bloody cheek!' Mike scowled, reading the letter Jessie had handed to him. 'He'll divorce you! It should be the other way round.'
    'No, it can't be. To cite my sister would be a far worse scandal than having Corby divorce me for desertion.'
    'Jessie,' Mike warned, 'he's likely to add other charges as well. He's already on record for claiming that I was having an affair with you and trying to shoot me, which adds fuel to the fire. Don't let him do this.'
    She smiled. 'We mustn't be hypocrites. Corby's charges are true now, aren't they? Anyway, by the sound of things, Corby isn't in any hurry for a divorce. He wouldn't care that Sylvia is pregnant. She's the one frantic to marry him. I think I ought to stand by my sister, don't you? I shall reply immediately, congratulating her on the forthcoming event and agreeing to the divorce to rescue her reputation. The sooner the better.'

Pompey was calling to Mike. 'Strange fellers coming down the road, boss. Who are these fellers?'

'How the hell do I know?' he yelled from the veranda. 'I'll be along in a minute.' He kissed Jessie. 'Are you sure you want to let them do this?'

'Very sure. I'm relieved, Mike. We can get on with our lives now.'

Mike rode down to meet a gang of men who were trudging up the road, packs on their backs. They were an odd lot, in coloured shirts and velveteen trousers, swarthy young men wearing dusty cloth caps.

'Who are you?' he demanded.

The spokesman, a curly-haired chap with a big grin, rushed forward and grabbed Mike's hands as he dismounted. 'We come to work for you, sir! Maria sent us.'

'What? Are you the Italians?'

They all nodded enthusiastically.

'But I only wanted two, and there are ten of you. I don't need ten foremen.'

'No, no. You listen, I tell you. These others, they do not speak English. You got a big farm here. Maria said you need more men. We do not ask much, put us to work in the fields, sir, and we will show you good workers.'

Mike was bewildered. 'You want to work in the canefields?'

'This is correct.'

They were a short, wiry lot, and Mike couldn't imagine how they'd shape up beside the Kanakas. 'Have you any idea how tough that job is in this climate?'

The Italian translated the conversation and his friends burst into an agitated chorus, pushing him forward again. 'Sir,' he said, 'you do not know the hard life we have left. This country has food and it has room for us. All we ask is a chance to prove we are worth our keep.'

'You'll have to camp out for a while,' Mike said, relenting. 'I haven't got any barracks for you.'

The young man saw a glimmer of hope. He snatched his cap from his head and threw his arms about Mike. 'You are a fine man, sir! God bless you! You will never be sorry! I am the happiest man in the world.'

At that, Mike was mobbed by the man's excited compatriots, who all insisted on hugging him and shaking his hand. 'All right!' he called. 'Settle down. Did you lot walk out here?'

'Yes, sir.'

'Well,' he admitted, 'I guess you're determined. Come with me and I'll find you a feed and somewhere to camp.'

'So I hired them,' he told Jessie later. 'They're keen and they seem decent chaps. We'll have to pay them more than the Kanakas but not as much as those union men are demanding. If this experiment works then it'll help us with the transition from Kanaka to European labour. And now there's another job for you.'

'Settling their wages?'

344

'No. Learning their names, they're all beyond me.'

'I'll be glad to. It'll be interesting having other Europeans working here, Mike. Providence is really growing up now, we won't be a backwater much longer.'

'Just as long as Cairns doesn't disappear from the map.'

'We'll worry about that when it happens.'

From the trees below them they could hear the Kanakas singing, their fine clear voices as true as any choir.

'I'll miss them,' Mike said. 'I wonder if Queensland will ever know how much we owe the Kanakas?'

Postword

Italian migrant labour became the mainstay of the massive Queensland sugar industry, and generations of Italian families still prosper in the industry along the 'sugar' coast.

Kanaka labour was phased out as scheduled, but many South Sea Islanders did remain in the country. There are estimated to be about 40,000 descendants of the islanders living in Queensland today, proud of the contribution made by their forebears.

The original Australians fought gallantly for their land during the long guerrilla wars. Some tribes were wiped out, others scattered, but the Aborigine people did not succumb and they now form an important and integral part of our society.

Port Douglas, the booming gold town, crashed and almost died. A proposed railway to the inland mineral fields caused bitter rivalry between Cairns and Port Douglas, but Cairns won the day as a slightly less difficult route over the mountains, isolating Port Douglas. The gold ran out and nature delivered the final blow to the little port with a severe cyclone that wrecked the town.

Recently, though, the high-rollers discovered this green and gorgeous sleepy hollow looking out over the Coral Sea. The rough old diggers would be amazed if they could see the languid luxury now nestling between the palm trees in the former frontier town.

Cairns had to deal with tropical hazards, battling floods and cyclones and shipwrecks until the administrators learned to cope. The sugar industry provided economic support and it was proclaimed a town in 1903. Sugar is still a major income earner and the rich tablelands produce tobacco, tea and other crops. However, tourism is now important.

Cairns, Queensland's most northern city, is one of Australia's premier tourist destinations. This lovely tropical city provides easy access to the Great Barrier Reef and the Wet Tropics rain forests, both World Heritage listings.